AF395505

VOIDSCARRED

An Aeldari Corsairs novel

VOIDSCARRED

MIKE BROOKS

BLACK LIBRARY

A BLACK LIBRARY PUBLICATION

First published in 2025.
This edition published in Great Britain in 2026 by
Black Library, Games Workshop Ltd., Willow Road,
Nottingham, NG7 2WS, UK.

Represented by: Games Workshop Limited – Irish branch,
Unit 3, Lower Liffey Street, Dublin 1,
D01 K199, Ireland.

10 9 8 7 6 5 4 3 2 1

Produced by Games Workshop in Nottingham.
Cover illustration by Christopher Cant.

A CIP record for this book is available from the British Library.

ISBN 13: 978-1-83609-364-0

See Black Library on the internet at

blacklibrary.com

Find out more about Games Workshop
and the worlds of Warhammer at

warhammer.com

Printed and bound in the UK.

For the Scriptorum Recaff Station. May our teeth remain forever safe.

For more than a hundred centuries the Emperor
has sat immobile on the Golden Throne of Earth.
He is the Master of Mankind. By the might of his
inexhaustible armies a million worlds stand
against the dark.

Yet, he is a rotting carcass, the Carrion Lord of
the Imperium held in life by marvels from the
Dark Age of Technology and the thousand souls
sacrificed each day so his may continue to burn.

To be a man in such times is to be one amongst
untold billions. It is to live in the cruelest and
most bloody regime imaginable. It is to suffer an
eternity of carnage and slaughter. It is to have cries
of anguish and sorrow drowned by the thirsting
laughter of dark gods.

This is a dark and terrible era where you will find
little comfort or hope. Forget the power of technology
and science. Forget the promise of progress and
advancement. Forget any notion of common
humanity or compassion.

There is no peace amongst the stars, for in the grim
darkness of the far future, there is only war.

DRAMATIS PERSONAE

AELDARI

THE STARSPLINTERS

Myrin Stormdawn	Corsair Baron, Lord of *Light of Heaven*
Xela Flickerstep	Shade Runner, First Mate and Bladesworn
Taranath	Bladesworn
Issarel	Bladesworn
Jhanandra	Bladesworn
Ellisar Elasandor	Captain of *The Yearning Stars*
Saraan Skyhand	First Mate of *The Yearning Stars*
Meliandril Anarra	Ranger of Alaitoc
Siriolas Wynlar	Captain of *Revenge's First Cut*
Princess Tishria	Leader of the Starsplinters, Lady of *A Beautiful Indifference*
Kraveth	Princess Tishria's Bladesworn
Idarael Mennatyr	Princess Tishria's Way Seeker
Arrerith Elwin	Corsair Baroness, Lady of *Isha's Portent*
Kruvell Darkspear	Corsair Baron, former Archon
Ellanelle Jadefall	Captain of *Feverbreak*
Aemesa	Corsair of *The Yearning Stars*

ILMAREN

Taenar Leotharan	Admiral-in-exile
Ra'thar Kyldran	Warlock-in-exile

Cithriel Shelwe-nin	Striking Scorpion Exarch
Faerys Asuthien	Captain of *Dance of Dying Seasons*
Elthorn Caman	Farseer
Amonvar	Healer on *Dance of Dying Seasons*
Arissys Caellanar	Admiral, Captain of *Dawn of Endurance*
Taevela Dumeril	Farseer

ORKS

BADSKAB BUKKANEERS

Uzgul da Magnificent	Da Grand Kaptin, Kaptin of *Sunstompa*
Bazgit	Lookout
Gazruk Hackspanna	Badmek
Runk	Grot
Skizz	Grot
Snip	Grot
Bashgut	Spanner
Kruggob	Spanner
Zaggit	Spanner

LEAGUES OF VOTANN

| Kôttak | Rumour-monger |

There is little that gives a commander of the Navy such a feeling of dread as the sight of a vessel of the accursed aeldari. Fear, yes – we should not baulk at admitting our fear, for we are not the Emperor's Angels, and weakening nerves can be steadied by catechisms of faith. The twisted ships of the traitor fleets, the brutal monstrosities of the orks, and other, stranger things can all inspire fear. However, they call only for a simple response – battle.

The aeldari are the great unknown of the void. At times they will strike without warning, murder-swift and with merciless precision, until some unknowable aim has been achieved, at which point they will withdraw. At others, their vessels will slide by without acknowledgement, ignoring us as we might ignore braying livestock caged for transport in port. Sometimes they will appear as saviours and drive away our enemies, though only the witless and faithless would think that they perform such actions for our benefit. And yet when the mood takes them, they engage in the cruellest of sport, harrying and disabling our ships before boarding to make red ruin of the crew, and taking many more for some foul purpose or amusement in whatever hell they call home.

This is why I feel the cold fingers of dread when I see those wasp-waisted vessels flickering in and out of view against the stars, for how can I make the best strategic decision when this enemy is so unknowable? A traitor or an ork or the creatures of a hive fleet are always an enemy, whereas today, aeldari interests may align with ours. At the least, to engage them without thought is to invite retribution, and perhaps find our fleets crushed between them and some other threat against whom, on another day and without a second enemy, we might have prevailed.

Against whom, on another day, they might even have aided us.

And yet, my duty is to safeguard the Imperium against all threats, and these arrogant xenos most certainly count as one. If I do not strike first, I might surrender the advantage to them if war is their intent. If I do not strike at all, and they leave us be in turn, might yet those same ships not darken the skies of an Imperial world tomorrow, or next week, or next year?

They are a conundrum, and a scourge, and most vexatious. Those scholars I have met who claim some knowledge of the aeldari declare that they are but the remnants of an ancient empire, and even now are fading from the stars regardless of our actions.

I can only pray to the Emperor that they fade faster.

– Journal extract of Captain Winderson Vorsingrass,
of the Lunar-class cruiser *Benevolent Fury*,
51st Gothic Fleet

ONE

Eluadhri, beautiful Eluadhri, the Lady of the Waters. A maiden world, seeded with life before the Fall, now grown into grand maturity. Her oceans rolled vast and cold and deep, supporting great blooms and shoals, from the moon algae that sparkled and glowed at night to the mighty kelp-dragons that wound their sinuous bodies around the trunks of the enormous deep-trees. The warm, sun-kissed shallows had bred species by the thousand, each brighter than the last. And the lakes; oh, the lakes! Great iridescent jewels capable of piercing the eye and the heart in equal measure, when caught by the young, vibrant sun. Eluadhri was a picture of perfection, proof that even in a cruel, destructive galaxy there was still a place for an unblemished mote of wonder.

So long as it could be kept free from pests.

Myrin Stormdawn stood with his eyes closed in the transport pod of his Falcon. She was *Veil of Night*, which could also be rendered as *Morning Mist*, depending on tone and intention. Even now, her armaments were extinguishing lives, such as they were. In mere moments, as the shroud of smoke cleared, she would bring a ferocious new dawn. Myrin smiled and fingered the hilt of his void sabre. This duty was one he had undertaken because no one else, it seemed, cared about maiden worlds like these. He would never abandon the freedom of the void for a dirtbound existence, but they must be kept pristine for those of the aeldari as might require them.

However, just because something was a duty did not mean it could not be invigorating. Enjoyable, even. The craftworlds might not agree, but had he and they seen eye to eye then he might still be there now, and Myrin Stormdawn would not have swapped this life for anything.

He adjusted his stance minutely as he felt *Veil of Night* begin to spin, holding himself steady despite centrifugal forces that would have sent one of the lesser species tumbling clumsily. He was ready at the moment that the doors slid aside, and leaped through them like an apex predator descending upon its quarry, his Bladesworn at his back.

The *mon-keigh* had been here for less time than it took for Eluadhri to swing around her sun once, and already they had brought a blight down upon her. Their hideous, blocky structures of unnatural metal and stone composites squatted in artificial clearings formed by butchery of the forest, and they had gouged great holes in her crust in search of the raw minerals from which they fashioned their crude weaponry and tools. Had they come here and made some attempt to live in harmony with the planet then they would still have had to be removed, but Myrin might have offered them an opportunity to leave of their own accord first, even though he knew the offer would almost certainly not be accepted. However, there could be no compromise with despoilers such as these.

He and his Starsplinters would slit the humans' throats and let their souls fall into the maws of whatever gods waited to catch them, and their bodies would be left to decay – a small reimbursement for what they had taken from the world. There were few true warriors here; he had known that before he ordered the attack, and was unconcerned by it. If the humans cared not for their own wellbeing, Myrin Stormdawn certainly would not either.

His boots touched the ground – soft dirt, yielding, so unlike the firm deck plates of the ships he now called home – and he slew his first human of the day a moment later, piercing the fragile skin of its throat with the merest flick of his void sabre's point. The creature had been staring up at *Veil of Night* in fear, and had barely registered that superior beings were emerging from the vehicle, let alone raised its weapon, before its life was ended. The anathematic crystal interlaced through Myrin's weapon hummed in delight at its first taste of blood, and the human fell to its knees as the wound immediately began to darken. The void sabre was not an envenomed weapon in the classical sense, in that no toxin coated the blade, but its very nature was inimical to life.

The first death took but a moment. Myrin slew two more of the mon-keigh within a second, his sabre whipping back and forth before either of them could bring their clumsy weapons to bear. His Bladesworn took down the rest of the first squad, and then they were sprinting into the very teeth of the humans' woefully imprecise las-fire.

The mining outpost had already been hit hard by the Starsplinters' vehicles – Myrin had sent Falcons, Hornets, and Nightwings screaming down from the skies, easily evading the few hard-point defences before disabling them with focused blasts from pulse lasers and bright lances. Like insects whose nest had been damaged, the humans came swarming out in the vain hope that their handheld weapons could succeed where the tools specifically created for the task had already failed.

This was where Myrin and his warriors came in. Other commanders might have turned their starships' weapons upon the colony from orbit, and trusted that any humans who survived the titanic blasts would soon fall victim to their own ineptitude once deprived of their artificial shelter. After all, even maiden worlds had predators – the ebb and flow of life and death was a crucial balance. One species of plant could not strangle its competitors, because it would be grazed upon; the grazers could not strip the land bare, because they were preyed upon in turn; and so it went, around and around, each organism occupying its niche in the web of life.

Humans had no place here, and Myrin would not leave Eluadhri to deal with them herself; she had already suffered enough at their hands. Myrin would ensure that each and every one of the invaders died, the infestation rooted out and cleansed, since humans were second only to orks for their stubbornness. Although individually weak, as a collective they showed an irritating tenacity if you left any alive, so his warriors poured from Falcons and Venoms, Wave Serpents and Vampire Raiders, and dropped from the skies on jet packs, bringing overdue death.

'No prisoners,' he stated, messenger waves bearing his words to the ears and minds of his warriors. He casually stepped aside from the projectile of a primitive percussive weapon aimed at point-blank range, and ran the human in question through with his sabre. 'Let the Dark Kin find their own playthings.'

A new wave of humans charged him, their blunt, plain features easy to read despite their alien nature. They were gripped by fear and desperation, well aware that their actions were, in all likelihood, futile, but hoping that some fluke of fate might turn proceedings in their favour. Their apparent commander, marked out by a higher quality of equipment, was in amongst them – not in the first wave, but it was at least not hanging back and cowering in fear while sending its underlings to their death. Myrin could grudgingly respect the humans' choice of shaky courage over shivering cowardice, even while he scoffed at their lack of intellect. Still, he reflected as he swayed away from a clumsy strike and disembowelled the offending creature, at least they were obliging enough to present themselves to him and his warriors, instead of making him root around the depths of their warren.

The world trembled slightly, just to Myrin's left and slightly behind him. There was no noise, no flash of light, nothing that his physical senses could detect. It was felt on a far deeper level, the faintest sensation of something sucking at his soul. Then a black-clad shape appeared in front of him, and a human fell as twin gouts of blood erupted from parallel cuts across its torso. The shape flickered and disappeared, reappeared again further away, and another human died, its heart pierced by a pair of blades that were gone again in a moment. The next one's throat was opened, and now the clumsy charge was failing as the mon-keigh realised that something was cutting them apart from within.

Myrin sighed, raised his fusion pistol, and fired. The human commander didn't even have time to scream. Most of its upper body was flash-blasted away into nothingness, and it was already slumping backwards to the ground by the time a pair of knives scythed through where its head had been only a moment before.

'You forget yourself, Xela,' Myrin said sharply. 'That kill was mine.'

Xela Flickerstep turned to look at him, her eyes sharp above her half-mask. The shade runner's blink pack allowed her to make tiny warp jumps – only a few paces at a time, but that was worth miles in combat. She spun her blades through her fingers and tossed her head derisively.

'You said no prisoners,' the former wych replied. 'What does it matter who kills whom?'

'What matters is what I say matters, as always,' Myrin said, casually disintegrating another human with his pistol as he strode towards her. 'What use to me is a first mate who does not understand that?'

Xela blinked out of existence for a moment, then reappeared behind a human who had been charging her from behind, and severed its spine with a single blow. Her eyes took on a calculating, hungry expression as she refocused on Myrin.

'And will I be punished for my inattention later, captain?'

Myrin snorted. 'Once more, you show an inability to predict my desires.' He blocked a blow from a human's weapon without looking, and with sufficient force to cause the wretch to drop the offending implement, then ripped his sabre up its front. Primitive armour parted along with cloth, and the human fell backwards to the ground while Myrin's weapon sang its quiet song of joy. Some considered void sabres to be cursed, but Myrin knew better. They were simply not meant to be handled by those of insufficient will; if the corsair life demanded anything of an aeldari, it was strength of will.

Taranath danced past, chuckling as his twin pistols hissed death. He used them almost as a duellist might use their weapons, taking off a hand, a foot, incapacitating his enemy before delivering the kill under the chin, or into the side of the neck or the chest cavity. Issarel, the second of Myrin's Bladesworn, was a duellist of a more traditional sort, wielding their twin powerblades in shining, precise arcs. Their kills were functional – as opposed to those of Xela, who had perfected her skills in the arenas of Commorragh, where death was almost a disappointment without an accompanying show – but no less effective. Jhanandra, more prosaic still, simply threw a plasma grenade with a flick of her wrist. The explosive detonated, burning the last three humans alive where they stood.

'Are we done here?' she asked, shouldering her shuriken rifle and looking around pointedly. Myrin surveyed the scene. His warriors had quickly overwhelmed the paltry resistance, and Eluadhri's ground was being watered by the blood of those who had sought to ravage her.

'We are done here,' he confirmed, 'but there is more work yet to do.' He raised his sabre, and pointed at the main complex.

'I want every room, ever tunnel, every crevice scoured. Leave none alive.'

TWO

Eluadhri was one of only three planets within its system, flanked by a baked ball of rock further in towards its star, and a frigid gas giant farther out. Beyond this lay a collection of planetoids and orphaned moons – lonely travellers through the void, conglomerations of ice and rock scattered in a wide orbit, without even sufficient gravity of their own to become fully spherical. It was around one of these, a nameless proto-world that glistened only faintly in the weak light from its distant parent, that the waygate hung.

It was a giant circle of wraithbone, and at fully five miles across it was of sufficient size for even the largest of aeldari warships to pass through it with their solar sails furled. *Light of Heaven*, Myrin's flagship, was not one of those giants – indeed, it could have passed through the waygate crossways – although it was a formidable vessel nonetheless. Beyond that wraithbone threshold lay the realm of the webway, and the freedom of the galaxy.

Most of the galaxy, anyway. There were many areas to which the webway could not now take an aeldari in safety. The foulness of the warp had corrupted entire branches and nodes, leaving whole swathes of the stars out of reach. Still, there was nothing to be done. Humanity might submerse itself fully into the warp and risk its lives attempting to cheat the laws of space and time, but such was not an option for the aeldari. Daemons flocked to the paltry spark of human souls with hunger enough. Their desperation to reach the burning spirits of the aeldari would overwhelm any defences.

'You seem maudlin,' Xela commented, coming up to stand alongside Myrin at the helm. Myrin smirked.

'Have your abilities finally resurfaced, then?'

Xela glowered at him. The natural psychic talents that usually marked the aeldari race were suppressed in those born in the Dark City, due to millennia of selective breeding. Asdrubael Vect, Master of Commorragh, ordered the execution of any individual gifted with such abilities, lest they inadvertently provide a foothold for daemons to invade his realm. Such were the perils of hiding from your species' doom forever. Drukhari who left Commorragh – and who were willing to be guided by another – might recover some small part of their denied birthright, but it was a slow process, and not without danger. Xela had not shown any inclination to attempt it.

'Don't try to change the subject,' his first mate said. 'If even I can tell that you're caught in one of your moods, it won't have gone unnoticed elsewhere.' She idly flipped one of her blades through her fingers. 'What concerns you?'

'I was considering the mon-keigh we just killed,' Myrin conceded after a moment. Xela snorted in response.

'A sad lack of plunder for a raid, I agree. Your dedication to your precious maiden worlds isn't profitable.'

Myrin sighed. 'I was not considering the loot, or lack thereof.'

Xela's knife froze in its rotations, and she narrowed her eyes at him. 'Don't tell me you're feeling *guilty*.'

'Don't be ridiculous,' Myrin scoffed. 'I was simply thinking about how they came here. No waygates, no webway, no ever-decreasing list of stars they can visit. They just throw themselves headfirst into the warp and, through brute ignorance and sheer numbers, extend their tarnish to any system they please. They can build their empires beyond our reach, but we can never be beyond theirs. Unless we retreat to the webway itself,' he added.

'There are humans in the webway,' Xela commented, spinning her knife again. Her lips peeled back in a sharp-toothed grin that had been honed in the depths of the Dark City. 'Very few of them voluntarily, I will concede.'

'It grinds at my spirit,' Myrin said, making a slight adjustment to *Light of Heaven*'s helm and feeling his instructions thrum out through the psychoactive wraithbone of the ship's superstructure. 'Why should those savages have free run of the stars? There must be some method of creating webway tunnels anew.'

'And you don't think that if there were, someone would have done so by now?' Xela asked mischievously, flipping her blade from one hand to another behind her back without looking. 'I'm sure you are not the first to give voice to these frustrations.'

'I'm sure I am not,' Myrin acknowledged. 'But you know as well as I how reluctant our so-called leaders are to do anything except cling to what they still have.' He hissed in frustration. 'It was done once, so it can surely be done again, but the secret certainly won't be found within a craftworld.'

'I would have said that it won't be found within Commorragh either, but it would take a thousand lifetimes to search all its corners,' Xela said. She frowned as something began flashing on her vambrace. 'Wait, my sensors are getting something…'

The drukhari might have lacked psychic awareness, but they made up for it with not only their physical skill, but their harnessing of technology. Myrin had been to Commorragh and had seen the *Ilmaea*. Even as someone birthed on a craftworld, a vessel the size of a continent, he struggled to imagine the forces necessary for the drukhari to have captured whole suns in order to power their dark realm. Xela and her fellow Commorraghan outcasts could not easily access the wraithbone networks of ships like his, but they knew enough to be able to integrate their own, more mundane systems.

Light of Heaven's own sensors alerted Myrin a moment later, by dint of an uneasy shudder running through him. There was something amiss, and the ship's spirit, given form by the awarenesses of the crew connected to it, recognised that. Myrin closed his eyes, seeking clarification. His own vision would be useless in identifying the threat, but flying by sight was for the galaxy's cruder beings.

'*Arakhia!*' Xela snapped, her instruments a hairsbreadth faster.

'Yes,' Myrin murmured as his mindscape swam into focus. Arakhia, the Children of Destruction; orks, as they were otherwise known. *Light of Heaven* had them now, burning around from the other side of the planetoid. They had used it as cover, accelerating up to full speed without exposing themselves even to the Starsplinters' advanced sensors, and he took a moment to marvel at their low cunning. It was easy for those who had never set foot outside a craftworld to scoff at the orks' uncivilised nature, their crude ships and weaponry, and assume that they were mindless brutes of no intellect. That was not the case. Orks were wonderfully suited for warfare, to the point that their perfection of function was almost a thing of beauty despite the horror that accompanied it. The sheltered ascetics who had ruled Myrin's former life would never have seen it like that, but they were scared to experience anything too fully, lest they get swept away entirely.

'Badskab Bukkaneers,' he said, allowing the ugly syllables to drip from his tongue. 'I would dearly like to know how they came to be awaiting us in this place.'

'And I would dearly like to know what we intend to do about them,' Xela replied tightly. 'At their current speed and trajectory, they will intersect us just as we reach the waygate.'

'They will,' Myrin confirmed. 'A remarkably well-sprung trap, even for Uzgul the Magnificent.' He flexed his fingers. 'I wonder if it is present.'

'Baron,' Xela said, and Myrin started at her unexpected use of his official title; the former wych only did that when she was deadly serious about something. 'You cannot be considering a boarding action in search of their commander. We would lose the fleet.'

'But think what we might gain,' Myrin said, smiling. He loved the dance of the void, where you pitted your wits and your reflexes against the weapons of a distant enemy, but nothing matched the sheer exhilaration of wetting your blade with the blood of a bridge crew who had assumed that their shields and hull would keep them safe from such an ignominious end. He could remember the face and expression of every such enemy who had breathed their last on the other end of his void sabre, from human shipmasters to t'au air caste to kaptins of the Badskab Bukkaneers themselves... But never the monster who ruled that freebooter crew. Never Uzgul da Magnificent.

'We would gain only death,' Xela snapped. Myrin heard the tapping of her fingers as she consulted her vambrace interface. 'If we put on full speed, we can manage a very limited engagement. We may well be able to achieve the webway before they can properly range their guns. Insofar as they ever do,' she added with a snort.

Myrin nodded. Xela was as eager for bloodshed as any other corsair, but her true strength lay in her analytical mind. An upbringing in Commorragh had given her a great awareness for traps and betrayal, not to mention preservation of her own life.

She would probably never have the charisma needed to rise to full command in the Starsplinters, but her insight was invaluable. She provided Myrin with opinions, and he provided his ships with orders.

'All ships to full speed,' he declared. 'Gunners, to your stations. Darkstar pilots, prepare to engage.'

Solar sails were extended to their full capacity, and his fleet surged forward. Even this far from the system's star, the photo-active membranes were still capable of harnessing its light and speeding them onwards at velocities that the ships of other species would struggle to match. However, one of his vessels was starting to lag. Myrin's awareness shimmered, and part of it formed into a signal from Ellisar Elasandor of *The Yearning Stars*.

'*Stormdawn. We should lead them away from the waygate, then pick them off at our leisure. The beasts cannot match us in open battle.*'

'I will not be turned from my course by a pack of animals,' Myrin replied stridently. In truth, he had been making similar calculations to Ellisar, and suspected the same thing. In an open engagement, his fleet could cut the orks to ribbons over time. Hit and run, hit and run, evade the firing arcs of their bulky, cumbersome vessels and gradually flense them until their superstructure was laid open to the pitiless sight of the stars. It was a tactic that had served the aeldari well time and time again. Only a nagging voice of caution stopped Myrin from giving that order, and it was not a voice that belonged solely to Xela Flickerstep.

This ambush from the orks was unexpected, and Myrin had not achieved command based on his personality alone. He understood void combat like few others, and he was not so naive as to think the brutes capable of only one surprise. There might be more ships lurking within the system, just out of range of his sensors; ships that would only reveal themselves once he gave up his one chance of a quick escape, and took the bait of a prolonged battle and the glory it promised. The waygate itself was virtually indestructible, but should the orks manage to blockade it then Myrin's ships were stranded. They could not flee to the system's edge and jump into the warp like human vessels, or even the orks themselves.

Once more, his options were constrained by the failure of his ancestors and those crystal-spined weaklings who called themselves the aeldari's current leaders. Having ships that could outpace any foe was fine in and of itself, but if the foe had identified the only place within reach from whence you could effect a withdrawal from the combat, then such a speed advantage was essentially negated. The combat would then forever be taking place on their terms, and Myrin Stormdawn refused to dance to anyone else's tune.

'So you would have us run like animals ourselves?' Ellisar demanded. *'To flee past them like* suathi *driven by a herder?'* He was a razor-sharp warrior, and one of the captains who had followed Myrin after he was betrayed by the craftworld of Ilmaren. However, abandoning the Path of the Mariner for the wild ways of the corsairs had lit a fire under Ellisar's ambition, and he grew increasingly bold in his defiance.

'You may do as you please,' Myrin replied shortly. 'Seek glory alone, if you wish. We may return one day and search for your spirit stones in the drifting wreckage of your ship. Assuming Uzgul leaves any behind,' he added. 'I hear the monster has a fondness for them.'

There was no reply, but Myrin could feel the tension and resentment through the link. Ellisar was convinced he was right, but the other captains had readily followed Myrin's orders without question, so he had few options. For a moment Myrin thought that *The Yearning Stars* was actually going to peel off and seek a glorious doom, and he hardened himself to continue without one of his best captains. If he would not be turned from his course by a pack of animals, then he certainly would not be by one rebellious ship.

Then *The Yearning Stars* put out full sail, and stopped falling behind.

'A problem?' Xela asked.

'Ellisar wished for combat,' Myrin replied, running his fingers over the shaped wraithbone of his command station and feeling *Light of Heaven*'s weapon systems respond. 'He will get it, of course, but not to the extent that he desires.'

'He's still lagging,' Xela observed. 'He will be an obvious target for the arakhia.' Her eyes narrowed as she calculated range and vectors. 'But if we slow in order to allow *The Yearning Stars* to rejoin the main formation, we will have to fight through the orks in order to reach the waygate.'

Myrin considered for a moment, then dismissed the possibility. 'Ellisar could have run out his sails the moment I gave the order, then tried to bring me around. I will not endanger my fleet because one captain did not have the sense to immediately obey me.' He activated the short-ranged messenger waves that allowed him to communicate with his crew. 'Gunners, stand ready.'

Every Asuryani voidship was a masterwork of the bonesingers' craft, miles of psychoactive substance that had been drawn forth from the warp and shaped into vessels of war or transport, and an aeldari could simply mesh their mind with the part of the ship's system they wished to use. Some adjustments tended to be made in corsair fleets, with more practical, physical controls incorporated for the use of less psychically active crew hailing from Commorragh, but the general principle remained the same. Technically, Myrin could have controlled the entire vessel himself from his command station – legend stated that this was possible in ancient times, before the Fall – but in practical terms, such a feat would be beyond any mortal mind. *Light of Heaven* had gunners assigned to each individual weapon, all of them trained in the focus and discipline needed to acquire a target, maintain lock, predict their enemy's likely movements, and pursue it to destruction.

The ork ships were closing fast on their intercept course now, each one a miniature eclipse just visible through the viewports, their shapes part-silhouetted by the raging fires of their drives. Myrin watched them, partly through his own eyes and partly with the sensors of *Light of Heaven*, waiting for the beasts to make the first move. Would they change course to present their heavier guns to his fleet as a punishing broadside while sacrificing their chance to blockade the waygate, or would their kaptins hold their approach vector and content themselves with unleashing their comparatively fewer forward-facing weapons in the hope of getting in close? Either option was just as likely as the other, and niceties of strategy did not need to enter into it. An ork might find just as much gratification in the thunder of guns as it did in ramming its vessel prow-first into an enemy, without any consideration of which approach better fitted any tactical preferences of their commander – if such a thing even existed.

'They're holding course,' Xela reported uneasily. 'All of them. No stragglers, no mavericks.'

'It's there,' Myrin declared, abruptly certain. 'Uzgul. A formidable will indeed must be present for us to face such a unified threat.'

'Baron…' Xela said, her tone one of warning, but Myrin simply smiled.

'Worry not, I will not go headhunting today. The monster will breathe its last on the end of my blade, but that hunt will be at a time of my choosing. Prepare to engage,' he added, for the benefit of everyone on board. 'We are coming into weapons range.'

Light of Heaven pulsed as the weapons batteries and pulsar lances opened fire. Strobing columns of tightly focused light stabbed outwards, standing out stark against the dark surface of the planetoid below, and seeking targets amidst the ork horde. A couple of blossoming flowers of destruction signified some initial success.

Then, a few moments later, the orks fired back.

They had fewer energy lances – despite the power of those weapons, Myrin suspected that such things were insufficiently tactile for a mentality which refused to believe that anything was happening unless accompanied by loud noise and vibration – but they had many more guns. The ork fleet lit up like the bioluminescent display of deep-sea creatures, each momentary flash the birthing pains of a gigantic, high-explosive shell streaking in the general direction of the Starsplinters.

'Here comes the storm…' Xela muttered, and a storm it was indeed.

Asuryani ships such as *Light of Heaven* were sheathed in holo-fields – flickering shrouds of disruptive light that made it all but impossible for even the most advanced enemy targeting systems to firmly lock on to their positions. Imperial ships or their Chaos-corrupted cousins, the compact ships of the t'au, and even the strange, angular vessels of the necrons would all struggle to pick out their targets from the squalling blizzard of contradictory sensor returns. Orks, however, rarely used such devices. An ork's approach to gunnery was to point their weapon broadly towards their foe and fire enthusiastically and rapidly, but without much in the way of accuracy. Insofar as they had an ideology of warfare, it was very much that if they saturated an area with firepower – 'enough dakka', in their crude tongue – then they had to hit *something*.

Therefore, somewhat counterintuitively, the Starsplinters' defences were the least effective against their least accurate enemies, since when marksmanship was never the aim, measures to disrupt marksmanship were of only limited use. In such situations, everything relied on a pilot's ability to steer their ship through wave after wave of artillery fire whilst taking minimal damage.

Myrin spread his senses out, letting his consciousness merge more fully with the rudimentary awareness of *Light of Heaven*. It was not a discrete entity – not in the same way as humans described their so-called 'machine spirits' – but the psychoactive wraithbone superstructure took on and magnified the imprint of the minds connected to it. Joined with it in this manner, Myrin could sense what his ship's instruments were detecting far more immediately than even he could have interpreted readouts and notifications. His reactions were similarly swift. Aetheric engines and solar sails felt like extensions of his own body, but whereas a novice pilot might have been overwhelmed by the scale, not allowing for the difference from the four-limbed frame they were used to controlling under the constraints of gravity, Myrin was experienced with guiding this miles-long form and compensating for its bulk and inertia.

Still, there were limits. Fleet and agile though Asuryani ships were, even they could not come unscathed through shellfire of sufficient density. Like a pugilist seeing a blow coming but unable to do anything more than roll with the punch, Myrin immediately realised that his options were limited to a certain choice over how and where to take damage, rather than evading it entirely.

A detonation on the aft portside fin made him clench his teeth as the icy shock of telepathic pain roiled back through his nerves. A desperate half-roll saw another shell pass by so close that the heat of its propellant fires scorched his hull, only for it to strike *Day of Falling Leaves* behind him. Psychic screams echoed through the communication network binding his fleet together, and Myrin recognised the voice of Ahshala Cloudfall before it was cut off with an ominous finality.

'Gunners!' he snapped, but *Light of Heaven*'s weapons were already lashing out again. Through the ship's sensors he registered ork cruisers flaring and dying as heavy starcannons found and detonated fuel reserves or ammunition stores, fusion beamers melted away great swathes of enemy hulls, and pulsar lances bisected bridges and crew decks.

'Darkstars, launch!' Myrin ordered. Other captains might have already sent their fighters out, but Myrin knew better than to risk them a moment longer than he had to amidst the hail of fire coming their way. Now, however, he could see the distinctive flare of torpedo waves, and in amongst them, he had no doubt, were ork boarding craft. Aeldari ships needed far fewer crew members than those of many of their enemies, thanks to their advanced systems. However, that left them vulnerable to boarding actions, and if there was one place you did not want orks to be, it was on your ship.

Most orks were far from skilled fighters, but they made up for it with brute strength and a stubborn refusal to acknowledge when they were beaten, or indeed dead. Besides, although the vast majority of their warriors were little more than slabs of aggressive muscle armed with primitive blades and large-calibre ballistic weapons, there were some with an innate instinct for causing far greater damage who would seek out important parts of the ship itself, rather than contenting themselves with the slaughter of living beings. Their own survival rarely seemed to register with them. For most, the sheer act of destruction appeared to be a satisfactory life goal, and so explosives would be placed on engines without the saboteurs giving any consideration for how they would escape the blast, leaving very limited time for countermeasures.

The sleek shapes of Darkstar fighters accelerated away from their launch bays, weapons already sparkling as they swept out to shoot down the incoming orkish ordnance. Myrin rolled *Light of Heaven* again, but was unable to prevent the main dorsal sail being strafed by a volley from some anonymous ork kroozer's guns. It was a calculated sacrifice; the loss in speed would be negligible thanks to their forward momentum, and the solar sails would be of no use once they reached the webway in any case. In there, engine power would carry them onwards to their destination, so better to take the hit on the mainmast and sail rather than let those shells strike an occupied part of the vessel.

'We'll be exchanging fire at point-blank range before we can get through,' Xela warned. She had one of her knives out again, and was rolling it through her fingers as she made her calculations.

'I am aware of that,' Myrin replied testily, attempting to keep a tactical overview of the battle while simultaneously guiding *Light of Heaven* through the least punishing path to safety. The task would have taxed a lesser mind to breaking point – most other captains in his fleet left the piloting to a crew member – and even he was struggling, but Myrin refused to leave his ship in lesser hands unless he had no option. 'But we will only be doing so briefly.'

'Briefly will be enough,' Xela muttered. Her head snapped up, pale hair swishing, as she focused on something through a viewport. 'They've missed one.'

Myrin, his consciousness skating through an almost over-whelming flood of sensation and information, realised what she meant – an ork assault boat coming at them fast on an intercept course, having somehow evaded the fighters he had sent out to prevent just such an occurrence. His fingers twitched reflexively, but he had very few options. To twist them far enough out of their current path to prevent the assault boat from being able to turn and match them meant either steering straight through a wave of torpedoes, or breaking so far from the main formation that they would become an isolated target and very unlikely to make the waygate.

'Hold course!' Xela shouted, drawing a second knife and sprinting for the bridge doors. 'I can't kill a torpedo, but I can kill boarders!'

'There could be a hundred of them in there!' Myrin retorted. A hundred orks on a battlefield was a problem, but an addressable one, depending on the circumstances. The same number loose in a voidship's corridors was a very different proposition.

'Not for long,' Xela replied with a razor-sharp grin, and then she was gone.

'Go with her,' Myrin ordered his other Bladesworn, gritting his teeth as he twitched *Light of Heaven*'s course slightly. At the very least, he could try to ensure the assault boat impacted on an area relatively distant from anything particularly important…

'Lord,' Taranath said with one of his infuriating chuckles, 'our place is–'

Light of Heaven juddered as the boarding craft rammed home, and Myrin grimaced as the heat of fusion cutters and the jagged edges of drills ground against the wraithbone hull his mind currently inhabited.

'Your place is where I tell you it is!' he snapped at his Bladesworn. 'Go, and go now!'

They at least had the sense not to argue with him further. Taranath, Issarel and Jhanandra ran for the doors, and although none of them could match Xela's pace aided by her blink pack, they would be fleet enough to arrive not too long after her. The shade runner would pick up other warriors on her way, Myrin knew, but he had no idea if it would be enough. He could do nothing about it, however, as much as he wished he could cut down the boarders himself. He needed to get *Light of Heaven*, and the rest of the fleet, to safety.

'Focus fire on the lead ships,' he ordered. 'I don't care which of the enemy has the biggest guns, we just need to stop them from physically blockading us.'

Terse acknowledgements came from his captains. None liked the idea of leaving larger ships unmolested, but they recognised the importance of his words. The fleet was committed to their escape action now, and it was to that they needed to bend their will with all the single-minded focus of an exarch on the Path of the Warrior. Any attempt to turn this into a battle would see their utter destruction, for they were far, far too close to the enemy.

Memory of Sorrow's Thorns came apart under heavy gunfire, its holofield flickering and dying to reveal a cracked-open shell spilling atmosphere into the void. A sharp-nosed ork ship, little more than a giant beak attached to massive engines, dived towards *Wind of the Falcon's Wings* with such speed that the aeldari captain was unable to evade it, and it plunged straight into the bridge. Myrin could not understand how any of the attacking crew would survive such an impact, but orks were astonishingly resilient; besides, such a consideration might well not have entered their heads before they embarked on their final run.

His fleet was taking casualties, but they were dealing out damage in return. His gunners' accuracy was near-perfect at this close range, even with the evasive manoeuvres taken by the ships to which they belonged, and ork vessels were cut to pieces with surgical precision. Even as Myrin watched, one heavily damaged enemy veered involuntarily to its starboard side, and was rammed by a sister vessel either too clumsy or too unwilling to alter course to avoid it. Another came apart in a cataclysmic explosion that briefly lit up the hulls all around it.

And there it was. The leering grin painted across the blunt, ugly prow. Rank after rank of weapons batteries, firing near constantly. The largest, most notorious ship in the entire Badskab Bukkaneers fleet.

Sunstompa.

It was a ludicrously named vessel, but deadly nonetheless. The flagship of Uzgul da Magnificent had claimed nearly two-score Starsplinters kills of which Myrin was aware over the course of the two fleets' long-running war, which spanned the past three decades. The sight of the massive kroozer was nearly enough to sway Myrin from his course. He yearned to bring *Light of Heaven*'s prow around, brave the full firepower of the freebooter fleet, and strike directly at the monster's heart. To take his Bladesworn, board the vessel, and–

Another impact jarred him from the momentary reverie. He had told Ellisar that he would not be moved by these animals, he had told Xela that any hunt of Uzgul would occur on his terms, and he was not so weak-minded as to break his word simply because he had sighted his enemy with his own eyes.

'Prepare to activate waygate,' he ordered. 'Priority is to get through. We can deal with any of the enemy that come with us once we are on the other side and the entrance is sealed.' He smiled viciously. With the enemy cut off from the numbers that made them dangerous, that would be a short fight, and a brutal one. He half-hoped that *Sunstompa* would somehow make it through, at which point it could be dissected at his leisure, but he could already tell that the hulking flagship was too far off the pace.

Once more, temptation dangled its lure in front of him. He could leave the waygate open, try to tempt his foe in after him, and then…

But there was no guarantee of success. For *Sunstompa* to come in, many of its attendant vessels would make it in as well, and then the Starsplinters' advantage would be gone. The battle would still be brutal, but far more even. It might even lead to the orks triumphing, at which point the remainder of their fleet would undoubtedly scour what tunnels they could and kill or enslave any other aeldari they encountered, which was an outcome Myrin was not prepared to let come to pass. He might have cut himself away from the path Ilmaren had laid out for him, but that did not make him uncaring for his fellow aeldari. Indeed, it might be argued that he cared too much – had the Seer Council of Ilmaren been more willing to take action to safeguard the future for all aeldari, rather than content to skulk through the shadows between the stars and hope to evade notice by any notable powers, Myrin and his fleet might still be there now.

'All ships, hold course,' he ordered. 'No slowing, no indulging yourselves. And we wait for no one…'

THREE

Uzgul da Magnificent glared at the space through which the skrawnie ships had just disappeared, and ground his teeth together.

'Zoggin' skrawnies!' he bellowed, and kicked the nearest grot. The wretched little creature sailed through the air, impacted somewhat wetly on a bulkhead, and dropped to the deck with a noise like someone punching a pile of squiggoth dung. The other grots near Uzgul's feet applauded wildly and squeaked praise for the distance, trajectory, and accuracy of his kick, with the desperate sincerity and bowel-emptying fear of runts who knew their only purpose was to be the next projectile when something else annoyed their kaptin.

'Dey disappeared into dere hole again, boss!' reported Bazgit, peering through the make-bigger tubes.

'I can see dat!' Uzgul snapped. *Sunstompa* was roaring past that strange bolthole right now, but the space within the skrawnie-made ring was empty and lifeless again, far different from the rippling sheen of energy which had filled it until a few moments ago. One of his gunships flew hopefully through it, just in case, but with no effect; it came out the other side. One or two vessels had managed to slip through along with the skrawnie fleet, but their communicators went dead a moment later. Besides,

Uzgul knew how that worked. None of his ships that went into a skrawnie tunnel were ever seen again.

'Yoo see how dey're scared of me?' he thundered, slapping his chest. The sound of the blow was somewhat muffled by the layers of gold brocade that adorned the front of his mighty greatcoat, but it was still enough to make the orks on *Sunstompa*'s bridge jerk to something like attention and look around at their kaptin. Uzgul surveyed their faces, searching for any sign of mutiny. He wanted to tear *something* apart right now, and a grot really wasn't going to satisfy that need, so he was hoping for an overambitious krewer who'd decided that the kaptin coming up just short on his target meant he was ripe for overthrow.

Nothing. Every single ork cheered raucously, waving fists and weapons in the air, completely on board with the idea that the skrawnies had fled from his might. Jovial shouts of 'Yoo'll get 'em next time, kaptin!' and the like should have gladdened Uzgul's heart, but the lack of an obvious target for his frustration just festered all the more, and he turned away from them in disgust.

Skrawnie holes. What *were* they? Why did the little gits zip in and out of them instead of flying around like normal folk? If you wanted to travel to another star then you lashed your weirdboy to the wheel, got the meks to activate the warp engines, and went for it. You usually got an entertaining fight out of the weird things what lived in the warp, and then you came out the other side again. Sometimes you were where you'd aimed for, sometimes you'd missed a bit. But that was no real problem – there was often another fight waiting there anyway, and if not, you just dropped back into the warp and did the whole thing again.

Skrawnies, though… Uzgul had done a fair bit of thinking about them, and he'd realised that their ships only ever came and went from these holes – or at least, other bigger stuff what might have one of these holes somewhere inside it. If things ever got hairy then they just ducked back inside and you couldn't chase them, couldn't do nothing. How could he bash in a door to get at them when the cowardly little gits even took the zoggin' *door* with them? He'd tried blowing the rings up, but they were annoyingly hard to damage; he'd wondered about setting them to spinning round and round so the skrawnies inside got dizzy, but he wasn't sure that would work. When the damned things weren't actively being doorways they didn't really seem to be *anything*. Just empty holes, hanging in space and being no use to no one.

It was frustrating, was what it was. Uzgul's shoota was always a shoota even if he wasn't shooting it. It was still a shoota even if it didn't have any ammo in it (although if that state of affairs ever occurred then he'd be having serious words with the mek who'd rigged up the multiple magazines and selector switches). He didn't hold with this notion of a thing stopping being a thing just because someone wasn't using it at that moment. How could you get anything done if things stopped being things?

Uzgul pulled a skrawnie stone out of his pouch. He didn't really know what they were either, but most skrawnies he'd ever met had one, and very occasionally more than one. They were flashy to look at, that much was certainly true. He had more than a few sewn into his coat, to make it all sparkly and impressive when they caught the light.

He held this one between his knuckles for a moment, then tossed it up into his mouth, and bit down. It resisted for a moment, then gave way under the crushing force of his jaws, and his mouth was full of cold shards that sliced at his tongue and gums. He tasted blood, and grinned.

Uzgul had seen a weird warp-fing do this once: some big git with four arms and horns. It seemed to enjoy it a lot – before

Uzgul and his ladz had dakka'd it into a pile of goo, anyway – and although Uzgul couldn't really claim to have had a similar experience yet, that didn't mean he wasn't going to keep trying when the mood took him. Besides, if eating skrawnie stones gave you horns then that was great – he'd have to stop wearing hats, but he'd take that trade-off – and if it meant you grew an extra pair of arms then you could hold twice as much dakka.

Plus, it was fun watching the little gits struggle when you prised the gems off the front of their armour, like it was some critical part of their own body you were removing. Uzgul chuckled, his mood slightly improved by the memories, and turned back to his bridge krew.

'How many didn't make it froo?' he barked. 'Oi, Gazruk! Wot's yer machines sayin'?'

Gazruk Hackspanna the badmek looked up from his scannerz. 'Two little kroozers, boss, plus a bunch of tiddlers wot probably ain't worf boverin' wiv.'

'I'll be da judge of dat!' Uzgul growled, and Gazruk ducked his head deferentially. Gazruk's old warboss had sent him packing after one too many incidents of exploding bioniks, but Uzgul had recognised the badmek's natural talent. He had also, however, made it clear that the first instance of an explosion happening within the ranks of the Bukkaneers, as opposed to whomever they were currently fighting, would result in Gazruk himself being in dire need of a bionik head on account of Uzgul removing the one currently sitting atop his shoulders. The warning seemed to have had the desired effect, and Gazruk had so far busied himself with gadgets and gizmos and weapons, without getting overenthusiastic and blowing up anyone Uzgul found particularly useful.

'Lemme see dat,' Uzgul said, clomping down the steps from his gold-plated command throne to where Gazruk's instruments and screens were whirring and fizzing away. Sure enough, a couple of the skrawnie ships hadn't made it through the gate as part of their desperate escape plan. They were now drifting, blazing with fire where their leaking atmosphere provided enough oxygen to sustain the flames, and harried and pounded by fighta-bommerz.

'Cut it out!' Uzgul bellowed, picking up the handset that would send his voice booming through the entire fleet. 'Dis is da kaptin shoutin'! I want any skrawnies wot ain't already dead to be captured an' thrown in da brig, is dat clear? I got a use for 'em, and it ain't as target practice for yoo lot!'

He didn't wait for an answer, instead heading back to his throne and pulling down the massive choppa that rested crossways above the seat. Most boyz would have needed two hands to use it, but Uzgul da Magnificent could wield it in one. He pointed at Gazruk with the other.

'Shout down to da launch bays, an' have 'em get me skiff ready!' he ordered, adjusting his hat to ensure it was balanced at the most impressive angle. 'I got places to be, an' skrawnies to capture!'

'Yes, boss!' Gazruk said hastily, then paused with the handset halfway to his mouth. 'Boss... do you fink we're ever gonna nail 'em down prop'ly? Da skrawnies, I mean?'

'Dere's only free fings wot're certain in life,' Uzgul replied. 'Death, dakka, an' da Badskab Bukkaneers! We'll get 'em, my lad.'

He headed for the hatch, choppa balanced over his shoulder, and snarled his next words at the corroded metal in front of him.

'Dey're runnin' out of places to hide...'

FOUR

Myrin disliked the webway. It was a dead, sterile place that was not properly understood even by its masters. All aeldari used it as a matter of course, not to mention necessity, but there were few he knew who actually enjoyed the experience. The Asuryani, by and large, did not linger within its tunnels longer than they had to. There was always the risk of discovering – or being discovered by – something that should not have gained access to the network; not to mention the threat of drukhari, for whom the webway was home, and who knew its ways better than any craftworlder save for the most experienced of rangers. Then there were the Harlequins, whose knowledge made a mockery even of the drukhari's… And yet, even the Harlequins to whom Myrin had spoken viewed the webway as a place of which they had stewardship, a vital piece in the ongoing survival of the aeldari people, but not as a paradise they were lucky to inhabit.

The aeldari had once ruled the galaxy. Myrin knew that they were made to stand on the surface of worlds and smell the air; to sail between the stars, and bend their fires to their will. These pale grey ways were not, and should never be, the limit or nature of his species' dominion. He was unfailingly glad to leave them, once he had reached his destination.

Except when he emerged into the middle of a battle he had neither expected, nor for which he had been prepared.

The Starsplinters had bases scattered throughout the galaxy. Most were ruled by a particular commander – often the one who had built or adapted them – but such personal fiefdoms were only tolerated so long as tribute was ultimately paid to Princess Tishria, Grand Lady of the Stars and the Scourge of the Calexis Nebula. The Well of the Long Death was Myrin Stormdawn's preferred base of operations – a planetoid hollowed out by some unknown force in millennia past and within which was located a waygate large enough for even the largest capital ships in an aeldari fleet. *Light of Heaven* was barely through that waygate when something exploded off the port bow.

'Xela!' Myrin barked, leaping across the bridge to his command post. The corsair who had been directing the ship for its supposedly uneventful docking stood back, and Myrin hastily subsumed his consciousness into the limited infinity circuit of *Light of Heaven*. 'Give me something!'

'Orks,' Xela replied, her voice flat in disbelief and rage. 'Judging by their colours, more Badskab Bukkaneers!' She turned her deathly pale face towards him, eyes smouldering. 'How did they find us? Only we know the route through the fissures in the crust!'

'Such considerations are for another time,' Myrin said shortly, then switched to messenger waves to broadcast to the entire crew. 'Prepare for war!'

He was already cursing his own laxity. His vessel would emerge from most waygates at battle readiness, but never before had any enemy tracked him back to this nameless rock, let alone to the Well itself, hidden deep within it. How had the arakhia, of all beings, come to find their way here?

At least his crew were fast to respond. He was getting readings back from *Light of Heaven* now, which confirmed Xela's analysis. Throughout the grand chamber of the Well, a massive cavern several hundred miles across in all directions, ork warships were raining destruction on any aeldari construction they could find. Habitat zones and agriculture blisters were being blasted open to the central void, the moisture in their atmosphere crystallising out as their protective shells were cracked by orkish weaponry. The gigantic spiderweb of gantries with which his fleet would dock was coming apart, miles-long sections of wraithbone torn loose to pinwheel lazily away from their moorings. Myrin had seen a home subjected to destruction like this before, but he thought he had left such things behind him when he abandoned Ilmaren to forge his own path.

'Gunners, fire!' he ordered, and *Light of Heaven* began to retaliate against the raiders.

He was not alone, of course. Not all of his ships had gone with him on the cleansing mission to Eluadhri, but the ones in port when the orks attacked had clearly been both vastly outnumbered and outgunned. He scanned the Well and quickly ascertained the pattern of the battle – ork ships had entered through the openings that, after many miles of manoeuvring through great cracks and chasms, led to the planetoid's surface and out into the larger system. His ships had moved to engage, but then realised that they were outmatched. Some died there, while others had made a run for the webway gate, but were cut down from behind and their burnt-out wreckage had slammed into the habitation blisters. He was getting contacts back from the few still operational, but they were a handful at best. They were fighting doggedly on, attempting to stay ahead of orkish guns in what was, for voidships, a relatively confined space; and doing so with only their aetheric engines at that, since solar sails were of no use in the stygian blackness of the Well.

Light of Heaven opened fire, its weapon systems focusing all their fury on an orkish light cruiser a mere stone's throw away, in voidship terms. The vessel erupted in chained explosions, and Myrin felt a surge of fierce joy through the wraithbone as his crew took delight in the carnage they had wrought.

'That got their attention,' Xela commented tightly. Sure enough, orkish warships were starting to heel clumsily around. Myrin realised that he had, if anything, overestimated his adversaries' capabilities – he and his crew had reacted before most of the arakhia had even realised that the waygate had activated, and now they were suddenly aware of this new, prime target that had emerged into their midst.

'Do we retreat?' Xela asked. It was a sensible question, Myrin realised, even while fury rose within him at these animals daring to attack his fortress. They had fled one fight into another for which they were woefully underprepared.

But that was the point. He had already fled one fight this day, and it was not in his nature to do so twice.

'No,' he said firmly. 'We cannot make the chasms, and our ships are still emerging from the gate. If we attempt to withdraw there, we will simply collide with one of our own coming the other way.' His gunners fired again, picking their targets with polished efficiency, seeking to combat the orks' vast output of munitions with precision damage. A ship did not have to be in pieces to be ineffective; it could be disabled with far fewer shots.

'We will die if we remain here,' Xela warned. Her hand had gone to the spirit stone she now wore on her armour. She had left Commorragh while still young by any aeldari's reckoning, let alone those of the Dark Kin, but that did not mean she had never felt the lingering malice of She Who Thirsts awaiting her. Xela had chosen a cold, crystal afterlife as her way of escaping that fate, instead of feeding on the essence of tormented souls to sustain her. Nonetheless, she was not eager to experience it before she had to.

'And how do you think the Scourge will treat us if she learns we fled from this filth?' Myrin said grimly. 'I would rather make my stand here and, if I must die, die in combat, than be hunted down by Princess Tishria for my perceived cowardice.'

He threw *Light of Heaven* into a roll, and did not even wince when an ork mega-kannon strafed shots across his dorsal sail. In this space, lit only by explosions and sensor returns, solar sails were fully expendable. Indeed, if he could tempt the orks into shooting those instead of *Light of Heaven*'s superstructure, it would be to his benefit.

'Keep signalling those who are emerging behind us,' he ordered. They could not contact the vessels still in the webway, since that realm existed outside mortal distances, but at least the ones emerging could understand the situation as soon as possible. 'If there is a way to win this, we will find it.'

There was no way to win it. Of that, Myrin was now certain.

His captains had fought well, but this environment played almost entirely into their enemies' advantages. The orks had numbers and massed firepower, and the interior of the planetoid had become a kill-zone. It was like being trapped inside a small cage with an angry *ghor'vash* – you could perhaps avoid any one of the beast's strikes at you, but you could never get out of its reach, so you had to avoid the next, and the next, and the next, and any one of them could be your end.

That was where they were now. The enemy was badly wounded, but still hale enough to strike hard, and Myrin's fleet was in tatters. The orks pounced on any weakness, so a disabled ship fast became an obliterated one. The situation would have been even worse had that tactic not sometimes led the beasts to pass up a more strategic target in their eagerness for outright destruction, and, indeed, to occasionally engage each other. Myrin had initially taken this to simply be bad marksmanship, but he had concluded it was in fact born of dispute over who got to make the kill.

Nonetheless, the mathematics of attrition had never been in his favour. *Cry of the Stars*, *Cerulean Memories*, *Azure Blade* and more were gutted hulks now, and it was impossible to strike and fade with nowhere to fade to. The orks might have been undisciplined, but there was at least one mind amongst them that had some capacity for tactical thinking. No matter what ugly chaos was occurring, there were always some ships covering both the chasms that led to the surface, and the waygate. Whether or not the Badskabs' commander had expected Myrin's fleet to emerge, it was clearly not willing to let them escape now they were here.

'Find me that flagship!' he snarled, heeling *Light of Heaven* into a sharper turn than it liked, and wincing as he felt the strain on the superstructure as though it were his own bones. Decapitating the orkish leadership was a tried-and-tested tactic, although it was of less immediate use in the middle of a battle, since even the most belligerent of the beasts were unlikely to engage in protracted conflicts with their own kind while there were still obvious enemies to be killed. At this point, however, Myrin was willing to try anything.

'Trying to decipher their communications is like wading through filth,' Xela replied, her face twisted in disgust. 'There's no order, no direction. I can't tell who is ordering what!'

'We will be wading through the void soon, unless we can change something rapidly!' Myrin spat. *Light of Heaven*'s guns spoke again, and a handful of ork gunboats exploded – hardly the most dangerous enemy left in the crowded skies around them, but this was point-blank, moment-to-moment fighting, where you simply tried to kill what was in front of you and avoid your own death in return. It was the closest Myrin had come to experiencing the thrill and rush of hand-to-hand combat while piloting a ship, and a part of him – the wild, self-destructive part that lurked in every aeldari's heart to one degree or another – relished it even while he cursed the arakhia's very existence, and mourned every aeldari death.

Still, this was how he'd long suspected his life would end. Not for Myrin Stormdawn the gradual sputtering out of a flame that had already diminished for centuries. A craftworld was immense, but it was as nothing when set against the incomprehensible vastness of the galaxy as a whole, and it was for that freedom that Myrin had traded greater certainty. What purpose was there to a long life if all but minor personal variations within it were dictated by a seer council? What use was it to have the means and the will to act for the good of your people, but to be con-strained by those who insisted that they knew better? Had the gift of foresight been flawless, then surely the aeldari would never have been reduced to their current state, limping around the galaxy while younger, brasher races warred over supremacy amongst the stars. No, this was life: to live and die by your own decisions; to feel the silken joys of success set against the bitter sting of regret; to walk the blade's edge of sensation and emotion, and truly *experience* existence in a way unimaginable to those who cleaved to the narrow paths of the craftworlds, the self-serving scrum of Commorragh, the puritanical asceti-cism of the Exodites, or the life of servitude and performance of the Harlequins.

He dived and rolled, pulling *Light of Heaven* under and around another orkish barrage that nearly disembowelled his ship, then felt a stab of psychoflux pain as a kroozer he hadn't seen trans-fixed his hull with a lance strike. The energy beam flickered and died after a moment as the orks' crude power generators burned out and failed, but the blast had clipped a power relay serving at least one of the aetheric engines.

'I'm losing manoeuvrability,' Myrin announced, fighting against a ship no longer able to match its capabilities to his desires. He had no need to say anything further; every member of his bridge crew knew what that statement meant. Orkish accuracy was poor, but even holofields had limited ability to hide the truth, and the beasts were usually capable of hitting a blurry target moving at a steady pace and changing course only slowly, if at all.

Myrin began mentally composing his death hymn. His family would never get a chance to sing it, since he had left them all behind, but it felt fitting to face his doom with a tune of his own devising on his lips, even if he managed only a few bars before his life was claimed…

'The waygate!' Xela shouted. 'It's activating!'

Myrin did his best to shunt aside *Light of Heaven*'s battle wounds from his consciousness and focus on the information the ship's sensors were still gathering. Xela was right, as always. The waygate had flickered into life, and the familiar shimmering, roiling curtain of energy was once more stretched out from edge to edge. He paid as much attention to it as he dared, hoping against hope that somehow another branch of the Starsplinters had come to their aid. It didn't matter who it was, whether it was a commander he knew or of whom he'd never heard, a close ally or one of the several with whom he had crossed blades in the past – any warrior who faced this peril with him would have his gratitude and his friendship in the aftermath, assuming he had anything left to give.

The waygate flickered, and something slipped through. It was tiny, and it was alone.

'A single Aconite?' Myrin said, the sudden hope that had

surged in his heart draining away like a dying sea. Although well armed for a ship its size, Aconite frigates were nothing more than footnotes in a battle like this – his own fleet had boasted a dozen or more, although his readings suggested that only four remained operational. What was more, the Aconite was already turning, using its exceptional manoeuvrability to heel around and flee back through the waygate before its presence was noted by any of the nearest ork vessels. Myrin could not blame the captain, since this was a battle in which that small ship would make no discernible difference, and which would almost certainly be a death sentence for the crew. He hoped for a moment that some of the ork ships *would* notice the frigate, or at least the active waygate, and would pursue the Aconite back inside, thus taking them out of the fight. Considerations of orks loose in the webway were of rather less import to him when set against his remaining fleet's chances of survival.

To Myrin's mixed relief and chagrin, it looked like his wishes were to be answered in part. One of the kroozers was indeed changing course, having apparently seen the active waygate and deciding to investigate what was on the other side of it. Myrin cursed quietly, and tore his attention away. Half the ork force would have had to disappear suddenly for this battle to be conceivably winnable, and the waygate would not remain active for that long, even assuming enough of the arakhia wished to leave their current fight behind in order to pursue an entirely theoretical one elsewhere.

'That ship,' Xela said as the frigate fled back into the webway. 'Did you see its colours?'

Myrin blinked uncertainly. Had he? He had been so focused on its size, nature, and solitude that he had paid attention to little else, not that he could have made out much from visuals alone in the dim and constantly shifting light of this subterranean war.

'Why?' he asked, fighting the helm as he tried to put orkish wreckage between him and an enemy intent on reducing him to the same state. He could dredge back through *Light of Heaven*'s sensory memory and see if the ship had received any sense of the new arrival's allegiance, but that would take concentration he could ill-afford to spare.

'I'm not certain,' Xela said, 'but I think–'

The waygate erupted.

Not a single vessel this time, nor just a frigate. Ship after ship emerged through the portal at full speed – aeldari ships, cruisers and escorts, fighters and bombers, all sweeping out in attack formation. They wasted not a moment, opening fire immediately, and the carnage they wrought was instant and devastating. Two ork warships – including the one that had been heading for the waygate – died within the first few seconds, breaking apart under the impact of guns, pulsar lance strikes, and torpedoes. The wave of ships came on, acquiring new targets and engaging them with ruthless precision.

'Those aren't Starsplinters,' Xela said, her tone halfway between awestruck and suspicious.

'No,' Myrin replied, his soul twisting uncomfortably within him. One aeldari fleet's movements looked much like any other to many commanders, but there was a world of difference to the experienced eye between the swashbuckling, individualistic style of a corsair fleet where every captain was out for their own glory, and the tight, well-ordered forms of a craftworld armada. One approach embraced the thrill of the moment, of having to adjust on the fly not just to your enemies but to your allies, making it all but impossible for the enemy to predict; the other subsumed individual expression into the collective goal, sacrificing spontaneity for a cohesion that, when executed correctly, could cut most foes to pieces.

'These are no corsairs,' Myrin said. 'These are craftworlders. *Ilmaren* craftworlders,' he added bitterly.

'You recognise their manoeuvres?' Xela asked.

Myrin sighed. 'I invented some of them.' He could feel the connection through *Light of Heaven* as well now. The vessel had been a part of this same Ilmaren fleet, and their shared heritage of wraithbone sang out like blood calling to blood.

'Look to yourselves,' he broadcast to his remaining captains. 'Let the intruders deal with the orks, since they have a mind to do just that. You all know my history, many of you share it. This may not be a rescue, so let us save what strength we can in case we find ourselves in need of it again.'

No sooner had he sent that signal than he became aware of a new pressure on his consciousness, that of an unfamiliar identity. One of the Ilmaren ships was attempting to make contact; it seemed that they too recognised their kin, and were able to pick out *Light of Heaven* as one of their former brethren. Any thoughts that this might be a chance encounter, unlikely though that was, were swept away.

Myrin opened the channel. Once he might have done so cautiously, attempting to gain some idea of the other party's intentions before deciding upon what approach to take, but that was not the corsair way. This was *his* citadel, besieged though it was, and it was no longer in his nature to show deference.

'Identify yourselves,' he ordered, as crisp and sharp as ever he had been when an admiral of the Ilmaren fleet.

'*This is Taenar Leotharan of the* Dance of Dying Seasons,' a male voice replied, matching Myrin tone for tone. '*Our scout was sent through to ascertain what manner of welcome we might receive. When they returned immediately with word of a battle, we came through to assist. You have my apologies for our intrusion, admiral.*'

'That has not been my title for many years,' Myrin snapped,

trying to put more space between him and an ork kroozer in the hope that it would focus on the aeldari ships that were coming towards it, obviously spoiling for a fight. 'What business does Ilmaren have here?'

'*Ilmaren is not present here, Myrin Stormdawn,*' Leotharan responded. '*You are looking at independent ships, no longer tied to any craftworld.*

'*And, if you will have us, an addition to your fleet.*'

FIVE

The battle of the Well of the Long Death was over. The orks, their attention focused inwards in an effort to hunt down the remaining Starsplinters, had been swept aside in short order by the newcomers. Now the arakhia were either dead, or scattered remnants in their smallest vessels that were being exterminated in their turn by kill squadrons. The commander of the newly arrived fleet could have taken the ruins of the Well of the Long Death for his own, should he have wished to; Myrin certainly did not have the ships to stop him. Instead, Leotharan had merely asked for an audience aboard *Light of Heaven*, which was a simple enough request to grant. Albeit not one without its problems.

'I don't like it,' Xela Flickerstep said. She had one of her knives out again, and was spinning it between her fingers. It had taken Myrin many years to work out that this was not necessarily a precursor to her using it on someone, and was in fact as close a sign to nerves as the shade runner ever displayed.

'I'm not without my misgivings,' Myrin admitted, 'but what would you have me do? We would be dead if not for them, I'm not too proud to admit that. Our fleet is in tatters and we are vulnerable. It would take too long to recall my other captains to make us strong again, even if they did not decide to switch allegiances to another commander.'

'He might be seeking to depose you,' Xela hissed. Her knife's rotations increased in speed.

'Then he is giving up a strong position to place himself at my mercy by coming aboard,' Myrin pointed out. He gestured to his stateroom and its occupants from the comfort of his throne. Such an extravagance would have been seen as evidence of dangerous pride in Ilmaren, but the life of a corsair baron required a certain amount of theatricality to remind his crew who was in command. 'That in itself intrigues me sufficiently to grant his request.'

'And perhaps he brings news from home?' Xela added, her tone tinged with sarcasm. She stepped back hastily as Myrin's void sabre cleared its scabbard, and the point flashed out to where her chin had been a moment before.

'This *is* home,' Myrin said flatly, fixing the former wych with a glare. 'Ilmaren is no more home to me than Commorragh is to you. Do not make me repeat myself.'

'*Captain.*' The messenger wave arrived in his ear, from Issarel. '*The visitors are here.*'

'Bring them in,' Myrin ordered, sheathing his sabre. He had sent one of his Bladesworn with the greeting party as a gesture of respect – although he had no idea if this Leotharan would understand that – and he had chosen Issarel as the one least likely to raise hackles on the trip from the landing bay. Taranath laughed too much and too often, and at the wrong things, while Jhanandra was sullen at the best of times, and as for Xela… Well, it did not take even a worldly Asuryani to look at her and see a wych. Perhaps that would have been the best test of these newcomers' proclivities, and how far they had extricated themselves from their former lives and mindsets, but

Myrin had no wish to see fights break out on his ship due to misunderstandings.

Of course, what he wished for and what transpired did not necessarily bear close relation to each other. There was discipline amongst his crew, and most knew better than to test their captain's patience, but neither *Light of Heaven* nor any of his other ships operated with the solemnity and unthinking adherence to authority of a craftworld fleet. Bosuns carrying whips that owed their heritage to drukhari agonisers were on hand to ensure order was maintained, but there were limits to what such methods could achieve. Rank in a corsair fleet was an organic affair, and many a captain had lost their position – and, if they fought the change too hard, their life – when their crew grew tired of failure or poor treatment, and someone else with popular support rose up to challenge them.

All of which meant that when the grand double doors to Myrin's stateroom opened, what greeted the new arrivals was not the refined sanctum of contemplation they might have expected, with water features and sculptures and other sober expressions of Asuryani art and reflection; possibly a cultivated garden flourishing under soft lights mimicking sunlight, and delicately misted by inconspicuous devices. Such had been the state of this chamber at one point, but that was long ago, and such things had now been repurposed for the less fettered life of a corsair. This was where Myrin held court, and his court was in attendance: the captains of other capital ships – considerably fewer than they had been – and their officers, as well as the inevitable miscellany they had picked up along the way.

There was a Bard of Twilight, one who had become lost on the Path of the Player and whose dedication to performing the ancient lays and songs had taken him far from whatever craftworld had once been his home. He had discarded his own name in the service of keeping alive the names of heroes, and around him were others who sought to learn from him in much the same way that Aspect Warriors of a shrine would be taught by an exarch. There was Meliandril Anarra, one of the many rangers of Alaitoc wandering the galaxy, who had decided to travel with the Starsplinters for a time. She was not under Myrin's command as such, but she had lent her long rifle to their cause more than once, and she accepted his rule while aboard his vessel. There was even a small band of Harlequins. Myrin had given up trying to work out when and how they came and went, and knew better than to try to oppose them so long as the murder-acrobats did not meddle in his affairs. Harlequins were also about the only thing that could dampen Taranath's humour, which only served to add fuel to Myrin's private speculations about what life the smiling gunslinger had led before he found his way into the Starsplinters.

'Make way!' Issarel shouted, and Myrin saw the flash as they drew one of their powerblades to emphasise the point. The laughing, revelling crowd began to part, drawing back to leave the way to Myrin's throne unimpeded. They did not withdraw too far, however, since all of them were eager to lay eyes on the newcomers, and see who had come to the Starsplinters' rescue. Myrin did not doubt that some in the room would be weighing up the arrivals, and assessing whether the balance of power had changed. A corsair fleet was not as cutthroat an environment as Commorragh, where a single perceived crack in a shell of power could be the trigger for a dozen knives in the back – and other, less pleasant places – but it was dynamic nonetheless, and often uncomfortably so.

As the last straggler hastened to one side, Myrin finally got a proper look at his guests. They were almost entirely what he'd expected.

Almost, but not quite.

Taenar Leotharan was certainly the very image of an Ilmaren admiral. He had not yet even altered his uniform, which was still the burgundy-and-ash bodysuit that Myrin remembered so well, decorated with the wraithbone tags that indicated his rank and achievements – lower and fewer than Myrin's own before he left, Myrin noted idly. A powerblade rode on Leotharan's right hip along with a shuriken pistol, both of which would be standard for a warrior of that rank. An admiral should never have to fight to defend their ship, but should be armed properly in case that dire eventuality came to pass.

Leotharan himself was tall, with blunt, pale features that almost veered towards human, although somehow without the inherent ugliness that would imply. His long, straight, red hair was bound up in a high topknot, and he carried himself with the air of a fighter. He had spent some time as an Aspect Warrior, or Myrin was no judge. That was good. Regardless of Myrin's opinion of the Paths, a history of the Path of the Warrior implied a certain tried-and-tested strength that could be relied upon in battle.

Leotharan had five others with him, three of whom were clad in much the same way as their admiral. One captain, by Myrin's reading – presumably the ranking officer of Leotharan's flagship – and two senior crew members. The remaining two, however, he found far more intriguing.

The first was a warlock, clad in the intricate, rune-encrusted robes of those travelling the Path of the Seer. His helm was tucked under one arm, and the hilt of a witchblade rose above his right shoulder. His blue-black, curly hair was cropped short and close to his skull, and a shiny scar marred the smooth surface of his dark brown skin, running as it did down over his left cheek. Seers often appeared serene and aloof, an impression

Myrin suspected they deliberately cultivated. This one, however, just looked… bored. Which was in itself an interesting demeanour for someone who had just walked into a corsair baron's lair.

The second, watching her surroundings with distrustful eyes set into a bronze-skinned face, was clad in the segmented green armour of the Striking Scorpions aspect shrine. What was more, the quality of her wargear and the number of spirit stones set into her armour marked her out as an exarch – one who had trodden the Path of the Warrior too long for her mind to ever readjust to a different life. She was doomed to that existence, now, and her soul would be gradually merging with those of the other aeldari who had worn the armour before her.

'Welcome!' Myrin declared, having studied them enough for the moment. He was lounging on his throne with his right leg draped over one arm, and he did not rise. Rescuers or not, they needed to know whose realm this was. 'Will you have some refreshments?'

The fountains still ran, but no longer with water. Myrin waved his hand, and his courtiers dipped goblets into the dark purple flow, then brought them forward to proffer them to the newcomers with sharp-edged smiles. The ship crewers eyed the drinks with the alarmed wariness of a pet avian that had just seen a predator prowl into the room, and attempted to distance themselves from the offer without doing anything so obvious or crass as refusing. The exarch simply stared a hole into the corsair holding a goblet out to her until he fell backwards, his smile faltering. Leotharan took a goblet but did not drink, and held it with as little of his hand touching the stem as possible.

The warlock ignored the offer and the corsair making it, until she laid a hand upon his shoulder and pushed it up under his nose with a mocking smile, relishing his discomfort. Then the warlock raised his other hand and, without even looking at her, made a simple gesture. The corsair was thrown away from him by an invisible force. She landed hard on her back, the drink spilling onto the ground.

'Don't touch me,' the warlock said calmly into the moment of shocked silence that followed, his voice deep and steady.

The stateroom erupted into noise as the assembled corsairs began yelling, and the crowd began to surge inwards. Leotharan's jaw clenched, and he immediately ducked his head into a bow.

'Baron, please forgive Warlock Kyldran,' he said hastily. 'He–'

Myrin held one hand up to forestall his apology. 'Peace, admiral. All is not as you think.'

The swarm of corsairs crowded around the new arrivals, laughing and slapping them on the shoulders in a comradely fashion, all save for Kyldran, of course, whom everyone was careful not to touch, although he still found himself at the centre of a circle of amused faces. The corsair who'd fallen victim to his psykana was hauled up by others, who began to ridicule her.

'Well?' Myrin said softly to Xela, as Leotharan's attention was momentarily diverted by someone draping herself around him in a way clearly intended to be welcoming.

'I can practically smell the stink of Asuryani still clinging to them,' Xela muttered back. 'Uptight, sanctimonious prigs, probably with no initiative. They'll be a liability.'

'Perhaps,' Myrin agreed. 'Still, there's no harm in seeing if they loosen up a little.' He slid off his throne and descended from its dais, brushing his courtiers aside until he found himself face to face with Leotharan. The former Ilmaren admiral was a shade taller than him, with clear lilac eyes that would have been piercing had they not currently been full of uncertainty. Myrin slid his arm through the other aeldari's before Leotharan had properly registered his presence, and began to steer him gently but firmly away from the crush.

'I have several questions,' Myrin said without preamble. Leotharan's head twisted around, clearly wishing for some support in this unexpected development, but the rest of his coterie were anchored in place by the Starsplinters' welcome. 'Let us start with how you found me, followed swiftly by *why* you found me.'

'Baron Stormdawn,' Leotharan began uncertainly, but Myrin raised a finger on his other hand to cut him off.

'None of that. No awkward titles, no stammering or stuttering, no hiding behind stiff formality. I'll have honesty out of you, Leotharan, or you won't be leaving this room alive.' He tightened his grip on Leotharan's arm as the admiral tensed at the threat. 'Don't try anything foolish. My shade runner can be at your side before you can blink, and have her knives into your spine before you can react. She was one of the very best of Commorragh's fighting pits until she decided she wanted to see the galaxy, and she already doesn't like you very much.'

Leotharan relaxed a little, although it was clearly a conscious effort. 'Is this the gratitude you show to the commander who rescued you?'

'We'll get to gratitude after you've answered my questions,' Myrin said, putting some of the sternness Leotharan might expect from a former Ilmaren admiral into his voice. 'This is my last time of asking. How did you find me, and why?'

'In truth, I'm surprised you need to ask,' Leotharan replied. 'You are a famed commander of the Starsplinters, the mightiest corsair fleet in this part of the galaxy. This port of yours might not be widely known, but word travels amongst aeldari. It took us many months of searching, but someone with sufficient interest can find out, so long as he has… sufficient means to persuade others to answer his questions.'

Myrin thought of Leotharan's fleet, and smiled wryly. That was certainly a great deal of persuasive power.

'As to why,' Leotharan continued, 'you may not know me, since I had not risen to prominence in the fleet when you left Ilmaren, but I know you. Your very public argument with Farseer Caman and your subsequent departure with half a fleet was shocking. It dominated conversation across the craftworld for several years, and we mariners spoke of little else amongst ourselves.'

Myrin snorted. 'I imagine I was cast as the villain of the piece.'

'That was certainly the prevailing opinion,' Leotharan acknowledged cautiously. 'Caman themself was fairly close-mouthed on the issue, at least publicly, but others had opinions which they shared at great length. "Traitor" was a word that cropped up with fair frequency, given the state of our... of the craftworld's defences even before your departure.'

Myrin smiled again, catching the slip. 'And you, Admiral Leotharan? I notice you do not express your opinion on the matter, and yet here you are with what must be, by my estimation, a fair chunk of a fleet of your own.'

'I did not think of you favourably at first,' Leotharan admitted. 'No, that is incorrect. I thought of you very favourably, at first. We all knew you as a talented and devoted servant of Ilmaren, an admiral under whom any mariner would be proud to serve. I felt the stab of betrayal when you left. However, when I achieved your former rank, although I initially intended to become a commander of your equal who could fill the void you had left behind, I found myself... frustrated.'

'Indeed?' Myrin asked neutrally, steering the pair of them around a sculpture that somehow managed to be both abstract and intensely sensual at the same time. Leotharan's eyes lingered on it for a long moment as they passed.

'The Farseer Council,' Leotharan said a moment later in answer to Myrin's half-question. His voice was tinged with shame, yet also defiance. 'Even now I doubt myself, wondering if I should not have trusted to their wisdom, but I could see precious little evidence of it. We were wounded, isolated. Repairs from the orkish attack were progressing, but too slowly. The seers appeared to have no plan other than avoiding notice until our wounds were healed, but I could see only folly in that approach. The galaxy is a harsh and vicious place, and our enemies would not give us that time. We needed to eliminate threats before they found us, not duck our heads and hope to hide our weakness. We should have ventured forth and courted allies, not hamstrung ourselves with stiff-necked pride.'

Myrin chuckled. 'And did you express these opinions?'

'I did.'

'And how were they received?'

'I was told that I was young and foolhardy, and too eager to drag us into conflicts which we might otherwise evade entirely,' Leotharan replied. 'I was assured that the Seer Council knew better than I. I was instructed to see to my ships and my crews, and to be ready to respond to any threats against which their foretellings could not entirely shield us. I was told, in short, to *mind my own business*, despite the fact that precious few of those worthies had served amongst a ship's crew, and none for centuries.' He sighed. 'And then the Queen of Knives came.'

Myrin looked up sharply. 'Lelith Hesperax came to Ilmaren?' He knew that name; precious few aeldari did not, save for the most isolated Exodites. The grand succubus of the Cult of Strife, the greatest gladiatorial fighter ever to emerge from the Dark City, and utterly merciless.

'Aye, and as an enemy,' Leotharan said, bitterness curdling his voice. 'A raiding party that overwhelmed our defences, slaughtered many of those who rushed to the craftworld's defence, and carried off many more. We had no warning, no *foretellings*.

The drukhari struck and faded with such force and swiftness that we could do little but harry them as they were already retreating, and we knew better than to pursue the Dark Kin into the webway on their terms. Another grievous blow, which we might have rebuffed had we made alliances for our own protection, and which might never have fallen at all had our reputation been more warlike, and less that of a dying world limping towards its own doom.'

'And your response was to leave?' Myrin asked.

'I could see no other honourable course,' Leotharan said tightly. 'Our leaders could not protect us, and what should I have done? Attempted to overthrow the Seer Council? Such a civil war would be unheard of. I would never have gained enough support to succeed, and if I failed then my fate would likely be death. At best, it would be the one I have taken upon myself now – to gather to me those who shared my views and make our own way, rather than stay to watch the world we called home drift blindly into oblivion while still expecting us to give our lives for it.'

Myrin nodded soberly. 'A sad tale. But I fail to see how this relates to you seeking me out.'

'I find that hard to believe,' Leotharan said levelly. He stopped, and the tug on Myrin's arm pulled him around in a quarter-circle to face the other aeldari.

'I admired you before, as a defender of Ilmaren,' Leotharan said, his voice quiet but steady. 'I was hurt by what I considered your betrayal, but only until I encountered the same problems, the same… obstinance. Rumours of your more recent exploits still filter back to the craftworld of your birth – the defeat of the Szarekh Dynastic fleet at the Helmingvar shipyards, your gambit with the black hole against the Chaos filth sworn to the Despoiler, and so on.' He straightened. 'You may consider this "stiff formality" if you wish, but if Ilmaren cannot be worthy of my loyalty then I will find someone who is, and I believe that to be you.'

Myrin ran a thumb across his lower lip, grinning. 'Such pretty words from a pretty face!' Leotharan's eyes widened slightly, and Myrin chuckled. 'My friend, you know nothing about me. As you may have gathered from our surroundings, I am far from the same Myrin Stormdawn who led a fleet in defence of a craftworld.'

He unhooked his arm, and gestured about them. 'There are no Paths out here. We chart our own courses, and they can take you to some strange places indeed. The life of a corsair is dangerous, and not just from battle. The weak-willed find themselves pulled one way and another, until they lose themselves in something and never return. Some go mad. Some fall into the clutches of She Who Thirsts.' He smiled cruelly at Leotharan's expression. 'Oh yes, worse than any of the Dark Kin. Too much freedom is a very dangerous thing. Even Commorragh has inviolable rules, rules that you go against on pain of a very final death. Asdrubael Vect is a tyrant, but a tyrant who will tolerate no threat to his miserable city. Out here, we must control ourselves...'

He drew one forefinger down Leotharan's arm.

'...lest others control us.'

As he predicted, Leotharan's response to the touch was to stiffen. A corsair would have laughed, or thrown an insult, or punched Myrin in the face, and would have been perfectly within their rights to do any of those things. Had Myrin ever been *this* uptight? Xela had not been wrong in her assessment of the newcomers.

Still... there was an underlying strength in Taenar Leotharan, Myrin could sense that much. It was held in check at the moment, and it kept his spine straight and his limbs tense. Myrin wondered what it would take to bring it out of him.

Wondered what it would look like if and when that happened.

'Tell me about your companions,' he said, looking back at them. 'The interesting ones, I mean. I would have expected other crew members to have come with you, but a warlock? And an exarch, I see.'

'Ra'thar Kyldran shared my frustrations with the Seer Council,' Leotharan said. 'He was a Dark Reaper once, and I'm not sure he ever fully left it behind. He's been grim of countenance and minded towards the destruction of our foes ever since, so he was just as impatient with the council's inaction.'

'He does not strike me as the patient type,' Myrin agreed easily, and Leotharan flushed.

'It was wrong of him to strike your...' He hesitated, clearly searching for the correct term to describe someone who, to him, had no obvious rank or role. 'Person.'

'Not at all,' Myrin said with a smile. 'She had no right to touch him without his permission. Had he drawn blood then remonstrances might have followed, but as it is, your warlock has probably endeared himself more than any others in your crew so far. We appreciate a bit of swagger, around here.'

Leotharan looked at him, and Myrin could almost feel the calculation going on behind the other's eyes. No craftworlder relished conflict with other aeldari, and their instincts were honed to avoid it where possible – to step aside, to make allowances, to keep weapons sheathed and insults behind one's teeth. Such measures did not always work, of course, since sometimes others' transgressions could not be ignored, but even then no Asuryani took up arms without reluctance – save perhaps for the exarchs, who knew no other way of living. The notion that braggadocio might be admired was clearly something that Leotharan was struggling to process.

'Cithriel Shelwe-nin is, as you say, an exarch,' Leotharan continued after a moment. 'She and some of her shrine's warriors would travel with us, seeking combat in boarding actions, or repelling enemies attempting the same thing. I was as surprised as you that she left her shrine to come with us, but she is adamant that she will return there some day. Or her armour will,' he added with a shrug. 'Which to her, I suppose, is now more or less one and the same.'

'Fascinating,' Myrin murmured. 'Shelwe-nin, you say? I knew of a Striking Scorpion exarch named Rhidhal Shelwe-nin when I served in the fleet, although I never met him. This is his successor?'

'Indeed,' Leotharan said, nodding. 'Rhidhal trained me in the ways of his shrine. Cithriel was my squad leader. When she lost herself on the Path she inherited Rhidhal's armour, and the exarch lineage.'

'You are very lucky to have a warrior of such skill with you,' Myrin said with complete honesty. 'With any luck, we can avoid any of my crew provoking her to the point that she kills one.' He smiled. 'Although anyone foolish enough to do so will not be a great loss.'

Leotharan's expression flickered again, and Myrin laughed. 'It will take time for you to lose that reflex, my friend. You are used to thinking of our people as a precious resource, lives that must be treasured and preserved above all other considerations.'

'You do not believe that to be the case?' Leotharan replied, his tone a challenge to which Myrin did not rise.

'I told you, we must control ourselves out here. We have no capacity for those who do not add value, in whatever form that takes. I am not saying that we sacrifice the weak,' he added, taking a guess at the mindset behind Leotharan's darkening expression, 'for they can still contribute. But the foolish, the unwise, those who make bad decisions even when the con-sequences have been laid out for them... They have no place. There are no craftworld domes here for such wastrels to shelter in while the rest of us bleed to protect them. Everyone pulls together, or they are abandoned.'

'And who are you to make that judgement?' Leotharan asked. Myrin smiled inwardly. Leotharan had played the perfect Asuryani guest so far, but there was the tantalising hint of more underneath.

'I am Baron Myrin Stormdawn, Lord of the Well of the Long Death, and the one to whom you came of your own free will in exile,' he said. 'You apparently thought enough of me to follow in my footsteps and leave the craftworld behind, but you baulk at the first sign that things here may be different?'

He gestured back to his court. 'There you see the finest of the aeldari. Why? Because they are only those who can cope with the pressure of freedom.'

Leotharan nodded slowly. 'And how did they cope with the pressure of an ork fleet invading their fortress?'

Myrin chuckled. 'Oh, so the admiral has teeth after all!' He sobered again. 'That was unexpected, I will admit. No enemy has tracked us here before. My fleet was engaged by another fragment of theirs before we entered the webway. I cannot credit the beasts with the wit to drive us from one ambush into another, especially since they could not know that we were coming here. It appears Uzgul is escalating the conflict between us.'

'Uzgul?' Leotharan asked.

'The leader of the Badskab Bukkaneers, as they call themselves,' Myrin replied wearily. 'A wily monster. At first, we thought it simply objected to other pirates in the area of the galaxy it viewed as its own. After a while, we realised that it wanted slaves, for some purpose we have still not determined, and it seems to favour aeldari. We know it will take the spirit stones from the dead as well, though we have no idea what it does with them.'

Leotharan shuddered. 'I dread to think.'

'Precisely.' Myrin sighed. 'But you bring me back to the important point. Somehow, at least one element of the Badskabs found us. It would be foolish for me to assume that they cannot manage it again, and in greater force. The Well is no longer a refuge.'

'You will be leaving here?' Leotharan asked.

'For now,' Myrin agreed. 'But here is where we differ from the craftworlds, Leotharan. Ilmaren would seek to melt into the shadows after a battle such as this, but I intend to take this fight to Uzgul. I must contact other commanders and find out if they have been similarly targeted. If so, perhaps I can leverage decisive action.'

'Baron–'

'Please,' Myrin laughed, knocking his knuckles into Leotharan's chest. 'You, at least, may call me Myrin.'

'Myrin,' Leotharan said after a moment's hesitation. 'When we first spoke, I offered you my ships.'

'Thinking better of it now?'

'No!' Leotharan protested. His eyes narrowed as he saw Myrin's sly smile, and realised he had again been needled into a reaction. 'No. I merely wish to know if you accept my offer.'

'I haven't decided yet,' Myrin said lazily. 'You'll need to prove yourselves to me.'

'Beyond destroying an orkish fleet for you?' Leotharan demanded.

'Yes,' Myrin said, deadly serious. 'Have you not been listening? Void battle with your ships following your orders is what you know, it's as close to craftworld life as anything you'll find out here. You're a good leader, with good crews, but that's only half of what you'll need now. I must know that you can cope with this life, all of it. I must know that you're not going to panic and abandon me when the reality of your situation sets in, that you won't fall prey to the laughter of the thirsting gods between the stars, and that you won't *embarrass* me.'

He took a step back towards the rest, and beckoned. 'Come. We have work to do.'

SIX

'Da Dakkaplanet,' Uzgul da Magnificent said, clearly enjoying the sound of the words. He clapped Gazruk Hackspanna on the back hard enough for the badmek to feel his teeth shift. 'Ain't dat da greatest fing ever created by an ork?'

'Ever created by *anyone*, boss!' Runk the grot squeaked obsequiously by Uzgul's right ankle.

'Obviously!' Skizz, the other grot, snorted from Uzgul's other side. 'Nuffin's gonna be better'n wot an ork's created, so dat's superflu… soupy… souperful! Dat's a souperful description!'

'Your *face* is souperful!' Runk retorted angrily, and the two of them fell to brawling with much squawking, long fingers rammed up noses, and tugging of ears. Uzgul ignored them, and Gazruk did his best to imitate his kaptin. One did not squash the boss' grots flat, even if they were making an infuriating racket, since otherwise the boss might not have a grot around to flatten when he really wanted one.

'Da greatest fing ever created by an ork,' Uzgul repeated, apparently on the basis that it had lost a bit of impact after the gretchin's interruptions.

'Sure is impressive, boss,' Gazruk admitted. It was the badmek's first time seeing it since joining the Bukkaneers, and he didn't want to seem underwhelmed. However, looking down at it from orbit, it didn't really look much different to any number of other worlds he'd seen. 'Don't take dis da wrong way,' Gazruk said cautiously, 'but didja really *create* it? Da planet, I mean,' he added hastily.

'Of course I didn't create da *planet*!' Uzgul barked, rounding on the badmek. 'Wot sort of nonsense question is dat? I'm talkin' about wot I did to it to make it da *Dakkaplanet*, obviously! Used to be just a planet, right? Nuffin' important or interestin' about it. Den I came wiv me ladz an' made it into da Dakkaplanet!' He folded his arms. 'Don't see why dat's so hard to understand.'

'How's da progress?' Gazruk asked. Uzgul looked at him suspiciously, but Gazruk schooled his features into complete earnestness.

'It's got four rokkit boostas now,' Uzgul said proudly. 'All on da same side of da planet, for maximum "go". Dere was a bunch of islands wot weren't really doing nuffin', so we had da slaves build da rokkits on 'em, one on each.'

'Maximum "go",' Gazruk repeated, feeling the words in his mouth and trying to connect them to a concept that made sense.

'Dat's right.'

'Wot about turnin'?' Gazruk asked after a few seconds. 'Or stoppin'?'

'Eh, we'll deal wiv dat when it happens,' Uzgul said dismissively.

'Stoppin's for cowards!' Skizz squeaked from where it had Runk in a headlock. 'Da boss said so!'

'Boss?' Gazruk said.

'Aye?'

'Permisshun to whack yer grot?'

'Aye!' Uzgul agreed happily. Gazruk rounded on the two gretchin, who broke apart from their pathetic scrap with the self-preservation instincts of creatures recognising that something truly dangerous was coming, and fled in opposite directions into the shadows of *Sunstompa*'s bridge. Gazruk growled under his breath, then returned to his previous position.

'So wot about da gun?' he asked, hoping that at least this bit would make more sense.

'Da gun?' Uzgul beamed in delight. 'Dat's da best part! See, everyone knows big gunz are shootier, right?'

'Yup,' Gazruk nodded. 'Dat's why we build 'em so big.'

'Right, now y'see, dis ain't somefing wot most kaptins would know,' Uzgul said, winking as though to let Gazruk in on the secret of how much smarter he was than the average freebooter. 'But cos I'm clever, like, *I* know dat if da gun gets *really* big, da barrel might droop a bit. So if I wanted to build da biggest gun wot an ork's ever built, stickin' outta da ground, it's gonna need lots of stuff to hold it up, right?'

Gazruk nodded again. 'Wiv ya so far, boss.' And yes, this part was true. Strength-to-weight ratio, warping of material with heat and use… these were all concepts that meks understood on an instinctual basis, even if they couldn't put them into, y'know, *words*.

'But dat's a lot of work!' Uzgul said theatrically, waving one arm towards the planet. 'An' fine, we got slaves to do da work, but dat still don't make it *quick*. So dat's when I had wot might be me best idea yet.' He paused expectantly.

'An' wot's dat, boss?' Gazruk asked, a moment later than Uzgul would have preferred, but not so late that he couldn't pass it off as slow-wittedness instead of lack of interest. Not that it mattered. Uzgul was enjoying pontificating about his grand project.

'We'z had da slaves hollow out da tallest mountain!' the freebooter kaptin said triumphantly. 'All da way down to da ground, an' beyond! Da *mountain* is gonna be da *barrel*! It's taller'n anyfing we could get da gits to build on dere own.'

'Yoo dug a hole… right down da middle of a mountain?'

Gazruk said. Luckily, his frank disbelief was apparently taken as an appropriate reaction.

'Dat's right!' Uzgul crowed. 'No one ain't gonna see *dat* comin'! Oh look, here's a perfectly normal planet comin' into dis solar system, no gunz on it, den *whoomp*!'

'Whoomp?'

'Well, dat's a rough approx-er-mayshun of da sound it's gonna make, I reckon,' Uzgul said, waving one hand dismissively. 'I might be da greatest kaptin in da galaxy, but I ain't got da ability to give ya da sound of one planet shootin' anuvver one an' blowin' it up. Ain't heard it yet, for one fing.'

'Right, right,' Gazruk said. He took a step to one side, very graciously giving Uzgul space to bask in the glory of his achievements, and definitely not because he was starting to have definite doubts about which one of them was actually more likely to blow up something important. 'An' about da gun… Wot's it gonna shoot?'

'Wondered about dat,' Uzgul admitted. 'Fort of a few fings. Big ol' rokkits, maybe – basically a small kroozer wiv explosives in it. Some sort of electro-zappy fing, like reverse lightning. Dat'd look well snazzy, and shouldn't be too hard to get rigged up.'

'Yeah, not too hard,' Gazruk muttered, looking out of the viewport in the vain hope that he'd find some sort of answers or salvation there.

'*But*, I settled on da best option,' Uzgul said. 'Just like wiv da mountain, we get da planet to do da work for us!'

'Do da work for ya?' Gazruk asked. He should have held his tongue, but his natural mek curiosity propelled him onwards. 'I fort yoo'd dug da hole into da mountain?'

'Well, yeah, but digging *down* is easier'n building *up*, innit?' Uzgul said. 'Cos gravity, right? C'mon, yoo're a mek. I fort you'd know dis stuff!'

'But how'd dey get da rock dey'd dug back up out of… Ya know wot? Sorry, boss,' Gazruk apologised, ducking his head. 'Carry on.'

'Y'know how planets've got dat hot rock in 'em?' Uzgul said, leaning a bit closer in a conspiratorial manner. 'Comes shootin' right out? Dat's wot we're usin'! It's genius!'

'Genius,' Gazruk said. At this point it was probably safer just to repeat words. 'Yeah, I can see dat. Definitely.'

'I'm callin' it da Gun-cano,' Uzgul said. 'Dat's like a gun, but *also* a volcano, right? It's better when ya mash two words togevva to make one word, dat's how ya know a fing's gonna be good.'

'Dat's definitely sense, kaptin,' Gazruk said, hoping this bit of praise would be spread out and applied to all of Uzgul's other statements, even though it blatantly shouldn't be. 'So, dat hot rock…'

'Gonna use it for da rokkits, too,' Uzgul said proudly. 'See, fing is usually, when planets have dese fings goin' off, dey're on opposite sides, so it all cancels out. *We've* got all our rokkits on one side, and dere's no uvvers about!'

'How're yoo gonna make it erupt when you want it to, boss?' Gazruk asked. Surely, if he did his own digging, sense would emerge?

'Simple,' Uzgul said with a snort. 'Drop a bomb in it, get da stuff all riled up. Same wiv da gun.'

Gazruk scratched his cheek, hoping that provided an excuse for his grimace. 'An' how're yoo gonna keep it from comin' out when ya *don't* want it to?'

'Lid,' Uzgul said, looking at him dubiously. 'Obviously. Y'know, Gazruk, yoo don't seem too smart about dis sorta fing. Maybe you should stick to smaller gunz 'n' whatnot.'

'Yeah, sorry about dat, boss,' Gazruk said, fiddling with a spanner. 'So… how long yoo been doing dis? Wiv da Dakka-planet, I mean?'

'Been a few years,' Uzgul said, turning to survey the jewel of his domain once more. 'Uvver orks would've lost patience by now, but I got a *dream*, Gazruk! I got a *vision*, maybe sent by Gork 'n' Mork 'emselves! Everyfing da Bukkaneers are doin', all da slaves, all da tek – it's all goin' into dis.'

'All of it,' Gazruk repeated numbly. 'Goin' into dis.' He shook his head and let out a long, low whistle. It was a long-established mek tradition; a shorthand for when you came across one of the worst bodge jobs you'd seen. It was vastly insufficient in this instance.

'Only one problem,' Uzgul began.

'Only one?' Gazruk responded absently, then jerked to alert. 'Sorry, kaptin. An' wot's dat one problem?'

'Need more slaves!' Uzgul said simply, gesturing at the Dakka-planet. 'I know it don't look it from up here, but dat's a big place! Dere's still a lot of work to do, an' we need more hands down dere. Humies ain't much use – da gits keel over an' die after a few weeks. Sure, yoo can easily find more, but dat takes time too. Skrawnies, on da uvver hand…' He looked meaning-fully at Gazruk. 'Dey're da real deal. Stronger'n dey look, an' a powerful will to keep alive, speshully if yoo take dere stones off 'em first. I don't fink dere's an ork in da galaxy wot's got more skrawnies of his own in one place.'

'An' dat's why yoo've been after dese Starsplinter gits?' Gazruk asked. That'd always been the rumour, that Kaptin Uzgul da Magnificent really had it in for the skrawnies. It just turned out that there was a more practical side to it.

'Well, dat an' dey've been annoyin' me for ages,' Uzgul said. 'Weird, tho. Used to be we'd never know where dey woz, dey'd take us by surprise. Now, it's like I just got dis *idea* of where dey're gonna be. Yoo fight somefing for a while, yoo start to know how it finks.' He tapped the side of his head, and winked.

Gazruk tried to get his mental balance. All he'd ever wanted from life was the chance to throw together some scrap and make weapons and vehicles and other things that went fast and/or bang. He didn't really care where he did it, and nor was he particularly bothered about who he nominally did it for, because at the end of the day he was doing it for *him*. It was just that Warboss Uvrik had been quite fussy about exactly where those explosions took place, so Gazruk had needed to find another place to do it, and then he found his way into the Badskab Bukkaneers, and…

And, well, Uzgul was clearly loony.

Not loony in a normal way. Not loony in that he heard Gork and/or Mork in his head, or spoke in random, high-pitched gibberish, or would only ever wear a boot on his left foot. Gazruk had met orks with those traits and thought nothing more about it. He liked making things. Doks liked sewing orks up, or chopping bits off and sewing other things on in their place. Runtherds liked training and herding squigs, or prodding grots until they obeyed orders. That was all part of how orks were, endlessly different flavours of Gork and Mork, and, so far as Gazruk was concerned, maybe there was a place for orks who only wanted to wear a boot on their left foot. So long as they got stuck in with a choppa when a fight showed up and didn't try to stop him from building things, he didn't care.

Uzgul, though…

Uzgul had looked at a planet and decided, so far as Gazruk could work out, that he wanted to turn it into a sort of spaceship. That was well over the one-boot-only threshold, and accelerating fast towards the horizon. It wouldn't have been so bad, except that Uzgul was clearly very capable of other things, like commanding a krew and krumping other spaceships. That success meant that he thought he should be able to do this – that because he was good at one or two things, he should be good at *everything*. And because he was in charge, he was going to assume it was someone else's fault if his ridiculous, nonsense plan didn't work.

Which it couldn't. Gazruk couldn't even begin to think how it would work. The problems with it were so big and so many he couldn't even begin to think how it *wouldn't* work. It was like trying to explain to your boss that he couldn't swallow the sun. Where did you start?

So Gazruk knew better than to express any interest in da Dakkaplanet, or give any indication that maybe he could help with whatever the next problem with it was going to be, because as soon as they reached a problem he couldn't overcome, Uzgul would blame him. However, Gazruk also needed to make sure he stayed useful. Fine. Just because he couldn't do anything about the planet, that didn't mean he couldn't do anything about the stuff the boss wanted *for* the planet.

'So yoo want more skrawnies,' he said slowly.

'Always,' Uzgul said, nodding.

'An' yoo've got some of da stones dey wear?'

'Yeah.' Uzgul looked at him suspiciously. 'Why?'

Gazruk tapped one finger thoughtfully on his teeth. 'Might take me a little while, but maybe I could rig up somefing wot could help...'

SEVEN

'You intend to abandon the Well?' demanded the aeldari Taenar had learned was named Ellisar Elasandor, captain of *The Yearning Stars*. 'We built this place! It is as close to a home as anything we have!' He slammed his palm down on the tabletop around which the assembled captains sat. The limb was a false one with the appearance of marble, Taenar noticed; it seemed Elasandor had elected not to seek the assistance of healers after whatever injury had taken his left arm.

'And it is compromised,' Myrin Stormdawn said. His voice and expression were calm, although his drukhari first mate – no, his *corsair* first mate, Taenar corrected himself – standing behind his chair at his right shoulder looked far less happy.

'The arakhia found their way in through routes we thought only we knew,' Stormdawn continued. 'Some certainly escaped, and we must presume they found their way out again, and could lead others of their kind back to us. What is more, who is to say that another foe could not duplicate their feat?' He leaned back in his chair, the very image of a languid commander, but Taenar noticed his eyes glittering beneath half-closed lids. Stormdawn was nowhere near as relaxed as he seemed.

For that matter, Taenar could not imagine how Stormdawn

could be relaxed at all. His home berth was all but destroyed, his forces were in tatters, and he was facing down something which in the Ilmaren fleet would have been considered a mutiny. Mariners were expected to obey their senior officers, not hit the furniture and shout. Taenar had known it would be a very different world out here, but it was one thing to know it, and quite another to actually *experience* it. He took a small sip of his drink. He would have expected a delicately spiced water at a war council, but here his glass was filled with something thick and almost treacly on the tongue, the sweetness not quite hiding the potent alcoholic kick, nor the copperish aftertaste.

'Then why do we not seal off the fissures?' Elasandor was protesting, to which Myrin simply rolled his eyes.

'And leave yourselves solely dependent on the webway to come and go?' Taenar found himself saying as his sip spread a pleasant heat down through his chest. 'What if that branch becomes corrupted? What if the Dark Kin come hunting? You will have boxed yourselves in, and done your enemies' work for them.'

'Why is the stripling speaking?' Elasandor asked the room in general, waving one hand dismissively in Taenar's direction.

'My ships are the reason you are still alive!' Taenar snapped, nettled by the other's manner, but Elasandor simply snorted.

'Your arrival and subsequent actions came about through no doing of mine,' he retorted, to Taenar's amazement. 'You would place me in your debt because you came to my home unannounced, and killed a foe you would have engaged no matter where you had encountered them?'

'I did not speak of debt–' Taenar began.

'Let me be clear, *admiral*,' Elasandor said, leaning forward and fixing Taenar with a stare. 'You walked a different Path before you chose that of the Mariner, correct? When you pulled on your first uniform and set foot on your first void-craft, did you expect everyone to listen to your opinions because you had achieved some prominence as an artisan, or a poet?'

'Of course not!' Taenar said, irritated at being spoken to like a fool.

'Then you understand!' Elasandor said, sitting back again and gesturing to Taenar with his marble palm, as though the discussion was concluded. 'You are no corsair. You are not one of us. Why should we listen – no, why should you even *speak* – when you have no familiarity with our ways? If the ships are, as you say, *your* ships, then you are not a part of our fraternity. If you *have* joined the Starsplinters then your ships come under the command of Baron Stormdawn, and you have nothing more than your own vessel.'

Taenar felt a flush rising in his cheeks. He wanted to throw the corsair's words back into his face, but the truth – that Stormdawn would not accept Taenar's fealty until he knew that he could trust him – was hardly the stinging rejoinder he would have wished. He glanced at the baron, but Stormdawn was simply watching them both with one fist tucked under his chin, apparently enjoying himself. Taenar should have known better than to expect support from that quarter; the sort of structure and discipline to which he was used was almost completely absent here.

'My apologies,' he said tightly. 'I believe you were suggesting leaving yourselves with only one way in or out. Please continue.'

'It is not a matter for debate,' Stormdawn broke in before Elasandor could respond. 'I, and all ships of my fleet, will depart the Well as soon as we have finished those repairs we can achieve, and salvaged all that can be saved from the docks and living quarters. Any captain wishing to stay behind to lay claim to the Well as their own may of course do so, but they will do so alone, and they will deal with any further threats alone.' He rose from his chair, and motioned lazily for the rest of them to do the same.

'What will be our heading?' asked another captain, who wore around her shoulders the furry pelt of a beast with which Taenar was unfamiliar.

'The Farmarket,' Stormdawn replied, garnering a few intakes of breath and surprised, furtive glances amongst his assembled captains. Taenar, who had no idea what that destination might be, kept his expression carefully neutral.

'Do you think that's wise, baron?' Elasandor asked, although his tone was more respectful this time, a genuine question rather than a challenge. 'With the fleet in this condition–'

'Uzgul found where we lived and sent its ships to murder us should we escape the trap it set for us at Eluadhri,' Stormdawn declared. 'I think it high time that we return the favour. Someone at the Farmarket will know from whence the Badskab Bukkaneers embark, and I wish to have that information before I approach the princess with any calls for a raid. Ergo, with no safe harbour of our own, we go to the Farmarket together.' He snapped his fingers. 'To your ships, all of you. Not you just yet, Leotharan,' he added as Taenar began to turn away. 'A moment, please.'

Taenar remained awkwardly in place as the rest of the council filed out of the war room, Elasandor staring provocatively at him as he passed. Taenar initially averted his eyes, then deliberately met the other captain's stare. He needed to get used to these new ways if he wanted anyone to take him seriously, and he desperately needed them to take him seriously.

'Did you know Elasandor from the Ilmaren fleet?' Stormdawn asked, when the doors had shut again. He was leaning on the ornate back of the chair in which he had been sitting, and running his thumb around the pommel of his sabre without looking at Taenar.

'No,' Taenar replied, then surprised himself by adding, 'my dislike of him is entirely new.'

'He's a good captain,' Stormdawn said, looking up. The quirk of his lips suggested that he had found Taenar's quip amusing, but his eyes were serious. 'Talented, instinctual… These things are important to us. More important than strict adherence to a command structure we left behind us many years ago.'

Taenar nodded soberly. 'I understand.'

'I sincerely doubt that you do,' Stormdawn replied, pushing away from his chair and coming fully upright in a manner so effortless that it seemed to simply involve some rearrangement of his personal gravity. There was a grace to him that reminded Taenar of a dancer; every movement was perfectly balanced, and any imprecise gesture gave the impression of being a deliberate choice. 'I will not come to your defence,' Stormdawn continued, stepping closer to Taenar. He smelled, somehow, of woodsmoke and pine resin – a wild, invigorating scent, very different from the fresh, clean air of the natural domes in which Taenar had walked on Ilmaren. 'Do not assume that shared ancestry – even our shared former home – will count for anything with him, or any other captain here. Disputes will not end at playing politics for his advancement and your detriment, or barbed comments over the voidwine. If you aggravate him sufficiently then he will attempt to kill you. Perhaps in single combat, or perhaps by turning his guns on you when you are aboard your vessel.'

'So I should shut my mouth, avert my eyes, and let him speak to me as though I am a foolish child?' Taenar said.

Stormdawn laughed. 'Not unless that is your wish! I do not say these things to dissuade you from speaking your mind, Leotharan. I merely wish to warn you what the consequences might be for doing so. Thus advised, you may make whatever choice seems best to you.'

'He neglects to mention that there are other ways to prevent such an eventuality from coming to pass,' Xela Flickerstep said, spinning a knife through her fingers. Stormdawn looked over his shoulder with a smirk, but Flickerstep was staring straight at Taenar.

'And those would be?' Taenar asked, frustrated by the drukhari's – the *corsair's* – manner, but intrigued nonetheless by what she might have to say.

'Firstly, you make yourself so obviously capable that he dare not try anything,' Xela said, weaving her way around her captain to look him straight in the eyes. 'Elasandor has no wish to die, so if he believes that any attempt on your life will see him lose his own then he will refrain from taking that risk. At the least, the ways in which he will be willing to attempt it will be considerably fewer, and contingent on circumstances he perceives as beneficial.'

'I see,' Taenar said slowly. 'And the second?'

'Simple,' Flickerstep said with a snort. 'You kill him first.'

Stormdawn smiled. 'My first mate always sees to the heart of the issue, mainly in order to work out how to thrust a knife into it.' Flickerstep hissed in vexation, and the speed of her blade's rotation increased, but Stormdawn ignored her. 'I do hope you will not take the second part of her advice in this instance, Leotharan. As I said, Elasandor is a good captain, despite his manner, and I would not like to lose him. Besides which, he is not without allies in my fleet, and by removing one enemy you may find yourself making more.'

'There are solutions to that as well,' Xela muttered under her breath, but Taenar raised his hands.

'Please!' he protested. 'This talk of "enemies" is premature! I have no wish to kill anyone, let alone a fellow captain, and one of your fleet to boot.'

'Are you sure?' Stormdawn asked, raising an eyebrow. Taenar blinked in surprise.

'I beg your pardon?'

'Are you *sure* you don't wish to kill *anyone*?' Stormdawn emphasised with a lazy smile. 'You are a warrior of the void, Leotharan, and you must have claimed many lives during your time in Ilmaren's fleet. You walked the Path of the Warrior before that, and I suspect your weapons then also tasted an enemy's lifeblood.'

Taenar looked from one to the other, and realised he'd licked his lips nervously. 'Indeed.'

'It's a glorious red feeling, isn't it?' Stormdawn asked. 'And the Paths and the elders and everything in that world will tell you that this is forbidden, that it is dangerous, that it is something to be locked away and never spoken of. We all feel our blood heating when the Avatar of Kaela Mensha Khaine awakens and leads us to war, but in the aftermath of that we feel–'

'Shame,' Taenar said, nodding. 'I have experienced that.'

'Why should we feel shame?' Stormdawn asked, spreading his arms. 'The battle-lust is a part of who we are! It is a heritage that the craftworlds seek to lock away! Certainly, it cannot be *all* that we are, but why should we shun it when there are so many beings in this galaxy for whom death is the only acceptable fate?'

Flickerstep sighed noisily. 'Asuryani. These truths have been known for ten thousand years in Commorragh, yet you proselytise as though you were the first to discover them.'

'I do not think we will be taking Commorragh as an example of anything to which we should aspire,' Stormdawn said primly, prompting another snort from his first mate. 'However, you raise a valid point. Perhaps our new friend would benefit from a perspective more different to his own than mine, as we attempt to get him used to our ways and render him less likely to fall prey to unexpected death.'

Flickerstep stiffened, suspicion darkening her sharp features. 'What precisely did you have in mind?'

'You will go back to *Dance of Dying Seasons* with Captain Leotharan,' Stormdawn said smoothly. 'There you will advise him, until I recall you to my side.'

'I am your Bladesworn!' Flickerstep hissed. 'I am not some trinket to be traded–'

Stormdawn's left hand shot out, faster than Taenar could have reacted. The corsair baron's fingers threaded themselves through Flickerstep's ice-white hair, close to the scalp, and yanked her head backwards to expose her throat. Taenar, startled into immobility, saw her pupils dilate slightly. He watched her hands, expecting the knife held in one to be plunged upwards and backwards into Stormdawn's chest, but the first mate's arm hung limply at her side.

'You are, as is everything else in my fleet, whatever I require you to be,' Stormdawn whispered to the air next to Flickerstep's ear, his eyes focused on an unremarkable point on the ceiling. 'You will go with Leotharan. Do not make me ask again.'

He released her, and left the room without another word.

Xela said nothing as she walked with Taenar to his shuttle. Nor did she say anything once they'd taken off. Finally, he could stand the tension no longer.

'Your baron's court is…' he began, then paused, aware of to whom he was speaking. However, he had started now. 'More like Commorragh than I was expecting.'

Xela snorted. 'Have you been to Commorragh, Asuryani? Do not bother to answer, I know you have not. Firstly, you are still alive, and secondly, if you had, you would not utter such foolishness.'

Taenar flushed again. 'I meant only that his choice of decor–'

'In Commorragh, the statues would be living creatures flesh-crafted into shapes their owners find pleasing, or crystallised by the glass plague,' Xela cut him off, sounding bored. 'The fountains would be running with blood, not narcotic-laced firewine. Stormdawn's court may be extravagant compared to the sterile places in which you have lived, but it is nothing like Commorragh.'

Taenar bit his lip, chastened. However, at least the drukhari – *former* drukhari – was speaking now, and he had no idea how long this would last. 'I can understand what led Stormdawn to leave his former life, for I experienced a similar thing myself. But if I may be so bold, what provokes someone from the Dark City to take up with those she would once have fought? I ask not in judgement,' he added hastily, 'but to understand those I would join.'

Xela glanced at him as though sizing him up, a process which Taenar found most uncomfortable. Then she sighed.

'Freedom.'

'Freedom?' Taenar echoed. 'Forgive me, but it is the understanding of the Asuryani that Commorraghans indulge whatever impulses they please, no matter how vile or debased. What freedoms did you lack?'

Xela laughed mirthlessly. 'Your own frustrations give you away, Asuryani. Your first thought when someone says "freedom" is being able to do whatever you wish without care or consequence. What desires are locked away in *your* mind, I wonder, that you felt unable to act upon in your craftworld home?'

Taenar gritted his teeth. 'If you do not wish to answer the question–'

'Commorragh is a dark place of muted colour,' Xela interrupted him. 'Everything is… How can I best describe it to someone who has never seen it? *Everything* is sharp. Edges, weapons, screams – everything. It shelters its inhabitants, yet it kills them at the same time. Everything there is done with thought only given to how it benefits one's own survival. Nothing can be done simply for the sake of it. Do you understand?' she asked, and Taenar realised the question was a genuine one, her pale eyes searching his face.

'I think I may,' he said slowly. 'In Ilmaren, everything is done in service to the craftworld. Whatever Paths we walk, our actions are expected to benefit all. It is… a weight that forever sits around one's shoulders. It sounds completely opposite.'

'A poor analogy, but a serviceable one,' Xela said with a shrug. 'There is little freedom in Commorragh. The drukhari hide in the webway from She Who Thirsts, fearing to walk too long in realspace lest their souls are drained away. They are the galaxy's parasites,' she said, and Taenar was shocked to hear genuine loathing in her voice. 'They steal extended life at the expense of others, but they do nothing with it save for lurking in their shadowed palaces and plotting against one another. Do you know the first thing I did when I left? When I stole a small ship and escaped through the webway, venturing outside Commorragh for the first time not as part of a raiding party?'

'I do not,' Taenar admitted. Xela looked away from him, and stared straight ahead at the wall.

'I flew to a small webway gate on an airless moon, in a place where half the sky is taken up by the great spread of the Calexis Nebula. A titanic cloud of gas and dust, light-years distant, yet so vast it was as though it hung in the air directly in front of me. And I sat in my ship, and I looked at it for a day.'

'Just that?' Taenar asked.

'Just that,' Xela said quietly. 'For the first time, I had the freedom to do something that *did not matter*. No one could use my inaction against me. No one could leverage it into an advantage over me, and I did not do it in order to advance myself.' She looked at Taenar again, her eyes hard. 'The drukhari do not see how well they have caged themselves. They lurk in Commorragh and congratulate themselves on escaping the clutches of She Who Thirsts, without realising that by doing so they deny themselves anything worth experiencing. They are just as constrained as any one of you craftworlders on your Paths. The difference is that they are kept in their place by the knives of their fellows, rather than by ancient dogma.'

She drew a knife, and started spinning it through her fingers. 'I know my life here among the stars will be far shorter than the existence I could have eked out in the Dark City, if I were careful and lucky. I also know that I will see things, experience things, that I never would have had I continued to hide there, rationing my time in realspace to lightning raids in order to seize new victims. It is a trade with which I am content.'

'I thank you for your honesty,' Taenar said, inclining his head respectfully. Drukhari were the nightmares of the craftworlds, rapacious predators who could sometimes, perhaps, be bargained or bartered with, but could never be trusted. She Who Thirsts was the doom of the aeldari, and its machinations were to be guarded against at all times, but it was the drukhari who were more likely to be the cause of untimely death. They were the Asuryani's dark shadows peering back at them from the mirror, an unrepentant reminder of what had brought about their species' downfall; terrifyingly alien in some ways, yet similar enough to know exactly how best to hurt you.

To meet one who had been born into that life but had chosen to leave it – who was not exiled for failing to meet Commorragh's standards, but had abandoned it because it did not meet hers – was a revelation. It simultaneously heartened Taenar, and angered him. Heartened, because it was a sign that the Dark

Kin were not the monolith of blood-crazed murderers many assumed they were. Angered, because Xela's choice demonstrated that all the others, including those who had recently attacked Ilmaren with the Queen of Knives, had made their own choice.

'Why should I hide the truth from you?' Xela asked, tossing her head disdainfully. 'Neither it nor you can hurt me.'

'I have no desire to hurt you,' Taenar protested, but Xela simply snorted.

'There you go again, speaking about desire. You *cannot* hurt me, Asuryani. I could kill you before your blade left its scabbard, and you have no standing within the Starsplinters. Besides,' she added, 'you may simply consider what Myrin would do to you, should something happen to his first mate aboard your vessel.'

Taenar straightened. 'He did not seem overly concerned about your wellbeing earlier.'

Xela rolled her eyes. 'Spare me.'

'When I spoke with him in his court, he made clear that Ra'thar had crossed no lines by attacking someone who laid their hands on him without his permission,' Taenar persisted, attempting to make sense of it. 'Yet you suffered Stormdawn's actions without protest. There, too, I felt as though we were in Commorragh. Was I incorrect?'

'More than you know,' Xela said, baring her pointed teeth in a grin. 'In Commorragh, no one would have risked handling a free warrior with a weapon in her hand in such a manner. That is not how the Dark City's denizens achieve their long lives. They tread only on the powerless, knowing that their victims have no ability to strike back, either through genuine inability, or layers of subtle countermeasures and consequences that shackles them with mental chains. I, however, could have killed Stormdawn in that moment, or in any other, should I have wished to.' She shrugged. 'Of course, I suspect he thinks the same, only in reverse.'

'Then why submit to his abuses?' Taenar demanded, exasperated. He wanted to like Stormdawn – it would make the entire process much easier. And there was indeed much to like about him, for he was handsome and graceful, and had been welcoming in a strange, wild fashion. However, it had been drummed into Taenar that a commander should always be concerned about the wellbeing of those beneath them, and Stormdawn, it seemed, was not that.

'Because that is the game, is it not?' Xela replied, licking her lips and smiling at him. 'He has earned my loyalty, and now he tests it. He does not provoke me because I cannot stop him. He provokes me because I *can*. He pushes his luck, because he delights in walking as close as he can to that edge. I let him, because by so doing he repeatedly places his life in my hands, and refraining from taking a life when you have the power to do so can be a thrill far sweeter than giving in to the impulse.' She sighed. 'But at any point, I may decide I am bored with the game, and then he may lose a finger, or a hand, or whatever else I choose.'

'But *why*?' Taenar said. 'Why play this game at all?'

'For the same reason I do anything, Asuryani,' Xela said seriously. 'For the same reason we – all of us – became corsairs in the first place.

'To feel alive.'

EIGHT

Taenar had asked what the Farmarket was, but Flickerstep refused to answer other than to say that if he didn't know, then no description would suffice. He had debated with himself what course to take from there – should he argue the point, and assert himself? Or would it be seen as more in keeping with the corsair mentality to accept this new adventure at face value? He decided on the latter, not least because he had no doubt that Xela Flickerstep would take her knives to him should he vex her overly, and that was not a contest in which he wished to engage. So it was that his ships fell in behind the Starsplinters as they traversed the webway, and he fielded his captains' queries as to their destination with responses that attempted to balance vagueness and certainty.

'These ways have an ill aspect to them,' Faerys Asuthien commented to Flickerstep on the second day, by ship's time, after they had left the Well of the Long Death. Asuthien was *Dance of Dying Seasons'* captain, and as the commander of the flagship she would, under most circumstances, be expected to take command of a fleet if the admiral was incapacitated. However, Taenar was not quite sure how matters would resolve themselves given the presence on board of Ra'thar Kyldran. He hoped he never had to find out.

'Just remain alert,' Flickerstep said in response, spinning her blade through her fingers again, which was far more disconcerting to Taenar than had she loudly ridiculed his crewer. The webway was never a welcoming place, even for its nominal masters, but in most places it simply felt somewhat alien. Here, shadows seemed to congeal in the corners, or out of sight, and the ship's sensors reported strange returns that Taenar could not fully understand.

They reached the webway gate without incident, however, and came out into the clear vastness of space on the outskirts of a planetary system Taenar did not know. To his surprise, *Light of Heaven* did not set course for the solar system, instead heading outwards, into the black. Although, Taenar noticed, it was less black than usual.

'We are somewhere near the galactic core,' he commented, taking in the proliferation of stars strewn across the sky. Mere pinpricks only, from his vantage point, but so many of them that it was as though they were grain scattered by hand across the dark soil of a field. Wherever he looked, the space between two points of light resolved into yet another, smaller and fainter point of light.

'We are,' Flickerstep confirmed. She pointed. 'Behold, our destination.'

Taenar frowned at the smudge ahead of them, obscuring some of the stars beyond. 'That nebula?' But he knew as soon as the words left his mouth that he was incorrect, the perspectives were all wrong. The object was massive, certainly, but it was nowhere near large enough to be a nebula.

'Wait and see,' Flickerstep said with an infuriating smile.

They made good speed with the planetary system's parent star behind them, and it was a mere hour or so before they were close enough for Taenar to get a proper reading on the gigantic formation swelling in front of them. It filled the field of view now, thousands of miles long: a dull brown flank the size of a continent, peppered with literally mountainous warts; the great pale shape of a bone protruding from the void-frosted flesh, as long as a fault line and broken off by some unimaginable force; a massive sunken eye the size of a human city; fleshy tendrils, each one of sufficient size to kill an entire fleet, extending out from around a mouth that could have swallowed a small moon; and dense layers of noisome gas, still held tight around the central form by its own gravity.

'A void whale?' Faerys asked, incredulous.

'The corpse of one,' Flickerstep confirmed. 'We do not know what killed it, but here it is – a veritable treasure trove that many would seek to claim, but one faction has declared the beast as its own.'

Indeed, Taenar had already noted the vessels positioned at strategic intervals along the dead monster's bulk. They were huge, blocky ships, considerably larger than any one of those in the Starsplinters fleet. The nearest one was close enough for him to make out the cloud of smaller, snub-nosed craft surrounding it, which even now were boiling outwards towards them.

'The Leagues of Votann,' he said, casting an eye over their design. The predominant colour scheme was orange, and he delved into his memory to recall the name this particular group of grotesque, stunted creatures gave themselves.

'The Trans-Hyperian Alliance,' Faerys said, a moment before the words came to Taenar's mind. His captain bit her lip thoughtfully. 'Not the friendliest creatures, but not the worst of their kind.'

'If you say so,' Flickerstep said, her tone bored. 'Hold formation with the baron, and do not make any aggressive moves. The Kin will give us no trouble so long as we do not initiate it, and give no sign that we are intending to jump their claim.'

The doors to the bridge opened, and Ra'thar Kyldran entered. The warlock had avoided the bridge since Xela Flickerstep came aboard, and Taenar had not needed to ask why – he could positively feel Ra'thar's bristling animosity towards the former wych.

'Admiral,' Ra'thar said without preamble. 'I have consulted the runes, and...' He tailed off, staring out of the bow viewport. 'Isha's tears.'

Taenar could not imagine why anyone would want to jump the Kin's claim, as Flickerstep put it, since he could think of little worse than scavenging on a vast corpse such as this. However, he could not deny that the sight was an impressive one, and he did not blame Ra'thar for being momentarily derailed.

'Void carrion,' Ra'thar said after taking a moment to compose himself. 'What a delightful surprise.' He cast a glare at Flickerstep. 'The inside of a dead world, and now this? Your master truly knows how to find the greatest sights of the galaxy. What are we doing here?'

'Gathering intelligence,' Taenar said before Flickerstep could respond. It was his ship, and Ra'thar should rightly have addressed the question to him, albeit in a more respectful manner. Besides, he was not about to have the warlock start cross-questioning Myrin Stormdawn's first mate, given what had happened the last time Ra'thar had interacted with the Starsplinters. 'The baron intends to determine the location of the Badskab Bukkaneers in order to launch a raid against them, and he believes that someone here will have that information.'

'Amongst the Kin?' Ra'thar said with a dubious sniff. 'They barely bother to look farther than the ends of their own noses.'

'There are more than just Kin here, witchling,' Flickerstep replied. 'They will suffer no competitors, but they trade willingly, and tolerate other merchants so long as they do not step outside the zone the Kin have demarcated for them.'

'And the purpose of our welcoming committee?' Taenar asked, gesturing to the Votann ships that were clustering around the Starsplinters fleet.

'The one redeeming feature of the Leagues is that they kill the servants of Chaos on sight,' Flickerstep said. 'They are making sure that we do not serve the Great Enemy. Relax,' she added with a wicked grin, as Taenar, Faerys, and Ra'thar exchanged glances. 'I'm sure they will have many opinions about us, you stiff-necked Asuryani in particular, but they will not mistake your vessels for those of Chaos worshippers. Even drukhari can come here unmolested, although it is a rare archon who seeks out a trading post such as this, and only a brave or foolish one who seeks to engage in their usual pursuits here. The Kin pay little attention to what occurs in their satellite fiefdom, but "little" is not "none", and they appreciate neither slavery nor wanton butchery.'

'How encouraging,' Ra'thar bit out, his eyes nearly as sharp as the witchblade sheathed across his back.

'You had something to tell me about the runes?' Taenar prompted, attempting to interrupt the staring match between the two of them.

'I do,' Ra'thar confirmed. 'In private.'

'Feel free to leave,' Xela Flickerstep said, not bothering to conceal her amusement.

'You can leave,' Ra'thar countered. He raised his left hand. 'One way, or another.'

'Your presence is not currently required on the bridge,' Taenar said to Xela before she could respond. She shifted a murderous gaze towards him, and he met it steadily. 'This is my vessel and you are here as my guest. If Baron Stormdawn wishes to accept my fealty, he can place his people aboard my ships as he sees fit. Until then, you stay or leave at my word.' He panicked for a moment even as he spoke, certain that Xela was going to refuse him, and he added his next sentence on a sudden impulse. 'Or I will have you cast into the void, and explain to the baron how you attempted to slit my warlock's throat.'

Xela snorted. 'He would never believe you.'

'Perhaps not,' Taenar allowed, his heart racing, doing his best to ignore Faerys' shocked expression. 'But in what do you think he will place more weight? His suspicions about the fate of a single crew member? Or the very real fact of my ships' guns?'

Xela Flickerstep took a moment to weigh him up, and another moment to cast a similarly evaluating stare over Ra'thar Kyldran. Then she snorted again and departed.

'Did you just threaten to murder her if she disobeyed you, and then to open fire on the baron if he took issue with your cover story?' Ra'thar asked in a low voice as soon as Flickerstep had left the bridge.

'You backed me into a corner,' Taenar said, his voice wound as tight as his nerves. 'Stormdawn is accommodating us for now, in part because he knows that our forces can defeat his should he attempt to eliminate us, but his fleet is already making repairs and recovering their strength. There is no goodwill here other than that which we can purchase with our actions, so we *must* be in the baron's good graces by the time he has the strength to confront us. The corsairs do not respect command structure, Ra'thar, nor do they set much stall by niceties and kindness. They respect *strength*. If you were to go against my wishes then they would expect me to punish you, so by confronting Flickerstep you forced me to show that you were acting in accordance with my own thoughts. You threatened to strike her with your powers, so in order to not be seen as following *your* lead, I had to go further and threaten her life.'

'Would you have done it?' Faerys asked. Her expression was

studiously neutral, but Taenar could sense the tension beneath the surface. Ra'thar's face was a cool mask, as usual, but Taenar felt as though the warlock was weighing and assessing him.

'Kill her? I would have, yes,' he admitted, somewhat surprising even himself. 'To threaten such a thing and then back down would have endangered us all.' He pictured Xela's desperate face on the wrong side of an airlock door – features that would have been near-perfect had they not borne lines of cruelty – swelling up and bruising as her blood boiled, with trails of flash-freezing moisture leaking from her nose and mouth and eyes. He deliberately pushed the image from his mind. The sensations it raised were… complicated. 'Open fire on Stormdawn, though? Not unless he attacked first.'

'A dangerous game of brinksmanship, nonetheless,' Ra'thar mused.

'Then do not force my hand again by initiating a conflict with those with whom we intend to ally,' Taenar snapped. He waved a hand to brush the matter aside. 'You spoke of the runes.'

'I did,' Ra'thar said after a moment. 'You understand that our path is clouded.'

'It always is, or so I am led to believe.'

'Nonetheless, we are more adrift than most,' Ra'thar continued, 'and I am not a farseer. My understandings of the skeins of fate are limited. Still, I can sense a twist in our futures, and one that has recently developed. If we continue this course, conflict and death *will* follow, of that I am certain.'

'Conflict with whom?' Taenar asked.

'I cannot see.'

'And the death of whom?' Faerys put in.

'Aeldari lives will be lost,' Ra'thar said soberly, looking from one of them to the other. 'Of that, I have no doubt.'

Taenar pondered for a moment, but almost immediately realised that he was not going to make any drastic changes based upon the warlock's counsel. It was a liberating moment. Ra'thar did not command these ships as the Farseer Council commanded Ilmaren. The ultimate responsibility lay with Taenar, and out here in the strange world of the corsairs, he did not need to please others with his actions.

'We will stay the course,' he said, his voice soft but firm. 'We knew the risks of coming here in this manner. I will not crawl back to Ilmaren with my tail between my legs, begging for forgiveness. Even if lives are to be lost, they may not be ours.'

Ra'thar nodded slowly, but his eyes did not leave Taenar's face.

NINE

There were many things that could be created or refined from the raw materials of a dead void whale, or so Myrin was given to understand. The vast majority were utterly disgusting, to his mind, and so he paid little attention to them, but the prospect attracted traders like flies attended a corpse of a more standard size. The Kin didn't object, as it meant they could sell some of their spoils without needing to transport it any real distance, and, as in most cases, once trade of a certain sort had sprung up, other sorts followed. Wherever there were life forms with a concept of exchanging items of value for different items of a different sort of value, a market would inevitably appear.

The Kin had been harvesting this corpse for five years now, and the Farmarket had been here for most of that time. It was vast – nowhere near the size of a craftworld, but the equal to many of the galaxy's sprawling metropolises. It had moved since Myrin's last visit, shifting several miles in a nominally upward direction along the massive rib to follow the work progress, but the marker beacons had been updated, and his fleet settled into their allocated corral some way above the thriving sprawl of commerce. From there, shuttles bore the captains and their close crew members down to the surface, and Myrin stepped off the ramp onto thruster-charred bone. The gravity was a little weaker than on most planets solid enough to set foot on, but otherwise it was very easy to forget that he was standing on something which had once been alive.

'Is there a possibility of the orks being present, if the Kin welcome all?' Taenar Leotharan asked. He, like the rest of them, was dressed in a void-sealed suit. The market itself was enclosed in giant, temporary domes of durable translucent material, with an atmosphere amenable to most of the galaxy's sapient species, but the walk to the airlock from the space port took place through whatever gases formed the corpse's thin atmosphere.

'Unlikely,' Myrin replied. 'You have not been to a place like this before?'

'The fleet of Ilmaren has not frequented such haunts since your day,' Taenar replied, slightly stiffly, 'so I have not previously had the opportunity.'

'"Opportunity" is not the term I would have chosen,' the warlock Kyldran commented, the crystal lenses of his witch helm somehow managing to convey contempt for their surroundings.

'A few orks can restrain their brutal instincts sufficiently to conduct trade with more sophisticated species,' Myrin informed them as they approached the airlock. 'The majority, however, will simply open fire with no more thought than it takes to breathe. Some corners of the galaxy harbour markets where even those beasts can trade, but the Kin are too protective of their bounty to risk it being damaged by wanton destruction. All vessels are inspected to see if they bear any marks of Chaos, but ork vessels would not gain even that courtesy.'

'And if the beasts have taken the vessels of another species?' Kyldran asked.

'Without "improving" them to their own specifications, and without giving themselves away by attacking the Kin's craft?'

Myrin replied. 'Then they would likely be some of those very rare orks I mentioned. Regardless, the Badskab Bukkaneers certainly do not fall into that category. They take a positive delight in displaying their barbaric totems, and the prowess of their guns.'

The other set of airlock doors opened, and he removed his helm and stepped into the Farmarket.

It was not, Myrin had to admit, the most fragrant place in the galaxy. Breathable the air might be, but there was no salt tang of a sea here, no fresh, green smell of forests or the hard, dry scent of a desert's hot sands. It was not a *living* atmosphere; it was one quite literally built on death. The stink of processed flesh, rendered fat, and gaseous byproducts wound through it without any natural odours to balance them out, and underneath them all was layered the strange, almost metallic smell of the bare bone upon which they stood.

'How delightful,' Taenar commented. He had removed his own helm and was wrinkling his nose.

'Would you like a scented pomander, Asuryani?' Xela sneered at him. The shade runner shook out her hair and took a deep breath. Myrin had always thought she seemed at home in environments like the Farmarket in ways she never did aboard a ship. Perhaps it was the similarity to the place in which she'd been raised. Xela might have detested Commorragh, but only someone who truly understood that sort of anarchic place could have survived it long enough to get away.

'You all know what we're looking for,' Myrin told his captains. 'See what you can unearth. Anyone who finds information about the location of the Bukkaneers will have their name mentioned to Princess Tishria.' That was a threat as much as it was a promise of a reward, since if the information did not pan out then the Scourge of the Calexis Nebula would have an obvious target for her inevitable anger. Myrin trusted that the prospect of the princess' displeasure would make his captains wary about whom they trusted, but he had no illusions that he could fully pass off any blame onto someone else. They were *his* captains, after all, which implied that he trusted their judgement, and Tishria had a notable history of punishing her underlings for their failings in such matters while ignoring the logic implying her own judgement was equally flawed. Such was the capriciousness afforded to a corsair princess, who ultimately answered to no authority save her own.

'I must confess that my captains and I do not,' Taenar said awkwardly. 'We are, of course, ready to assist.'

'Of course he is,' Ellisar Elasandor scoffed. 'But what *use* can you be, boy?'

'What use are *you*?' Taenar snapped. 'You appear to offer nothing to this fleet save complaints.'

Myrin blinked in surprise, then smiled in sly delight. He had expected more stiff formality and attempts to defuse tension in response to Ellisar's rudeness, not that sort of retort.

'Did I tell you that he threatened my life?' Xela murmured at Myrin's elbow as an ugly mutter ran through Ellisar's followers.

'You know very well that you did not,' Myrin replied softly. Taenar's captains were eyeing the corsairs in a manner that suggested they were considering drawing their weapons. 'Not very straight-laced and Asuryani of him, eh?'

'You would be surprised how many Asuryani have threatened my life,' Xela muttered, and Myrin snorted in amusement. However, Kyldran's hand had gone to the hilt of his witchblade, which Myrin somewhat regretfully took as his cue to step forward. Whatever the warlock's qualities, restraint in the face of provocation was probably not to be easily found amongst them.

'We have only just arrived here,' Myrin said, smiling widely at them all. 'Let us at least get what we came for before we fall out and bring the Kin's displeasure down on our heads, shall we?'

'Why do you persist in lumbering us with these fools?' Ellisar demanded, turning to Myrin. 'They do not understand how we live–'

'We were just like them, not so long ago,' Myrin interrupted him. 'And look at us now! A unified fraternity, with never an ill word to say about each other!'

A low, ironic chuckle ran through the Starsplinters, and even some of Taenar's folk cracked slight smiles. Myrin waited for a moment to let his humour leach some of the tension from the air, then raised his hands.

'However, the esteemed Captain Elasandor is correct,' he continued, gesturing at Ellisar. 'These newcomers do *not* understand how we live. Therefore, it behoves us to educate them. Each of you will take one or more of our new captains and their companions under your wing.' He watched with mild amusement as his corsairs' faces fell. 'Show them how places like this work. Teach them where things of value are to be found, and where they should avoid at all costs. Preferably with as few casualties as possible,' he added casually, provoking another round of chuckles from his mariners. Taenar's followers, by contrast, appeared unsure of exactly how much he was joking.

'Don't just stand there,' Myrin added a moment later, when no one moved. 'Get to it! Pick someone who intrigues or attracts you, or whom you think you might find useful. Two restrictions only,' he added. 'Captain Elasandor gets no company until he learns to be more polite, and Admiral Leotharan comes with my Bladesworn and me.' He snapped his fingers. 'Move.'

'So do I intrigue you, or attract you?' Taenar said with raised eyebrows as he stepped to Myrin's side. 'Or is it, perhaps, that you find me of use?'

'Yes,' Myrin agreed with a smile. 'Ah, Warlock Kyldran. You will be joining us as well?'

'I can confidently predict that the greatest trouble will be found wherever you go, and therefore my presence might be required,' Kyldran replied. Of all their group, he alone had not removed his helm.

'Yes to which?' Taenar demanded of Myrin, almost before the warlock had finished speaking.

'Which what?' Myrin replied brightly, turning away from him. 'Come, the Farmarket has much changed since I was last here, but I suspect I can still find our best chance of getting that which we require.'

'I find it hard to believe that all this is predicated upon the butchery of this corpse,' Taenar said as Myrin led them into yet another of the Farmarket's domes. The former admiral gestured around them. On their right stood a palatial tent of gaudy, shimmering fabrics, in which others of a similar sort were on sale, and next to that was something that looked almost like a giant hive of some sort of colonial insect, and in front of which were displayed jagged and pointed lengths of a dull, matt-grey substance, which were clearly some form of stabbing or hacking weapon. Meanwhile, on their left was a veritable maze of food stalls, the various scents overpowering the background smell. That was not to say that the resulting concoction was a pleasant one, of course. Taenar looked quite uncertain about it.

'Of course not,' Myrin replied. 'But people came here to trade with the Kin, and then some of them settled to refine the raw materials on site, and those people needed all the things that people usually need in order to live, and word got out that there was an opportunity here to supply them.' He spread his arms. 'And so the Farmarket came to be – an example that no matter how the galaxy's self-proclaimed great empires quarrel and war, there will always be places where their renegades and outcasts gather and suppress their natural enmity in the hope of making profit off a stranger.'

'You sound almost proud,' Taenar said with distaste.

'Are we not renegades and outcasts?' Myrin asked, wandering over to one of the food stalls. 'Here! You must try some of this.'

'If it is made from void whale, I am not eating it,' Taenar said steadfastly, and Myrin nearly burst out laughing.

'Void whale? No one *eats* void whale, my friend. The flesh is used by lesser species as fuel, as construction material, and many other things besides, but I doubt even the most depraved worshipper of She Who Thirsts would consider *eating* it.' He held up two fingers to the four-armed biped at the stall, and pushed a finely crafted knife across the counter as trade.

'That surely cannot be fair value,' Taenar said, but Myrin placed two fingers on the admiral's wrist to shush him, and leaned in close.

'This is part of being Baron Stormdawn,' he said into the other aeldari's ear. 'This is part of being a Starsplinter, but it is *especially* a part of being me. I buy things for more than they are worth, because a corsair baron should not care about such petty sentiments as "price". Confident, wealthy, swaggering, deadly – I must be all these things, and more, if I am to maintain my position.'

'It is… an act?' Taenar asked, his voice low, and Myrin smiled.

'Think of it more as a *performance*, my friend. I am not one of our masked cousins in the rillietann, but I still have my part that I must play. We are far from the glacial pace of the craftworlds here. A situation may turn at any moment, and if it does then we must have already done all we can to indicate that we are no easy meat. I must display my wealth openly, so that everyone can see I have no fear of it being taken from me, and ask themselves what it is that gives me such confidence. I must carry myself as though I am at home wherever I step, so that others will assume that I have allies all around. This is what it means to be a Starsplinter. Do you understand?'

Taenar nodded slowly. 'I believe that I do.'

'You do not,' Myrin told him, and watched the other's cheek twitch. 'But you may be learning, and that is good.' He stepped back, took the two proffered food items from the vendor, and handed one to Taenar.

'What is this?' Taenar asked, inspecting it.

'I have no idea,' Myrin admitted, 'but they taste marvellous.' He bit through the warm, crisp outer shell and into the richly seasoned filling, which exploded into his mouth. He truly did not know what these particular foodstuffs were, but he'd eaten them before without dying, which was all that really concerned him. Taenar, apparently unwilling to be upstaged, followed his lead, and Myrin watched in some amusement as his eyes widened.

'I think he likes it,' Taranath said, chuckling. 'A bit different from craftworld food, hey?'

'You should try one,' Myrin said to Kyldran, who shook his head.

'I will pass,' the warlock declared, his voice echoing hollowly inside his witch helm. 'Baron. You spoke of finding information, yet all you have done so far is parade us around this grotesquerie as though it was your own, and you thought that we would somehow be impressed at its contents.'

'Perhaps your mood would improve somewhat if you removed your helm, friend,' Taranath said with a grin that was some distance from actually friendly. 'You're not getting the full experience of this place.'

'My mood would improve somewhat if you were to spontaneously perish,' Kyldran replied levelly. His helm turned so that its huge, blank lenses were studying Taranath. 'Of the two, which do you consider is more likely to occur?'

Tanarath's face fell, but Issarel snorted a laugh. 'I like him.'

'For a seer, you appear remarkably direct,' Myrin said to Kyldran as he led their group onwards through the market. 'That Path never called to me, but is it not concerned with observing the shape of the future, then manipulating small events in order to orchestrate the changes you wish to come to pass?'

'I have, at times, been chastised for my lack of patience,' Kyldran replied.

'And did you heed those admonishments?' Myrin asked, smiling.

'I left my craftworld and joined Admiral Leotharan's fleet in exile,' Kyldran said, 'so it is fair to assume that I did not. It is true that the runes rarely show me much in great detail, or with any particular specificity.' He gestured with his right hand, and pale witchfire blossomed into life around his fingers, causing Xela to take a step away from him with a sharp hiss. 'However, what I lack in precognitive abilities, I make up for with the ability to respond to unexpected events with violence. Do not assume I have not considered the possibility that you brought us here not in order to seek information, but to trade us away for your own gain.'

Myrin saw the briefest flicker of a glance Taenar shot at his warlock, but he could not decipher it. Was Taenar shocked, having trusted Myrin? Or had he also been on the lookout for a double-cross, and was angry that Kyldran might have tipped their hand? Sometimes Taenar seemed an open book, with every page laid out for Myrin's inspection – mainly awkwardness, confusion, or embarrassment, as Taenar was constantly surprised by the realities of corsair life. Every now and then, however, there were moments when Myrin had no idea what was going on in his new ally's head.

'It is always sensible to be cautious,' he agreed easily, 'and it is true that the pair of you might fetch a handsome price on the open market, if we were interested in selling–'

'Selling?' Taenar said, his head snapping up. 'Selling to whom?'

'There are more potential buyers than I could easily name,'

Myrin said. 'The drukhari are the most obvious, of course, although they would have to fetter Master Kyldran's powers somehow before bringing him into Commorragh.' He fell in between the two of them, and tucked his arm through Taenar's. The other aeldari stiffened for a moment again, then relaxed into it far more swiftly than he had done upon their first meeting.

'Uzgul the Magnificent takes aeldari slaves, but orks would most likely seek to capture us as well, and would have little appreciation for the individual value the two of you represent. Besides which, in Uzgul's case in particular, there is the little matter of me wishing to deprive him of his head,' Myrin continued, ticking off on his fingers. 'The Imperium are far too wary of us in general to trade, and are more likely to kill aeldari than own them, but there are always some renegades among their number. The followers of the Great Enemy would be far more interested – especially in Master Kyldran, I suspect – but we are unlikely to find them here. And, of course,' he added, 'I kill them on general principle wherever I discover them. The only difference is that I do not have to check with a seer council to ensure that I am not disrupting a millennia-long plan by doing so.'

'Did that happen, when you served Ilmaren?' Kyldran asked, sounding surprised. Myrin nodded.

'I became aware of a particularly foul warband operating in our vicinity. A handful of Space Marines and their retinue of corrupted humans, as well as allies from perhaps a dozen other species, all of whom had fallen to the worship of She Who Thirsts. I petitioned to exterminate them, but was denied.' He sighed in regret. 'They were not a mighty force, and we had the numbers and firepower. I cannot imagine that our leaders feared retaliation, so I can only assume that it was viewed that the scum had a more important role to play in the future of the craftworld by being left alive. What that might be, I do not know, but I knew that whatever benefit our world might have gained from it, it would come at the cost of the suffering of thousands, and the glorification of a name I wish eradicated from the galaxy.'

Taenar and Kyldran exchanged another glance, and this time Myrin was able to read it as it flashed across him: unease.

'So you didn't do it?' Taenar asked, and Myrin chuckled.

'Oh, I did, but only once I'd left Ilmaren. My fleet's annihilation of that vermin was what brought us to the attention of Princess Tishria, as it happens.' He surveyed the stalls past which they were walking, and nodded in satisfaction. 'We turn left here.'

'So what *is* our destination?' Kyldran persisted. 'Whatever it is, we have not taken a direct route.'

'The market shifts over time, and stalls come and go,' Myrin said. 'However, many vendors tend to pick new plots near their former neighbours. So, either the particular individual I am looking for has ceased trading, or...' He tailed off in triumph as a familiar glyph came into view. It might bear some resemblance to an aeldari rune to the uninitiated, constructed as it was of multiple parallel and interlinked lines, but the differences were obvious to Myrin – the design was less flowing, more tightly packed, and drawn with blocky solidity instead of flowing grace.

'What is that, and what does it mean?' Taenar asked.

'It is a Votann glyph, and while I am sure it has some other, deeper meaning, in the market as a whole it is taken to stand for "information",' Myrin explained as they approached. 'Do you speak the mon-keigh tongue they know as "Low Gothic"?'

'I understand it,' Taenar said with some disdain. 'I will not speak it.'

Myrin grinned at him. 'Our quarry today barely speaks in it either, but not because he is not fluent. The Kin's communication in person relies a lot on physical gestures, or so I am given to understand. Unfortunately, I do not understand *those*, and so that leaves us in a situation where we are both speaking a language not our own, in very different ways. My advice is to pay attention purely to the information in his words, and disregard the manner in which it may be delivered.' He turned away from Taenar's serious face, and switched languages. '*Kôttak! Are you still cheating death?*'

A red flare in the shadowed depths of the stall turned into the end of a lit cigar as the Kin sucking on it stepped forward into the light. Kôttak was just as disgustingly short, broad, and hirsute as he had been when Myrin had last seen him, and the glowering distrust was still prominent in his expression. The Kin rolled the cigar to the left side of his mouth and clamped it firmly between his teeth to spit out of the other side.

'*Stormdawn,*' he grunted in reply with the faintest nod of his head. Kôttak was clad in a full bodysuit suitable for hard physical work, covered with patches and pouches, despite the fact that to the best of Myrin's knowledge the Kin did nothing more exhausting than mind his stall. Perhaps it was that unless he looked as though he was ready at any moment to climb into a seat and start operating heavy machinery, he would not be taken seriously as a Kin. Myrin, who had spent most of his life in carefully curated mindsets designed to blinker his emotional stimulation, considered that to be far from the strangest possible cultural explanation for such an affectation.

Kôttak's eyes slid over Myrin's Bladesworn, whom he had seen before, then lingered for a moment on Taenar and Kyldran. '*Ilmaren.*'

'How does he know our colours?' Taenar demanded.

'Kôttak knows a great deal,' Myrin replied in their shared tongue. 'That's why we're here.'

'*Old friends?*' Kôttak asked, still looking at Taenar and Kyldran, and Myrin switched back to Low Gothic.

'*You should know better than to try to glean such information for free, Kôttak,*' he chided the Kin. '*How about a trade? I'm in the*

*market for a particular piece of knowledge, and I thought you might
be able to help. If you can, I can tell you all about these two.'*

Kôttak sucked on his cigar and blew the resulting smoke from
his nose while he studied Myrin. Then the corner of his mouth
twitched in a manner Myrin had come to interpret as being
open to beginning negotiations.

'What?'

'The Badskab Bukkaneers,' Myrin said. *'Specifically their leader,
Uzgul the Magnificent. I want to know where its base of operations
is – where it is most likely to be found, or where I can strike to
draw it out.'*

Kôttak inspected a tool on his belt for a few seconds. *'No.'*

'I am truly impressed by your contacts, Baron Stormdawn,'
Kyldran said acidly. 'I can only hope your lesser captains are
having similar luck.'

'No, you don't know?' Myrin said to Kôttak, ignoring the warlock as best he could. *'Or no, you won't tell me?'*

Kôttak looked up at him from under bristling brows, and
held one hand out.

'A charge simply to know if you have the information?' Myrin
protested. *'This is outrageous.'*

Kôttak shrugged. *'Then go.'*

Myrin snorted. *'And leave you with the free information that
I'm looking for a particular ork, with me none the better off?'* He
fished into his belt pouch, and pulled out three gems, which he
dropped into the Kin's palm. The routine was a standard one:
Kôttak charged for telling people if he knew what they wanted
to know, and traded the actual information for other information, thereby keeping himself in stock. That didn't mean
that Myrin had to like it, and even a notably extravagant corsair
baron could express his frustration with extortion.

Kôttak's fingers curled around the gems and tucked them away in a pouch. *'No, not enough.'* The Kin gestured at Taenar and Kyldran to make his meaning clear.

'Well, you two are clearly insufficiently interesting,' Myrin commented. He sighed. *'Very well, Kôttak. What morsel might pry this loose from your lips?'*

Kôttak's brows twitched as if to suggest that Myrin should make him an offer. Myrin sighed. He would happily face an enemy with a weapon in his hand or a starship under his command, but haggling was a tool with which he still felt clumsy. Surely the whole point of being a corsair baron was that you could either buy or threaten loose whatever information you wanted? Yet Kôttak had always steadfastly refused to let his information go for gems, exotic weaponry, or any other form of physical remuneration, and so Myrin was reduced to sorting through the things he had seen and learned since his last visit, and working out which the Kin might consider that he could sell on.

'I could try,' Kyldran suggested. His tone was neutral, but Myrin already knew the warlock well enough to know what he was thinking.

'Absolutely not!' he snapped, rounding on him. 'The Trans-Hyperian Alliance might take only a loose interest in the general affairs of this market, but they will not ignore threats or violence against one of their own!'

'I could try,' Taenar said slowly.

'You will not even speak the language!' Xela protested, but Taenar waved her objections aside.

'Perhaps it is time to adapt. Besides, I am still attempting to persuade the baron that we are worthy of joining his fleet.'

Myrin hesitated only for a moment before curiosity took over. He took a step back, and gestured towards Kôttak. 'By all means, my friend, if you think you have something the trader will value.'

'I believe I may,' Taenar said, nodding. He cast a glance over them all. 'However, if I am to exchange information then I suspect the exclusivity of it will be important. You will all need to withdraw.'

'Very well,' Myrin said, gesturing to his Bladesworn. He was exceptionally curious now, as much about how Taenar would handle this exchange as in the information to be traded. They retreated a few paces; after a moment or two, and at a meaningful look from Taenar, Ra'thar Kyldran joined them.

'You don't know what he is offering?' Myrin murmured to the warlock, who shook his head.

'No. But I do not like this.'

'Is there anything you *do* like?' Taranath asked with a chortle.

'You should have some trust in your admiral,' Myrin said to Kyldran as Taenar leant in close to Kôttak. 'He may be more suited to this life than he realises.'

Kyldran said nothing, but his fingers flexed a few times. Witchfire did not appear, however, for which Myrin was grateful. He had never killed a warlock before, and he did not relish his first time coming in an attempt to prevent one from bringing the wrath of an entire League down on their heads, and potentially starting the sort of war that could bring ruin to the Starsplinters.

To his surprise, after a minute or so of discussion, Kôttak brought out what appeared to be a star chart. There followed a brief back-and-forth between the Kin and Taenar, before Taenar turned around and walked back to them.

'I have the location,' Taenar reported with a hint of pride, then exhaled in mild frustration. 'Most of the time was spent trying to get him to communicate it in a manner I could understand. Your quarry has apparently made its home on the fourth planet around the star the mon-keigh call Darmeer. I will be able to pinpoint it more accurately in our terms when I have access to my own charts, but I am aware of its rough location.'

A wide, genuine grin spread across Myrin's face, accompanied by a fierce excitement in his soul at the prospect of driving a blade, metaphorical or literal, into Uzgul's designs. 'How marvellous! And what, may I ask, was the price?'

'I traded a location for a location,' Taenar said calmly as they moved off. 'That of the Well of the Long Death, to be precise.'

Myrin's grin faded. 'You did *what*?'

'The lair of Baron Stormdawn of the Starsplinters,' Taenar continued, as though Myrin had not spoken, although Myrin could now see the faint tightness at the corners of his eyes. 'A renegade outcast from my craftworld, whose company I was only tolerating in order for him to lead me to my real quarry.' He shrugged. 'The information is barely out of date, and you left sufficient evidence of your presence there that anyone hunting you will recognise that you *were* there at some point. In truth, the prospect of me betraying you under your nose appeared to sweeten the deal for the Kin somewhat.'

'He will surely work out that you've told us!' Xela snapped. 'That even had we not left, that we will soon!'

'Then he should not have made the deal,' Taenar said. 'Besides, I suspect he cares less whether the information is accurate, and more whether it will look to have been accurate to whoever might buy it.'

Myrin bit his lip. Taenar's improvisation was a flagrant breach of trust, an intrusion into Myrin's life, a guarantee that he could never return to his former home, no matter what changes he made to it…

…and it had got the required result. Myrin left Ilmaren because the craftworld was too focused on the past, and on preserving what they had out of fear of reaching for anything new. Myrin Stormdawn would not make the same mistake.

'Taenar Leotharan,' he said, putting his arm around the other's shoulders. 'I think you will make a *fine* corsair.'

TEN

'How's da inkremental defuser comin' on?' Gazruk barked, furiously tightening bolts. 'Kaptin Uzgul said he's comin' to look at da machine today!'

'Wot's an inky-metal defoozer, boss?' Snip the grot asked helplessly.

'Da fing wiv all da tubes wot yoo're sittin' on!' Gazruk snapped, pointing at it. Snip was more or less useless, because it was a grot, but it did at least have a basic understanding of worky bitz and gubbinz. 'Get it wired in!'

'Yes, boss!' Snip yelped, getting to work. It might well not get all of the wires in the right places, but that was fine – Gazruk had always adhered more to an approach of quantity over quality when it came to wires, on the basis that if everything was connected to everything else then 'da joose', as he liked to call it, definitely went where it was supposed to go. If it took a bit of a detour on the way there, then so what? Gazruk knew that da joose moved very fast, so having to double back on itself shouldn't really pose many problems. And thinking of da joose…

'Bashgut!' Gazruk said, snapping his fingers. 'Are da fans workin' yet?'

'Nah, boss, all da snotlings ran away,' Bashgut said, shamefaced.

He was Gazruk's chief spannerboy, mainly because unlike many of Gazruk's former apprentices, the badmek hadn't accidentally blown him up yet. However, Gazruk was starting to consider whether a deliberate explosion might be the solution here, since while Bashgut appeared to be a natural survivor, he was not a particularly natural mek. It happened sometimes. Most orks gravitated to whatever role they were best suited to, as organically as a dropped grot hitting the ground. Every now and then, though, you got one who either drifted around, uncertain as to what his purpose might be, or who was very certain about what he should be doing but simply wasn't very good at it. Those orks didn't tend to last long, whether they be choppa boy, painboy, or even a brewboy (the ladz took their fungus beer very seriously, and anyone peddling a substandard cask was asking to have his head removed and left in the dregs).

'*Why* were dere gonna be *snotlings* in da *fans*, Bashgut?' Gazruk demanded, speaking slowly and clearly in an effort to emphasise exactly how much he shouldn't have to be asking the question.

'...to make 'em turn?' Bashgut replied, his expression and tone one of an ork who was fairly sure he didn't know the correct answer to the question, and also knew he couldn't figure it out in time.

'Can yoo believe dis nonsense?' Gazruk said, addressing the room in general. 'Right, get over dere and hold dat fing. No, da uvver one, da sticky-out one wiv da knob on it. Got it?'

'Yes, boss,' Bashgut said, holding on to the metal protuberance with some relief at the very simple, achievable task he'd been given.

'Now grab hold of dat buncha wires on yer left,' Gazruk said, tightening the last couple of bolts.

'Dis one, boss?'

'Probably,' Gazruk muttered. 'Let's find out.' He threw a lever, and beamed as da joose flowed right across the luckless Bashgut, causing him to stiffen and convulse in a thoroughly amusing manner. Gazruk waited until green foam started to leak out between the spanner's teeth, then reluctantly returned the lever to its original position. 'Now, unkink da quantum flanja, an' if yoo ever fink about puttin' snotlings into somefing of mine again, I'll tie ya down an' let a painboy's grots operate on ya, is we clear?'

'Yes, boss,' Bashgut said weakly, staggering in the general direction of the component Gazruk had mentioned. It probably didn't need unkinking, but right now Gazruk's main goal was to keep Bashgut from wrecking anything until he could try to knock some sense into the git and see if there was any sort of decent mek brain in there worth saving. Now he came to think about it, maybe he should just call in a painboy anyway; Gazruk was pretty sure he'd know a good brain if he saw it up close...

He snapped himself out of it. There were still things to do! Uzgul was expecting a demonstration of the machine, and if Gazruk wanted to avoid getting sent to achieve something infeasible and probably impossible on the Dakkaplanet, he had to be able to convince the freebooter kaptin that what he was doing here was useful. 'Kruggob! Pump da warp flush!' he ordered one of his other underlings, who leaped to obey. 'Zaggit! Stand by da temporal relays, and *don't* get 'em mixed up dis time, unless yoo wanna be seein' yesterday for a week!'

'Yes, boss!' his other spanners chorused, hurriedly carrying out his orders. Gazruk pinched his nose, squeezed his eyes shut for a moment, then opened them again to survey his creation in full.

It hadn't been an easy build. Most of the time Gazruk just constructed whatever came into his head, safe in the knowledge that it would be useful for something, at some point, and in any case he could probably convince someone to give him a bag of teef for it – especially true amongst freebooterz, who were notoriously extravagant and flashy. However, this had been different. This time Gazruk hadn't been able to follow the whims of his neurones, throwing in parts to meet the needs of whatever mechanical monstrosity he would end up with. *This time* he'd been trying to build a specific thing, which necessitated a level of focus he had not needed before. He'd had to resist the urge to spiral off into new and interesting creative directions, which had required frenzied sketching to ensure the new ideas didn't dissipate for good before he had a chance to make them real.

He'd done it, though. By Gork and Mork, he'd only gone and zoggin' done it. The resulting creation now took up most of a chamber in *Sunstompa*, but Gazruk knew on a certain pit-of-the-stomach level that it was going to *work*.

That still, of course, left the question of whether it was going to work *in time*, but Gazruk was confident he would be able to get something out of it. It wasn't going to bring about an immediate result, in any case. All he needed to do was convince Uzgul that it was working, and that would buy him the time to make tweaks and adjustments under the pretence of 'takin' readings' without the kaptin realising what was going on.

As though summoned by the thought – in actuality, turning up just as he'd said he would – there came a great metallic hammering on the chamber door.

'Snip!' Gazruk yelled, and the grot scampered away from its just-completed wiring – well, it had better be completed, or Gazruk would wring the scrawny little git's neck – and to the door, where it leaped up and grabbed hold of a lever. For a moment it seemed as though the grot's weight wasn't going to be enough to shift it, designed as it was to be moved by an ork's prodigious strength, but then Snip kicked its feet a couple of times, and something caught. The lever jerked down, and the door swung inwards.

'Kaptin!' Gazruk barked, whacking himself in the temple with a salute. It was stormboy nonsense to his mind, but Uzgul seemed to like it, so Gazruk did it. His spanners followed suit. Snip did as well, but no one noticed or cared.

'Gazruk,' Uzgul said, swaggering in and surveying the machinery as though he knew what he was looking at. He was wearing his favourite, five-cornered hat today – on the basis, apparently, that 'any git can wear a three-cornered one, an' four-cornered ones are just squares wiv pretenshuns' – and an overcoat of truly monumental proportions, not to mention eye-bleeding colour combinations. It was laden with gewgaws and bits of shiny loot, pieces that Uzgul either had no better use for or that he simply wanted to display about his person, as well as entire swathes of gold-plated teef… and dangling here and there, sparkling oddly in the light, were the skrawnie stones.

'Great dat yoo're here, kaptin,' Gazruk said with as much enthusiasm as he could muster. 'We woz just about to do da first test run.'

'An' dis… fing… will show us how to find more skrawnies?' Uzgul said dubiously.

Expectation management, Gazruk had learned, was an important part of keeping your boss onside. Well, that and not blowing up his favourite stuff. 'Should do, kaptin, should do,' Gazruk said cheerfully. 'Fing is, y'see–'

'Wotcha mean, "should do"?' Uzgul said, glowering at him.

'Dat's wot I'm gettin' to!' Gazruk said hurriedly. 'So, dere ain't no way to just *find* skrawnies, right?' He had no idea if that was true, but if you sounded certain enough about the opening proposition of your argument then you could take your audience just about anywhere. 'But wot I *can* do is find skrawnie *stones*!'

'Skrawnie stones?' Uzgul repeated, his brow furrowing. Gazruk knew he had to remember that despite the absolute nonsense of the Dakkaplanet, Uzgul wasn't stupid. Da Grand Kaptin was, in fact, very canny about many things; he simply had a planet-sized and planet-shaped blind spot where all his common sense apparently went to die.

'Dat's right,' Gazruk said encouragingly, hastily recalibrating the omnidirector without taking his eyes off his benefactor and, if he played this wrong, executioner. 'Dey're quite specific fings, skrawnie stones. Ain't nat'rul, if ya get my meanin'. Ya don't just see 'em lyin' around – ya only find 'em wiv skrawnies. So I fort, da kaptin's a smart ork, he's got a bunch of da fings, just wot we need to find more of 'em!'

'Is dat right?' Uzgul asked. He was preening slightly at the compliment, but he still didn't seem entirely won over.

'Yup!' Gazruk said with all the confidence of a charlatan who knew that a false promise today might get him killed tomorrow, but a lack of that promise would certainly see him killed today. 'Dere's a *resso-nance*, see? Da weirdboyz I've talked to say most skrawnies are all a bit weirdboy, speshully da ones wiv da stones, an' dere stones are too. So all we gotta do is find da stones, and we'll find da skrawnies wot are *wiv* dose stones!'

'Dat's an interestin' propasishun,' Uzgul said, stroking his luxuriant hair squig beard and studying Gazruk with narrowed eyes. 'Wotcha need?'

'Skrawnie stones, kaptin,' Gazruk said. 'As many as ya can spare for da machine.' He said it with a little trepidation, since everyone knew how much Uzgul liked his loot, and especially his skrawnie stones. However, this was the only way Gazruk could think of making this work, so he had to hope that Uzgul's desire for more slaves would outweigh the freebooter's attachment to his hoard.

'Hmm,' Uzgul rumbled, apparently deep in thought. 'An' I'll get 'em back?'

'Should do, kaptin, should do,' Gazruk said. 'Course, dis is krumpin'-edge tek, so dere's no way to be sure, but I can't see no reason why anyfing should happen to 'em.'

He eyed Uzgul warily, waiting for the kaptin to make his decision. With any luck, Uzgul would consider it a risk worth taking. Gazruk had thrown in the bit about his machine's innovative nature not just to brag – although also to brag – but because the whole point of being a Flash Git like Uzgul was to have the best, newest, and most impressive stuff. A device that not only did something useful, but which no other kaptin would have, *should* be irresistible…

'Alright, Gazruk,' Uzgul said. He pulled a pouch off his belt, and tossed it underhanded. 'Take 'em. Ain't like I don't got plenty more!' He chuckled jovially, which was another thing Gazruk had been counting on – you could get quite a bit out of a freebooter if they thought it made them look wealthy. After all, having the stuff was pointless if you couldn't *show off* about having it.

Now Gazruk just had to put it to good use.

'Everyone to yer stations!' he barked, and his spanners poised themselves by wheels, levers, and switches. Fear of the kaptin or not, every mek lived for the moment when their endeavours were rewarded with the sizzle of electronics, the hum and whirr of power relays and fans – *without* snotlings in them – and the sort of glowing lights and static discharge that were the signs of a really good piece of inventing. Often there was explosions and so on involved as well, if the invention was a weapon, but there was always a certain gleeful delight in having built a machine that no one else but you understood, whether it blew something else up or not.

So long as it worked. Having a machine that no one else but you understood and didn't work was less impressive, because that made it look like you didn't understand it either, and it was actually just a lot of junk arranged to look impressive. Gazruk simply had to hope that this wasn't going to be one of those times. It *shouldn't* be – he was pretty sure he had a firm grasp of the theory of it – but only the youngest, most foolish meks assumed that everything would work first time. Unfortunately, warbosses and freebooter kaptins alike ranked somewhere below the youngest, most foolish meks in the realism of their expectations, but far above them in terms of their ability to cause trouble about it.

Gazruk upended the pouch, and the skrawnie stones fell into the resonance chamber with a skittering clatter. They seemed to swirl back and forth for longer than they should have, given their size and weight, but Gazruk had no time to investigate that any further.

'Fire it up!' he ordered, and threw the master switch.

Da joose began to crackle and surge throughout and around the chamber. Dial after dial flipped from 'nuffin" to 'lotz', the needles hitting the far end of their range with tiny, tinny clangs. Lights blazed into existence, every one an angry blood red, which was how you could tell everything was working properly. The inkremental diffuser began to wheeze in steadily descending notes, so at least Snip had done an adequate job with the wires. Gazruk pointed at Kruggob, who hit the button to release the warp flush, and the air suddenly became cloying on the tongue, like someone had set something sweet on fire.

'Wot's dis?' Uzgul demanded, holding up one hand and scowling at it as pale fire collected around his fingertips. He waved the limb about experimentally, and the fire not only came with him, but there was a momentary, blurry afterimage where his arm had been a second beforehand too.

'Just an expected part of da process!' Gazruk replied, while making furious gestures at Zaggit. The spanner jerked in alarm as he realised he had a job to do, and threw every temporal relay from 'weird' to 'more weird'. Both of Gazruk's ears popped at once, along with his brain, and then the air returned to normal – no more burned-sweet taste, no more fuzzy afterimages, and no more screaming faces collecting in the dancing shadows cast by the machine's lights and sparks. Not that Gazruk objected to screaming faces in general, and a few weird gits clawing their way out of the walls would certainly occupy the kaptin for a bit, but right now he was determined to prove that his machine would do what he said it would.

All that was left now was the hum of a high-powered machine functioning properly, and the occasional zap and whine as little bits of excess charge fired off from one of the bleed-rods Gazruk had installed for just this purpose. He rubbed his hands together in delight. Nothing had blown up!

'Well?' Uzgul demanded. 'Wot's it say?'

'One second, kaptin,' Gazruk said, turning back to the omni-director. This was the final step. He just needed *something* out of this, and he could claim success. If he fine-tuned it and it turned out they had to change direction after a while then he could just claim the skrawnies had moved…

He flicked the switch, and the omnidirector juddered into life. To the untrained eye it looked like nothing more than a big metal needle, but to a technological expert like Gazruk it was obviously a big metal needle *powered by genius*.

Unfortunately, the needle itself didn't seem to know this.

Gazruk had expected a few moments of uncertainty as his machine's precision calculations were translated into phys-ical form. What he hadn't expected was the needle see-sawing unsteadily, and with no discernible rhythm, as though it was being batted backwards and forwards by a pair of high-spirited and very invisible grots. He stared at it for a moment in confusion and mounting horror, because there was no way that he could pass *this* off as a successful result.

'Is dere a problem, Gazruk?' Uzgul asked, his tone of voice suggesting that he thought that there might be, and that if there was, he was going to make zogging sure that more problems swiftly followed.

'Dis don't make no sense,' Gazruk muttered, rubbing his neck with the creeping awareness that something terminal might happen to it quite soon. 'It's like da fing can't work out...'

Light dawned.

'Bashgut!' he bellowed. 'Did you activate da quantum flanja?'

'...Woz dat my job, boss?' Bashgut asked, and Gazruk groaned.

'Of course it zoggin' was!' he yelled. 'Dat's why yoo're stood next to it, ain't it? Just get it... No, ya know wot? Zog it. Bashgut, walk over dere, and don't touch nuffin'! *Snip!*'

'Yes, boss?' Snip piped up, its face giddy with glee at being noticed.

'Activate da quantum flanja,' Gazruk said, fixing Bashgut with a stare to really drive home how incompetent he was if a *grot* could do his job. Snip whooped with glee and scampered over to the piece of machinery in question, big feet flapping on the floor, and yanked on the appropriate lever.

The hum in the room changed pitch slightly, everything wobbled for a moment, and then the wobbling settled down along with the omnidirector, which swung around smoothly to point steadily in a single direction.

'Da quantum flanja cancels out da contents of dis ship, kaptin,' Gazruk said proudly, and not without a certain amount of relief. 'Da machine was gettin' stuck between yoor stash of stones, an' da uvvers what it could pick up.'

'So it *is* pickin' 'em up?' Uzgul asked suspiciously.

'Definitely!' Gazruk replied, and he wasn't even feigning the confidence. 'Yoo just follow da machine's directions, kaptin, an' yoo'll find yerself a whole new pack of skrawnies!'

Uzgul stared at him for a few moments longer, then bellowed a laugh. 'Very good, Gazruk! I knew dere was a reason I picked yoo up off dat asteroid, rather'n leavin' yoo to get very slowly torn apart by da monsters what woz on it wiv ya!'

Gazruk smiled, but he knew a threat when he heard one. 'Ta, kaptin!'

'Get somefing to patch dis up to da bridge,' Uzgul said, pointing at the omnidirector. 'I don't wanna have to shout down here all da zoggin' time. But uvverwise...' He looked around the room, fixing all the assembled spanners with a stare for a few moments. 'Good work.'

He turned and left, slamming the door shut behind him.

'Wahoo!' shouted Snip, leaping into the air and waving its arms. Kruggob kicked it.

Gazruk exhaled. Well, that was one more day of not being the subject of one of Uzgul's inventive punishments. More importantly, his invention had worked! Now it was going to bring them closer to the skrawnies, and a good scrap.

He grunted. Something was nagging at him, something that he'd missed. Well, no matter. If it was important, he'd certainly figure it out before Uzgul did.

After all, he was a genius.

ELEVEN

Taenar might have been able to prise Uzgul's location loose from Kôttak's lips, but he still couldn't navigate the Farmarket with any surety, and Myrin had to lead their group back towards the rendezvous. The former admiral seemed to be adjusting well, which Myrin had suspected might be the case, but it was encouraging that there were still some things which he had not fully mastered.

'I do hope my impulsiveness will not prejudice you against me,' Taenar said quietly, brushing up against Myrin as their group squeezed through a press of other bodies – mainly the short, solid shapes of the Kin, but also others, including a few aeldari of various origins, the tall, gaunt, beaked shape of kroot, and even an intermittent scattering of humans, as well as other, stranger – or at least, more rarely seen – patrons.

'My dear Taenar, it positively delights me,' Myrin replied with a chuckle. 'Do you think I could not have returned to a craftworld if I so chose? If not to Ilmaren, then to another which might have welcomed my ships, and my talents? No, I am still here because I prefer this life, and I view it as the better course. Why would I not celebrate to see another starting to realise how much more fulfilled he can be if he discards the oppressive mindsets of the Paths?'

'Nonetheless, I feel that–'

'There you go, tensing up again,' Myrin said, placing his hand on the other aeldari's shoulder. 'And you had been getting more relaxed, too – very different from when we met.' He was not speaking purely figuratively, since the muscles of Taenar's shoulder were hard against his palm.

'I think it is only natural to be tense when leaving one's way of life behind,' Taenar said, a trifle defensively. 'When we met, I had no idea how we would be received.'

'It's not just that, though, is it?' Myrin said, leaning closer to speak softly into Taenar's ear as they waited for a bellowing, six-legged reptilian beast to be led across their path by a gaggle of small, chittering bipeds in ragged robes and fully enclosed helmets with opaque visors. 'You can feel how much more natural this is. How much closer to how we were meant to live, yes? The other factions within aeldari culture experience only a part of how our society existed before the Fall, whereas we have freedom to sample the whole gamut of life.'

'It seems unwise, even foolish,' Taenar replied stiffly, 'to speak in idealised terms of life before the Fall, without acknowledging the self-evident reality of what that led to. As though the Fall was something that just *happened*, like a supernova or an earthquake, as opposed to a calamity brought about directly by our people's own actions.'

'I told you, did I not, that this life pulls the weak-willed this way and that?' Myrin asked. 'But fear not. We are wiser than our forebears, and know the dangers of overindulgence in practices that can irrevocably taint the soul. However, just because the ocean may contain currents that can drown does not mean that one should be content with simply dipping one's toes into the water.' He shrugged. 'To live fully means to accept the possibility of death. To know that you can find your own way, you must leave the path. To truly succeed, one has to have the chance to fail. Otherwise, what have you overcome?'

'I am starting to wonder whether your decision to leave Ilmaren was accurately reported,' Taenar commented as the flow of foot traffic began to move again. 'This feels far more like a philosophical difference than a tactical one.'

'Philosophy influences tactics, as any military student knows,' Myrin said, 'but you are correct. Although I did not realise it at the time, when I look back I can see that there was a yearning in my soul that the Paths could never fulfil. I externalised that dissatisfaction to focus it solely on orders which, yes, were short-sighted. In truth, perhaps I should thank Elthorn Caman, since without their infuriating manner I may not have ever had the impetus I needed to break the bonds with my unsatisfying life.' He chuckled. 'It was only once I shed my chains that I realised what weight I had been carrying.'

Taenar nodded without speaking, and Myrin linked arms with him. The other aeldari no longer stiffened at such a gesture, instead simply leaning into Myrin slightly.

'How about you, Taenar?' Myrin asked. 'Can you feel the lightness now your chains have gone? Or do you miss the surety of your old boundaries?'

'I may have to come back to you on that, once I am more certain in my own mind,' Taenar replied. He smiled, but it was an uncertain thing, and made Myrin think of an animal scenting the air outside its burrow, ready to turn tail and flee at the first sign of danger. It made Myrin want to crack him open, to wrench apart his stiff, armoured shell and plunge into the vulnerability within to find out who Taenar Leotharan *really* was. Myrin was getting flashes, mere tantalising glimpses of the true aeldari soul beneath the layers of formality and constant second-guessing, and what he saw hinted at something beautiful and wild that deserved to run free and unfettered.

Hints were not truth, however, and freedom could not be forced. To break a beautiful thing was an indulgence that Myrin allowed himself only rarely, lest he travel too far down a path upon which he did not wish to tarry. To impose his will or vision on Taenar would be to break the other, in truth. Whatever then emerged would not be Taenar's genuine soul but a cracked and flawed reflection of Myrin's desires. Some aeldari – particularly those of Commorragh – might find satisfaction in controlling and shaping another's nature in order to be surrounded by nothing but facets of themselves, but Myrin placed too high a value on individuality. No, he would have to leave Taenar be for now, and do nothing more than urge him on and see where he landed. That might take some time, but Myrin had no intentions of dying soon, and sometimes delayed gratification was all the more satisfying.

'Tell me, baron,' Ra'thar Kyldran said, drawing level with them, 'what is the likelihood of your subordinates having completed their assignments and returned to meet us, as opposed to losing themselves in… this?' He gestured at the market surrounding them with one hand, the rune-encrusted sleeve of his robe slipping down to reveal the tight-fitting vambrace beneath.

'You're the seer, you tell me,' Myrin replied lightly, then chuckled at how Kyldran's helm managed to look disapproving. The angle of the warlock's head changed slightly, implying a condemnatory glance at Myrin and Taenar's interlinked arms before he forged ahead of them.

'You really shouldn't mock him,' Taenar said quietly.

'Why?' Myrin asked. He placed his free hand on his chest, fingers splayed above his heart, and adopted a melodramatic expression. 'Is he a good soul, wounded by my callous wit?'

'No, I mean that if you provoke him enough, he *will* kill you.' Taenar ran his tongue over his teeth thoughtfully. 'I know you despise the Paths, but you should be grateful for them. Ra'thar has the soul of a Dark Reaper, and access to powers far more destructive than any mere weapon. Out here, away from the control of the Seer Council, I worry to what methods he may resort if he concludes that there is no good reason to control himself.'

'My dear Taenar,' Myrin said seriously. 'I am Baron Myrin Stormdawn of the Starsplinters. I left Ilmaren because I refused to be dictated to by farseers. Do you think I will hold my tongue over your fears about a warlock's temper? I live as I please, and if that involves making fun of dangerous individuals then I will take the consequences of that.'

'I did not say that my worry was for you,' Taenar said. 'I would hate to see Ra'thar lose himself.'

'Then you should not have brought him with you,' Myrin replied. 'And you should give him the credit not to lose himself, but to find himself.' The crowd parted in front of them again, and he raised his voice slightly. 'You see, Master Kyldran? You had no reason to worry.'

Most of his captains, along with their companions from Taenar's fleet, were already assembled. In part that was due to a large tent selling powerful alcohol brewed by the Kin, which Myrin had known would be a draw for his underlings. Kyldran was studying the assembled Starsplinters with the air of one displeased, yet also utterly unsurprised.

'What in the name of all the gods are they drinking?' Taenar asked, wrinkling his nose.

'It doesn't have any name that you could easily pronounce,' Myrin told him. 'In truth, it's more of an endurance sport than refreshment – the taste can be most charitably described as "bold", and Kin brewing reacts in some slightly odd ways with aeldari biology.'

'He means that it tastes like sucking raw alcohol through mildewed animal hide, and leaves a hangover that feels like your head being drilled open,' Xela said, pushing past them and heading for the tent.

'And yet you are eager to drink it?' Taenar asked the back of her head as the other Starsplinters raised their tankards to greet the shade runner.

'You clearly were not raised in Commorragh,' Xela said without turning. Myrin smirked as he saw one of Taenar's captains take first a cautious sniff and then a mouthful of the drink, urged on by Siriolas Wynlar of *Revenge's First Cut*, then nearly spit it out again as her eyes bulged. To her credit, the officer managed to swallow it at the second attempt, and when she went on to drain the tankard she received a resounding cheer from the Starsplinters around her.

'Is this to what you referred when you referenced "learning your ways"?' Taenar asked dryly.

'In part,' Myrin agreed. 'Now, let us see what results they have achieved together.'

'Baron!' Siriolas shouted, looking around and spotting him as Xela pushed past her. 'What luck?'

'No luck, Siriolas, merely talent, as always,' Myrin said easily. 'What have we learned?'

Several of his captains had not managed to uncover anything relating to the freebooters, though there were some other items that would normally have been of interest. Fian Tor of *Sorrow's Death in Exile* had found rumours of a hrud migration in the galactic north, while Halthir Orksbane of *Storm of a Thousand Nights* brought word of a new, if probably temporary, corridor through the great warp storm that bisected the galaxy – meaningless to those who travelled via the webway, but a new route meant the ships of other species gathering to chance the voyage, or regroup after having done so, and that meant fine opportunities for plunder.

However, some of the Starsplinters had better luck with their enquiries. Lladrin Seonar of *Flame in the Night* and Siriolas Wynlar had both heard rumours placing Uzgul's base in the same rough area, but it was Meliandril of Alaitoc who surprised everyone by stepping forward.

'The ork is most likely to be found in the system of the star Ashaonnir, known to the humans as Darmeer,' the ranger declared. She smiled at their surprise. 'Someone or something has put a bounty on its head. A ranger must eat as they travel the galaxy, and I have collected such bounties in my time, when the price has been right and the quarry felt… deserving. I still know how to find the places where such contracts may be entered into, and the reward claimed. The brokers will not give information out about known haunts and last location freely, lest it spook the prey, but they want their cut of the fee, and so they will disclose such things to those whom they consider likely to have a chance at collecting.'

'Impressive,' Myrin acknowledged. He had not given much thought to how rangers lived as they travelled, but it made sense. He wondered briefly what other galaxy-spanning networks there might be, outside the control of any one species' organised ruling body, of which even he was not aware. 'Can anyone do better?'

'You can.'

The voice was as sharp and cold as a sliver of ice, and it came from behind him. Myrin turned to see Ellisar Elasandor and his companions striding towards him, the captain's face set in an expression not far short of murderous.

'Well,' Xela said into her tankard. 'This looks interesting.'

TWELVE

'Ellisar,' Myrin said, unlinking his arm from Taenar's and stepping away from the former admiral. 'You have something you wish to say?'

'I knew where the best chance was of finding what we sought,' Ellisar declared, pointing at Myrin with the pale fingers of his marble arm. 'The Kin whisper-merchant, Kôttak – an unpleasant individual, but well informed. However, when I got there he informed me that he had already sold that information, and would not part with it again.'

'Remarkably decent of him, all things considered,' Myrin remarked. 'I would not have expected him to practise such exclusivity for his customers. However, since you have apparently deduced that my party were the ones who garnered this information, I am confused by your anger.'

'He told me what price he had charged,' Ellisar spat. 'You bartered away the location of our *home*, Stormdawn!'

There was a generalised shifting amongst the assembled captains. Even, Myrin realised, amongst some of Taenar's folk. He always considered himself to be the centre of attention, but now he really felt it, as pair after pair of eyes focused on him. It was not anger, nor outright hostility. Not yet. It was definitely uncertainty, however.

He could offer up Taenar, he realised. Shove the newcomer forwards, announce – completely truthfully – what Taenar had done, and that he had done it without consulting Myrin first. It would not completely discharge Myrin's responsibility, since he had elected to take Taenar with him and would be judged for letting him speak to Kôttak alone while knowing such sensitive information, but it would give a new focus for Ellisar's fury. For someone with Myrin's skill with words, it would be a simple enough matter to glide aside from the issue as effortlessly as he had done many times before, with Taenar as the sacrifice that would allow him to do so.

The cost, of course, would be Taenar. Ellisar was a fearsome warrior, and seemed blessed by the Bloody-Handed God himself when blades were drawn. The captain of *The Yearning Stars* was out for blood, and unless Taenar was either unusually skilled or got unexpectedly lucky, Elasandor would kill him.

And that was not, Myrin realised within a moment of the concept occurring to him, a price that he wished to pay.

'Our *former* home, Captain Elasandor,' he declared, spreading his arms wide. 'We've left it, or had you not realised? The location is already out there in the galaxy. Why not profit from it while we still can?'

'The entire point of this was to find the location of the beast Uzgul, and then slay it!' Ellisar snapped. 'With that threat removed, we could have returned to the Well of the Long Death!'

'You clearly grew too fond of that place,' Myrin said, shaking his head in genuine regret. 'You know that is not the life of a corsair, Ellisar! All things are transient to us. It is better this way.'

'No!' Ellisar shouted. 'This is not turning with the wind, this is running before it like a coward! The day will come when you will abandon all of us to save your own precious skin!' He drew his blade – a long, silvered sword, inlaid with crystals and a fine power matrix. 'I invoke the Gauntlet of Blood!'

Myrin opened his mouth to reply, then hesitated when he saw Ellisar's eyes.

'Well?' Ellisar demanded, his entire form quivering with tension.

'Oh, Ellisar,' Myrin said sadly. 'I am sorry I did not see it sooner.'

'See what?'

'The madness,' Myrin said, his chest hollowing out. 'It's been creeping up on you, hasn't it? Whispering in your ear. Telling you that we were wrong to leave Ilmaren, so we must make a new home and fight for it as we never did for our craftworld. That anyone who doesn't stand with you on these matters cannot be trusted. That there is only one true way to live, and it is your way. That those who see things differently will ultimately betray you.'

'You *have* betrayed us!' Ellisar snapped. 'Me, and all the rest of us who were foolish enough to let ourselves be led by you! If there is madness here, Stormdawn, it lies with the one who claims to know his course when he will abandon anything at the first sign of danger! The one who thinks he can hold fast when he has nothing firm on which to stand!'

'I have myself, and I know myself!' Myrin retorted, slapping his own chest. 'I am neither defined by nor bound to anything else! I need no home, I need no ship, I need no companions to know my own nature. I know my course, for it is mine, and I will take with me any who wish to join me on that journey.' He gestured to Ellisar's sword. 'Put that away, Ellisar. If you have lost faith in my leadership then you are free to leave, and take with you any who will follow. You can find another branch of the Starsplinters if that is to your liking, or you can strike out on your own and find whatever home eases your heart. Settle with the Exodites, or wander the stars, even go back to Ilmaren, if you wish. Do not make me draw my blade against you.'

Ellisar wavered, and for a moment Myrin thought that he would listen, that he might sheathe his sword and leave, perhaps taking a couple of captains and their ships with him, and depart in peace, if not harmony. But then the spark of madness flared up in his eyes again, and Myrin knew that his hope was forlorn even before Ellisar spoke again.

'You do not deserve to be left to lead good aeldari to their dooms, sacrificing them one after another for your convenience,' Ellisar growled. 'My blade is drawn, and I have invoked the Gauntlet of Blood! Either face me in combat, or surrender your weapons and allow your life to be taken!'

Myrin sighed. 'So be it.' It took corsairs like this, sometimes. Oh, there were those who lost themselves in dark pleasures, or whose minds simply shattered from the pressures put upon them without the cocooning structure of aeldari society, but they were easily identified and dealt with. This was the creeping, subversive threat – the never-ending, subtle stress that slowly cracked the mind and distorted the images within. Ellisar might have pinpointed Myrin as the villain, but in truth, he would never be happy again. There would always be someone else whom Ellisar would blame; someone else who would not match up to his standards, not through any specific action of their own, but because Ellisar's mind would demand that such a subject be found in order to externalise the pressure he felt.

'What is the Gauntlet of Blood?' Myrin heard Taenar whisper.

'Starsplinters challenge for leadership,' Xela whispered back. 'Single combat.'

'You consider yourself the baron's superior,' Taenar replied, to which Myrin cocked an eyebrow. 'Can he not call upon you to fight it for him?'

'No other Starsplinter can intervene,' Xela said. 'Not even his Bladesworn.'

'And is it to the death?' Ra'thar Kyldran asked as Myrin unsheathed his void sabre.

'Of course,' Xela confirmed.

'Of course,' Kyldran echoed, his helm turning to look at Taenar, for some reason. 'Whoever could have foreseen this?'

Myrin put their slightly confusing discussion from his mind, since puzzling over the warlock's words was not going to help him. He raised his weapon to Ellisar in salute.

'You are certain you wish to do this here?' he asked, gesturing at the market. 'I would be happy for this to take place in my chambers on *Light of Heaven*.'

'No delays,' Ellisar snarled, twirling his sword – an expert loosening his wrist and fingers, not an overconfident fool showing off. 'No chances for you to run away from another fight, or another hard decision. The Kin care not what happens here so long as their own are not harmed, and the only one who will be harmed is you.'

'As you wish,' Myrin sighed, then smiled and stretched. His body felt strong and invigorated, as though energy was flowing through it at the prospect of danger. 'At the very least, it will be fascinating to cross blades with you, Ellisar. I have no intention of dying at your hand, but if that is to be my fate, then this feels like a suitably exhilarating way for my life to end.'

'Enough words,' Ellisar said shortly. 'Are you ready?'

Myrin assumed a guard position. 'I am ready.'

There were few rules on the nature of the combat in the Gauntlet of Blood, save that projectile weapons were not permitted. You could run an opponent through with your own blade, claim theirs and use that instead, attack them with anything in the immediate environment, or even throttle them.

The end simply had to be brought about by your own hand, rather than at range. Ellisar had technically not needed to get verbal confirmation of Myrin's readiness once both their weapons were drawn, but Ellisar still thought he was being the reasonable one.

Ellisar moved with no further warning, his blade flashing and dancing in minuscule feints, before stabbing out for Myrin's heart. Myrin knocked the tip of his opponent's weapon away, fighting the urge to give ground, well aware that letting himself be put on the back foot was to invite disaster. He parried another cut and launched an attack of his own, but his thrust landed a fingers-breadth short of Ellisar's throat. Ellisar circled to Myrin's left, looking for a way past his guard, and Myrin mirrored him. He was dimly aware of the Starsplinters looking on in tense silence, but some of the market's other occupants had realised that a duel was occurring, and had begun to gather around and whoop in encouragement. Someone was probably already taking bets, Myrin thought wryly, and the thought distracted him enough that he almost did not react in time to Ellisar's next attack. He managed to beat it away, knocking his opponent's weapon up and stepping forward to ram his shoulder into Ellisar's chest and knock him back a step, but his counter-cut was clumsy, and Ellisar had his guard back in place to catch it. The captain of *The Yearning Stars* was good – very good, in fact, but Myrin thought that he might be better–

Ellisar staggered, and a handspan of narrow, sizzling power-blade emerged from his chest. He looked down at it in shock and uncomprehending horror, his sword already sagging in his hand. Then the blade twisted, bringing about an instantaneous and corresponding contortion of agony on Ellisar's face, and withdrew. Ellisar slumped down to his knees as blood leaked gently out over his void suit, his ruined heart no longer even having the strength to pump. Myrin looked up from his dying opponent's face in shock, and met the eyes of Taenar Leotharan.

'I was told no Starsplinter could interfere,' Taenar said, Ellisar's blood already drying and atomising off the surface of his energised blade. His expression was outwardly calm, but his eyes were a tempest. 'However, as Ellisar himself was quick to point out, I am not a Starsplinter.'

To his shock, Myrin found himself speechless. Conflicting emotions whiplashed through him. His body was still pumping with energy from the barely begun fight, and the snarling, animal part of himself raged at being denied its kill – the entirely justified kill, the kill that had presented itself to him and demanded he fight for his life, the kill he could have made with no compunction, or thoughts of morality. This warred with relief. Relief that he did not have to kill Ellisar Elasandor, a commander who had fought well both in the Ilmaren fleet and that of the Starsplinters, and who had been brought to this pass not by treachery but by the weakness of his own mind; and relief, too, that he was no longer at risk of being killed *by* Ellisar Elasandor, should he have stumbled or miscalculated. Then there was guilt at not noticing Ellisar's decline until too late, gratitude to Taenar for removing this hardest of choices from his hands, and anger that this newcomer – still in his Ilmaren uniform! – should think that Myrin could possibly *need* his help.

Underpinning it all, however, was a dark and fierce joy at seeing Taenar unmasked. There he was, sword bloody and eyes tumultuous, having just taken a life. This was as raw, as genuine, as a being could be, and Myrin drank the moment in with a hunger he had not known was in him, fixing every facet of the moment in his mind: Taenar's expression; the tilt of his blade; the fragility of his posture as it tried to suggest bravado, yet communicated an expectation of chastisement or retribution.

Perhaps there was even a subconscious desire for it as a reassurance that yes, there were still rules to which he would be held, and that the galaxy was not truly his to do with as he wished. There was little that could be so terrifying to the aeldari mind.

And yet, retribution was indeed to hand, since Ellisar's crew were already drawing their weapons. Taenar's followers responded in kind, and Ra'thar Kyldran pulled his witchblade from his back with a growl of frustration. The other Starsplinters – those who had owed Ellisar no particular allegiance – looked back and forth uncertainly between the two groups, hands on weapons but making no move as yet to openly side with one or the other.

'Don't just stand there,' Xela hissed at Myrin, her knives appearing in her hands. 'Get control of this!'

Part of Myrin honestly did not want to. There was an impulse just to let events unfold and see what happened. Everyone there was an experienced crewer or warrior, after all, and who was he to interfere if they decided they wanted to spill blood? Still, there was his own position to consider, and a corsair baron who let his subordinates cut each other into pieces would suffer in standing as a result.

'Hold!' he commanded loudly. 'Stand down!'

'That snivelling princeling just killed the captain!' shouted Ellisar's second, a mariner by the name of Saraan Skyhand. They had joined the Starsplinters from an Exodite planet – as demonstrated by the feathers and scrimshaw that somewhat anachronistically adorned their void suit – after Ellisar's crew had killed a drukhari slaver force preying on their world. Some Exodites received protection from craftworlds, but there was often tension between them and the followers of Asuryan. The craftworlders saw the Exodites as rustic and unsophisticated, and the warrior clans in their turn tended to view their spacefaring cousins as pretentious and condescending, and still far too close to the lifestyles that had led to the Fall. No corsair was likely to take their captain's death well, barring the existence of a personal grudge, but Skyhand had owed Ellisar Elasandor a personal debt.

'I am losing my patience with this entire charade,' Ra'thar Kyldran declared, the air around his witchblade shimmering with force. 'Attack, if you wish your souls to enter whatever afterlife you have chosen for them.'

'You are not helping matters, master warlock,' Myrin snapped, pointing at him. 'This is–'

He broke off as the ground shifted beneath his feet. He staggered and managed to retain his balance, but he was not the only one affected. The rest of his party were similarly jolted, with some thrown from their feet entirely. The market was shaking, with other bipedal patrons who lacked an aeldari's natural grace falling this way and that.

'Kyldran!' Myrin shouted. 'Stop this!'

'This is not my doing!' the warlock responded, his feet planted and his helm swivelling this way and that as he searched for threats. 'Nor is it any psykana that I can detect! How stable is this giant corpse?'

'It's a damned void whale, it doesn't have tectonic activity!' Xela shouted at him. A large pole holding up part of the brewing tent began to fall towards her, and she momentarily blinked out of existence, reappearing a few feet away as it crashed down. 'This is no natural disturbance!'

Unless it was. Myrin sheathed his void sabre, ripped off his void suit's glove and pressed his palm to the surface beneath him. What should have been cool, hard bone was rapidly growing warmer to the touch, as well as increasingly spongy. In fact, the ground was starting to sag beneath him, his own weight causing him to sink into it as though he was standing on a thick bed of moss. The bone was softening and weakening, and Myrin knew of only one thing that could do that.

'*Cruevar!*' he shouted. 'To the ships!'

He took a moment to clamp his helm on – not for protection against the cruevar, but against the atmosphere outside. His crew were already moving towards the airlock, and Taenar's were thankfully going with them, all animosity between the two forgotten for now in the face of a far more pressing threat. The Ilmarens might not know what a cruevar was, but they could at least gather that they did not want to find out first-hand.

Unfortunately, they were not to be so lucky.

The ground directly in front of Myrin began to bubble and liquify, the pale surface darkening to a sticky, smoking brown. Most of the Starsplinters managed to pull up in time, but a couple who had been farther ahead found themselves starting to sink up to their knees in corrosive muck. An aeldari's usual response to danger was to leap away, counting on their agility to protect them against the galaxy's slower and clumsier species, but on such foul footing their efforts merely mired them deeper. A few of their companions tried to reach out for them, but Myrin grabbed one such would-be rescuer by the shoulder and wrenched him away.

'Back! Back!' he shouted at the others. 'You can do nothing for them now!'

The cruevar did not emerge from the ground so much as the ground fell away around and into it: a disc-shaped mouth as wide across as a Falcon grav-tank, into which drained the liqui-fied bone its acidic saliva had already part-dissolved, along with the screaming Starsplinters. The other corsairs reacted instinc-tively, drawing and firing weapons at the gigantic parasite that had just devoured two of their own.

'No!' Xela yelled at them. 'Don't attract its–'

The cruevar, las-blasts and shuriken discs ricocheting off its carapace, emerged further from its burrow to tower above them, tall as a Phantom Titan despite the fact that the bulk of its serpentine body remained hidden. Its head swayed blindly this way and that for a moment, and the Starsplinters froze instinctively.

It did no good. The cruevar lunged downwards towards the greatest concentration of aeldari, an avalanche of acidic chitin seeking to rid itself of an irritation. Myrin staggered to one side on the unsteady footing, and could only watch as a handful of his finest captains and their crews were instantly ground into paste by the titanic impact. For a moment he thought that would be it – that the monster would simply dissolve its way back into the bone, and be gone – but then it began to sweep its head sideways towards him.

There was no way to evade it in time on such treacherous ground. Xela disappeared from existence just before she would have been killed by the cruevar's bulk, and the last Myrin saw of her was the agonised expression in her pale eyes as she looked back at him, unable to take him with her but unwilling to die alongside him. He understood. He would have made the same decision in her place.

Of all the ways the galaxy might hold for Myrin Stormdawn to die, being crushed to death by a colossal parasite was not the end for which he might have hoped. It was not a fate worthy of a song. Indeed, his last thought was that he hoped very much that no one *did* compose a ballad about it, since it was undoubtedly better to perish anonymously than live on in mockery.

The air by his right ear exploded linearly, and a bolt of horizontal purple lightning seared past him to bore right through the cruevar's carapace and into what passed for its brain. The head exploded with a wet thud that reverberated through Myrin's body and shook the air in his lungs, and semi-solid matter poured out of the cruevar's corpse as it ground to a halt within arm's reach of where he was standing. He stared at it for a moment in confusion as his brain struggled to catch up with the fact that he still existed.

'Are there likely to be more of these things?' Ra'thar Kyldran asked, stepping into view. He turned his helm to look at Myrin, and let the witchfire playing around his fingers die away in what felt like a gesture intended to draw attention to exactly what he could do should Myrin displease him.

'Quite possibly,' Myrin managed. Even as he spoke, a new chorus of screams and shouts arose, away off to his right, towards the Farmarket's centre. 'There! We must leave, now.'

'I do not disagree,' Kyldran said, keeping pace with him as he suited actions to words. 'However, that creature does at least seem to be some distance away.'

'It's no longer them that worry me,' Myrin told him. 'At least not directly. The Kin take their claims very seriously, and they will defend them as vigorously against parasites as they would any invading force. I suspect their ships are already on their way to purge the infestation, and they have a tendency to value efficacy over precision!' He pointed towards the translucent roof of the Farmarket dome, through which could just be made out the running lights of Kin ships, gradually increasing in size and brightness as they began to descend. 'Taenar! With me!'

'Baron!' Taenar Leotharan said, joining them in their uneven, stumbling run around the cruevar's corpse and the mire surrounding it. 'I apologise if–'

'Later!' Myrin snapped. 'In seeking to solve one problem, you have merely landed me with another, far more complex one. For now, although it might simplify matters if you were to die, try to remain alive…'

THIRTEEN

The Starsplinters fleet had left its position at high anchor above the void whale corpse, and were making for the webway once more. The immediate crisis appeared to have delayed any fallout from Taenar's slaying of Ellisar Elasandor, but Taenar had ordered his crew to be alert for an attack from any angle, especially from *The Yearning Stars*. He had then retired to his chambers, ostensibly to meditate.

He did not need to ask who was at his door when the chime went off. He was not as psychically sensitive as some of his people, and he had never heard the calling of a Path that would develop those abilities, but neither was he a blunt-souled creature of Commorragh. He could sense the sullen, swirling maelstrom of Ra'thar Kyldran's mind from here.

The doors to his chambers slid open, and Ra'thar stepped inside with his usual brusque manner. However, the warlock came to a halt after one pace, and seemed to barely register the doors closing again behind him, even though they nearly caught the hem of his robes.

'What have you done in here?' Ra'thar asked, looking around with a frown. He sniffed. 'What's burning?'

'Nothing important,' Taenar replied. He waved a hand towards a brazier. 'I found that I desired the smell of woodsmoke, for some reason.' The item in question had been a small, carved wooden box – a gift from a partner from whom he had separated a few centuries ago. He had kept it more out of habit than any real lasting attachment to the one from whom he had received it, and no one would have known or cared what he did with it, but the act of breaking it down and setting the flame had given him a small thrill of transgression. And besides, as it turned out, the wood did indeed give off a pleasing fragrance when burned.

'Perhaps you're seeking to mask the scent of blood,' Ra'thar said coldly, crossing his arms.

Taenar sighed. 'Don't you think you're being slightly over-dramatic?'

'You killed an aeldari, Taenar!' Ra'thar snapped, pointing at him. 'I told you that my visions foretold death if we went to the market, and they were borne out!'

'We have both killed many aeldari,' Taenar said flatly, rising from his chair. 'Drukhari are aeldari, Ra'thar, and we have defended Ilmaren from them before. I do not recall you raising such objections then.' He shrugged. 'Besides, I trusted your visions. If death was to come, better that I fulfil that doom in a way that best benefitted us.'

'Do not attempt to turn my words back upon me!' Ra'thar said sternly, not in any way mollified. 'You stabbed him *in the back*! He was not threatening you! He was not an *enemy*!'

'No?' Taenar demanded, walking to stand in front of the warlock and folding his arms. 'Perhaps you had not heard the same words from Ellisar Elasandor as I had. He had no love for us. He did not trust us! He spoke constantly of how we should not be with the Starsplinters. It was merely a matter of time before he took matters into his own hands anyway, quite apart from the fact that he initiated a combat that might have killed Myrin! My main concern,' he added, 'is whether my actions, justified though they were, might force Myrin to banish us, or worse.'

'I do wonder exactly how personal your attachment to this corsair baron has become,' Ra'thar said, his tone sharp.

'And I wonder if you have forgotten the reason we're here!' Taenar said, exasperated. 'Have you? I remember the words Farseer Caman said to me very clearly! We are to aid Myrin Stormdawn, and ensure his survival, so that he can fulfil his role in Ilmaren's future!'

Ra'thar's face went blank. 'You should not–'

'Who else is here to overhear?' Taenar asked, his throat suddenly tight. The words had snagged on the way out, the very utterance of them feeling like a betrayal. Until this moment, Taenar had been able to pretend to himself that perhaps he had not been deceiving Myrin Stormdawn from the very beginning, even though that had been the point of this whole affair. Taenar's resolve had lasted until the moment he had set eyes on the baron, at which point things had got… complicated.

Stormdawn's personality – or at least his persona, which Taenar had come to understand was something deliberate and projected – was magnetic, that was the problem. He had the handsome features of a hero from legend, or at least a hero before they suffered the wounds that broke them, as was the fate of most aeldari heroes. However, he was also possessed of an easy-going air which was a stark contrast to the serious councils and doom-laden meetings of Ilmaren. The Starsplinters did not interrogate every action, every possibility to exhaustion, until no matter how worthy your purpose you felt like merely a piece in a machine, with no option but to perform your role. They considered and consulted to an extent, but then they simply *acted*, and it was wild and chaotic and glorious and wonderful and *free*, and Myrin Stormdawn was at the centre of it. He was the calm eye of the storm, the singularity to which the observer was drawn.

'The more it is spoken of, the more likely it is that the truth will get out,' Ra'thar said firmly, dragging Taenar's attention back from his musings. 'We cannot afford for that to occur.'

'No,' Taenar agreed. Myrin Stormdawn was not someone whom he wished to deceive. Part of that was because of the inevitable consequences should such a deception be discovered, consequences that would involve Xela Flickerstep and her knives, or the guns of the Starsplinters fleet turning on *Dance of Dying Seasons* suddenly, and without warning. However, at least an equal part was that despite the fact Stormdawn had turned his back on his craftworld, despite his mercurial and apparently self-serving nature, Taenar found him fascinating. Why had Stormdawn taken Taenar's story at face value, as he apparently had? It did not seem in the nature of a corsair baron who had survived and thrived in the role for any length of time, which Stormdawn had clearly done. To break the trust of someone who had no reason to be trusting, yet still offered it freely, felt... wasteful.

'I can feel the conflict within you,' Ra'thar said. 'Do not dwell on it. Let it flow over you and disappear. Yes, we wish to aid Myrin Stormdawn, so in what way are we hurting him? He would most likely already be dead, were it not for our intervention at the Well of the Long Death.'

'I would have thought that a seer, of all people, would understand the difference between something being done for the right reason and the wrong one,' Taenar said. He would have continued, but Ra'thar's expression darkened.

'For the wrong reason?' the warlock echoed. 'What reason could be better than the survival of our craftworld?'

'That's not what I meant!' Taenar protested. 'Don't pretend that you do not understand me!' He slapped his chest, and felt the cold shape of his spirit stone beneath his palm. 'Lies, Ra'thar! My very presence here is a lie, and I hate that I must continue to let him believe the falsehoods I have fed him!'

'It is entirely possible that he does not believe you at all,' Ra'thar said, studying Taenar's face. He sniffed. 'The question will be whether the dynamic between us changes when he has more ships of his own around him.'

'It will not,' Taenar said with a sudden certainty. 'You have met him and spoken with him. Do you honestly think he is the sort to pretend with us?'

'I wonder why it appears to pain you so much to consider that he might be,' Ra'thar said, his eyes narrowing.

'Nothing of the sort!' Taenar lied, ignoring the sharp hollow that had opened in his chest at the notion. 'I mean that he is the sort to speak his mind no matter the consequences. Had he distrusted us, I am sure he would not have allowed us to accompany him.'

'And *I* am sure a corsair baron is cognisant of the benefits of our fleet being at his apparent command,' Ra'thar said, 'and will use us for his own ends for so long as we show an inclination to obey him, all the while waiting for us to slip up and confirm his suspicions.'

Taenar forced back the harsh words that threatened to spill out from between his teeth. 'Well, perhaps it is of no importance. As you say, we are here to aid him, whatever our motives. If he is willing to allow our aid then that is what matters, whatever *his* motives.'

'And his motives do not concern you?' Ra'thar pressed. 'You are focused solely on our success, and not on whether or not this corsair is playing with you?'

'I am focused on the fact that you appear to be trying to antagonise me,' Taenar said tightly. 'Farseer Caman charged me with this mission, and so far I do not believe that they would have any cause to take issue with its progress. Do you disagree?'

Ra'thar's jaw shifted slightly. 'If I did, it would not be my decision.'

'You are in contact with them?' Taenar asked, astonished. 'Even here?'

'My abilities do not extend solely to destructive forces,' Ra'thar said with an icy smile. 'And more importantly, neither do the farseer's. We are not as alone out here as you might think. Something to consider, perhaps.' He looked around Taenar's chambers once more, and sighed. 'I will leave you to your... meditations.'

Taenar said nothing to stop him. He said nothing, in fact – simply stood and watched as Ra'thar opened the doors and stepped out again without a backward glance. He did not move until the doors were shut and he had privacy once more, whereupon he returned to his seat and slumped back down into it in an attempt to find some solid base for his body, even if his mind and spirit were in a whirl.

The thought of Ra'thar reporting back to Elthorn Caman was more disconcerting than it should have been. The prospect of oversight, or indeed potential guidance from Ilmaren's foremost farseer, should have gladdened Taenar's heart. Instead, it made him twitchy, as though he had just become aware of someone who had been looking over his shoulder for a long time.

More prevalent, however, was the ongoing churn of emotions concerning the issue that Ra'thar had apparently come to bring up: Taenar's killing – in fact, it would not be unreasonable to call it *murder* – of Ellisar Elasandor. On Ilmaren, he would be facing the strongest censure for his actions. Out here... he wasn't sure.

Everything Taenar had said to Ra'thar was true. Elasandor

had been hostile towards the supposed Ilmaren outcasts; had he triumphed over Stormdawn, the Starsplinters would almost certainly have turned on Taenar and his people. And it was certainly true that had Elasandor pursued the combat to the death, as seemed to be the way, then that would have ruined Taenar's mission. Elthorn Caman had been extremely clear that his scryings had shown Myrin Stormdawn playing a critical role in Ilmaren's future, and so they needed to ensure that the corsair remained alive. With Elasandor having made his move so swiftly, and without warning, Taenar was not certain what other course he could have taken.

However, all of that was secondary. When it came down to it, in the depths of his soul, Taenar was willing to admit that he had *wanted* to kill the other aeldari. The bubbling undercurrent of his ego, so often repressed, wanted to lash out at the source of the thinly veiled threats that had been sneered in his direction. He had wanted to shut Elasandor up and teach him why he should have minded his words and his manners.

But it was more than that, too. There was something in Taenar's soul that thirsted for blood, and cared not from whence it came, or what might justify its spilling. It was an old hunger, one which looked at the galaxy and declared it to be the plaything of him and his kind, with the lives of others having no more value than that he chose to give them. His time as an Aspect Warrior had sated it to an extent, as had the combats in which he'd engaged as a warrior of Ilmaren's fleet, but those killings at the behest of others had still been staid and stale by comparison – akin to sucking on a damp cloth when in the grip of a raging thirst. Now he had taken his first true draught of pure, clean water, and for the first time he properly appreciated the difference.

Taenar forced himself to calm. Elasandor's death had delighted him in ways he had never experienced before, and there was no point in denying that to himself. However, that did not mean he had to pursue that feeling again. He had mastered himself for his centuries of life so far, and he would not devolve into degeneracy after a single misstep. This was a test, nothing more. If Farseer Caman hadn't thought that Taenar could cope with the unique challenges of living amongst corsairs, they would not have chosen him for this task.

Taenar's soul had settled again. He would not hide from what he had done, but nor would he let himself be defined by it. In ancient aeldari legend, murderers were marked out by a hawk hovering above their heads, which Taenar had always taken to be a metaphor for their guilt. Such emotions could have impacts on an aeldari's spirit, and indeed their whole existence, in a way lesser species couldn't comprehend. In the same way as an aeldari could persist by sheer force of will through physical trauma that would kill a human, a broken heart could slay them, and guilt could hollow out a body and leave it rotten and dying. She Who Thirsts was not the only danger that awaited an aeldari who let themselves be ruled by their emotions, and Taenar would not let such things get the better of him.

The featherlight touch of a messenger wave brushed across his awareness, and Taenar acknowledged the signal with a flutter in his stomach. He was not generally given to nervousness, but he had not spoken to Myrin Stormdawn since their terse exchange during the Starsplinters' hurried escape from the Farmarket, and from the destructive cruevars. Stormdawn was the focus of Taenar's mission, and the one into whose affairs he had so recently and so violently interjected himself. He could not afford to alienate him now, and his mouth was dry at the thought that the message might be an angry banishment.

'Taenar. Attend me. We have much to discuss.'

FOURTEEN

I have been waiting for an update.

Forgive me. I did not wish to pre-emptively declare success. However, I am confident now that matters are progressing smoothly. Relatively so, at least.

And he suspects nothing?

No, the deception is intact.

Good. That must remain the case. We cannot predict how he will react, otherwise.

I would contend that his reaction would be rather predictable.

Do not make the mistake of thinking that you know him as well as I. But regardless of that, he must not learn the truth until our purpose is achieved. See to this.

Of course, farseer.

FIFTEEN

No languid preamble, as Taenar had come to expect from Myrin. No urbane wit, nor even barbed humour. Simply a peremptory instruction delivered with an apparent absolute conviction that Taenar would obey, and then instant cessation of communication.

Taenar would have bristled at such treatment from anyone else. Even Farseer Caman, wisest of all of Ilmaren's guiding council, would not have spoken to him in such a manner – they always emphasised choice and reason, even to those from whom they commanded unquestioning loyalty. Had Caman ordered Taenar into this mission outright, he might have baulked. It was only after the farseer had explained to him its importance, and the dire consequences that might befall Ilmaren were the mission unsuccessful, that Taenar had agreed to take on the role of deserter.

Here, however, he had no choice, and reason was only a fleeting companion. To continue his mission, Taenar needed to remain close to Myrin, and to do that, he had to keep the corsair happy. Now was not the time for posturing, or displays of wounded pride, so he boarded a Vampire Raider and took the short trip through the fleet to *Light of Heaven*. It was a tense journey, aware as he was that he would now make a very tempting target for anyone seeking revenge for Elasandor's death, but he reached his destination without incident.

The incident was instead waiting for him as soon as his ramp descended, in the form of Xela Flickerstep and a dozen Starsplinters.

'Leave your weapons on board,' Xela said, indicating the dropship with a nod of her head.

'And if I do not?' Taenar demanded. A direct instruction from Myrin Stormdawn was one thing, but he was not enthused at the notion of being ordered around by this Commorraghan refugee.

Xela drew her knives, and the other Starsplinters' shuriken rifles made faint whirring noises as their graviton accelerators powered up. 'Then we kill you here and flush the parts out into the void.'

Taenar's lip twisted, but he felt he knew Xela well enough by now to tell when she might be bluffing, or indulging in her strange, bloodthirsty humour, and this did not seem like one of those occasions. He kept his expression otherwise serene as he unbuckled his weapons belt and tossed it casually behind him into the Raider's passenger bay, and decided that here, at least, some corsair swagger might be appropriate. He descended the ramp towards them, arms spread slightly as though to reassure that he had nothing else hidden about his person. 'Should I be flattered at how dangerous you think I am?'

'Fools can be dangerous,' Xela said bluntly as the Starsplinters arranged themselves around him and they began to walk. 'Be flattered by that, if you wish.'

In the Ilmaren navy, officers did not quarrel in front of regular crewers – it was considered unseemly, and bad for morale. Taenar had already learned that things were done differently amongst the Starsplinters, and besides, he had no particular investment in the crew morale of *Light of Heaven*.

'If this is about Elasandor's death, you were the one who suggested that I might wish to kill him,' he said with deliberate lightness.

Xela's intake of breath was a sharp-edged hiss. 'In practically any situation *other* than when he'd just challenged the baron to the Gauntlet of Blood!'

Taenar grunted, his stomach tightening as doubt reasserted itself. 'I wondered if you were so specific in your wording of the combat's nature in order to hint at what you felt my best course of action was. It seems I may have been mistaken.'

'Dead gods and black suns preserve me,' Xela groaned. 'They have a saying in Commorragh. *The only thing more pathetic than an Asuryani who does not understand intrigue, is one who thinks he does.* You are the embodiment of that.'

Taenar felt the urge to rise to her needling, but restrained himself. He simply smiled slightly instead. 'Were I Asuryani, I would still be on my Path.'

'Would that you had stayed there,' Xela muttered. She held her hand up when Taenar opened his mouth to respond. 'No more words from you. Stormdawn would probably prefer it if I delivered you with your tongue still attached, but he did not specify it, and I am prepared to risk his displeasure.'

Their destination was neither the grand, opulent stateroom in which Taenar had first been received, nor the council chamber where Xela had first offered her murderous advice. Xela did not announce Taenar when they arrived, or even sound a door chime. She simply palmed the doors open and shoved him through them.

Taenar found himself in a set of rooms not too dissimilar from his own in terms of style and layout, which was not especially surprising. Craftworld ships were sung from wraithbone rather than constructed from baser materials, and bore the individual signature of their artisans rather than being put together in accordance with staid plans and schematics, but most were variations on a theme. Besides which, each craftworld had its own bonesinging traditions, and while an Ilmaren ship might differ somewhat from a Saim-Hain or an Alaitoc one, one Ilmaren ship was usually going to be much like another.

As a result, and much like he had in the throne room, Taenar found himself momentarily disorientated by the sheer contrast in presentation. His own chambers might have most recently been scented by the sharp tang of woodsmoke, but that was as nothing compared to the thick aroma of perfumed oils that hung languorously in the air here, much like the many-layered, multi-coloured fabrics that swooped from pillar to pillar. One entire side of the main room was given over to a riot of crystal, which Taenar realised after a moment was an enormous, open-fronted cabinet that contained dozens of bottles, each cut from the same sparkling glass yet subtly individual in size, shape, or number of planes, and holding a different liquid. Another wall held a warren of shelves and storage nests, home to a small library of books and scrolls. They were ordered, it seemed, neither by age nor type nor language nor even author, probably, but instead by some haphazard system of whatever the owner had been reading on a certain subject at a certain moment.

The room's light came from many sources, but never directly. Extravagant shades of carved wood or shaped metal blocked any overt glare, while the clusters of holes or flowing gouges in their surfaces permitted illumination to escape, which was then reflected by mirrors, or refracted through other crystals. The chambers hovered on the edge of dimness, yet so pervasive was the light that there was barely a proper shadow to be seen.

'Taenar.'

Myrin Stormdawn emerged from a door to the right, clad in nothing more than a pair of simple breeches of dark green with silver stitching, padding soundlessly across the floor on bare feet. Taenar got a glimpse of a torso criss-crossed with pale, faint scars, including a thick collection on his left flank, and his first proper look at the full extent of the tattoos of coiling thorns across Myrin's collarbones and up the sides of his neck, before Myrin pulled on a loose-laced shirt and tied his long, damp, purple-black hair back with a braided leather cord.

'Myrin,' Taenar managed. It felt hugely personal to use Stormdawn's first name in his chambers, but Stormdawn had been adamant from the start that this was how he wished Taenar to address him.

'Regicide,' Myrin said, nodding at a square black-and-white checked board with similarly coloured playing pieces, which Taenar had not previously noticed, sitting on a small table to one side of the bed. 'Are you familiar with it? It's a mon-keigh game.'

'I… am not,' Taenar acknowledged. Of all the reasons he had expected for his summons, discussion of barbarian games was not one of them.

'It is short, simple, and brutal, much like their lives,' Myrin said, still looking at the board. 'However, despite that, it is not without some merit. There is the possibility for crude strategy, and it has a pleasing finality – a piece once removed from the board cannot be returned. It is a far cry from the games of farseers, plotted out centuries in advance with their myriad failsafes and contingencies, where few pawns have much individual value, and most can be replaced by another.'

Taenar's throat went dry. Was Myrin's mention of farseer games a veiled allusion to Taenar's presence here? Had his deception been discovered?

'Speaking of pieces that have been removed and cannot be returned,' Myrin said, turning to face Taenar properly for the first time, 'I cannot ignore the issue of Ellisar Elasandor.'

Taenar's instincts shouted at him to avoid confrontation, to be the good craftworld servant he had always been and minimise the conflict so far as was possible, to apologise – for taking a life, for interfering – but he straightened his back instead, and looked down at Myrin from his slightly greater height. 'I will not say that I am sorry, and I will not say that I was wrong, for I believe neither to be true.'

'Indeed?' Myrin said. His expression was unreadable, his eyes like dark gems that bored into Taenar's face. Taenar could feel the pressure to cave in, to read that one word as a criticism and capitulate; could feel the urging that it was not too late to back down. He steeled his spine and nodded.

'Indeed.'

'And why,' Myrin asked, stepping slightly closer, 'do you not believe that?'

Taenar swallowed. Myrin was near enough to lay a hand on now, which meant he was also near enough to land a blow. Taenar had not seen any weapons, but he was not so much of a fool as to think it impossible that Myrin might have something about his person despite the lack of obvious places where such a thing might be concealed.

'I was not wrong, because I am not a Starsplinter, and therefore nothing prevented me from interfering,' he began.

'A craftworld answer,' Myrin said dismissively, 'hiding behind technicalities. Are you nothing more than that? Was it not wrong to take Ellisar's life?'

'No, it was not,' Taenar replied. He could smell Myrin. Not the fragrances with which the corsair usually adorned himself, but the simple scents of warm skin and wet hair, and the faintest hint of what might have been spiced wine upon his breath. 'Had Elasandor won the combat, he would have undoubtedly turned on me and mine, and more lives would be lost. Had you won the combat, he would have died anyway. I merely expedited the process.'

Myrin's cheek twitched. 'And are you not sorry for interfering in my affairs?'

'No,' Taenar said through a tight throat.

'Why not?'

'Because…' Taenar paused, considered his words for a moment, then pressed on. 'Because I value your life far higher than I valued his.'

A slow, savage smile spread across Myrin's face. 'Ah. Flattery.'

'Truth,' Taenar insisted, honestly.

Myrin reached out a hand and cupped Taenar's cheek, running his thumb along Taenar's jaw. It was another transgression, for Taenar to allow himself to be touched in a manner more in accordance with a lover than the virtual strangers that he and Myrin were, but he allowed it nonetheless, and did not shy away. This was certainly not an action he would have expected or allowed from another officer in the Ilmaren fleet, but he was not there any more. Conduct was different out here, and his mission hinged on him convincing Myrin that he was here in spirit, not just in body. That he was – or wished to be – a corsair, not an admiral, and he did not hold to the norms of his old life.

Besides which, Taenar suspected that the touch of one of his fellow admirals would not have sent lightning shooting through his nerves in such a manner.

'You have left me with a pretty problem, my pretty friend,' Myrin said, his voice low and his eyes glinting in the gentle shadows of his face. 'You are not a Starsplinter, and so it is true that there was nothing forbidding you from interfering in the

Gauntlet of Blood. However, that does not mean that there can be no consequences. The very fact that you are not a Starsplinter means that, by murdering one of my captains, you have declared war on us. Your ships are accompanying mine at the moment simply because I have not acted upon that provocation. Give me a reason not to.'

Taenar licked his lips. 'The only reason I am not a Starsplinter is because you have not accepted my fealty. Do that, and we are yours to command. And I am yours to punish,' he added, not without some hesitance. If this was what Ilmaren required, it was a price he would pay. Kyldran might still bristle at the corsairs, but both the warlock and Faerys Asuthien knew what was needed. Even if Taenar died, fed to Elasandor's crew to appease them, others within his fleet would ensure that the mission was fulfilled.

'Negate the conflict by immediately conquering the aggressors?' Myrin asked, then snorted, his fingertips lingering on Taenar's chin. 'More technicalities. Elasandor's underlings will still want their blood price. Why is it worth me overlooking your interference in one of our rituals?'

Taenar took a deep breath. He thought he knew what Myrin wanted; thought he knew what Myrin had always wanted. Not an obedient underling, not someone who would take orders without question and fulfil them without comment, not someone who always sought to make the baron's life easy. Myrin Stormdawn valued strength, and independence, and will. Face up to him with conviction in your actions and certainty in why you had taken your course, and – Taenar hoped – he would respect you. Shrink back into trying to please him, attempting to second-guess his wishes and contorting yourself to fit into the shape of them, and you would lose him.

'Because I lied,' Taenar said in a whisper.

Myrin raised an eyebrow. 'You lied?'

'I did not kill him to save your life,' Taenar said, and although he told himself the words were part of his act, they tore free from his throat with the ragged sting of truth. 'I killed him because I wanted to. I killed him because he'd angered me. I killed him because he insulted me, and dismissed me, and then he turned his back on me as though I meant nothing! I did not *embarrass* you,' he hissed. 'I killed a warrior so convinced he knew my nature that he failed to perceive the threat I posed!'

Myrin's fingers snaked around Taenar's head to tangle in the hair at the back of his scalp, and he leaned closer. 'And did you enjoy it?'

Taenar swallowed. 'I…'

'Make no mistake, this is my fleet,' Myrin said when Taenar hesitated, 'and I can keep Saraan Skyhand in check. However, I need to know that it is worth my while to do so. My price for that is having the truth from you, Taenar. Did you enjoy it?'

Taenar closed his eyes. To say the word felt like a betrayal of his entire life until this point. More than that, it felt like opening himself up completely and totally, exposing the jagged core of his soul – not to a close friend or confidante, but to someone whom he had known for such a brief time as to be utterly insignificant against the centuries he had been alive.

Yet strangely, that made it easier in some ways, because Myrin Stormdawn had no deep-seated perceptions of who Taenar was. There were no decades of friendship which could be damaged by a shocking revelation. Despite all of Taenar's deceptions, despite the lies he had told and inhabited from the moment he first entered Myrin's presence, in this matter he could relax and take refuge in total honesty.

'Yes,' he whispered, opening his eyes again. 'I did.'

Myrin grinned. '*There* you are,' he said softly, the warmth of his breath washing over Taenar's face, and tickling his lips. 'Finally, the true self beneath the shell. The Taenar Leotharan I have wanted to meet since I first laid eyes on you.'

'And now that you have met me,' Taenar managed, 'what will you do with me?' Myrin's face seemed to fill the entire world, his eyes like black holes into which Taenar was falling. Taenar knew, intellectually, that he could break Myrin's grip on the back of his head and cease being held like a disobedient animal, but there was a freedom to this vulnerable proximity that he did not want to end.

Myrin released him anyway, and stood back imperiously. 'Kneel.'

Taenar had knelt to Rhidhal Shelwe-nin when accepting a suit of Striking Scorpion aspect armour, but that was part of an ancient ritual going back to the craftworld's beginnings. Myrin had no authority to demand this, and yet Taenar felt his legs folding beneath him. He sank to the floor. Once more, he knew that he could resist, could refuse, but he was choosing not to. What did it matter, in here? Out there he was an admiral – or a former admiral – and the image he portrayed to others was all-important. They looked up to him as their commander, or looked askance at him as a newcomer, or a rival. Perceived weakness could lead to uncertainty in those under his command, or opportunism in others. Whereas in here…

He had to maintain the lie about why he was here, in terms of why he was with the Starsplinters at all. But as to why he was *here*, in Myrin Stormdawn's chambers, there was no lie about that. He was here because Myrin had commanded his presence, and because he had obeyed. Just as he was obeying now. There was a relief in that simplicity.

'You still wish to join the Starsplinters?' Myrin said from above him.

'Yes,' Taenar said, staring up at him. It was true, yet not, he told himself. He wanted to join them in order to fulfil his mission, and nothing more. His heart still belonged to Ilmaren, and that would not change. The freedom he felt out here was simply another Path along which he could walk for a time before he returned to his real home.

'And you will obey me as your lord?' Myrin asked. His arms were folded, the very image of a severe corsair baron staring down at his subordinate.

'Yes,' Taenar replied again. He tensed as Myrin moved closer, but Stormdawn simply squatted down in front of him so their eyes were level.

'Then I accept your fealty,' Myrin said softly, trailing his fingers down the side of Taenar's face again, 'and that of your crews. You are bound to me, and I do not readily relinquish that which is mine.'

'I understand,' Taenar breathed.

'Your orders, as a captain of the Starsplinters, are to finally and fully reject your former self,' Myrin said. 'I have no use for those still in thrall to their old way of life, be that craftworld or troupe, kabal or clan. The galaxy is ours to do with as we please. So long as you do not lose yourself along the way, you are to be what you wish, do as you wish, *take* what you wish.' He rose back to his feet, and Taenar rose with him. However, when Myrin went to step back, Taenar caught him by the wrist.

Myrin looked down at the fingers encircling his arm, then back up at Taenar. One eyebrow twitched upwards.

Taenar swallowed again. 'Is there... something in the oils? In the air? A psychotropic agent of some sort?'

The corner of Myrin's mouth crinkled in the faint hint of a smile. 'Do you want there to be?'

'No,' Taenar said. He could feel Myrin's pulse beneath his

fingertips, and although the corsair's expression was calm, his heart was racing as well. 'Whatever I am feeling, I want it to be real.'

'I assure you,' Myrin said, stepping closer again without taking his eyes from Taenar's, until Taenar could practically feel himself being pulled in by the strange gravity that had extended its tendrils between them. 'Whatever you are feeling, it is not my doing.'

'Liar,' Taenar managed, and fell into him.

SIXTEEN

What Gazruk Hackspanna had realised, not long after his machine's first and apparently successful activation, was that knowing which direction the skrawnies were in was not a massive amount of use unless you also knew *how far away* they were. As Uzgul explained to him, at some length and not inconsiderable volume, it was the difference between flying around a planet to see what was on the other side, and jumping into the warp for a couple of weeks to get somewhere entirely different.

'Dis machine's useless!' the kaptin had barked, kicking a bit of it with one steel-capped boot, whereupon Gazruk had fought down the urge to give Uzgul a brief but instructive dentistry lesson with a large wrench, and filed it away under *Stuff wot I'll get even for later if I get da chance.* 'I ain't got time to go wanderin' around da galaxy waitin' until dis fing starts pointin' a different way! Yoo're gonna find a way to make it more accurate, or I'll throw yoo out da airlock, an' yoo can find da skrawnies dat way!'

And so Gazruk had gone back to work, rewiring and recalibrating his work of genius to bring it more in line with demands from 'up da ladder' – quite literally, since the bridge was directly above the chamber in which his creation was situated, and Uzgul had cut a hole in the floor so he could open a hatch every now and then to bawl down and ask why things weren't ready yet.

Now, however, things *were* ready. Or so Gazruk hoped. He looked around. 'Everyone sorted?'

His assembled spanners nodded or gave a thumbs-up. Even Bashgut seemed ready this time. Gazruk took a deep breath, and threw the master switch again.

The machine buzzed and whirred and clicked and sizzled into life once more. It also screamed for a moment, but that turned out to be Snip the grot, who'd been standing too close to one of the Outlets for Unused CHarge, or OUCH. The omnidirector spun around a couple of times before settling on a heading, as it had done before – so far, so good. It was all going to come down to whether Gazruk's new addition functioned as he hoped it would.

Gazruk flicked three switches, turned a large wheel three times to the right, then pressed a large red button. It didn't make anything explode or go faster, which was the generally accepted function of red buttons, but Gazruk felt he probably needed every bit of help he could get on this one.

The device he'd tentatively titled the 'farscope' lit up, and multicoloured lights ran back and forth across its surface as it adjusted to the input flowing into it from the rest of the machine. For a moment it did nothing recognisable, and Gazruk had a brief moment of anxiety as he teetered between trying to fix it, and simply making up what it had said in the hopes of buying time to fix it without Uzgul realising that he was lying. However, after a few seconds the display settled down into one of the patterns he'd programmed. He squinted at it, wanting to be certain that he was interpreting it correctly.

'Wot's it say?' Uzgul demanded from above him.

Gazruk flicked the farscope with one claw, but other than a

brief buzz, there was no effect. The farscope stubbornly showed him nothing but green dots, and surprisingly few of them at that.

'Dey're close, kaptin,' he said with some surprise. 'Like… proper close. Not in da system, but it ain't gonna be a warp jump.' He looked up at Uzgul's suspicious features, really hoping that his technological skills – or more likely, the spanners who'd done various jobs for him – weren't letting him down. If he was wrong about this, he was going to have very little time to make good. 'A few days at full burn, maybe, if dey ain't movin' too sharpish? Somewhere out past da last planets.'

'Dat's a strange place for a bunch of skrawnies to be,' Uzgul opined, rubbing his broad chin with one ring-bedecked hand. His eyes hardened. 'Yoo sure about dis, Gazruk?'

'Dat's wot da machine says,' Gazruk replied with a shrug. 'Only way to find out is to go dere an' see, I guess.'

'Yoo don't do da guessin' around here!' Uzgul barked. 'I do! Except I don't do guessin', cos I *know* stuff, yoo got dat?'

'Yes, kaptin,' Gazruk said sharply. It was instinct, by now. Agree with Uzgul, don't give him an excuse to enact any of his virulently described favourite punishments on you, and wait for him to find fault with something else. There was no shortage of things on *Sunstompa* that Uzgul da Magnificent was prepared to get enraged about, from the quality of his grog to why the third engine kept making a rattling sound that could be heard throughout half the ship, so it usually didn't take long for the jewel-bedecked tyrant to get distracted by something else and leave Gazruk in something approaching peace.

Nonetheless, it was starting to occur to Gazruk Hackspanna that this was not the sort of life he thought Gork and Mork wanted for him. He was supposed to be creating mighty weapons of war, things that went *nyeoowww* and *boooom* and *dakka-dakka-dakka*, things that got the blood pumping and the heart racing and someone else's heart detonated over a wide area. He wasn't supposed to be stuck on a ship, fine-tuning a highly speculative device to satisfy the whims of a strangely obsessed freebooter kaptin who was hot squigshit at anything to do with freebootering and had more hats than sense when it came to anything else.

Still, Gazruk reflected, this was better than trying to make the Dakkaplanet functional. Assuming the omnidirector and the farscope worked in sync as they should, and the skrawnies really were where his machine suggested, that should be enough to hold Uzgul's attention for a bit. Then maybe Gazruk could take a couple of his spanners and have a wander of *Sunstompa* to check it over – y'know, see if there were any problematic loose parts, like maybe a shuttle what no one seemed to be needing right now, and quietly zog off. Leave Bashgut behind to take the blame, possibly feed a drive shunt into the main turbo breakers on the way out to cause a bit of a distraction, and then the great voyage of Gazruk Hackspanna could continue. That voyage had been a bit of a stop-start affair so far – he'd never really had the chance to get any *momentum* going, what with being kicked out of various Waaaghs! by various warbosses – but Gazruk was confident that his was a genius like what the galaxy had rarely seen. He just needed a chance, a break… or really, a boss who had a large pile of scrap, realistic time constraints, and a permissive attitude to localised explosions. Specifically, permissive about exactly how local they were.

'Give me dat,' Gazruk muttered, 'an' I can give yoo da galaxy…'

'Wot was dat?' Uzgul shouted from above him.

'I said, "Give me dat can, or I'll kick ya, happily,"' Gazruk said quickly. 'I was talkin' to da grot!'

Uzgul grunted. 'Yoo sending everyfing up to da bridge?'

'Yes, kaptin,' Gazruk replied. 'Yoo should 'ave it on yer screens now.'

'Good,' Uzgul growled. 'Dis'd better work, Gazruk.' His head disappeared from the hatch and he raised his voice. 'Get dis fing movin'! Half-halfway round, a quarter up, den hit da go button!'

Sunstompa began to shift, the floor tilting slightly as the spaceboyz in charge of moving the gigantic kroozer through the void obeyed their kaptin's instructions. Gazruk nodded in satisfaction – at least Uzgul was taking them in the right direction – then whistled. 'Hoi! Snip! C'mere!'

'Yes, boss?' Snip said eagerly, trotting up. It was still slightly singed from where da joose had discharged into it, but otherwise seemed healthy.

'Where's dat can?' Gazruk asked. It was important to keep the act up, just in case that wily git Uzgul was still listening.

'Wot can, boss?' Snip asked, big ears flopping as it tilted its head to one side in puzzlement.

'Da can yoo was supposed to bring me!' Gazruk barked.

'But–'

Gazruk booted it.

SEVENTEEN

Taenar knew that when the *Dathedian* had opened and ripped the galaxy in two – what the mon-keigh called the Great Rift – much was lost to the ravening energies of the warp. Entire star systems vanished, to be replaced by roiling madness. Perhaps even worse than that were the tortured margins, where the warp extruded its malign tendrils into the material universe to mis-shape it beyond all recognition. Whole populations descended into chaos overnight and fell upon each other with hungry teeth and grasping hands under sanity-twisting skies, all semblances of order and restraint gone. Other civilisations held on for longer, but the influence of Chaos was too powerful – fields were blighted and livestock either starved, or foamed at the mouth and slew each other with horn and hoof. Water sources became fouled no matter what purification measures were attempted, and crimes increased both in frequency and severity, until finally the few who had not succumbed were huddled behind whatever thick walls and locked doors they could find, living off scraps and drips, and eyeing each other with increasing paranoia.

The insanity did not end there. Even physics and matter did not escape the Dathedian's gruesome grasp. Voidships in orbit around surviving planets might find themselves assailed by acid-vomiting, multi-legged creatures that burned their way through hulls and viewports, causing catastrophic atmosphere leaks and suffocating the crews inside with vacuums they themselves should not have been able to survive. Hardened mariners saw shadows moving across moons and asteroids that took on the appearance of faces that whispered buried truths and barbed lies to them, causing the afflicted to take their own lives. Even the stars were not immune. Some, swollen and reddened, developed tendrils of super-hot plasma that reached out to encircle and incinerate the worlds which, until then, had bathed in their benign light. Others, pulled slowly into the warp's embrace, crushed their planets with wildly fluctuating gravitational forces, or flung them out of orbit entirely.

It was on one of these rogue worlds, cast adrift from its parent star and now drifting through the cold darkness of space with only the fitful, malignant glow of the Dathedian to illuminate it, that the Starsplinters had their court.

'I feel like I am viewing a spectacle from before the Fall,' Taenar said, not without a certain amount of awe. The fleet had come out of a webway gate held in orbit around the planet – whether it had always been there, he could not say. Now Taenar looked out from *Dance of Dying Seasons'* viewports at a darkened world on which life had nevertheless written the evidence of its existence in light, because the Starsplinters had colonised a great strip of frozen shoreline, where a mighty ocean sat hard and cold and stationary after being removed from the light of its former sun.

Small though the settlement was in comparison to the planet, Taenar had still never witnessed its like before. These were not Exodite encampments, not the simple hovels or tent villages of a rustic people who had abandoned the trappings of a species once capable of making the stars dance to their tune. Nor was it Commorragh, an endless nest of needle-pointed spires and unlikely geometry squatting in the webway; and it certainly was not a craftworld, a continent-sized edifice on a never-ending voyage through the stars. These were aeldari, flush with all the technological power still at their species' disposal, living on the face of a world, much like his ancestors had done tens of millennia before.

'And the behaviour exhibited there will likely be very similar to before the Fall,' Ra'thar Kyldran commented coldly from beside him. He leaned closer, and lowered his voice. 'Coming here was a mistake. Stormdawn may be vain and mercurial, but he is at least something of a known quality, and his fleet might contain deviants and murderers, but the core of it is still Ilmaren ships and Ilmaren crews. We do not know what manner of vileness might await us here, at the heart of the corsairs' empire.'

'It is somewhat too late for hesitation over such matters,' Taenar reproached him, trying to ignore the shiver Stormdawn's name sent through him. He and the baron had spoken since that charged encounter in Myrin's quarters, but only as two commanders, and with Stormdawn as the senior party. Just when Taenar felt he had started to puzzle out the nature of corsair society, he had fallen headlong into another dance, one where he knew none of the steps, or indeed whether he was actually still dancing at all.

'We knew the dangers of entering such a lawless culture before we even made it to the Well of the Long Death,' Faerys Asuthien cut in, pushing Taenar's thoughts away, which was just as well. They would not serve him here, other than to distract him at an inopportune moment. 'We had no certainty that we would not be attacked on sight,' the captain continued. 'Sadly, it was probably fortunate for us that the orks were already there, as it allowed us to demonstrate our good intentions.'

'And the Starsplinters' losses made it considerably less prudent for them to attack us, should they have objected to our presence,' Kyldran agreed. 'However, there is no such factor in our favour here. We have entered the realm of a corsair princess, and we will be beholden to her whims.'

That was not merely doomsaying. The channels had been alive with hails and greetings from other ships from the moment they'd arrived, some good-natured, some less so. Several appeared to owe fealty to Myrin Stormdawn to one extent or another, and Taenar's ships were no longer the largest element of Stormdawn's forces. Taenar was starting to grasp the scope of the Starsplinters fleet, and considered it to be significantly superior to that of Ilmaren. The balance of power had significantly changed, and it was his position that had suffered.

'But we have entered her realm *as* Starsplinters,' Taenar pointed out. 'We are no longer outsiders, merely newcomers, and we are under the protection of one of her greatest admirals.'

'You should know as well as I that his "protection" will count for nothing, should Tishria decide she wishes to make sport with us,' Kyldran insisted. 'She is not like Stormdawn, Taenar – I have heard that she is welcomed as a guest in Commorragh itself!'

'Then you should try not to antagonise her,' Taenar suggested. 'But regardless of your concerns, we are here. All we need do is wait while Myrin presents his case to Tishria regarding the ork menace.'

'And what of the crew of the captain you killed?' Kyldran demanded. 'They have not made a move against us yet, but–'

'Then perhaps they will not,' Taenar said, turning to him. 'Elasandor's second-in-command might be satisfied with being the new captain of *The Yearning Stars*. In any case, while I will be watching for an attack, I will not let myself be thought craven by refusing to go where others do.' He sighed. 'This is our new reality, Ra'thar. Here, the quiet, unremarkable ones are the most remarkable, and we do not wish to be remarkable. We must swagger with the rest of them. We must show our teeth, as you did upon our first meeting with the Starsplinters. We now exist in a world of bravado and bluster, and to deny that because we do not like it is to mark ourselves out as different and suspicious, if not potential prey.'

'*Do* you not like it?' Ra'thar asked, his piercing eyes searching Taenar's face. 'Have you not found some satisfaction in this hedonism, which you claim to be adopting simply for the sake of our mission?'

'You are attempting to provoke the admiral again,' Faerys said, her temper leashed, but clearly evident. 'Perhaps you should spend more time working to convince our new allies that you want to be here, and less time criticising him for fitting in.'

Taenar smiled tightly at Ra'thar, and turned away. 'Come. Myrin will not wait, and if your concerns about the character of Tishria are correct then we do not want to be isolated when we arrive.'

They descended to the planet's surface in a cluster of shuttle-craft, each one containing a captain and their closest officers and advisors, or however the command structure went on each individual ship. Taenar had already gathered that things did not operate in the same way as the Ilmaren fleet, no matter what the origin of many of those ships had been. *Autumn of Years* was commanded by a pair of sisters, Aywin and Haryn Glyn-dark, who might have made excellent pilots for a Phantom Titan given their near unity of thought and speech, while *Spear Parting Water*'s captain, Caerador Torthana, hid his face behind a veil of metal scales, and took advice only from a small council of such seers as operated with the corsair ranks. They had many different titles and roles, apparently, such as soul weaver, way seeker, and void dreamer. Ra'thar had not said anything, but Taenar could tell that the warlock viewed his wild-spirited kin with a suspicion that bordered on contempt.

'Where are we setting down?' Ra'thar asked as they followed the craft in front past the first string of lights. 'On the surface?'

'This planet has lost its sun,' Taenar reminded him. He pointed at the pale landscape, twinkling under the faint starlight. 'Water is frozen as hard as iron. To step out into this would be to court death in short order.'

'It could be done,' Ra'thar pointed out. Indeed, although swathed in robes, his rune armour was void-sealed and would protect him against even a hard vacuum, at least for a while.

'It could,' Taenar admitted with a small smile as the dark shape of an oceanside mountain loomed up ahead of them. 'But you are not yet thinking like a corsair. Functionality must sometimes come second to appearances – none of our companions wish to disembark clad in utilitarian void suits. And why be content with setting down on ice-blasted rock...'

Ahead of them, a thin, vertical slit of light appeared in the mountain's side, widening as they approached.

'...when you can set down *inside* it, instead?' Taenar finished, gratified that his hunch had been proven correct. The mountain was opening before them, revealing a far more inviting, hollowed-out interior. Shuttle after shuttle swooped gracefully in through the cavernous entry, and touched down delicately on a huge landing pad. Taenar's brought up the rear, the landing skids taking its weight just as the massive doors – the original mountainside itself, if Taenar was any judge, but repurposed and articulated by his species' technological mastery – ground shut again behind them.

'And so we are trapped,' Ra'thar intoned.

Taenar sighed. 'Your countenance and mannerisms merely make it more likely that we will encounter misfortune here. Wear your helm so that none might see you rolling your eyes, and feel free to keep your thoughts to yourself.'

For all the corsairs' lack of discipline – or at the least, markedly different forms of discipline – that did not extend to encroaching into the path of void-craft. The landing pad had been clear of intruders or trespassers, and it was only once engines had powered down that figures began to approach from the edges of the cavern. Taenar led Ra'thar Kyldran and Cithriel Shelwe-nin close to Myrin and his Bladesworn – all but Jhanandra, who had stayed behind to command *Light of Heaven* – hoping to blend in with the crowd of Starsplinters, and piece together from overheard greetings and conversations that which he did not know.

'Mind your surroundings,' Cithriel murmured in his ear. Taenar saw the brief flicker of the exarch's eyes and found Saraan Skyhand, the former Exodite, a mere three or four yards away. They were not looking at him, but Taenar got the impression that this was deliberate, rather than simply not having registered his presence. He was happy for this state of affairs to continue, but was also well aware that such studied indifference could merely be a cover prior to an attempt on his life. He shifted the angle of his body slightly, the easier to keep Skyhand in the corner of his eye, and to know if they attempted to slip behind him.

'Myrin!' a voice cried, and Taenar's attention shifted to the welcoming party, if that was what it was. The figure in the lead had spread his arms wide, which – given the amount of feathers attached to his sleeves – gave him the appearance of a giant avian about to take flight. In fact, the feathers were not just on his sleeves but all over the long coat he wore, and when he tilted his head, Taenar realised that what he had initially taken to be a headdress of some kind was in fact feathers inserted into the otherwise bald skin of the corsair's skull. Taenar had seen such things before, but only on the bodies of the winged warriors that sometimes accompanied drukhari raiding parties. This individual's bodily modifications appeared to be merely cosmetic, however, and without any extra limbs.

'Kraveth!' Myrin responded with an apparently equal level of enthusiasm. 'It's been too long!'

'Too long indeed,' Kraveth said. He reached Myrin, and closed his arms around the baron in an embrace which Myrin returned. They held each other for a few moments, before Kraveth stepped back. 'How do you fare? I hope you've brought Her Highness' customary tribute.'

The other corsair was serious, Taenar realised, despite the light-hearted delivery of the words, and the smile on his face. This was not a jest. Should Myrin not have whatever was expected of him, things had the potential to turn sour.

'Worry not, my friend,' Myrin said, patting Kraveth on the shoulder. 'I would never disappoint our mistress like that. Still, we've not had the easiest time of it. Matters have worsened with the Bukkaneers, and–'

'Speak not of that here,' Kraveth interrupted, raising two fingers as though to deflect Myrin's words to one side. 'Those conversations should be had with the princess first, not with me.'

'You are correct, of course,' Myrin said, nodding. 'Very well, lead on. It has been some years since I attended the princess' court, and I suspect she may have altered the layout since I was last here.'

'Perceptive as always,' Kraveth said with a smile, but his eyes were roving over Myrin's crowd. Taenar, watching their interaction, dropped his gaze a moment too late to be inconspicuous.

'But who is this?' Kraveth said, waving a hand towards Taenar.

The words and tone were still good-natured, but Taenar could feel the genuine curiosity behind them. 'You have some new additions to your captains, Myrin!'

'Taenar,' Myrin said, beckoning. 'Come. This is Kraveth, Bladesworn of Princess Tishria herself, and one of my oldest friends within the Starsplinters.'

Bladesworn. This was exactly the kind of attention that Taenar had hoped to avoid. However, to hesitate would invite further scrutiny and potentially displeasure, so he pushed his way forward with an attempt at the sort of easy confidence he hoped would see him assessed as simply another corsair captain, and of no particular note.

'Kraveth, this is Taenar Leotharan,' Myrin said. 'Another soul who found Ilmaren's structures too strict and defeatist for his liking.'

'I see,' Kraveth said, reaching out to clasp Taenar's forearm. Taenar returned the grip and met Kraveth's gaze, and was startled to realise that the corsair's irises appeared to have been somehow replaced or covered with glittering emeralds, still surrounded by white, and leaving the pupil as a dark hole in the centre. 'And how are you finding the Starsplinters, Taenar Leotharan?'

'Illuminating,' Taenar said with a small smile. He did not want to be drawn into any lengthy conversation, so he was more than content to be a momentary curio, greeted and then dismissed. Thankfully, it seemed that Kraveth was of a similar mind.

'We should not tarry,' the Bladesworn said, relaxing his grip and returning his attention to Myrin after a moment of studying Taenar's face. 'The princess knows of your arrival, of course, and she will be expecting you.'

'Of course,' Myrin echoed, and Taenar did not think he was imagining the slight tension in Stormdawn's jaw. One did not become a corsair princess without amassing a formidable reputation, but Taenar had not expected to detect unease, even fear, in Myrin Stormdawn. The corsair baron took everything in his stride, from mutinous captains to monstrous cruevar, so the notion of him being actively afraid of his commander was one to which Taenar would need to adjust his mind.

However, he was not likely to have long in which to do so. Kraveth and his small escort led Myrin's party away from the landing pad at a brisk pace, and plunged into one of the tunnel entrances that dotted the sides of the cavern. Taenar had anticipated darkness and rough rock within, but the walls were glass-smooth, and delicately illuminated by lights that caught the gently flowing bas-relief carvings. He saw scenes of rolling hillsides and thick forests, towering mountains and plunging waterfalls, and many strange and varied beasts and birds.

'Do you like our home, Captain Leotharan?' Kraveth asked, dropping back a few steps and extending one hand towards the walls as they progressed downwards.

'It is very impressive,' Taenar said honestly. 'Not exactly what I expected… but then, I am not certain what I *did* expect.'

'One of the many advantages of our life is the ability to choose the manner in which we live,' Kraveth said. 'Those who do not understand us assume us to be uncultured savages, simply taking what we want from others. They do not realise that we are perfectly capable of creating things for ourselves. Indeed, we enjoy it as much as any other aeldari. This world was not welcoming to our kind when it still held its position in orbit, but now it has been freed we have claimed it as our own, and we alter it to our whims.'

'It does not appear particularly welcoming even now,' Taenar commented, and Kraveth laughed.

'More so than it was, I assure you. It was a radiation-blasted place harbouring little life, and that which survived was hostile.

We may lack the light of a sun here now, but the planet's geothermal energy powers all that we need.'

'I am surprised to hear you speak of this as your home,' Taenar said. He got the sense that Kraveth was testing him, and decided he needed to show a little corsair arrogance. 'I would find it hard to abandon my ship, and the stars.'

'We are the rightful rulers of the galaxy,' Kraveth replied with the slightest hint of reproach. 'Our homes should be anywhere and everywhere. Why should we leave planets for the mon-keigh, or the arakhia, or even the Exodites?'

'Because we would be overwhelmed and overrun,' Myrin broke in, sounding both bored and exasperated. 'Which is exactly what happens to the Exodites every time one of their worlds is discovered, unless those of us who don't rely on giant reptiles to fight our battles for us intervene. That's why the Starsplinters are *here*, on an orphaned planet no one else could find, let alone would want. Please don't tell me Tishria intends some new colonisation mission in the galaxy at large.'

'You can speak to the princess about that yourself, if you wish,' Kraveth said. He snorted. 'Although given your position on the matter, I wouldn't recommend it.'

'Wonderful,' Myrin muttered. 'You're her Bladesworn, Kraveth, can't you talk to her about it?'

'My responsibility is the princess' safety,' Kraveth said with a shrug that jostled the blade he wore across his back as a companion to the whip on his hip, 'and that alone. She is my commander, and it is not my position to advise her on strategy unless she specifically requests it.'

'As one Bladesworn to another,' Xela said from Myrin's far side, 'it's sometimes necessary to ensure your commander's safety by telling them that they're being a bloody fool *before* they get themselves into trouble.'

'Xela is speaking hypothetically, of course,' Myrin said, chuckling. 'As we all know, I have never been foolish in my life.'

'Of course not,' Kraveth said. He smiled mischievously. 'I am definitely not, right at this moment, thinking of that incident with the greater daemon on the cursed craftworld of Shilea-Jar.'

'It left me with some very fetching scars,' Myrin replied, surreptitiously winking at Taenar, who abruptly remembered the thick, rough skin on Myrin's left flank.

'And only one working lung, until we got you to the healers,' Xela added acidly.

'I banished the accursed thing, though,' Myrin said stubbornly. He sighed. 'But I admit, I should have listened to you first.'

'Of course you should have,' Xela muttered, scowling at him.

'Princess Tishria has never been impaled by a greater daemon,' Kraveth said lightly, then sobered. 'More importantly, her temperament is not that of my friend Baron Myrin Stormdawn.' He shot a quick glance at Taenar. 'And you would all do well to remember that.'

EIGHTEEN

The Grand Hall of the Starsplinters got grander each time Myrin saw it, as Princess Tishria's fancies changed. The last time he had been here, several years before, it had mimicked a boreal forest, with pillars textured like rough bark. The floor had been lit patchily, to simulate shafts of sunlight striking down in the gaps between branches laden with tightly spaced needles, the air smelled of resin and earth, and occasionally carried to the ear the high, eerie call of a wilderness avian or a mountain predator. Tishria had been enthroned in the heart of it like a woodland deity out of old legend, wearing a crown of bones taken from slain enemies, and with her face painted in runes so old that not even the Starsplinters knew what all of them meant. The time before, it had been an ice cavern, with light reflecting off every shining surface. Breath had steamed in the air, courtiers had sipped hot spiced wine, and Tishria had sat on a pile of furs draped across a frozen throne so bright beneath the illuminations that it was almost impossible to look at her without averting your eyes.

This time…

'Black suns,' Xela swore softly.

The hall was near as bright as it had been in its ice cavern era, but this was achieved not by frozen water, but by jewels and precious metals. Every raised surface was piled high with them, in endless forms, and from innumerable cultures. There were coins and ingots, chains and pendants and statues, bracelets and diadems, weapons that Myrin presumed to have been ceremonial or purely decorative, and other pieces the nature or significance of which he could not guess. The entire display did not impose itself on the beholder so much as hold them down and stamp on their eyes. It was a wild roundhouse punch of pure excess, a guttural scream of ostentation.

'Rather gaudy,' Myrin heard Taenar murmur disapprovingly, and he stifled a smirk. His mirth did not last long, however, washed away as it was by a cold anxiety.

'Kraveth,' he said in a low voice, despite the air being filled by the chatter and shouts and song of the Starsplinters already present. 'How long has it been like this?'

'It's a fairly recent change,' Kraveth said. His expression was neutral, but Myrin knew him well enough to see that his old friend was disconcerted as well. 'A celebration of our success, she calls it. This is what she does with her tribute that she deems pleasing enough to display.'

The treasures lay not just on the many ledges that were carved into the walls, but on raised plinths of rock that flowed through the hall in semi-concentric patterns. Like water running downhill, Myrin's eyes were drawn by the lines to the far side. There, seated in a blazing golden edifice nearly the height of a Wraithlord, was Princess Tishria, Scourge of the Calexis Nebula.

A many-rayed sun design of gem-encrusted gold capped the throne, and towered above her head. The seat itself was backed and upholstered in rich blood-red fabric, and was perfectly proportioned to its occupant; it was simply the rest of the throne that was gargantuan. Half a dozen golden steps led up to where the princess sat, easily raising her above the rest of her court.

'A word to the wise,' Kraveth said quietly. 'Do not make any comparison to the mon-keigh god.'

Myrin looked at him in astonishment. 'Someone did that?'

'Briefly.'

+Baron Stormdawn,+ a voice said in his head, and Myrin winced at the unwelcome intrusion. +Please approach the throne.+

'You really don't have to shout, Idarael,' he muttered, focusing his gaze on the white-robed figure standing next to the throne's steps. Idarael Mennatyr, the princess' personal way seeker, tilted his head in response.

+Believe me, Stormdawn, you will know if I shout.+

'Kraveth, we have been summoned,' Myrin said, doing his best to ignore both Mennatyr's supercilious mind-voice, and the mild unease he felt about the spectacle in front of him. Who was Tishria attempting to impress? Her captains? She had always been extravagant, with a taste for dramatic entrances and exits, and thrived on attention and admiration. She was knife-sharp though, despite that, and only a fool would take her indolent, spoiled demeanour at face value.

'Then come,' Kraveth replied, and began to lead the way across the Grand Hall, weaving between tables carrying delicacies, and the golden platforms.

There were two explanations that Myrin could think of for this vulgar display of wealth. The first was that Tishria simply wanted to flaunt it in front of those who had, in part, collected it for her. That felt unwise, since Myrin did not imagine that he was the only one here who was bristling at it. He paid his tributes to his leader, as was right and proper to call himself a Starsplinter, but that didn't mean he enjoyed parting with it, or was eager to walk past it again.

The other possibility was that Tishria was attempting to impress someone else, and that was no more encouraging. What potential allies could the Starsplinters need, or Tishria want? And why? Myrin took a goblet of voidwine from a tray proffered by a passing servant wearing a fetching golden collar, and took a small sip as he studied the room, but no one was obviously out of place. He recognised many faces, although not all, but all present were aeldari of one stripe or another. There were none of the galaxy's more primitive species – human inquisitors, or varsine bloodsages, or londaxi technocrats – who might sometimes seek to capitalise on corsairs' reputation as mercenaries in support of their own designs. No one was holding themselves apart from everyone else, or dressed in a way that obviously suggested a different allegiance. Even Taenar's contingent had left behind their staid uniforms of craftworld colours, and were now attired rather more like corsairs.

All in all, Myrin was no closer to puzzling out the reason for the golden hall by the time he had reached the foot of Tishria's throne, at which point he had more pressing matters demanding his attention.

'Baron Stormdawn,' Idarael Mennatyr said once more, using his mouth this time. Although aeldari were obviously the most beautiful species in the galaxy, Myrin had always thought that Idarael was one of the ugliest amongst them. The proportions of the seer's face were wrong: his mouth was too narrow and too low-set beneath his nose, his cheekbones jutting aggressively as though trying to force their way free of his face, and his eyes were too large and too widely spaced. He never looked directly at whomever he was addressing, either, which gave him the air of always peering into the future, or at something no one else could see. Myrin considered it an annoying and deliberate affectation.

'Idarael,' Myrin said as neutrally as he could, then turned

his attention to the throne and went down to one knee, head bowed with his hands splayed out in front of him. His followers copied him, all showing obeisance to the Scourge of the Calexis Nebula. To Myrin's great relief, Taenar and his captains did likewise; even Ra'thar Kyldran, who at least appeared to be aware of the likely ramifications if he offended, though Myrin suspected the warlock would be bristling inside.

'Do get up, Myrin,' a voice said lazily from above him. Myrin obeyed without hesitation, yet not swiftly enough to risk being accused of resentment, and looked up.

For Myrin, as for all aeldari, the time before the Fall was lost to myth, legend, and the few piecemeal records that had survived. He did not know the nature of that ancient empire, and suspected that even his wildest imaginings could barely conceive of its breadth and majesty. He had no knowledge of what its rulers might have looked like, or how they would have presented themselves, but he suspected they would have been something like what now met his eyes.

Princess Tishria was ageless; not in the sense of looking forever young, but in that time itself appeared to have stood aside in acknowledgement of her strength and beauty. She still radiated the vital vibrancy of youth, tempered by the knowledge and wisdom of maturity and experience. However, Myrin had not mistaken her for the same kind of soul as a senior farseer even back when he had first laid eyes on her. Tishria's eyes did not gaze upon the deep mysteries of the universe, and her tongue did not parcel out prophecy or cryptic counsel. She was a warrior first and foremost, and while strategy and planning was a vital piece of any warrior's mind, Tishria also exemplified the spontaneity and mercurial nature of the corsairs. She was powerful and confident, capable and terrifying.

'Your Highness,' Myrin said with a respect he did not have to fake. Tishria was clad in loose-fitting golden robes with cream and maroon accents, which hung open in places to reveal glimpses of the skintight, blood-coloured bodysuit she wore beneath. A star glaive leaned against one arm of her throne, within easy reach should she need it, and a fusion pistol was tucked into her wide golden waistband. A diadem of black metal inset with red gems sat atop her waves of pure black hair, and her neck was encircled by a choker of her enemies' finger bones, bound together with silver wire. She was a vision of power and martial fury inextricably woven together, and an exemplar of how the aeldari should appear to the rest of the galaxy.

'What brings you back here, Myrin?' Tishria asked, her eyes roving over his assembled captains before snapping back to his face. 'I get the impression that it is more than just a passing visit to renew old acquaintances and give me my tribute.'

Myrin swallowed. He had wondered how best to bring up the reason for his visit with the princess, since it was rarely wise to derail things in order to bring up your own agenda. Being asked outright like this did at least solve that problem, but brought others with it, namely the worry of whether Tishria thought he viewed the Starsplinters as a means to his own ends rather than hers, not to mention whether someone on his crew had been secretly reporting his intentions back to her.

Still, it was best to focus on the problem that had been solved, for now, and deal with the others if and when they raised their heads.

'The Well of the Long Death is destroyed, Your Highness,' he said as calmly and clearly as he could manage. 'It was attacked by a force of ork freebooters, part of the Badskab Bukkaneers. We drove them off, but I lost many of my ships in the process, and the Well is not only damaged beyond reasonable repair, but its location is now no longer a secret.'

'That is unfortunate,' Tishria murmured, leaning her chin on the palm of one hand, the elbow of which rested in turn on her throne's arm. Her nails were pointed, and lacquered in a gold just as bright as that of her clothes. 'Still, it was a joyless, dark hole. More of a smugglers' den than anything worthy of a Starsplinter. Perhaps those orks did you a favour.'

'It was certainly nothing so grand as this,' Myrin acknowledged, gesturing around them. He wondered a moment later whether he should have done so, but Tishria's expression gave no indication that she had taken his words as criticism, so he continued on as smoothly as he could, so as not to call attention to it. 'Nonetheless, it was a part of your empire.'

'A part that you failed to defend,' Idarael put in softly from beside him. Myrin shot the seer a glare, then did his best to put him out of his mind.

'Your Highness, this is just one of many altercations that my captains and I, and I believe other Starsplinters as well, have had with the Badskab Bukkaneers of Uzgul the so-called Magnificent,' he said, trying to hint at the gravity of the situation without sounding like he was chiding, or implying that Tishria was unaware of what had been happening. 'The beasts grow ever more bold, and presume to challenge our dominance of the stars.'

'How very tiresome,' Tishria commented. Her perfect eyebrows rose a fraction. 'Did you have a course of action you wished to propose, my baron, or are you simply here to lay your grievance at my feet in the hopes that I will solve it for you?'

Myrin took a moment to congratulate himself on his own foresight. Tishria valued competence and individualism in her commanders, and gave short shrift to those who wasted her time.

'Your Highness, I have obtained what I believe to be accurate information on Uzgul's location,' he said. 'Even my own fleet would struggle against the numbers I believe it can bring to bear, but if you would be willing to grant me the authority to lead some of my fellow barons and baronesses against the orks, I am confident that we could annihilate this threat.'

'You seek prominence over your fellows, is that it?' Tishria asked with a throaty chuckle.

'For the purposes of this, yes,' Myrin admitted, but he could sense the trap in her words. A baron with such a successful venture under his belt would be a potential threat to the standing of any prince or princess. 'Of course, I would be most honoured if you chose to lead us yourself.'

Tishria regarded him thoughtfully for a moment. 'Some commanders would not be honoured, Myrin. Some commanders would feel that having identified the threat themselves, and composed the plan for its eradication, their sovereign's intervention would steal their glory.'

'Some commanders are fools, Your Highness,' Myrin said. 'My concern is with eliminating the bestial orks from our systems, safe in the knowledge that my sovereign would remember my contribution to these efforts and would reward them, or not, as she saw fit.'

Tishria laughed. 'Very fine words! You have always known when to play the soldier and when the politician, Myrin. Forever focused on the task in hand, with an admirable lack of self-interest.'

Myrin allowed himself a tight smile. 'Thank you, Your Highness.'

'It was not necessarily intended as a compliment,' Tishria said, and Myrin's throat constricted.

'You are one of my most gifted commanders,' Tishria continued, 'with a reputation that has spread far and wide, yet I cannot help but feel that you are still a soldier at heart. You still perceive things from the perspective of a craftworld admiral – one who sees enemies, instead of opportunity. If the orks are taking our plunder or attacking our ships and our ports then that is certainly cause for concern, but I have to wonder why they started doing such things? Did you kick the nest, considering them a pest that it was your duty to exterminate?'

Myrin licked his lips nervously. 'Your Highness, I detest the orks as brutal, barbaric monsters that offend the galaxy by their sheer existence, but this is no crusade of mine. We have come into conflict with the Bukkaneers time and again, simply through existing in the same areas.'

'I note that you have some new captains in your ranks,' Tishria commented, apparently ignoring Myrin's words. 'How did you come by them?'

'They are from Ilmaren, Your Highness,' Myrin admitted. 'They sought me out, having also grown disillusioned with our former home.'

'A soldier, you see?' Tishria said rhetorically. 'A soldier who seeks the company of likeminded others who have worn the same uniform, fought the same battles, and who think in the same way.' She sighed. 'I might wonder, Myrin Stormdawn, whether your accumulation of captains who might be inclined to obey you *instinctively* could be evidence that you are tiring of my rule, and are thinking of attempting to supplant me.'

'Nothing could be further from the truth, Your Highness!' Myrin protested, aghast. 'I had no knowledge of their defection from Ilmaren! Our first contact with them was when they aided my ships against the orks and saved what remained of my fleet, even though they could have left us to our fate!'

'Then perhaps they led the orks to you in order to worm their way into your good graces?' Tishria suggested. Her tone was one of mild amusement, but her eyes were sharp. She had not yet decided that Myrin was planning treachery, or they would not still be talking, but Myrin was acutely aware that the Scourge had also not yet decided that he *wasn't* planning treachery, either. He took a breath, his mind racing as he desperately tried to construct a sentence that could allay his ruler's concerns without outright challenging her suggested narrative.

'This is outrageous!' someone blurted, and Myrin cursed inwardly as he recognised the voice of Taenar Leotharan.

'Outrageous?' Tishria echoed sharply, one hand going to the haft of her star glaive. 'And who might who you be, to make such a pronouncement?'

'Taenar Leotharan of *Dance of Dying Seasons*,' Taenar said, not without a hint of pride. He stepped forward to stand beside Myrin, who desperately wished he could usher Taenar backwards, but the damage was done now. Or at least, some of the damage was done. Taenar had the potential to do a lot more before this conversation was over, if he did not manage to mind his tongue far better than he just had.

'And you are one of Baron Stormdawn's new recruits?' Tishria asked.

'I am,' Taenar confirmed. 'And I will not stand by and hear it suggested, by Your Highness or by anyone else, that I deliberately put other aeldari lives in danger. Particularly not to orkish scum!'

'You are not in an Ilmaren war council now, *captain*,' Tishria said sharply.

'I should hope not,' Taenar replied brazenly. 'There, I would be expected to bite my tongue and accept what was said about me in the interests of the craftworld's *unity of purpose*. Here, I will speak as I please. And take the consequences of it,' he added defiantly.

Tishria stared at Taenar for a few long moments, during which Myrin began to hallucinate the sensation of the star glaive's powered blade biting into his neck. His mind began to spin wildly. If Tishria ordered his death, would his Bladesworn step in? They were theoretically loyal to him, but did that loyalty extend to defying Princess Tishria in her own throne room, especially when *he* was supposed to be loyal to *her* in the first place?

Then Tishria laughed. It was a momentary thing, but the tension that had its fingers around Myrin's throat drained away to nothing more than a lingering background presence.

'I like him,' Tishria said, gesturing lazily at Taenar with one finger. 'Not as mindlessly obedient as I might have expected. You have broken him in quickly, Myrin.'

Myrin coughed awkwardly, and resisted the temptation to glance at Taenar. 'Your Highness.'

'So, these freebooters,' Tishria said, as though the previous conversation about treachery and deception had never occurred. 'Other than any lingering Asuryani impulses you might have, Myrin, what in particular makes you think we should expend a large amount of our resources on a pitched battle against them, rather than continuing to live as we please and simply dealing with them as and when they cross our path?'

Myrin seized on his opportunity. 'They harry us and pursue us whenever they can, making it very hard for us to "live as we please", as you say. That in itself is an insult I am loath to bear. However, the greatest insult is that the beast takes aeldari as slaves, for purposes we do not yet know.' He shook his head. 'You may put my disgust for such things down to my history if you wish, Your Highness, but I cannot stand the thought of other aeldari, no matter their lineage, forced to labour by such a creature.'

'Hmm.' Princess Tishria slowly drummed her fingernails three times on the arm of her throne. 'I will not command this attack.'

Myrin bowed his head, acid churning in his gut.

'But neither will I prohibit it,' Tishria continued, and Myrin looked up again sharply. 'Take your seats when the feast is served, and speak to your fellow captains. If there is sufficient support for your cause, you may undertake it. Of course, you may undertake it alone if you wish,' she added with a sharp laugh. 'But I doubt even your outrage runs that deep, Baron Stormdawn.'

'Thank you, Your Highness,' Myrin said, bowing his head in acknowledgement and gratitude again, and turning away. Tishria's response was less than he had hoped for, but more than he had feared.

Now all he had to do was persuade a room full of some of the most self-interested aeldari in the galaxy that they wanted to follow him into a void battle.

NINETEEN

The feast was excellent, as Myrin had come to expect. Delicacies from across the galaxy were piled high, taken as plunder or purchased more legitimately with the proceeds of it. There were few aeldari who would admit that other cultures could produce foodstuffs as good as their own – and Myrin would count himself in that number – but the assembled Starsplinters nonetheless gorged themselves on devilled kraelfish, sizzling haunches of maurtan, and spiced kirikiri fruits, along with the finest examples of more standard fare.

'She feeds us well,' Baroness Arrerith Elwin said into her goblet of Zetruscian ale, as she walked the floor alongside him. 'Of course, she can clearly afford to.'

Myrin took a sip from his flagon of purest human amasec, with a shot of aeldari firequill to give it more of an alcoholic kick, before he replied. 'It is certainly an impressive display.'

'"Impressive"? My dear Myrin, this display borders on the obscene, and that is not a term I use frivolously,' the baroness replied. 'Look at it! It is self-aggrandisement of the most blatant sort.'

Myrin hissed in alarm. 'Keep your voice down!' He looked about him, but none were close enough to overhear. Even their respective Bladesworn were spread out, close enough to act if required, but allowed to enjoy the feast themselves in the meantime.

'I'm too old to be scared by Tishria,' Elwin said with a snort. She was old, that much was certainly true – her gait was stiffening and her hair was greying, and Myrin thought he could hear a rattle in her breathing that had not been present before. Aeldari lived long by the standards of most of the galaxy's species, but they were far from immortal, even assuming that death did not find them through violence or misadventure.

'Then you have become a fool in your dotage,' Myrin said bluntly. 'The princess is no less deadly than she has ever been.'

'Just as deadly, perhaps, but not as sharp,' Elwin replied levelly. 'I saw her speaking to you at some length earlier, Myrin. Are you telling me you did not realise this during your conversation? She was always the best of us, else I would not have followed her, but she is losing her way.' The old captain sighed. 'She is so caught up in her own legend that she forgets it was built on her deeds, not on anything inherent to her. You need only look around to see that.'

'What *is* this?' Myrin asked, careful to keep his voice down. The atmosphere was not quiet – it rarely was when corsair captains were gathered together – but that did not mean he could be careless with his words. He waited for a moment as another servant passed with a tray of drinks, and noted idly that this one was wearing a collar very similar in nature to the first one he'd seen. 'Why this display of wealth?'

'Lost in her own legend, as I said,' Elwin replied with what sounded like some genuine sadness. 'I remember when Tishria truly *was* the Scourge, and this place was merely somewhere for her to celebrate victories, repair ships at anchor, and let the injured regain their strength. Now it is her palace, her kingdom, and she rarely leaves it. I do not know the last time her ship saw combat. She simply sits here, holding court with whichever of us are currently passing through, and congratulating herself on the wealth she has gathered… or that we have gathered for her.'

Myrin grimaced. 'Hoarding is not our way. What is the point of amassing wealth if you do not spend it? I assumed she was trying to impress a potential ally of some sort.'

'An intriguing theory, Stormdawn,' a new voice whispered, and Myrin started as Kruvell Darkspear appeared at his left elbow. The former archon bared gold-lacquered teeth in a smile, and took a sip from a cup of what was almost certainly spiced blood, judging by the smell.

'You should announce yourself, if you do not wish to be stabbed,' Myrin said stiffly. Darkspear was far from the captain whom he found the most objectionable, and by no means as cruel as his former kin, but there was still something about him that raised Myrin's hackles. He glanced around to see where his Bladesworn were, and sighed at the sight of Xela with a goblet in one hand and the other between the shoulder blades of the unfamiliar Starsplinter nibbling at her neck. The force of Myrin's glare seemed to attract her attention, and she looked around lazily.

'You should keep better watch,' Darkspear replied with a soft chuckle. 'But tell me, Stormdawn, what ally could the princess be attempting to impress?'

'I was not sure,' Myrin admitted, still holding Xela's gaze. He jerked his head infinitesimally in Darkspear's direction, to signify *how did you let him get so close to me?* 'I could not think of another explanation.'

Xela visibly sighed and, without disturbing her new paramour, pulled a knife from its sheath and raised it between thumb and forefinger, then nodded questioningly at Darkspear's back.

Myrin shook his head sharply – there was no point now, after all – and Xela rolled her eyes, then spun her knife back into its sheath and returned her attention to the aeldari whose lips had now reached her collarbone.

'The explanation is simple,' Baroness Elwin said. 'She seeks to impress *us*. To remind us of her place above us.'

'No, I think not,' Darkspear replied. The smile slid from his lips like warm fat off a knife blade, and suddenly he was all seriousness. 'This is a more subtle game, hidden within an unsubtle one. The princess fears unrest, so rather than wait for it to develop in its own time and take her unaware, she seeks to provoke it prematurely with this display. Which of us objects? Who resents their own tributes being displayed in front of all, reminding them what they have handed over? They will either face her down publicly here, before they have had time to gather allies, and she will crush them, or she and her agents will pick up hints from the conversations throughout the hall, and then the unlucky captains may find themselves set upon far from home, and with none able to carry word back of who brought about their end.'

Myrin nodded slowly. 'That feels more like the Tishria I know.'

'Being able to spot such traps is a benefit of a life spent in Commorragh,' Darkspear said with a smile like a knife wound. 'The only downside being that you are so used to looking for blades in the shadows, you can forget that out here they some-times appear right in front of you.'

'But from whom might she fear such a challenge?' Myrin asked, looking around. Getting caught up in an impromptu power struggle was not on his agenda, but the more he thought about it, the more Darkspear's interpretation felt like the most likely one.

'If you set your trap too specifically, you may miss your quarry,' Darkspear said. 'However, bearing in mind the present company…

perhaps the baron who is seeking to lead a gloriously bold attack against a monstrous ork warlord?'

Myrin looked at him sharply. 'The princess did not forbid my plan, but I have spoken to no one but her of this yet. How–'

'You have not, but not all of your captains have been so reticent,' Darkspear replied mockingly. 'The handsome redhead, for example.'

The bottom of Myrin's stomach dropped away. 'Taenar?'

'Ah, so you *do* think he's handsome,' Darkspear said with a grin. 'I did wonder, from the way I saw you looking at him.'

'Where is he?' Myrin demanded, ignoring Darkspear's comment as he looked around. Taenar knew no one here, had no idea of the webs of power and influence that ran through the Starsplinters. Wreaking retribution on an ork who had dared attack their ships should be a cause all of the corsairs could get behind – or at least, not interfere with – but things were not so simple. Myrin might be baron rather than prince, but he still held greater standing than many within the Starsplinters, and his position was always the subject of scrutiny from envious eyes. If he led a disastrous raid then his head would likely be forfeit to Tishria, which would allow someone else to step up into the light of her favour, so sabotage of his plans was not out of the question if word leaked to the wrong people.

'When last I saw him, he was involved in some sort of contest involving blades over there,' Darkspear said, pointing. 'You really should keep a closer eye on your pets.'

'Do be quiet, Kruvell,' Baroness Elwin said as Myrin moved off as swiftly as he dared without rousing unwanted attention. 'You're not half so clever as you think you are.'

The sheer scope and luxury of the Starsplinters' base had shocked Taenar. He had assumed that corsairs lived mainly as he had seen so far – a nomadic life, primarily focused on their ships, with their lairs mere hideouts that could be abandoned at short notice. This, however, was something more.

'It is a new way of life,' he said with feeling. 'The craftworlds, Commorragh, the Exodites – they keep alive something that has existed for millennia, but they do so in the same form. It is like a sculptor recreating the same piece with only minor variations. This is something different, which takes the disparate pieces and folds them into an amalgamation. New society, new culture, new art… everything.'

'And are you going to take your throw, or are you going to keep explaining being a corsair to me?' asked Ellanelle Jadefall with a small smile. She was clad in a mish-mash of fabrics and armour which appeared to have been taken solely from defeated foes, although some plates had obviously been beaten down or otherwise altered in order to fit her frame. Taenar was uncertain whether the uneven garb would serve her better than a well-maintained aeldari warsuit, but it was clearly as much for the aesthetic as it was for functionality. That aesthetic – a brash wildness – was something of which Taenar would have been wary not long ago, but his time amongst the corsairs had already changed his perceptions, and now he found himself drawn to it. Drawn to it enough, at least, to be attempting to impress her by taking part in a game of knife-throwing.

'My apologies,' he said with a slight bow. Then, while Ellanelle's fellow crew members were still chuckling at his mannerisms, he straightened up and threw his blade in one smooth motion. It thudded point-first into the carving they were using as an impromptu target, so close to hers that the vibration of its impact caused the hilts to rattle against each other.

'Oh, so the silver-tongued craftworlder can throw!' Ellanelle exclaimed with a mischievous light in her eyes as her companions sent up a good-natured cheer of mixed congratulation and surprise. 'Back another five paces, then! And you can tell me more about this adventure of yours.'

'Truthfully, the plan is not mine,' Taenar admitted as they withdrew a few steps. Ellanelle whistled and gestured, and one of the collared servants wrenched their blades out of the carving, then brought them over. Taenar took his with a smile and nod of thanks, but the servant ducked away without meeting his eyes.

'Not claiming credit for something? I see you still have much to learn about our ways,' Ellanelle joked. 'I saw you enter with Stormdawn. It's his venture, then?'

She released her blade, and sent it tumbling end-over-end to land in the carving with a solid *thunk*. Her companions cheered again, and Taenar heard a few rowdy voices challenging him to match her once again.

'It is,' he confirmed. 'And one with which I heartily agree. The beast not only attacks us, but enslaves aeldari. The princess gave her blessing for Myrin to gather others for the venture, so I am merely spreading the word on his behalf.' Which was not necessarily wholly true, but Tishria had certainly given her *permission*, and everything after that was merely a matter of semantics.

'*Myrin*, is it?' Ellanelle asked, raising her eyebrows. 'First-name terms with the baron?'

'Well,' Taenar said modestly, 'I like to think I've made a good impression.' He pursed his lips. 'You called me "craftworlder", so indulge me – what is your origin?'

'Ah, a personal question,' Ellanelle said with a smile. 'Well, since I brought the subject up, I suppose that's fair enough. I was born a corsair, my new friend, and this life is all I've ever known.'

'It's always good to know against whom one is competing,'

Taenar said, bowing his head slightly. He threw again, without really looking, and his knife nestled in alongside hers once more. His casual manner appeared to spark delight amongst Ellanelle's crew, who cheered again, and slapped her on the shoulder to urge her on.

'Another five paces?' Ellanelle suggested, good-naturedly shrugging aside her companions' hands.

Taenar shrugged. 'Why not make it ten?'

Ellanelle's smile widened. 'You must have some confidence in your skill with a blade, Captain Leotharan.'

'He does,' a voice said from behind Taenar. 'But mainly when your back is turned.'

Ellanelle's smile dropped away into cautious neutrality as Saraan Skyhand stepped between the two of them, flanked by two of their crew. 'Skyhand. Still aboard *The Yearning Stars*?'

'Indeed,' Skyhand replied, not taking their eyes from Taenar's face. 'Of course, the ship is mine to command now, thanks to this one.'

'Is that so?' Ellanelle's eyes flickered from Skyhand to Taenar, then back again. 'You don't seem overly happy about it.'

'My captain had declared the Gauntlet of Blood on Baron Stormdawn,' Skyhand said. 'The challenge had been made and accepted, and then this cowardly worm *stabbed him in the back.*'

Ellanelle's attention turned back to Taenar, as did that of her companions. 'You violated the duel?'

'I was not a Starsplinter at that point,' Taenar said as confidently as he could manage. 'Captain Elasandor had repeatedly threatened and insulted me, and I did not care to find out what he would do if he won.' What had felt like a justified argument in his own quarters, and to Myrin Stormdawn aboard *Light of Heaven*, sounded weak in his own ears in front of this crowd of hardened corsairs. He spread his hands, and attempted to play the cocksure character for which they would surely have more respect. 'If he had been wise, he would not have turned his back to me.'

'I could have done to you as you did to him, just now,' Saraan said, their eyes flat and murderous. 'Run you through from behind.'

'You could have tried,' Ra'thar Kyldran said. It should not have been possible for the warlock to lurk unobtrusively, but he had managed it, only stepping forward now.

'Well, friends, it looks like we might have some more entertaining blade work to watch!' Ellanelle declared, waving her arms as she backed off, taking her crew with her. Taenar should not have found it surprising that she was encouraging a violent spectacle instead of attempting to help calm the situation, but he did find it somewhat disappointing.

'No one has said that blades will be drawn,' he pointed out.

'You do not have to draw yours if you do not wish to,' Saraan said. They sniffed. 'It will make this faster.'

Taenar sighed, and took a cautious step closer to the bristling corsair. 'I was an Aspect Warrior for many years,' he said in a low voice. 'You will not find me an easy kill.'

'I do not care whether it is *easy*, you craftworlder bastard!' Saraan hissed. The former Exodite took a step back and drew their blade, a powered wraithbone sabre of a design unfamiliar to Taenar. 'I ripped a mon-keigh's spine out with my bare hands when they came for my world, but your kind always thinks that we cannot look after ourselves and that we should be grateful for whatever crumbs of protection you choose to give us. Ellisar fought alongside us, and you *killed him*.'

Taenar became aware of shimmering power starting to gather around Ra'thar's fists, and raised his own hand in a calming motion. 'Peace, my friend. This is a personal grudge that must be settled.'

'It can be settled easily enough,' Ra'thar growled. The warlock was not wearing his witch helm, but his expression of furious scorn was probably even more intimidating than its blank, crystalline stare.

'Saraan Skyhand,' Taenar said, taking a deep breath to prepare himself, and placing one hand on his sword hilt. 'If we fight, then that is to be an end to the matter. My crew will not seek to avenge my death, and yours will not seek to avenge yours.'

'That is how it should be, except in cases of treachery and backstabbing,' Saraan spat. 'I did not order my ship to attack yours, because my quarrel is with you alone. Now we are here, and face to face, I will take your life.'

Taenar sighed again, and nodded. 'Very well.' He drew his own blade. He did not relish the prospect of this fight – he certainly did not feel the same animosity towards Skyhand as he had towards Elasandor, nor the same desire to spill their blood – but there was little he could do about it. Skyhand clearly wished to spill his, and appeared to be prepared to pay only scant courtesy to whether or not Taenar intended to defend himself, so his options were limited to accepting the challenge and limiting the fallout, or getting embroiled in a brawl that would inevitably suck in others.

Skyhand dropped into a guard position – an unfamiliar one, but Taenar had fought enough different enemies in enough desperate circumstances to pay little attention to that. The moment you assumed you knew how a foe was going to attack was the moment you died. He readied himself, watching for the faintest telltale sign of a balance shift.

'Stop this! Now!'

Myrin Stormdawn strode in from Taenar's left, his expression thunderous. Saraan Skyhand hissed and straightened from their crouch, turning to address the baron. 'He will pay for–'

Myrin backhanded them across the face with a casualness that made Taenar blink in surprise, then rounded on, of all people, Ellanelle. 'Is this your doing?' Stormdawn demanded. 'You always have enjoyed stirring conflict for your own amusement.'

'Don't look at me, baron,' Ellanelle said with a smirk. 'This is entirely the work of your own crew. But if you can't keep them in line,' she continued, smiling coyly, 'how will you hope to lead an attack on this ork menace I've been hearing about? And after my mother apparently gave you her blessing, too.'

Taenar cursed himself for a fool, and it seemed that he was not the only one to do so. Myrin shot a glare at Taenar that felt as though it speared right through his chest.

'And will *Feverbreak* be joining us?' Myrin bit out, turning his attention back to Ellanelle. 'Or does the daughter of a princess not care about the enslavement of her aeldari kin by these creatures?'

To Taenar's horror, Ellanelle and her crew simply laughed in Myrin's face.

'Those who are weak enough to get caught deserve their fate,' Ellanelle said scornfully, placing her hands on her hips and looking Myrin up and down as though he were a fool in motley, and a disappointing one at that. 'The only disappointment is that they are not being put to *good* use.'

Taenar blinked. How could any aeldari consider that enslaving aeldari could be a good thing? Other than the drukhari, of course, such as the ones who had predated on Ilmaren…

Such as the ones who apparently welcomed Princess Tishria when she chose to visit.

Taenar found himself staring at Saraan Skyhand, who had raised one hand to their cheek where Myrin had struck them, but had been so taken aback by Ellanelle's words that they now stood frozen in place. Then, as if drawn by some unseen force, they both turned to look at the collared servant who had returned Taenar and Ellanelle's knives. He was standing demurely to one side with his hands clasped in front of him, and was resolutely staring at the floor.

'Did the princess have these servants the last time you were here?' Taenar asked hoarsely.

'No,' Skyhand replied. They looked positively unwell. 'You! Take your collar off!'

The servant – the slave – twitched involuntarily, but did not move to obey. Skyhand took a step towards them, but was brought up short by Ellanelle's mocking laughter.

'That's a good way to kill him,' the corsair called. 'The collar is drukhari technology – any attempt to remove it will fry his nervous system. He knows that, and he'll fight you to keep it on!' She applauded sarcastically. 'Please try! It will be an entertaining spectacle!'

Taenar swallowed bile. 'This is not hedonism,' he found himself saying. 'This is barbarism!'

'You don't like it, craftworlder?' Ellanelle said. 'You think we should send them back to Commorragh? They won't be as well treated there, I can promise you that!'

'No,' Taenar said, turning towards her and flexing his fingers around the grip of his powerblade. 'You should release them all. You *will* release them!'

Ellanelle scoffed, and crossed her arms. 'You should have left this one where you found him, Stormdawn!' She fixed Taenar with a contemptuous stare. 'He doesn't have the spine to be one of us.'

'If being a corsair is about following your desires, then I know my desires very well!' Taenar shouted, pointing at her. 'These people are to be freed!'

'Taenar, we are not here for these people,' Ra'thar Kyldran

said tightly, appearing at his elbow. 'We are here for our own purposes!'

'If I ignore this abomination, I will no longer know myself!' Taenar snarled shaking the warlock's hand away. 'Captain Skyhand, I must ask your indulgence. I suspect I am about to die, and not at your hand.'

'If you die, you will not die alone,' Saraan Skyhand said, flexing their shoulders. 'Craftworlders might be arrogant bastards, but my people hate slavers above all. I will cut the rot out of this place, or I will perish in the attempt. If we both survive, we can resume this conversation.'

Ellanelle's face began to slide from amused disdain into open hostility. 'Baron Stormdawn, it appears that your captains are starting to get out of hand. Perhaps you would like to take action, before an example has to be made of them? And of you?'

Myrin sighed, and turned to look at Taenar. His expression was a turbulent war between anger and resignation. 'You are right. I should never have let things get this far.'

'Myrin,' Taenar began, trying to find the words to express himself properly. He wanted to grab the corsair by the shoulders to shake him, to hold him, to stare into his eyes and try to explain why he simply could not let this pass. He wondered if this was how it felt to be on the brink of losing yourself on a Path, to know that if you did not take this step back, your very nature would be forever and irrevocably altered.

'Enough, Taenar,' Myrin said wearily. 'You have said enough.' He drew his sword and Taenar tensed, ready for an attack, yet dreading it at the same time. Should he fight? *Could* he fight? Would it be better to let himself be slain by Myrin Stormdawn, rather than the inevitable and almost certainly crueller death that would follow at the hands of Tishria's followers, should Taenar somehow survive their combat?

Myrin raised his blade before his face in salute. Then he turned.

'Princess Tishria!' Baron Myrin Stormdawn bellowed. 'I invoke the Gauntlet of Blood!'

TWENTY

Myrin had the brief and very satisfying experience of seeing absolute shock wash over Ellanelle Jadefall's face, before the entire hall went virtually silent. Tishria sat forward on her throne, her eyes locking on to Myrin's even from across the room.

'Myrin,' she said, her voice sharp and clean as a blade, cutting through to the ears of all those present. 'Why would you do such a foolish thing?'

'Slaves!' Myrin shouted, pointing at the first collared aeldari he could see. He felt like every nerve was on fire, standing under the gazes of the other assembled captains and surely signing his own death warrant, but a part of him revelled in his own daring nonetheless. 'I spoke to you of how the orks are enslaving our people, and you said nothing! Were you ashamed of the purchases you had made from Commorragh? Or were you laughing at me in secret, waiting for the moment I discovered to what depths you had fallen?'

A murmur ran through the hall, and Myrin realised to his surprise and delight that he was not the only one who hadn't realised the true nature of those whom he had taken to be servants playing a role in Tishria's ostentatious display. Some captains were staring at him with amusement or contempt, it was true, but others were starting to mutter amongst themselves. The aeldari were a people of multitudes, each planet or craft-world or kabal with its own subtle variations on their faction's broad stances, and the corsairs embraced them all. In many ways that made them stronger than all, but it also meant they could fly apart along partisan lines over a suitably contentious issue.

Tishria tapped her lips with her finger as though considering her answer. 'The second one. It was certainly an amusing conversation. You were so *earnest* about it all!'

Myrin ground his teeth. 'The challenge has been issued.'

'Yes, and ignored,' Tishria said lazily, waving one hand as though to shoo away an annoying insect.

Myrin stared at her in amazement. 'This is the code of the Starsplinters! *Your* code!'

'And so I can ignore it as I see fit,' Tishria snapped. 'I rule here! Myrin, think about this for a moment – why would I make myself beholden to my own decrees?' She stretched on her throne, an apex predator relaxing in a shaft of sunlight, yet still utterly deadly. 'You all know that I will kill any of you who displease me. Most of you are simply intelligent enough to understand that you will undoubtedly benefit more from my favour than you would by seeking to supplant me.'

'You are a coward, then,' Myrin said through gritted teeth.

Tishria snorted. 'Am I going to have to listen to you whine for much longer?' She waited for a moment, looking at her court, then sighed. 'That was not a rhetorical question. Kill him.'

Myrin was so taken aback by her casual ordering of his death that he nearly didn't dodge the first blade thrust at his face. He parried the thrust of one of Ellanelle's crew, opened the warrior's throat with his return slash, and then the entire hall descended into madness.

There were no defined sides, no way of marking out who was

friend and who was foe; it was simply a case of killing anyone who seemed to be trying to kill you. Myrin had taken two steps towards the throne when Kruvell Darkspear appeared in front of him, his blade drawn and lips pulled back from his teeth in a bloodthirsty grimace, only for the air behind and beside the former archon to flicker, and Xela to step out of the disturbance and almost casually cut his throat. Darkspear toppled forwards, one hand on the wound in a futile attempt to staunch the blood. Myrin stepped nimbly past him and buried his void sabre in Darkspear's back on the way past, and felt the other baron go limp as his spinal cord was severed cleanly.

'You've decided to make me work for my living, then!' Xela shouted over the noise of combat. She had two blades out and was constantly spinning, almost like a dancer, as she scanned for the next overt threat amidst the chaos.

'It seemed like a good idea at the time!' Myrin replied. He ducked aside as he saw someone trying to draw a bead on him with a shuriken pistol, and felt the whisper in the air as mono-molecular discs sliced through the space where he had been standing a moment before.

'Really?'

'No! It seemed like an awful idea, but I did it anyway!' Myrin's answering fire seared his attacker's head clean off their shoulders, but his second shot flash-burned the shoulder of another com-batant just beyond. The aeldari in question screamed in pain, and failed to block the subsequent strike from the corsair she'd been fighting, which impaled her through the centre of her chest.

'I hope she was one who wanted to kill you,' Xela commented, blocking a wild swing from a fur-wearing enemy before kicking them backwards into an ongoing ruck.

'If she didn't before, it was probably her dying wish.' Myrin took a moment to glance about him, trying to get a fix on other allies, either definite or potential. His captains and their crews had been spread through the hall, as had everyone else's, and he could not be sure which of them might stand with him on this, but he hoped that at least his old Ilmaren colleagues might.

+Myrin Stormdawn!+

The voice thundered in Myrin's head, and nearly drove him to his knees with its force. He recognised the psychic intrusion of Idarael Mennatyr, but in a way he'd never experienced before. Previously, Tishria's seer had been a presence while communicating, vague and nebulous and irritating, like a shadow in the corner of Myrin's mind's eye. Now the shadow was a suffocating thundercloud with claws, digging into his temples and fogging his vision.

'Master Kyldran!' Myrin shouted desperately. He had no idea if the warlock could even hear him over the noise of battle, let alone whether Kyldran was at all interested in assisting, but Idarael's psychic pressure felt like it was going to burst Myrin's mind within moments. He staggered, dimly aware of Xela's arm wrapped around his chest holding him broadly upright.

A coruscating blast of pink-and-purple energy erupted from what Myrin was still just capable of recognising as his right, and seared across the hall. He had a momentary sense of panic, which he recognised a second later as bleeding through from Mennatyr as the seer hastily disengaged from his psychic attack and threw up a whirling vortex of force, upon which Ra'thar Kyldran's attack detonated and disintegrated. The warlock stormed past a moment later, helm in place and witchblade in hand. A corsair threw themselves at him, long knife in each hand and a snarl on their lips, only to be neatly bisected at the waist by one swing, crashing down to the floor in two bloody halves. Kyldran neither looked back nor slowed, but simply lifted his hand and sent another blazing attack towards Mennatyr's position at the base of Princess Tishria's throne.

'The warlock isn't playing,' Xela commented, awe mixing with disgust in her voice. Even after so long out of Commorragh, she still viewed psychic powers with distrust at best, and outright hostility at worst.

'At least he's decided he's on our side,' Myrin managed, shaking his head in an effort to clear it of Mennatyr's assault. He nearly lashed out with his void sabre at someone close by, only to realise at the last moment that it was Taenar.

'To be honest, I suspect Ra'thar has simply decided that he is *not* on Tishria's side,' Taenar said breathlessly, blood atomising off his powerblade as another flash and thunder heralded the two psykers throwing their power at each other again. 'He warned me of her nature before we set down, but now we are at war I suspect he will stop at nothing short of her destruction.' Taenar fired his shuriken pistol, although Myrin had no idea how he had determined the target was an enemy. 'He is thorough, above all else.'

At war. The two words rang around Myrin's head, reverberating with their simple, terrifying truth. A civil war amongst the Starsplinters had never been his intent when he drew his blade and challenged Tishria in outrage, but he had not foreseen the princess casually disregarding her own code and inciting his death.

Taenar was right. This *was* a war now, not just a corsair brawl, and Myrin needed to start treating it like one. Escalation was always a risky tactic, but it was better to be the one to escalate first than the one left burning.

'Jhanandra,' he said, broadcasting a messenger wave to *Light of Heaven* and hoping it would carry through the mountainside. 'Can you hear me?'

'*Faintly, captain,*' Jhanandra's voice came back a few moments later. She sounded as sullen as ever; unsurprising, given that so far as she knew, she was missing out on a feast. '*It sounds like celebrations are in full swing down there.*'

'Hardly,' Myrin replied. 'Listen closely. We have been betrayed. Tishria is enslaving aeldari, and has ordered my death. Take the fight to her ships, before they do the same to you!' He waited, hoping desperately that his Bladesworn would believe him, and, more importantly, would not betray him in turn. Commanding her to open fire on their princess' ships was not an order either of them had ever expected him to give.

'*Acknowledged,*' Jhanandra said after a moment of stunned silence. '*Who is with us?*'

'…I'll have to get back to you on that,' Myrin admitted. 'At the moment, all I have is who's trying to kill me!'

'*There are hundreds of ships up here, and you're asking me to start an orbital war when I don't even know how many are going to be on my side?!*'

'Then you're going to have to be persuasive!' Myrin snapped, looking around. 'Don't expect any help from Darkspear's or Jadefall's elements, but other than that…' His eyes lighted on Issarel fighting back-to-back with Arrerith Elwin and two of the old baroness' Bladesworn, and pointed towards them, guiding his little group in their direction. '*Isha's Portent* might assist!'

'*Elwin's faction?*' Jhanandra replied. '*I know her captain, I'll approach them first.*'

'Just don't delay!' Myrin ordered. 'Attack now, allies later, or it will be too late!' A welter of blood to his left announced the arrival of Cithriel Shelwe-nin, the Striking Scorpion exarch cutting her way to Taenar's side like a true servant of the Bloody-Handed God. Within a few more desperate seconds, Myrin and his companions had reached Issarel and Arrerith Elwin, and slain those attacking them.

'Stormdawn!' Elwin exclaimed, leaning on her spear in relief. 'Well, you have exposed the rot here, and no mistake.' She cocked her head for a moment. 'And I hear that *Light of Heaven* has opened fire on *A Beautiful Indifference*. Going after Tishria's flagship is a bold move.'

'I assume you will order your ships to assist?' Myrin said tightly. Jhanandra had certainly followed his orders; he simply hoped she had not doomed herself and *Light of Heaven* in the process.

'Are you intending to kill Tishria, or merely save your own hide and escape?' Elwin demanded, fixing him with a stare.

Myrin bit his lip. His military instincts were to avoid a pitched battle for which he had not prepared, capitalise on the confusion, and escape as soon as possible through the hole in the enemy's fleet that his warships were hopefully even now creating.

And then... what? Be cast out from the Starsplinters, blamed for the schism, and hunted down by Tishria and her underlings? That would benefit no one except the enemies Myrin had made today. His military instincts might advise retreat, but he could hear the echo of Elthorn Caman's voice there. His corsair instincts, on the other hand, were to press on and seize a decisive victory in a combat which until a few minutes ago, no one – including him – had dreamed might be occurring.

'To kill her,' he said flatly. He had intended that when he challenged her, so why not see it through now?

'Then you will have my assistance,' Elwin said. She raised her eyebrows. 'What is your command, Prince Myrin?'

'We corner Tishria,' Myrin said, thinking fast. 'We cannot let her get to her ship, where her death would be difficult to verify. I need her head.' He looked around at their small group: himself, Xela, Taenar, Issarel, Elwin, Cithriel... but here came two of Elwin's Bladesworn, and there was Siriolas Wynlar of *Revenge's First Cut* and a handful of his crew, and there was Taranath, dancing his way through the battle towards them, clearing a way for himself with his pistols, and there was Saraan Skyhand and a full half a dozen of *their* crew, and suddenly what had been a mere handful of warriors was looking more like a small army.

'For Stormdawn!' Xela Flickerstep yelled, raising her bloodied knives in the air. 'For freedom!'

'For Stormdawn!' Taenar echoed. 'For freedom!'

'For Stormdawn!' Myrin's followers thundered, taking up the chant. *'For freedom!'*

Taranath spun to a halt in front of them, and bowed low, one pistol in each hand. 'Apologies, my baron.'

'You always were late,' Xela snapped. Taranath looked up, grinning.

'That is not what I was apologising for.'

He levelled both of his pistols at Myrin.

TWENTY-ONE

It happened so fast that Myrin barely registered what had happened until after it was over. He was staring down the barrels of Taranath's pistols, frozen in a moment of incomprehension, starting to turn as he looked for the enemy that had to be behind him, the enemy that Taranath must be aiming at.

Then Taenar was there, lunging in front of him. There was a spray of blood and an agonised cry from Taenar, echoed a moment later by Taranath as one of Issarel's powerblades sliced through both of his outstretched wrists at once. The pair of pistols fell to the floor, traitorous hands still wrapped around their grips, and Issarel's other sword swept around to remove Taranath's head.

'Hold!' Myrin barked. Issarel's reflexes were equal to his command, and their swing stopped with the edge of their blade doing nothing more than nicking Taranath's throat. They swiftly brought the other one up to scissor their fellow Bladesworn's neck underneath the jaw, leaving him stretched uncomfortably upwards in an attempt to minimise the pressure.

'Were you always Tishria's agent?' Myrin demanded.

'We don't have time for this,' Xela hissed at his elbow, but Myrin ignored her and pointed his fusion pistol at Taranath's face.

'Well?'

Even handless, and with no fewer than three lethal weapons within inches of his skin, Taranath could still smile. It was an ugly thing now, though, sour as ruined milk.

'Tishria is worth no more to me than what she could give me,' Taranath said, leering at him, 'and I am a true corsair, always looking for opportunity. Imagine my reward if I had presented her with the head of the traitorous–'

His final words were lost in a flash of light and heat as Myrin fired his fusion pistol and blasted his former Bladesworn's head apart. Taranath had been with Myrin for decades, one of the first to join his corsair crew who had not followed him from Ilmaren. Clearly there were no ties of loyalty that ran deep enough to stifle the flames of ambition in some aeldari hearts.

'Princess Tishria must die!' he thundered, pointing. 'To the throne!' He couldn't see whether Tishria was still there, but the symbolism of the thing was important. Either he would confront her, or she would have abandoned her literal seat of power. More and more aeldari were rallying to him, forming a cohesive group amidst the chaos as they recognised the side with which they wished to stand. However, they had to move *now*, before they were surrounded.

'What about the craftworlder?' Elwin asked, pointing down at Taenar as the first of Myrin's followers surged towards the throne.

Myrin looked down. That was a mistake.

Blood hot with fury and the thrill of combat, he could have charged off and left Taenar to the mercy of gods and corsairs, neither of which was a tangible thing. He *should* have charged off. Myrin had not asked Taenar to take those shots for him, had not made his fellow former admiral his Bladesworn. Corsairs lived or died for glory, and perhaps for honour, but not for self-lessness. If Taenar wanted to court death when he could have kept himself hale and whole by simply doing nothing, that was his prerogative.

But then Myrin looked down and saw the red ruin of Taenar's torso, saw the rivulets of blood and the torn flesh and the gruesome pale flash of neatly severed bone. He saw the eye-squeezing agony written on Taenar's face, and even above the noise of battle, he heard the bubbling, rattling wheezing of his breathing.

And he couldn't do it.

This was not glory, but neither was it selflessness. It was, perhaps, honour, but it was something more than that as well. This was an ugly, twisting pain in his core, something which warned him that if he stepped away now he would wrench out a part of himself, and it too would lie here bleeding on the floor. It was not just who he was but who he wanted to be, and what he wanted for himself. Taenar was a glorious soul, one whose full nature Myrin had only just begun to lay bare, and Myrin wanted to keep peeling back the layers until the true Taenar stood in front of him. He wanted the galaxy to look upon Taenar Leotharan and marvel at what Myrin Stormdawn had brought forth from the staid, dutiful former admiral of Ilmaren, and Myrin wanted the galaxy's envy.

'Keep him alive,' he told Elwin.

The baroness' expression showed what she thought of that. 'I am no healer, and his body is ruined.'

'His spirit is strong!' Myrin snapped. 'Protect him, and he will have the strength to hold on for now.' He looked around at Cithriel Shelwe-nin. 'Exarch, would you–'

'Do not ask a priest of the Bloody-Handed God to stand apart from battle,' Cithriel Shelwe-nin said, her voice emerging harsh and laced with clicks from her sinister helm. Myrin knew better than to argue.

'Siriolas!' he ordered instead. 'Guard him!' He crouched down and took Taenar's hand in his.

'You are bound to me,' he whispered into Taenar's ear, 'and I do not readily relinquish that which is mine. Stay alive – your prince commands it.'

He had no more time to waste. He surged upright and ran for the throne amidst his followers, void sabre raised and fusion pistol in hand, Xela at his right and Issarel at his left, and Cithriel cutting her own bloody path. The only way to avoid a protracted war amongst the Starsplinters, a war that would weaken them all and leave them vulnerable to the galaxy's myriad predators, was to end it decisively here and now.

Tishria was still on her throne. Myrin could see her now, sitting calmly in place with her star glaive laid across her knees. No help was coming from her way finder. A psychic war raged away to Tishria's left as Mennatyr and Kyldran clashed with all the arcane energies at their disposal, both too caught up in their conflict to be able to spare an iota of energy for the battle at large. A loose screen of corsairs loyal to the princess had formed up in front of the steps up to the dais, and let loose with a withering hail of fire at Myrin's warriors. Several fell, but Tishria's protectors were dying as well, cut apart by shuriken or falling as energy beams burned holes through vital organs. Then the first wave of Myrin's corsairs hit, and blades buried themselves in flesh, and Tishria's remaining defenders were cut down – not without loss, but Myrin's followers stumbled forward over the dead and the dying, staring up at their former princess with hunger and fear and disbelief at their own daring in equal measure.

Tishria stood. Myrin just had time to see her smile, and then the force dome blinked into existence.

It was a translucent bubble of energy that extended out and down from the rayed sun design atop the throne, enclosing the entire dais. The second wave of Myrin's warriors rebounded off it, its superlative design stopping not just their bodies, but the projectiles and energy beams from their weapons. Tishria shrugged out of her robe and leaped athletically down from her seat to land like a vengeful god amongst those of Myrin's followers trapped inside the dome with her. He saw her star glaive flash, and then bodies began to fall.

'Down!' Xela shouted as a shape thundered down at Myrin from on high. Kraveth landed and spun in one motion, and monomolecular-edged feathers soared from his cloak, opening throats and embedding themselves in chests. Issarel's swords flashed as they cut projectiles out of the air to protect themself. Xela simply flickered out of existence and reappeared behind Kraveth, but her knife thrust was knocked aside by the other Bladesworn's jagged sword, and then he was on her with blade and agoniser whip.

'Help her!' Myrin barked at Issarel.

'My duty is to protect you,' Issarel replied, 'not her.'

'Your duty is to do as I command,' Myrin growled.

'She will not thank either of us for it.'

'I don't give a damn!' Myrin shouted in frustration as the very tip of Kraveth's agoniser licked at Xela's heel and she stumbled. He could no more abandon Xela to potential death than he could Taenar.

Issarel shrugged, and leaped into the attack with a scream. They no longer had the vocal amplification of the Banshee mask they had worn when following the Path of the Warrior, but the noise was still enough to draw Kraveth's attention for a moment. Xela blinked away from the thrust of Kraveth's blade, but she might have been a moment too late to avoid being skewered by it anyway had Kraveth not become aware of the incoming attack from behind. He whirled with consummate skill, lashing out with his agoniser. The tendril coiled around Issarel's right forearm, and Myrin's Bladesworn's legs gave out as pain shot through their body. Kraveth drew back his sword for the killing strike, but now Xela was attacking again from behind him, her Commorraghan conditioning shaking off the agoniser's effects, and Kraveth had to readjust and knock her knife strike away.

Issarel severed the agoniser around their forearm with their other blade, and lunged from the floor at Kraveth's thigh. He managed to sidestep and whirl with preternatural swiftness, his feathered cloak tangling Issarel's blade and knocking it aside, but now when he licked his agoniser out at Xela's face the truncated weapon came up short. Xela jerked her head back from it, allowing the sparking tip to flash by her nose, and locked both her knives around Kraveth's blade when he stabbed for her with it. She wrestled him around in a half-circle as he tried to maintain his grip, only for Issarel to step forward and plunge both of their blades into his chest as he turned towards them. They impaled him, piercing right through his body and jutting out of his back to lift his cloak away as though it were wings in truth.

Kraveth let out a gasp of pain and shock, and dropped to his knees. Xela opened his throat a moment later with a desultory slash of her knife, and Issarel's forearms were spattered with blood as they wrenched their blades out.

'That was unnecessary,' Myrin heard Issarel say as Kraveth collapsed forwards.

'So was your intervention,' Xela growled, turning away. She saw him watching the fight and glared at him. 'Are you happy?'

'Not at all,' Myrin said, fighting down his emotions. Kraveth had been as good a friend as was possible, for a warrior who might at any moment have received an order to end Myrin's life. Myrin had drunk with him, fought alongside him, sparred with him, discussed art and philosophy with him, and all the myriad other activities aeldari could partake in when free from the constraints of more limiting societies.

However, Kraveth had always been Tishria's Bladesworn, and Myrin had known him well enough to be sure that would never have changed. No persuasion, no reason could have broken Kraveth away from the Scourge's side. For Myrin to live once Tishria's decree had been made, Kraveth would have always had to die.

Just another body to lay at the princess' feet.

He looked about him. It was still difficult to ascertain exactly who was on what side – and he had no idea how the combatants were managing it – but the majority of the aeldari in the chamber were skilled warriors, and skilled warriors needed only a moment's inattention or minor mistake from their opponent in order to land a telling blow. Bodies were strewn everywhere, either dead or, like Taenar, fighting against death's clutches so hard that they were no longer a factor. Those left on their feet were largely turning towards him with uncertainty on their faces, not murderous intent. They had chosen their side in the brawl, and it had been his, and now they needed to know what he was going to do with this fragile, unexpected victory.

A shudder ran through the hall – not a shockwave so much as the inverse of one, as charged, shivering air calmed and stilled. Myrin looked around, and saw Idarael Mennatyr's body sliding off Ra'thar Kyldran's witchblade. The dying seer's eyes locked on Myrin's for a moment, then rolled back into his head as he hit the floor.

'A more prosaic end to that combat than I would have expected,' Xela commented.

'Master Kyldran is as much a warrior as any of us,' Myrin said, not without a little unease at the thought of what the warlock might do upon learning of Taenar's condition. 'If the battle of power was even, martial skill decided the contest.'

On the far side of the hall, beyond where Kyldran had just slain Mennatyr, Myrin saw Ellanelle Jadefall and her coterie withdrawing through a side door. The captain of *Feverbreak* flipped him a jaunty salute, before sending a few last shots into her pursuers and slamming the door behind them. It merged seamlessly with the carved frescoes of the wall, and Myrin suspected that forcing it would be near impossible. Ellanelle knew this palace as well as her mother did, and it undoubtedly had secrets that the rest of them would never discover.

'She does not seem concerned about Tishria's wellbeing,' Issarel said.

'Ellanelle has always been pragmatic,' Myrin replied. The words were almost automatic, his mind responding without thought while it grappled with the problem he was about to face. 'Nor has she ever displayed much filial duty beyond that due from a captain to her princess. Perhaps she views this as an opportunity to step out from her mother's shadow.'

He turned towards the throne, where Princess Tishria's shadow was laid bare for all to see.

The Scourge of the Calexis Nebula stood tall inside the protective force dome, star glaive in her hand and a dozen corsairs dead at her feet. A thin trickle of blood ran from just below her hairline on the right-hand side of her forehead, the only sign, apart from the viscera of others coating her weapon and her bodysuit, that she had been in a fight at all. A contemptuous smile crooked her lips as she watched Myrin walk towards her. Tishria was a tyrant, a pirate, a raider, and a murderer, but she had not become leader of the Starsplinters by being a fool. She knew that she was beaten, but she also knew that the only way she might escape her fate was to act as though the possibility of her defeat was so inconceivable that it had not even crossed her mind, and do so with such force and certainty that it convinced others. Even now, at bay and surrounded by those who had taken up arms against her, she projected an aura of one who was merely humouring them.

But that could not last. Myrin could see the tiny, telltale fractures in her poise. Tishria might act as though she could end their rebellion at any time, but with every passing moment that she did not, her pretence was exposed more and more. He could post guards and leave her, and rely on her ongoing powerlessness to erode her authority, but what guards could he trust against her charisma, or her lethality when she finally decided to drop that field? He could order his followers to throw everything they had against the dome, but he had no idea of its nature or its capabilities. Should they attack it without success, *he* would be the one looking powerless, while Tishria smirked at him from behind her protection.

That left a stalemate. Myrin could not truly lead the Starsplinters while Tishria lived, and remedying that state of affairs was near impossible in the short term, but Tishria was similarly trapped. She would not drop the force dome unless she thought she could escape, and neither hunger nor thirst would be a fast motivator against a spirit as resilient as hers. She might hold out in the hope of rescue from other captains – which was not an impossibility – and that meant Myrin would have to leave a huge portion of his strength here to guard her, or else he risked her escaping and hunting him down in vengeance.

He had to offer her a more appealing option.

'I invoked the Gauntlet of Blood,' he said loudly, making his way to where the force dome met the floor. Tishria stood a few paces on the other side of it, not taking her eyes from him.

'You tried,' the princess replied.

'Lower your field, and let us resolve this as we should have done originally,' Myrin said. There were no other realistic options. He could leave an enemy alive at his rear, trap himself here with her until she finally perished or attempted a desperate escape from her sanctuary, or risk it all.

'Single combat under the rules of the Gauntlet?' Tishria asked, raising an eyebrow. 'For command of the Starsplinters?'

'Single combat under the rules of the Gauntlet,' Myrin replied, holstering his fusion pistol and perfecting his grip on his void sabre. 'For command of the Starsplinters.'

'No interference from your Bladesworn?'

'No interference from my Bladesworn.'

Tishria studied him, weighing up his words. There was no warning before she dropped the field.

Myrin had not been expecting any sort of verbal acceptance. As soon as the field blinked out of existence, he went for his sidearm.

Tishria was bringing her star glaive up and around in a shimmering arc that would have likely ended with Myrin losing his head, but the first fusion bolt cooked her heart and burned through her spine, and her limbs went limp. Her weapon clattered to the floor and came to rest against Myrin's boot at the same time as her body thudded to the ground, but Myrin was not done. He kept firing, unleashing his weapon's power again and again until Princess Tishria, Scourge of the Calexis Nebula, was nothing more than a pile of cooked meat.

All except her head. That, Myrin left untouched. He might need it as a trophy, to prove she was dead.

'Tishria voided her own code when she called for my death instead of honouring the Gauntlet,' he said into the loud, hungry silence that surrounded him. 'I simply granted her the same courtesy.'

He turned to face the hall.

'I am Prince Myrin Stormdawn, commander of the Starsplinters,' he declared. 'Those of you who fought for me here shall be honoured. Put out the word – any who sided with Tishria will be spared so long as they lay down their arms as soon as they receive this offer. Those who do not will be executed. Those of our brethren abroad in the galaxy who cannot live under my rule should not return to us, on pain of the same fate.' He pointed to a small huddle of the slaves, cautiously emerging from where they had taken cover during the fight. 'And someone find a way to remove those damned collars.'

Xela knelt first. It was against her nature, Myrin knew, but the role of Bladesworn went deeper than just being his bodyguard. Issarel followed a moment later, and then the obeisance spread outwards in a wave. Corsair nobles and captains he had joked or feuded with, all going to one knee out of respect, or possibly fear, or possibly because they had just seen the removal of the person whom they had obeyed and wanted to make sure they had their feet under them before they considered the ramifications of doing it again so soon. Not everyone in this room was going to be content under Myrin's rule, he was wise enough to know that. But none of them seemed about to challenge him for leadership here and now, and that was good enough for the time being.

He wanted to bask in the glory of the moment. He, Myrin Stormdawn, had become a corsair prince without even ever truly intending to do so! But then his gaze found Baroness Elwin and Siriolas Wynlar crouched by Taenar Leotharan's body, and his chest froze.

'Rise, my friends,' he managed, striding forward. 'We have work to do.'

TWENTY-TWO

The void war had gone as well as could have been expected. Tishria's aura of invincibility meant less when not present in person, and the wildfire news of slavery combined with a lightning attack by Myrin's forces swayed some crews to his cause – or the likely winning side – even while their nominal commanders fought for Tishria on the planet below. *Feverbreak* could have been a bastion of opposition, but when Ellanelle Jadefall reached her ship and it darted for the waygate instead of continuing the fight, the battle was as good as over.

Myrin Stormdawn was Prince of the Starsplinters, unopposed and unchallenged. He should have been delighted.

He was not.

'This is your fault, you know,' Xela Flickerstep said. Myrin weighed the vase in his hand for a moment, then threw it at the wall of his chambers. It shattered, the lovingly preserved, millennia-old pottery disintegrating under the force of the impact. He rounded on her, but she gave no ground, a rock in the face of his flood of anger.

'It is *Tishria's* fault,' Myrin snarled, but Xela shook her head.

'It is *your* fault. Or possibly Taenar's.'

'He saved my life!' Myrin snapped. 'Don't put this on him

simply because he did a Bladesworn's duty while you were making snide comments at my would-be assassin!'

Xela's nostrils flared, and her fingers flexed, but she made no other move. This was not one of their dominance games; this was emotion, real and raw. If either of them drew a weapon or laid a hand on the other now, the consequences could be severe. Myrin was no longer sure that he cared. Xela, it seemed, was still holding back from that edge.

'That was my failure,' Xela acknowledged, the words slipping out between her teeth. 'But it was Taenar's words that sparked the conflict, and meant Taranath tried to kill you in the first place. If you had left him in orbit, or quietened him in the hall–'

'Are you saying that you approve of what Tishria was doing?' Myrin demanded. 'Laughing at me behind her hand as I tried to rally support to free aeldari slaves, when slaves had been serving us drinks and food all night?'

'Don't forget where I come from, Myrin,' Xela said. 'I grew up surrounded by the slaves of my masters. I could have been one myself, had I not shown aptitude for combat. It was a simple fact of life.'

'You left Commorragh behind,' Myrin reminded her, but Xela simply snorted.

'Yes. For my own reasons, not out of some high-minded objection to its culture. The galaxy is harsh and cruel, and the strong will always subjugate the weaker. Those raised in the ways of the Asuryani always seem to feel that there is some *right* way of the galaxy being ordered, and that if they look hard enough then they will find it, but there is not.' She shook her head. 'Don't be angry that your self-righteousness somehow failed to shield your latest lover from the consequences of your actions, and of his.'

'I do not need to look for the right way of ordering the galaxy,' Myrin said angrily. 'I *know* it! It is laced into the very structure of my bones, and it runs through my veins! That knowledge is why I left Ilmaren behind when it no longer lived up to my expectations, and that is why I challenged Tishria!'

'And that is why this is your fault!' Xela declared, throwing her arms up in frustration. 'Had you not done so, Taenar might not be under the healers' ministrations, which appears to be the thing that is most bothering you!'

'And I would also not have my fleet,' Myrin said. '*My* fleet. Not a ragtag group of captains recruited through pleas and flattery, but other barons beholden to me.' He took a deep breath, trying to focus. As a baron, he had enjoyed a great deal of authority, but always with the unseen presence of Tishria lurking behind him. Her favour had lent his words weight, but the risk of her displeasure had often tainted his actions. Now he answered to no one.

Save, of course, for those same barons and baronesses of whom Myrin had until recently been a peer. He needed to achieve success quickly. The strong might always subjugate the weak, but they were mostly content not to test themselves against each other so long as they did not lack for what they wanted.

Nonetheless, the challenge did not scare him. He too had been one of the strong, content with his position, but he had never assumed that it would be the end of his story. He had simply, and perhaps without consciously realising it, been waiting for the right moment to take his story further. That moment had arrived with Tishria's fall from grace, and he had seized it.

No, what was scaring him was on *Dance of Dying Seasons*.

'We have heard nothing from Kyldran?' he asked. Xela rolled her eyes, and shook her head.

'Nothing, save for the warlock reiterating that they will receive no visitors until Leotharan has recovered.'

Myrin ground his teeth. As prince, he should not be subject

to such petty territorialism from a ship in his fleet, but each vessel was akin to its captain's own fiefdom. To demand entry was to risk being seen as abusing his newfound power, and also left him with the dilemma of what to do if Kyldran – not notably tractable, from Myrin's interactions with him so far – held to his position. But should he meekly bow his head and accept such an ultimatum from someone who, eldritch powers or not, was not even a captain?

'Very well,' Myrin said reluctantly. He had not realised how intertwined his soul had become with Taenar's until the other had been left bleeding and shaking on the floor of the Starsplinters' Grand Hall. Perhaps it was best if Myrin did not pursue the matter for now. His new underlings believed – because it was true, he hastily added to himself – that Myrin had overthrown Tishria as a matter of principle over her taking of aeldari slaves, not because he had taken the side of one of his captains who had spoken out of turn. He would leave that perception as it was, rather than risk distorting matters by making a visit to Taenar's bedside.

'Ensure they keep pace with the rest of the fleet,' he ordered. 'I don't want Taenar's ships dropping back, or taking a different branch of the webway.'

'You don't trust him?' Xela asked, cocking her head.

'I don't trust *Kyldran*,' Myrin clarified. 'I don't know what he will do if…' He broke off, finding himself unable to put his fears into words. 'Fine. If the warlock will not allow us aboard, then he can come to us. Call a council of the captains. We need to discuss our strategy against the orks, and with Taenar incapacitated, Kyldran can take his place.' He paused. 'I take it there has been no sign of *Feverbreak*?'

Xela shook her head. 'None. I suspect Jadefall will seek support amongst the other Starsplinters before making a move against you, if that is her aim. Speaking of which, are you sure that combat against the Bukkaneers is your wisest first move as prince? You are asking much from your captains, with little in the way of reward.'

'Why would I change my aims now I have even more resources to achieve them?' Myrin replied. 'Some of these captains will have followed me simply because they viewed our side as the likely winners of the fight, but some aligned with us because they agreed with me. To abandon the Bukkaneers' captives now I am prince would risk alienating them. Besides,' he added, 'I'm offering them the opportunity of glorious combat and a chance to demonstrate our superiority over the brutish orks. Any captain who does not find their blood stirred by that prospect may find themselves at odds with their own crew.'

'Very well, *my prince*,' Xela said, drawing out the title. 'I will call the council. Just be certain what you're going to tell them. We will have nowhere to hide now.'

'You concern yourself with making sure none of them try to cut my throat,' Myrin told her, 'and let me handle the speaking.' He waved her away, and watched her until she had left his quarters and the door had slid shut again behind her. Then he poured himself a large glass of voidwine and stared into it, trying not to think of Taenar's wounds.

Taenar floated for a long time.

He was not unaware of the pain wracking his body, but it was at a distance, as though he were connected to it by a series of threads that allowed only some of the sensations to reach the rest of him. A part of him recognised the danger that if he became too disconnected from those sensations, unpleasant though they were, he would lose them altogether. However, another part of him could feel the tug of something else – the crystalline song of his spirit stone, its comforting presence nestled on his chest even though he was only dimly aware, in this moment, of exactly where his chest was. The spirit stone promised peace, and tranquillity, and stillness, whereas his body offered him only pain, and uncertainty, and fear. And yes, the spirit stone would be a lonely prison at first, if a peaceful one, but when it was placed into Ilmaren's infinity circuit his spirit would be free to join those of his kin and wander the craftworld's matrix.

Except, Taenar remembered dimly, he was not of Ilmaren any longer. He had abandoned it for the corsair life, and there was no guarantee that anyone would be able to return his stone to his home and set it in place. No, wait, that was a ruse in the service of his craftworld, he had only *pretended* to abandon Ilmaren…

When Taenar opened his eyes he was lying on cool sheets, and light was filtering down through what turned out, after a few blinks, to be a canopy of green leaves. He could smell the plant life around him, and the faint, rich scent of living soil, and could feel the gentlest of breezes on his skin.

He sat up gingerly, feeling the pull in his chest and stomach of tissue that had only recently mended. His fingers, questing under the plain, soft robe in which he had been dressed, found faint, diagonal scars across his torso, and a sudden whiplash of remembered pain nearly drove him back down again. He breathed hard, trying to push aside the thought that he was actually bleeding out on a floor, and that this was all a hallucination.

However, he recognised the healing rooms of *Dance of Dying Seasons*. Not for the aeldari the filthy worktables of the orks, or even the supposedly sterile surgical environments of the mon-keigh, where a body was stitched back together in surroundings completely removed from nourishment for their poor, feeble souls. Taenar's species might wander the stars – might have ruled the stars, indeed – but they knew better than to isolate themselves from the galaxy's life. There was something about the purity of nature that spoke to the aeldari soul, and so that was how Ilmarens healed their wounded, even when far from the craftworld and its cultivated green spaces.

'Admiral,' a voice said behind him, and Taenar turned to see one of the healers in question walking towards him. He was relatively young – probably younger than Taenar, at least – but with a serious expression and a heaviness of gaze, which, combined with his shaved head, made him seem far older. Taenar, who had made a point of knowing the names of as many of his crew as possible, recognised him as Amonvar, one of the chief healers, despite his age.

'How are you feeling?' Amonvar asked, coming to a halt beside Taenar's bed.

'Like I have been pulled apart and stitched back together again,' Taenar said ruefully. 'With no disrespect to your art, I hasten to add. I have never received such a grievous injury before, even when I was an Aspect Warrior.'

Amonvar placed his hands on either side of Taenar's face and stared into his eyes for a few long moments. Taenar stared back, neither embarrassed nor intimidated, since he was well aware that this was part of the process. A body would die if the soul abandoned it, but even a healed body might house a wounded spirit. An aeldari who had received life-threatening wounds might become fey and destructive if the soul that had so nearly been cleaved away did not reattach itself as it should.

'Good,' Amonvar said eventually, withdrawing his hands again. 'You were nearly lost to us for a while. Your spirit is strong, but had Master Kyldran not got you back to us when he did–'

'Ra'thar!' Taenar exclaimed as the events immediately prior to his injury reasserted themselves in his memory. 'Is he well? Myrin! The baron, is he…'

'Master Kyldran is alive and uninjured,' Amonvar said soothingly. 'Albeit not in a particularly good temper, the last time I saw him. I have no personal knowledge of Myrin Stormdawn, but I am told that he is alive thanks mainly to your intervention. What is more, it appears he has now achieved the rank of prince.'

'Prince?' Taenar blinked in astonishment. 'What of Princess Tishria?'

'Dead, from what I have gathered,' Amonvar said. He gave a small smile. 'Although I must admit, the details of these corsair politics are not my area of expertise.'

Taenar swung his legs off the bed. 'I must get to the bridge immediately.' All manner of possibilities were running through his head, but the most pressing was the risk of his ships being somehow separated from Myrin's. Farseer Caman's predictions might well be coming to fruition. If Myrin was now Prince of the Starsplinters he would have even more influence that would, at some point and in some way, be crucial to Ilmaren's survival. Ra'thar Kyldran knew the importance of their mission as much as Taenar did, but Taenar had no illusions that the warlock's personality was best suited for the task. Kyldran might have the sort of blunt manner that some corsairs apparently appreciated, but he had not proved himself adept at building bridges with their new allies. If Myrin took the opportunity to send Taenar's detachment away in order to rid himself of Kyldran for a while… Even worse, if Myrin decided that now he had command of the entire Starsplinters fleet he did not need his former comrades at all…

'Under normal circumstances I would advise further rest,' Amonvar said. 'However, I know that rest is not the same as enforced inactivity.' He extended his hand, and Taenar took it to ease himself off his bed. 'Just please, my admiral, try not to overexert yourself. I would not wish to see you back here.'

'I can promise nothing,' Taenar said with a wry smile that

Amonvar returned. 'But know that should that happen, it will be because of dire necessity, and not from a lack of appreciation for either your skills or your advice.'

The healing rooms were placed more or less centrally in the cruiser, to ensure that the wounded could receive treatment as soon as possible no matter where they were when injured, so Taenar's trip to the bridge did not take him long. He took a conveyer rather than risk overtaxing himself too soon, and managed to walk through the bridge doors without any winces.

He recognised the indistinct greyness outside the viewports as soon as he saw it. They were in the webway again. Faerys Asuthien turned towards him from the captain's command station, concern written over her face.

'Admiral,' she said with palpable joy. 'You are recovered?' Behind her, Ra'thar Kyldran's expression spoke of similar relief.

'Not completely, but sufficiently,' Taenar replied, making his way over to the pair of them, and nodding in acknowledgment to various members of the bridge crew as they greeted him. He lowered his voice. 'What is our situation? Ra'thar, what happened after I was incapacitated?'

'The princess was trapped behind her force dome. Stormdawn baited her into fighting him in single combat, then immediately broke the rules to murder her and claimed sovereignty over her domain,' Ra'thar said bluntly. He shrugged. 'Overall I cannot say that I disapprove of his methods, given the circumstances, which simply reinforces to me the abominable nature of our position.'

'And what of our *actual* position?' Taenar asked. 'Are we still with the rest of the Starsplinters fleet? What is our heading?'

'A few corsairs broke away, but most stayed to pledge their fealty,' Faerys reported. 'Stormdawn marshalled every ship under his command, and we are even now on our way to attack the ork warlord he has spoken of.'

Ra'thar sighed. 'The prince is determined to free aeldari captives, I will say that for him, but I have the feeling that his command is still fragile. If this venture encounters serious resistance then I fear many of the Starsplinters will break and flee from him. We must be prepared for what we will do if that occurs.'

Taenar eyed him. 'Are you speaking of an escape plan, or taking action to preserve his life?'

'If Farseer Caman has ascertained that this arrogant degenerate is somehow crucial for the craftworld's survival, then I must assume that their divinations are correct,' Ra'thar replied. 'As such, we should of course attempt to ensure Stormdawn's survival, despite how he vexes me. I merely suggest that you should consider how we might best achieve such a thing without support from many of his potentially fickle followers.'

Taenar bit his lip. 'In our time with the Starsplinters, and the observations you have made of them, how likely do you think it would be that Myrin Stormdawn could be persuaded to disengage from a combat from which he himself was not ready to be removed?'

'Not at all,' Ra'thar said with a snort.

'Then we shall have to keep him alive as best we may,' Taenar said, flexing his fingers as he stepped up to the command station. Faerys stood aside to allow Taenar to place his hands on the wraithbone controls, and the sensations of *Dance of Dying Seasons* ran through him once more. He had missed this – the Path of the Mariner still called to him as strongly as it ever had. Maybe this was why some corsairs made their choice, he thought idly as he reacquainted himself with the reaches and depths of the ship's spirit. He would certainly not appreciate anyone, even the most respected farseer of his craftworld, telling him that he was being removed from command.

His brow furrowed as he registered the full scope of the

webway passage down which they were travelling. Accurate distances were always tricky to ascertain in this ephemeral, half-real space, but there was no disguising the fact that there was space around *Dance of Dying Seasons* for many, many other ships. The webway varied in size from passages that would only admit travellers on foot, to the largest – and rarest – tunnels that would allow even a craftworld access, and then right up to the enormous, interconnected world-domes and sub-dimensions of Commorragh, which was supposedly so large that it would cover entire solar systems of planets were it to exist in realspace.

Dance of Dying Seasons was currently travelling, along with Taenar's other ships, in the middle of a fleet of vessels just as large as themselves, and in some cases larger. It was a collection of ships that could have stood proudly alongside that of any craftworld, already drawn up in battle formation, yet they still had to pay little attention to their surroundings. Taenar suspected that Ilmaren's knowledge of the webway was far patchier than that of the corsairs, let alone the drukhari or the Harlequins, but there were plenty of routes that were known to his people. He reached out with *Dance of Dying Seasons'* sensors, trying to determine their location, and received conformation almost immediately.

'We are coming up on the webway gate closest to Ashaonnir,' he said. 'It is enormous – easily large enough to accommodate us all, even arrayed as we are.'

'A craftworld-sized gate, then,' Ra'thar said. 'Well, at least we will arrive ready for battle, even if the orks are waiting for us.'

Taenar nodded, then looked sidelong at him. 'You consider that a possibility?'

'They were apparently waiting in ambush for the Starsplinters upon their return to the Well of the Long Death,' Ra'thar pointed out, staring ahead as though he could see through the distant webway gate ahead of time if he looked hard enough. 'We surely cannot presume that it is impossible for them to have somehow determined Stormdawn's intent, even if it is not likely for them to have done so.'

'Wise counsel as ever, my friend,' Taenar said. He checked their position again. The webway gate was fast approaching now, and the fleet was not reducing speed. It seemed that Myrin was not intending to exit cautiously, which came as no surprise.

'Ready weapons,' Taenar broadcast, and felt the synaptic resonances as *Dance of Dying Seasons'* crew obeyed, and graviton pulsars, heavy starcannons, and fusion beamers powered up. The internal song of the ship's infinity circuit took on a more warlike hum, and Taenar's skin tingled at the feedback.

A messenger wave came in immediately, a top-priority signal. 'Dance of Dying Seasons, *why are you readying weapons?'*

'Myrin?' Taenar blurted. He felt more than saw Ra'thar's look, and cleared his throat. 'Prince Myrin.'

'Taenar! You are well?'

'I am better,' Taenar confirmed, his heart lifting at the mixture of concern and relief he heard in Myrin's voice. He had not interceded in the manner he did out of any expectation of gratitude or appreciation – there had been no time for anything other than pure instinct – but he was honest enough with himself to admit that although he did not want Myrin to have suffered anxiety and uncertainty over his wellbeing, he would have been hurt had there been no evidence of it. Throwing oneself in front of guns was far from ideal either as a method of expressing affection, or for eliciting it from others, but it should at least serve as an unequivocal one.

'I am delighted to hear it,' Myrin said. *'Master Kyldran refused to allow visitors, or I would have come to see you myself.'*

Taenar glanced at Ra'thar, whose expression was studiously

neutral despite being unable to hear Myrin. The warlock was, it seemed, astute enough to guess what direction the conversation may have taken, which, Taenar realised with a flush of pleasure, perhaps indicated exactly how determined Myrin had been to visit him.

'You would have been most welcome,' Taenar said deliberately, watching Ra'thar from the corner of his eye. 'However, in regard to your initial question, Master Kyldran pointed out that if the orks ambushed you once, it is not impossible to assume they may ambush us all again.'

'The Bukkaneers have ambushed us twice, in fact,' Myrin replied. *'Once after we had finished cleansing a planet of its human invaders, and once at the other end of our webway journey in the Well of the Long Death. Your warlock is no fool. I cannot imagine what methods or strange technology the brutes are using to track us, but it appears that they might have such a capacity, so we will prepare for it. I was about to give the order to ready weapons myself, but wished to determine why a captain of my fleet had anticipated it.'*

'We await your command, my prince,' Taenar said. The words felt strange on his tongue. Records suggested that the ancient, pre-Fall aeldari civilisation likely had a myriad of different rulers, including those who had styled themselves as royalty. It was a far cry from the ways of the craftworlds, guided as they were by the wisest of those who had become lost on the Path of the Seer, but it felt more… *vibrant*, somehow. There was a kernel of truth in his cover story, Taenar was realising. Although he retained the utmost respect for the Council of Seers, and Elthorn Caman in particular, there was an appealing immediacy and directness to how the corsairs conducted themselves. That was not to say that he preferred the idea of a tyrant with ultimate power who could only be overruled by a coup, and corresponding complete upheaval, but… Well, perhaps with Myrin in charge, things would not be so bad?

'*All ships, prepare for battle,*' Myrin announced, broadcasting generally now. '*We anticipate our quarry to be located near this gate, but we do not know exactly where, nor whether they will be ready for us. These orks have proved themselves to be a cunning quarry before, and we will not underestimate them. Prepare to show this filth that the stars are ours!*'

Answering war cries flooded back as the Starsplinter captains shouted their approval. Taenar felt their fierce, infectious joy at the notion of impending battle. It was a marked contrast to the sober, businesslike demeanour encouraged in the Ilmaren fleet, where war was a risk that always extracted an unwelcome price. Nonetheless, it pulled at him, for he had never lost the thirst for an enemy's death that had marked his time as an Aspect Warrior. Besides, a small part of his mind whispered to him, the price only came from those who *failed* at war. Why should a competent commander fear battle, instead of embracing it?

Taenar forced such thoughts from his mind. Overconfidence was as deadly an enemy as any other that lurked between the stars. He checked and double-checked his ship's systems, confirming that the psychotropic links were functioning optimally, the sensors were at maximum sensitivity, and he had full control over the engines. He was as ready for whatever might greet them as he could be.

The outriders were through the gate, disappearing into the shimmering curtain of energy that marked the boundary between the strange half-place of the webway and realspace beyond. They blinked out of existence in Taenar's senses, and he wondered for a moment if the fleet should not have slowed and sent a couple of scouts ahead, much as he had done at the Well of the Long Death. On the other hand, what enemy could await that could stand before the full might of a Starsplinters war fleet, with weapons primed and captains alert?

Light of Heaven was through now, along with its escorts, and the gate surface was coming up fast. Taenar took a deep breath and prepared himself.

They hit the gate and were through in an instant, out of the misty grey of the webway and into the sharp black of the void, pinpricked with the light of stars, and one somewhat stronger glow from starboard – the star of the system in question, distant but still powerful enough for the solar sails to trap its photons and boost the vessel's speed.

'*–nfirm, it is weapons fire,*' Myrin's voice came to him. '*Determining the source now.*'

'Are we taking fire?' Taenar asked, scanning their surroundings.

'*No,*' Myrin replied tightly, just as Taenar's sensors got a fix on massive energy outputs. '*But someone is.*'

Taenar focused in on the readings, trying to make sense of what he was detecting through the haze of drives and holofields surrounding him. A battle was certainly taking place, that much was quickly obvious, and not far distant, either, although not in the immediate vicinity of the webway gate.

He frowned at what his sensors were telling him. They had found the Badskab Bukkaneers, judging by the weapons readings he was detecting, and a huge swarm of their ships at that. But what the orks were attacking…

'Myrin?' he said, unable to believe what he was seeing.

'*Taenar,*' Myrin replied, his voice tightly controlled. '*Do you have an explanation?*'

'No,' Taenar said, swallowing. 'No, I do not.'

Because there, shuddering under the barrages of orkish fire, swarmed about by a defensive fleet that was both numerous and yet hopelessly outnumbered, was the craftworld of Ilmaren.

TWENTY-THREE

Gazruk Hackspanna had only gone and zoggin' done it.

The skrawnie-finder – now simply dubbed Da Machine – had worked! It had led the Badskab Bukkaneers to the edge of the system, out past the orbit of the final planet, to where its sun had receded to the point that it was more just a star with an attitude. And sure, Uzgul hadn't been best pleased at first when there was no immediate sign of the skrawnies, but then the Bukkaneers' scanners had – erratically, and without a great deal of certainty – picked up something of absolutely monstrous size bearing down on them.

Gazruk had heard of the skrawnies' world-ships, the big chunks of whatever-the-zog on which a lot of them flew around the galaxy, but this was the first time he'd seen one. And honestly, he had to admit that he was kind of impressed. The sheer size of it put even the largest space hulks to shame, and it was obviously a lot more deliberate than a hulk. Their meks had clearly planned this out all proper, not just let stuff mash together in the warp until floors became ceilings and up became sideways. Of course, it didn't have nearly enough guns on it – if Gazruk had made it then he'd have included at least one kannon the size of a regular ship, or what was the point? – but it was a monumental feat of engineering nonetheless.

'Alright, ladz,' Uzgul da Magnificent had declared, a smoking cigar clamped between his teeth and his five-cornered hat pulled down at a suitably rakish angle. 'Let's give 'em a kickin'.'

And a kickin' had begun.

The skrawnies were game enough, Gazruk supposed. They launched their fleet, and even the big ones were zippy little buggers that dodged all over the place and usually looked like they were ahead or behind or next to where they *actually* were, which wasn't really in the spirit of things. And sure, their weapons hit hard, and were quite capable of blowing even a kill kroozer apart in a diverting shower of short-lived flame and high-velocity debris. There weren't that many of them, though, not in comparison to the Bukkaneers, and they didn't seem to be quite as effective as usual.

'See, Gazruk?' Uzgul said in a self-satisfied manner, pointing. 'Da nippy little gits ain't so hot once you pin 'em in place like dis. Yeah, so dey can outrun us when dey're runnin' away, so what? If dey run away now, we just get to put all da ladz down on dere doorstep wivout any bovver. If dey stay an' try to fight us off, we blow 'em out of da zoggin' stars, an' *still* put da ladz down!' He chuckled, took a long drag on his cigar, and puffed the smoke out happily. 'Dis was a marvellous idea of mine, it's gotta be said.'

Gazruk nodded silently, not trusting himself to answer. It had been *his* idea to build a machine to find the skrawnies, and *his* work that had actually managed it, too. And sure, he hadn't built it specifically to find a skrawnie world-ship, but the fact remained that were it not for him, Uzgul probably wouldn't be here at all. Huge though it was, the skrawnie vessel had been running with very few lights across its surface. It was entirely possible that it would have slunk quietly past the system without announcing itself in any way, and the Bukkaneers would have been none the wiser about its presence.

Gazruk frowned. 'So why's it here?'

'Wot?' Uzgul demanded, turning to look at him.

'Da gits don't wanna fight,' Gazruk said, puzzling it through. 'We… I mean, *yoo* are giving 'em a kickin', just like ya said. But dey didn't change course once dey saw us, just kept comin'. Skrawnies don't normally run into a fight unless dey're da ones wot're starting it, an' yoo're lookin' da uvver way.'

'We'd catch da big fing even if it ran,' Uzgul pointed out as though that ended it, but Gazruk wasn't convinced.

'Yes, boss, but–'

'*Kaptin.*'

'Yes, *kaptin*, but dat don't normally make no difference, do it?' Gazruk said. 'Skrawnies don't just charge straight into ya just for a scrap.'

'So wot're yoo sayin', Gazruk?' Uzgul demanded. 'Since yoo seem to fink yoo're da skrawnie expert around here.'

This was dangerous territory, Gazruk knew. He could hear the anger in Uzgul's voice at the suggestion that he, the all-powerful freebooter kaptin, might have missed something. However, Gazruk hadn't gone to all this trouble to build a skrawnie-finding machine only for the gits to slip out of sight unexpectedly and him somehow be landed with the blame. There had to be a reason for why they'd barrelled on without slowing or trying to evade…

Something clicked.

'To get to da uvver side!' Gazruk exclaimed. He hurried to the scanner and sensor arrays, and started flipping switches and fiddling with dials. He couldn't have told anyone exactly *why* he was doing any of it, because that wasn't how being a mekboy worked. Gazruk knew what needed to be done with technology, and so that was what he did. He couldn't imagine any other way of doing it.

'Wot're yoo doin'?' Uzgul thundered, while Runk and Skizz

gibbered and cackled behind his ankles at seeing their kaptin so riled, and the beating that would surely ensue.

'Dere!' Gazruk said triumphantly, pointing at the new reading the scanners had thrown up. 'Dat's wot da skrawnies are headin' for, an' dat's why dey kept goin'! Dey wanna get to da ring!'

'Wot ring?' Uzgul snapped, stomping over to peer at the readouts.

'One of da skrawnie rings wot dey're always zippin' in and out of,' Gazruk said proudly. 'Dere's a whoppin' great one not far off – big enough for dat fing to fit froo, I reckon!'

'Dat don't make no sense!' Uzgul protested. He slapped himself in the chest. 'If dere was a skrawnie ring dat size in *my* system, how come I ain't found it before now?'

Because yoo ain't half as smart as yoo fink yoo are, Gazruk's internal voice said. *An' yoo might know how to order a spaceship around, but yoo ain't dat hot wiv tek.*

'Well, it's big circle, innit?' his external voice said instead, well aware that it had the job of making sure his head stayed attached to the rest of his body. 'So da edges are a *long* way apart, but dere's also a whole lotta *middle*, wot ain't gonna show up on anyfing.' He frowned as a new string of glyphs ran over the screen. 'Also, its orbit is locked side-on to da star, so if yoo woz scannin' from inside da system…' He glanced sideways at Uzgul's thunderous expression, and did some hasty revisions. '*Or*, it's always possible dat it's shown up *just now* as part of some sneaky skrawnie trick, and da reason yoo never found it before is cos it weren't dere.'

'Dat sounds more likely,' Uzgul said firmly, glaring at him. 'Now, wot does it matter, anyway?'

'Well, kaptin,' Gazruk said carefully. 'If da big skrawnie-fing gets dere, it might get away, right? So dat means we ain't got as long to do wot we're doin'.'

A slow smile spread across Uzgul's face. 'Nah. Wot dat means is dat when dey try to get away, we're gonna be able to get inside dat ring wiv 'em!' He chuckled. 'No escape dis time, skrawnies! Anywhere yoo can go, we can go too!'

Gazruk rubbed his chin. He'd never been through a skrawnie-ring, and he'd never heard of an ork who had, either, or at least not one who'd come back out to talk about it. Something suggested to him that while out here belonged to the orks, *in there* was… well, it was skrawnie-space, and sneaky gits that they were, it might well give them some sort of advantage that he couldn't even imagine.

'Kaptin,' he said. 'Yoo ever been able to get a ship froo one of da rings wivout skrawnies doin' it first?'

'Nah,' Uzgul replied dismissively, 'da wibbly stuff just disappears.'

'So wot if, once we get *in*, we can't get *out* again wivout a skrawnie ship goin' froo first?' Gazruk asked. 'Den we'd be stuck in dere, and…' He tried to verbalise why his gut felt this was a bad thing, and quickly hit on something that might persuade Uzgul. 'An' den yoo'd be cut off from yer Dakkaplanet!'

'Wot!?' Uzgul bellowed, instantly outraged. 'Da little gits! So dat's dere plan! Well, I ain't fallin' for it! I ain't put all dose slaves to work just for dese gits to steal me away from it at da moment of triumph!' He grabbed the shouter-horn. 'All gits, listen up! Get da job done and get all yer captives loaded *before* da big skrawnie fing gets to the skrawnie-ring wot's just appeared!' He glared at Gazruk as he spoke, challenging the badmek to correct him, but Gazruk held his tongue.

At least, until new readings flashed into life on the scanner screens.

'Kaptin!' he said urgently, pointing at the sudden rise in detectable power levels. 'Da ring's activatin'!'

'Already?' Uzgul said, frowning in confusion. 'But even da skrawnies ain't anywhere near it yet.'

'Dose ones might not be,' Gazruk said as contact after contact appeared. 'I fink dey just got some friends!'

Uzgul clapped his massive hands together with a boom that sent Runk and Skizz diving for cover. 'Great! Da more da merrier, eh ladz?'

There was a resounding cheer from the bridge krew, with which Gazruk joined in. He was as happy as any other ork to see skrawnie ships get blasted into fine powder by orkish weapons, particularly the ones he'd helped design, although he'd have liked to have been able to fire some of them himself rather than just watch. Still, as more and more skrawnie ships appeared, it became apparent that this was not just a few reinforcements – this was an entire war fleet, and it was heading straight for them.

'Dis could get a bit tasty,' Uzgul muttered, apparently recognising the threat. He raised the shouter-horn again. 'Alright, ladz, looks like we've got some new gits comin' wot want a scrap. Nagrak! Guzbrag! Take yer ships and set up a screen, hit 'em when dey get in range. Mukkrug! Wait behind da uvvers, and krump any gits wot get froo…'

Gazruk tuned out Uzgul's orders – he had little interest in the tactical deployment of ships, which was something that came as naturally to Uzgul as technological know-how did to a mekboy – and focused on the readouts, looking to see if they'd missed anything important. Skrawnies could pull a surprise out of their sleeve at a moment's notice, and had a habit of wandering out of shadows you could have sworn you'd checked a moment before to knife you in the ribs. They were cunning, they were subtle, you had to be alert for the slightest hint–

'Uzgul!' the speakers bellowed, and Gazruk took a step backwards in surprise. That wasn't an ork voice, or even a grot – it was high, and thin, and though it was merely uttering a name it possessed such suffocating arrogance that it could have belonged to only one species in the whole galaxy.

'Uzgul! Your reign of terror ends today, and it will come at the end of my blade!'

'Wot's it sayin'?' Gazruk asked curiously as the unfamiliar syllables continued to erupt from the speakers.

'Dunno,' Uzgul said, killing the sound with a casual flick of a switch. 'But I recognise dat ship. Dat belongs to da head skrawnie freebooter wot keeps runnin' away from me. Looks like it's got tired of runnin'.'

He grinned.

'Big mistake. Bring us around, ladz, and ready all da dakka! Get da traktors an' da killsaws powered up, but don't bring 'em out until I tells ya! We got a skrawnie to krump!'

TWENTY-FOUR

Myrin Stormdawn, Prince of the Starsplinters, had hesitated.

Not from fear. Not from strategic uncertainty. The ork fleet attacking Ilmaren was a formidable foe, but his expert mind was already plotting vectors and battle lines, assessing threats and how he would counter them with the resources he had at his disposal.

No, the issue lay with Ilmaren itself. This was the first time Myrin had laid eyes on his former home since he had taken those of his fleet who would follow him – more than he'd expected – and left it behind. He had tried to put it from his mind in the decades since, but like an old love from whom the wounds had never properly healed, Ilmaren had always wormed its way back in. He had caught himself listening out for news, found himself gripped by a sick, self-hating joy when he heard of its hardships, subconsciously waiting for the impossible moment when Elthorn Caman would announce: *Yes, we were wrong and Myrin Stormdawn was right, our ways have only led us to doom.* But of course such an announcement never came, and so Myrin had watched from afar as his old home limped on, too stubborn to either change or to admit the faults that had driven him away in the first place.

His immediate response was denial. He wanted to turn around, plunge back into the webway, and leave Ilmaren to its fate. However, the accursed place was yet still too lodged in his heart for him to either take true pleasure in its demise, or just to let events take their course with a clear conscience. Even seeing it like this, dimly lit by stars and the distant light of the system's sun, reminded him of the good things he'd left behind – places and people and experiences that he had tried to forget, so that he could enjoy his life unfettered by regret.

'So… are we killing the orks?' Xela asked pointedly after Myrin had stared in silence for a few seconds.

'That's Ilmaren,' Issarel said quietly.

'I know damned well what it is,' Xela said in exasperation. 'You can all wallow in sentimental nostalgia later, if you wish. Right now, the Starsplinters will need direction from their new prince if he wants any hope of keeping them under his rule.'

She was correct. Myrin had brought his new fleet here with the promise of ork blood and freed captives – an idealistic notion perhaps, but a glorious one, and one that would disintegrate if he ordered his followers to abandon a craftworld to its fate, no matter how that craftworld had wronged him. Questions about exactly how this turn of events had come about could wait.

Besides, there were a lot of good people on Ilmaren who deserved better than the trouble they had been led into. That was what Myrin had been trying to say all along, so he would hardly look good if he turned down this opportunity to prove his point in favour of letting them die from the Seer Council's shortsightedness.

'Very well,' he muttered. 'Time to play the prodigal saviour.' He opened communications to all his ships again, cutting through the chatter of various captains demanding to know where they were, what craftworld that was, and what was happening.

'Starsplinters!' he declared. 'We have found our foe, albeit in unexpected company! I for one do not intend to let my former home take all the glory of their destruction! Strike hard, strike fast, get in amongst them, and we will cut them to pieces!' He closed the channel, and sent an impulse through the wraithbone circuits that sent the engines to full power. If he accelerated towards the combat then any of his corsairs who wanted to ask questions he couldn't answer – like how much of a coincidence it was that they had apparently come to the rescue of Ilmaren – would be faced with the choice of lagging behind and looking like cowards, or following him in anyway.

For a moment, as only a few of his escorts and closest allies began to move with *Light of Heaven*, Myrin thought he had miscalculated, that the rest of the Starsplinters would hang back, and then, in ones and twos, quietly retreat into the webway and leave him to die as he wished. Then the fleet sprang into action, solar sails run out and aetheric engines pushed to the maximum, and Myrin smiled wolfishly. Was there a greater feeling than this? To dive into an enemy's teeth and have others follow you, willing to fight and die at your command?

'I do hope Ilmaren isn't holding a grudge about you stealing some of their fleet,' Xela commented as they accelerated.

'I can't imagine that even they would be foolish enough to turn their guns on us once we've engaged the orks,' Myrin said with confidence. 'If they do, I will quite happily call for us to withdraw.'

'And you have no suspicions about its presence here?' Xela asked.

'What suspicions could I possibly have?' Myrin demanded.

'You don't think the fact we have a large contingent of ships that recently deserted from the craftworld–'

'Their leader has been unconscious!' Myrin pointed out, exasperated. 'They have had no input over our heading!'

'Leotharan was the one who provided us with the Bukkaneers' location!' Xela shouted, heedless of who else on the bridge heard her. Myrin opened his mouth to snap back again, but then paused. She was right.

'Yes,' he said slowly. 'He was. But Meliandril confirmed it independently, and as we can see, the information was accurate.' He sighed. 'It is not a coincidence that pleases me, but I led a fleet here to slay orks, and there are orks in front of us. What would you have me–' He broke off as Xela stiffened. 'What is it?'

'It's here,' Xela declared. '*Sunstompa*. Uzgul is leading this attack.'

'Good,' Myrin said, and he meant it. This was his opportunity to mark his ascension with a famous victory, not just over the Badskab Bukkaneers but over their vile leader as well. It was a well-known fact that killing an orkish warband's leader usually incapacitated it. Either its progress came to a standstill while the lieutenants fought each other for the command, or – if the warboss' end came in an ongoing battle rather than through an assassination – the brutes' cohesiveness would fall apart without a single voice and banner to rally behind.

'Set to broadcast on all wavelengths,' he said. 'I want the orks to hear this.'

'They won't understand it,' Xela said. 'Unless you've learned to speak their tongue, that is.'

'I don't care,' Myrin snapped. 'I want that abomination to know that I'm coming for it. It'll recognise its own name, if nothing else.'

Xela shrugged, and adjusted the controls. Myrin leaned forward.

'Uzgul!' he began forcefully, then paused, suddenly uncertain of what to say next. Perhaps Xela was right, and this *was* pointless, simply posturing into the void for the benefit of no one. However, he'd started now, and he needed to present a suitably impressive image to his followers, if nothing else. 'Uzgul! Your reign of terror ends today, and it will come at the end of my blade!'

That would probably suffice. He nodded at Xela, who killed the broadcast.

'Not your snappiest,' the former wych commented.

Myrin bristled. 'There was nothing wrong with it!'

'It was no "Shut up and die,"' Jhanandra put in. 'I thought that Space Marine Chaplain looked quite put out to be scolded in his own language, right before you put a blade through his throat.'

'He was being rather tiresome, and very repetitive,' Myrin recalled absently as he studied the changing layout of the battle. 'I find that the more fanatical the followers of their Emperor are, the more limited their vocabulary becomes.' He grunted. 'The orks are sending out a screen of light cruisers.'

'Break around them?' Xela suggested.

Myrin shook his head. 'The Bukkaneers tend to be well drilled, for all their savagery. My guess is that Uzgul would simply pivot them to keep them between us and the main body of its fleet, and then we will have lost both time and momentum.' He tapped his lips with his right forefinger. 'We shall have to break through.'

'That is surely what the orks want,' Issarel suggested cautiously.

'But not necessarily what they will expect,' Myrin pointed out. 'We have never engaged them head-on before, unless we were certain of victory. Let's give them a surprise. Of course,' he added, his fingers skating over the controls as he tweaked his fleet's approach, 'that doesn't mean we can't identify the inevitable weaknesses in their formation, and use those to our advantage.'

His ships adjusted their courses in response to his transmitted instructions… mainly.

'*Blade of Commorragh* isn't responding,' Xela reported. 'Baron Drazyth and his ships are going straight for that one with the horns on the prow.'

Myrin sighed. 'I am as great a proponent as anyone of the freedom and independence of the corsair life, but I must admit that the holdovers of Ilmaren fleet discipline are very useful to me as a commander.' He activated his messenger waves. 'Captain Wynlar, cover Drazyth's position on the right flank. Leotharan, on me, high and to starboard.'

'*Acknowledged, Prince Stormdawn,*' Taenar replied, and Myrin smirked for a moment at hearing his new honorific drop so easily from the lips of a former craftworlder. '*Will you be deploying grav-charges?*'

Myrin smiled. 'And here I was thinking I came up with that tactic *after* I'd left the Ilmaren fleet.'

'We are about to enter effective weapons range,' Xela warned. The ork ships had – mostly – held their fire to this point, which was another mark of the control Uzgul clearly had over its minions. Much as he hated the creature, Myrin was forced to acknowledge that it was obviously not simply a dull-witted brute, but had a clear grasp of both tactics and discipline. Only a fool underestimated their foe, despite their foe's appearance, and Myrin Stormdawn was no fool.

Now it was time to see if Uzgul had underestimated *him*.

'All ships, prepare for evasive manoeuvres,' Myrin instructed. 'Let them waste their ammunition, and don't get drawn into a firefight. Get into their midst, then pick your targets, and keep moving.' His words were probably unnecessary, since only a foolish aeldari captain would dally to exchange broadsides with an ork cruiser, but foolishness could overcome even the most level-headed in the heat of battle. That went double for corsairs, who were significantly more likely to put personal glory above collective success than, for example, the members of Ilmaren's beleaguered defensive fleet who were even now giving their lives in a futile attempt to prevent the orks from landing troops on their home.

Sparks of light were emanating from the ork ships now as their commanders activated their weapons batteries. Myrin waited until a gentle thrill ran through him from *Light of Heaven*'s sensors, indicating that its own weapons were at last in range. 'And... fire.'

The Starsplinters opened up as one, and the combat began in earnest. Myrin's ships danced and jinked and dodged, trusting to their agility and the confusing effect of their holofields to keep them safe from orkish ordnance as they flew into the teeth of the beasts' guns. It wasn't a perfect defence – the only perfect defence was not to be in the battle at all, as the saying went – but those firing the blazing batteries of huge-bore cannons and searing beams of energy more often than not found their intended targets were never quite where they had thought.

'Here they come,' Jhanandra muttered. Such discipline as the orkish screen had was never going to last once battle was joined and guns were firing. Their cruisers and escorts accelerated forwards with bellowing war cries broadcast across whatever frequencies they had access to, but this was no elegant dance of evasion such as the Starsplinters were performing. This was a brutish charge relying on speed alone, and their vectors were easy to calculate.

'As expected,' Myrin said with satisfaction. 'A screening tactic is only effective if correct distancing is maintained. A screen too close to the fleet's main body is no screen, whereas a screen too far removed is merely a collection of isolated targets that do not provide protection. Let us teach our foe how this game is played.'

He sent impulses out, and his gunnery crews obeyed. *Light of Heaven*'s manoeuvres meant their firing would be suboptimal, but Myrin had never intended for them to destroy the orks in their first pass. Ork ships were blocky, heavy things, usually fitted with layers of armour plating in addition to whatever unlikely energy shields their meks had cobbled together. Any damage his vanguard did would be useful, but these ships did not need to be destroyed to be removed from the battle.

He just needed to get between them, and with the orks accelerating towards them, that moment was approaching even faster than it would have done otherwise.

The two fleets raced towards each other at immense speed. Evading the orks' gunfire became more difficult as every second passed, but that same firing became more and more erratic as the kaptins stopped focusing on the damage their guns could do, and instead angled their craft with the intention of ramming headlong into the aeldari ships – an impact that would have devastating consequences for both sides, but from which the Starsplinters would inevitably come off worse.

They would never have the chance. If the battle of the Well of the Long Death had been like being trapped inside a small cage with a *ghor'vash*, this was like hunting the beast in the wild. You drew it out and used speed to avoid its strikes until it was exhausted and bleeding.

'Prepare to launch charges,' Myrin ordered as the two fleets closed on each other. An energy beam came within a hairsbreadth of clipping his main solar sail, but the orks had yet to land significant damage – only a couple of escorts and one of his smaller cruisers had been destroyed. These next few seconds would be crucial. Either the orks would get lucky as the two fleets passed each other at what was, for voidships, point-blank range, or sheer speed would defeat the enemy, and then Myrin's vanguard would be past and free.

That of course left the main body of his fleet, against whom the orks would undoubtedly happily fight and die while holding them up, but Myrin hopefully had a way of circumventing that.

'Three...' he said. 'Two... One... *Launch!*'

Ork and aeldari port and starboard batteries opened fire at similar times, brief and violent symphonies of destruction erupting outwards as the Starsplinter ships slipped away from their enemies' ramming attempts and aimed for the gaps in the orks' formation, such as it was. However, this was a secondary consideration. Myrin's ships deployed their grav-charges just before the two fleets flashed past each other, and the devices detonated scant seconds later. *Light of Heaven* felt the tug as the artificial gravity well blossomed into existence behind it, but it had enough momentum and distance to wrench itself clear, as did the other aeldari ships.

The orks, in contrast, were flying directly past the fields when they activated, and the sudden gravitational instability wrenched their ships off course. What had been gaps in their screen became gaping holes as their kroozers were pulled not only away from their intended trajectories, but towards each other. Wild gunfire lashed out from veering vessels, largely missing the Starsplinters, but increasingly raking across similarly beleaguered and rapidly closing allies. Orks being orks, such accidental fire quickly became deliberate, since each ship assumed it had been targeted on purpose and responded in kind, and short and violent conflicts erupted as they tore each other apart in anger and frustration.

'*Nicely done, Prince Stormdawn,*' Taenar said in his ear.

'That was merely the prelude,' Myrin replied with a smile. 'Now for the main performance.'

The rest of the orkish fleet was shifting position now, preparing for a battle on two fronts as those who had not been aware of the approaching Starsplinters picked up on their presence. Some of the largest battleships had already turned, however, and Myrin recognised *Sunstompa* amongst their number.

'I know that expression,' Xela said from beside him. 'You're not thinking of being literal about your threat, are you?'

'Not *literal,*' Myrin corrected her. 'I don't intend my blade to get involved. There seems little point in risking a boarding action where our craft might get shot out from beneath us. However, yes, I intend to be the one that strikes the killing blow to that monstrosity of a vessel.'

'Just don't lose sight of the wider picture,' Xela cautioned. 'There's no point ending Uzgul if we die in the process.'

'That's the problem with you drukhari,' Myrin said, winking at her. 'No sense of romance.'

Explosions behind them signified that some of the corsairs had slowed to execute those Bukkaneer screening ships that hadn't blown each other up, but the rest of Myrin's fleet were still inbound. The orks had not been expecting an attack from this angle, and while the Starsplinters would not have the advantage for long, it was long enough to count.

'Attention, warriors of Ilmaren,' Myrin broadcasted as *Light of Heaven*'s weapons opened up in earnest for the first time. 'This is Prince Myrin Stormdawn. Your deliverance is at hand, courtesy of the Starsplinters.'

'A bold claim to make before the battle has properly begun,' Issarel commented, but Myrin brushed their words away.

'If you wait until you have done something to claim that you will do it, the words are meaningless,' he said. 'Either we shall succeed and I will be vindicated, or I will die and I won't care.'

'Not a particularly encouraging sentiment for the rest of us,' Xela muttered.

'If you would like to broadcast your caveats, then by all means get your own ship and do so,' Myrin snapped at her. 'Until then, limit your words to updates, if you please.'

He relaxed into *Light of Heaven*'s circuits, feeling his consciousness flow through the ship until it was an extension of his very will. He relied on his crew to carry out his wishes, but the guiding mind, the genius behind every pitch, yaw and roll, and every weapon discharge, was Myrin Stormdawn.

'I have a battle to win.'

TWENTY-FIVE

'Did you know about this?' Taenar demanded as *Dance of Dying Seasons* plunged into battle alongside *Light of Heaven*.

'About what?' Ra'thar Kyldran replied. 'You knew as well as I that the purpose of our mission was to ensure Myrin Storm-dawn was able to fulfil his role in saving Ilmaren.'

'Yes, but here? So soon?' Taenar said. The starscape outside wheeled across the viewports as he rolled to evade the brunt of an orkish broadside, although the ship still shook as some shells clipped their flank.

'I must admit, I had been expecting to be absent for far longer,' Ra'thar said. 'I feared it would be years, perhaps even decades, before we saw our home again. Are you not glad that we can put this ridiculous charade behind us and return to a place where life makes sense, with rather fewer impulsive murders?'

The image of Ellisar Elasandor impaled on his powerblade invaded Taenar's mind, and his concentration faltered for a moment until he pushed away both the lingering guilt and the blood-red, blood-warm tendrils of pleasure that accompanied the memory.

'The farseers speak as though they are manipulating events that will come to fruition a long time from now,' he pointed out.

'This is hardly that.' Sharp-nosed ork assault boats speared at *Dance of Dying Seasons* from starboard, but disintegrated under concentrated fire. The last thing Taenar wanted was orks aboard. Cithriel would relish the fight, but Taenar had far too much respect for the brutes' ability to wreak havoc in the most unexpected ways.

'You sound almost resentful of efficiency,' Ra'thar commented. 'Our brief intervention ensured that Myrin survived to lead the Starsplinters here at near full force, to help our world in its time of need.'

'Yes,' Taenar agreed absently, pulling away from an ork kill kroozer that was trying to target him. The temptation to engage with it was great, but he knew better than to indulge. He would apparently flee, the orks would follow him, and the next ship in the battle line would strafe across them from above, leaving *Dance of Dying Seasons* free to move on and engage the next. Greater speed and manoeuvrability to stay one step ahead of their potent but sluggish enemies was how the Starsplinters would win this fight. And Ilmaren, he added hastily to himself. That was how *Ilmaren* would win this fight, with the Starsplinters as their allies. Their unwitting allies, not realising they were here simply due to farseer schemes…

His crews fired again, striking a medium-sized cruiser that appeared to be an amalgamation of three different human vessels, welded together with the inevitable orkish mix of innate ability and sheer optimism. His new quarry came around faster than he had anticipated, forcing him to cut to starboard, into the kill-zone of where his former pursuer would have been, had they not–

Dance of Dying Seasons shook under the impact of weapons fire, the feedback shooting through its wraithbone circuits like barbed lightning. Taenar desperately dived, trying to get out of range of the unexpected attack from the kill kroozer that should have been immobilised by now…

'*I understand you have recovered from your injuries enough to regain command, Leotharan,*' the voice of Saraan Skyhand said in his ear. '*I told you that we would resume this conversation if we both survived.*'

'And so you attack my ship now, in the midst of a different battle?' Taenar demanded desperately. But no, the kill kroozer *was* there, right where it shouldn't be, and *The Yearning Stars* was some distance away. In fact, *Dance of Dying Seasons* was rather further from help than Taenar had realised.

'*So melodramatic. I could have stabbed you in the back, as you did to my former captain. Instead, I merely left these creatures alive to deal with you for me. Worry not, I will avenge your death once their work is done.*'

'Or you could have faced me in single combat, and left my crew out of this!' Taenar retorted, desperately trying to find a vector that would minimise damage. The ship's superstructure was still intact, but he could feel the weaknesses where orkish artillery had struck home as though they were the shuriken scars in his own chest.

'*The betrayer does not get to choose how or where revenge finds him. Farewell, Taenar Leotharan.*'

'Starboard solar sail is badly damaged,' Faerys reported grimly from her station. 'The dorsal one is barely any better.'

'I know,' Taenar said through gritted teeth. Both cruisers he had just attacked were on them now, closing in from different directions. He forced *Dance of Dying Seasons* to accelerate, pushing ahead, but there was no salvation here, merely more ork ships. He was performing his own gauntlet run, just as the Starsplinters vanguard had in the opening engagement of this combat. However, this time he was on his own.

'I take it Skyhand has chosen the worst possible time to seek revenge?' Kyldran said as their ship shuddered from the impact of more orkish guns.

'Or the best, from their point of view,' Taenar said tightly. None of the damage *Dance of Dying Seasons* had taken was catastrophic – not yet – but that had the potential to change very quickly. Wraithbone was incredibly resilient, and could be grown back into a living whole rather than the crude welds or fixes of lesser species. Unfortunately, that was not something that could be done quickly, in the heat of battle.

He threw the ship into a disorientating spin, attempting to further confuse the guns of their hunters, but it was a tactic that could have only limited success. A cruiser was not a fighter craft, capable of rapid changes of direction or velocity such that it could come about and get the drop on a pursuing enemy. They were still more manoeuvrable than any individual ork ship, but no matter where Taenar turned, there were simply more orks.

A sharp warning notification alerted him to a hull breach, just fore of one of the main engines – ork assault boats had landed on the hull, and were boring their way in. Combat crews were already on their way to repel boarders, but it was yet another reason why they had to get clear.

'You wanted to go home, didn't you?' Taenar said to Ra'thar, putting everything they had into a sharp turn to port. 'Let's go home, then.'

It was a direct route, straight towards Ilmaren. The beleaguered craftworld might be under siege, but even a force the size of the Badskab Bukkaneers couldn't actually *stop* it short of somehow destroying its engines or seizing control of the helm, and it was still moving towards the massive webway gate through which the Starsplinters had arrived. Now Taenar was heading for it with all the speed he could coax from the engines of *Dance of*

Dying Seasons, and with an ever-increasing volume of ork ships in pursuit.

'What are you doing?' Ra'thar demanded. 'You're drawing them back towards the craftworld!'

'Exactly,' Taenar said through gritted teeth. 'I'm intending to make our problem *their* problem, and a large enough one that they won't be able to ignore it!'

'And if they destroy us along with the enemies on our tail?' Ra'thar said. *Dance of Dying Seasons* took another hit, and Taenar grimaced as the output of one of the engines began to fluctuate wildly.

'Then we will die a little closer to home than we would have done otherwise.' He opened a communications channel, connecting himself back into the Ilmaren command network. 'This is Admiral Taenar Leotharan aboard *Dance of Dying Seasons*, requesting immediate assistance.'

The channel chatter died down for a moment in shock. Taenar felt the sensors of other Ilmaren ships brushing over his own, confirming his identity as much through the familiarity of the wraithbone and its circuits as it was anything more prosaic.

'*Why should we help you, traitor?*' said a voice, which Taenar immediately recognised as Arissys Caellanar, a fellow admiral, and commander of *Dawn of Endurance*. '*You abandoned us, and come back now in the company of another traitor?*'

'Traitor?' Taenar echoed in disbelief. *Dance of Dying Seasons* was nearly through the ork fleet now, and still just about hanging together. The headlong flight had attracted the attention of a sizeable number of the orkish ships, and dragged them around and out of position. They were laid open for the guns of the remaining Ilmaren defenders, guns he could see pivoting towards him now.

'*What else would you call a commander who so badly degraded our defences?*' said another voice, one he could not place.

'We are here to save Ilmaren!' Taenar said desperately. Had the fleet's commanders not been informed of his mission? Yes, his meetings with Elthorn Caman had been circumspect, and he had been instructed not to talk about it, but...

'*You are more likely here to pick our bones,*' Caellanar retorted. '*Farewell, traitor.*'

'Wait,' Taenar tried, 'I–'

'*Help him.*'

The two words were spoken softly, but they carried both a weight of authority, and an inherent expectation of obedience. Taenar gritted his teeth, waiting for the volley of fire that would finally break *Dance of Dying Seasons* apart and seal his fate, and honestly wasn't sure if he wanted it to come from orkish or aeldari guns.

'*Of course, Farseer Caman,*' Arissys Caellanar said.

TWENTY-SIX

The battle was everything Myrin could have dreamed.

It was brutal, yes; unforgiving, yes. Ships were exploding and dying, leaving their crews to be flash-burned in raging fires or asphyxiated by the harsh void of space, assuming they didn't end up smeared across the prow of an entirely different vessel or blown apart by guffawing orkish gun crews. The messenger waves were filled with desperate shouts and cries as captains tried to hold their ships together or begged for help as they came under fire, or whooped in savage joy as they claimed another enemy. Many aeldari lives were being lost – precious lives, lives that had been cultivated over decades, centuries, even millennia, and each one worth far more on its own than those of the entire fleet of monstrosities against which they were opposed. This should have been a combat of miserable arithmetic, each loss digging into his soul like thorns of guilt and sorrow.

They didn't.

This was life at its most beautiful, riding the razor's edge with destruction's jaws yawning on either side. Myrin had no pity for those who shied away from such an experience, and little for those who succumbed to its perils. This was his moment. Every aeldari life here was in his hands. The Starsplinters were in combat because he had decreed it, and each death was simply a testament to his power, that he could drive such timeless, beautiful beings to their end simply through the force of his own will. Meanwhile, Ilmaren and its defenders would owe their lives to him at the end of this battle. They would have been lost, overwhelmed by the freebooters had Myrin and his ships not arrived, but the Starsplinters had swept down on the orks like vengeance incarnate. Their plan of attack was fluid, swift, deadly, and it was *working*.

'We're winning,' Xela announced cautiously, flicking from one readout to another as though making the pronouncement against her will. 'It's bloody, but we're winning. The orks' losses outpace ours by roughly three to one. At this pace they'll either break and flee, or we'll wipe them out. We'll have lost a lot of ships, us and Ilmaren both, but–'

'But nothing,' Myrin said. *Light of Heaven*'s guns raked across another enemy, which came apart like a child's toy crushed underfoot. He had lost track of *Sunstompa* in the chaos, but he would find it before long, even if he had to cut the entire orkish fleet apart in the process. 'We came here to break this beast and its forces, and that's what we'll have done.'

'I thought we were here to free slaves,' Issarel said.

'We would find it hard to do that with the orks harrying us at every turn,' Myrin replied. 'What purpose does it serve to free slaves, if Uzgul remains alive to capture more?'

'It would probably matter a great deal to the slaves in question,' Xela pointed out, but Myrin waved her words away.

'We are committed now.' He smiled wolfishly as another ork ship died, although whatever foul creature was at its helm managed to careen the vessel into a limping Starsplinter frigate, so that the final explosion took both ships down. Something new caught his attention on the sensors, and he frowned at it.

'Xela, why are all those ork ships breaking for Ilmaren? Is it some sort of last-ditch attack run?'

'Maybe,' Xela said, her fingers skating over her vambrace. Her brow furrowed in turn. 'Wait, they're being led by... No, they're *chasing* a single ship.' She looked up at him, her expression troubled. 'It's *Dance of Dying Seasons*.'

The words went through Myrin like an ice wind. 'Taenar. Why is he so far out of position?'

'And why is he making a run for Ilmaren, instead of back to us?' Jhanandra added meaningfully. Myrin shot her a glare, but his Bladesworn met his eyes with a defiant expression.

'Taenar,' he said, sending out a messenger wave. 'Taenar, what are you doing?'

Only silence met him, but Myrin knew this silence. This was not the simple emptiness of a message received and ignored. It was fuller, and more stifling.

'Ilmaren interference,' he said grimly. 'They're jamming him.'

'How can you be sure that they're jamming him, rather than *he's* jamming *us*?' Xela demanded, and Myrin found that he had no answer.

Ilmaren's defenders had taken the opportunity to get back into a defensive formation after the majority of the Badskab Bukkaneers had broken off to fight the Starsplinters, but now they began to shift, angling their guns towards the onrushing mass of ships. Myrin could imagine the commands flying back and forth across the fleet to which he had once belonged. One aeldari life was worth more than the entire orkish force, that was true enough, but what price the lives of aeldari deserters, fleeing towards you ahead of a cluster of enemies? The safest thing to do – and the lesson to other would-be traitors – would be to eliminate them all. Myrin could almost hear Farseer Caman's voice: better those aeldari die, and the orks along with them, than risk loyal Ilmaren lives through trying to place shots.

The Ilmaren fleet opened fire, and Myrin's hands clenched into fists. If those short-sighted fools destroyed *Dance of Dying Seasons*, he would not be satisfied with a victory over the orks. Visions seized him of ordering the Starsplinters into the attack on the very craftworld they had thrown themselves into battle to protect; of his ships, guided by his knowledge of this enemy, effortlessly predicting and avoiding Ilmaren's defensive patterns; of finally forcing Elthorn Caman to admit the grave mistake they'd made in forcing Myrin out…

'Your former people know how to shoot, I'll give them that,' Xela commented, her pale eyebrows rising as she studied her vambrace.

Myrin snapped out of his momentary reverie, and focused on the readouts again. The ork ships were being surgically dismantled. The guns of Ilmaren's defenders could barely miss, given how close together this group of Bukkaneers had packed themselves in their pursuit of Taenar's ship, and yet through the storm came the single point of light that was *Dance of Dying Seasons*. Unchallenged, untouched by Ilmaren fire… and not pulling away again, but settling into place amongst the Ilmaren ships as though it had never been away.

As though that had been its destination all along.

Rage rose up inside Myrin, fierce and hot and utterly directionless. He wanted to cut the Ilmaren fleet apart for their part in whatever this was. He wanted to blow that damned ship up, snatch Taenar Leotharan from its wreckage, and… And what? Make him *answer*, for one thing. Make him admit that he had been lying, had always been lying; or watch him sink to the floor and protest that he was now and forever a Starsplinter, sworn to do Myrin's bidding, and he would never–

'Myrin!' Xela yelled, and *Light of Heaven*'s motion was suddenly and violently arrested.

'What is it?' Myrin shouted, scanning his readouts, trying to *feel* the answer to his own question through *Light of Heaven*'s circuits. Something was wrong, something was very wrong indeed. It was as though they were an archaic sea-going vessel that had run aground on a reef or a sandbank. Yet there was no catastrophic damage to the hull – they had not been rammed, had not blundered into some massive broken spar of wreckage which now pinned them in place. What could be–

Sunstompa.

The accursed ork ship had managed to manoeuvre itself behind them without them noticing. It was out of line of fire of virtually all their guns, and was drawing them in with some sort of immense tractor beam. Myrin braced for the inevitable hail of fire, since even orkish gunners could barely miss a target of this size, at this range, without the ability to evade, but no such barrage came. Then two enormous, serrated metal discs unfolded on articulated arms from beneath *Sunstompa*'s prow, and Uzgul's plan became clear. He was going to rend *Light of Heaven* apart, piece by piece, with those gargantuan circular saws; the closest an ork starship kaptin could come to the beasts' love of brutal close combat.

Well. Not quite the closest.

Myrin threw the drives to full, just in case, but to no avail. Crude though orkish technology often was, it was usually both effective and durable, since Myrin had no doubt that those orks who made substandard devices were not permitted to survive long by their superiors. He could stay here and attempt to outpower something which had undoubtedly been designed to hold ships such as his in place until his engines were carved up and all hope was lost, or he could save as many of his crew as possible and take the fight to his enemy.

'Abandon ship,' he ordered, broadcasting the order to all. He wasted no more words than that; those who ignored his instruction could take responsibility for their own fate. 'Assault crews, to your shuttles. We will kill this monster ourselves.' He ended the communication and the bridge crew immediately began to obey him, leaving their stations and racing for the docking bays, but Myrin held up a hand to stop Jhanandra. 'I must ask to you remain here. Do whatever you can to keep Uzgul's focus on this ship, so it doesn't see us coming for him.'

Jhanandra scowled. 'We have had this argument before, but I *am* your Bladesworn.'

'And you will be protecting me in a different manner,' Myrin assured her.

Jhanandra rolled her eyes, but took his place at the control stations with barely a tremble in her lip to betray her acknowledgement of the likely death sentence she had just received. 'If you live, I expect you to come and find my spirit stone. And I expect you two to hold him to it,' she added, pointing at Issarel and Xela.

'Of course,' Myrin said, although he doubted their odds were going to be much better than hers. He smiled at Xela. 'It appears that the reference to "my blade" was not poetic licence after all.'

'Poets don't win battles, my prince,' Xela snapped, checking her knives and anchoring her helm in place. 'Let us hope that blade is still as sharp as your tongue.'

TWENTY-SEVEN

It was nice to see your work put to good use, Gazruk thought. The pilot of the skrawnie ship had thrown it around all over the place in a desperate attempt to escape, but Gazruk's supatraktors hauled it towards them nonetheless, and the megakillsaws he'd created began to tear into its hull. Ramming other ships was all well and good – it was very fun, and definitely made Gork and Mork happy – but there was something extremely satisfying about a more methodical approach. He was a mek, which meant he took delight in making machines, but he got a great deal of pleasure from taking them *apart*, as well. He watched with interest as the saw blades carved their way into the guts of the skrawnie vessel, slicing off chunks of strangely configured interior.

Of course, some orks took a less intellectual approach to the whole thing.

'Come out, skrawnie!' Uzgul da Magnificent bellowed. 'Where are ya? I'm wreckin' yer ship, ya cowardly little git!' He threw a lever forward, and the right-hand killsaw plunged even deeper. Gazruk opened his mouth to say something, as a premonition struck him, but he was slightly too slow.

Sunstompa rocked as the sky turned white in front of them.

When Gazruk picked himself up from the floor that had quite unexpectedly come up to meet him, and blinked the bright spots out of his vision, he saw that the killsaw Uzgul had just been plunging with so much glee into the skrawnie ship was now little more than a melted mass of metal. The enemy vessel, however, was now spread over a somewhat larger area than it had been a few moments before.

'Hah!' Uzgul said in slightly dazed triumph. 'Must've hit da engines! Dat was a good'un!' His expression soured somewhat. 'But still no bang. I tell ya, Gazruk, one day I'm gonna figure out how to make an explosion so big dat yoo can hear da bang in space!'

'Maybe da Dakkaplanet will do it, kaptin,' Gazruk muttered. He didn't know why you didn't get bangs in space, either. He'd heard that it was something to do with there not being any air, which didn't make any sense to him, since he'd not yet found a pair of lungs which had ears, nor ears that could breathe, so the two things seemed entirely unrelated. However, part of being a mek was not only being willing to push yourself into new frontiers of discovery, but also understanding when a certain frontier of discovery was just going to be *boring*. You didn't get bangs in space, and that was an end to the matter so far as Gazruk was concerned. He was better off focusing his attention on more interesting stuff, like whether he could fit cutta beams to his megakillsaws.

'Well, dat was fun,' Uzgul said, hitting the button that disengaged the traktors. The remains of the skrawnie ship began to drift away, and the kaptin looked around briskly. 'So wot's goin' on? I know da gunz have been firin', how many skrawnies are left?'

'Quite a lot, kaptin!' reported Bazgit the lookout, eyes affixed to the make-bigger tubes.

'Good, still plenty of fun to be had,' Uzgul said, rubbing his hands together in satisfaction. Gazruk, on the other hand, while not always the ork who paid the closest attention to anything not involving wires and electricity, had picked up on a certain amount of trepidation in Bazgit's voice.

'A fair few of da ladz've got krumped, kaptin,' Bazgit continued. Uzgul waved one massive hand dismissively.

'Eh, serves 'em right for somefing or uvver, I'm sure. Let's get–'

'So when I said "a fair few", I kinda meant "a lot",' Bazgit interrupted him, although he at least had the sense to remove his eyes from the viewfinder so he could see whether or not Uzgul was about to wallop him for his temerity. 'Da gits are winnin', kaptin!'

'Dat don't sound right,' Uzgul said with a snort. 'Skrawnies, overcomin' da Badskab Bukkaneers?' He strode over with shocking speed and shoved Bazgit out of the way so hard that the lookout collided with the far wall, then applied his own face to the eyepieces. 'Oi, Bazgit! Wot've yoo done to dis fing? I can't see hardly any of our ladz!'

'Dat's wot I was tryin' to tell ya, kaptin!' Bazgit protested. 'Da skrawnies've krumped 'em!'

Uzgul sucked his teeth noisily. 'Should've known dis lot couldn't handle 'emselves in a fight wivout me tellin' 'em wot to do all da time. Honestly, ya take a moment to enjoy slicin' up da ship of some git wot's been causin' ya problems for ages, an' half yer ladz go an' get scragged! It's like no one's got any *pride* any more.' He stood back from the viewfinder and snapped his fingers. 'Gazruk! Get on da shouta! I want Skagbad and Grimsnap to bring dere ships around! Tell Mozzgoff's lot to get dere arses back dis way, an'–'

But Gazruk never found out what Mozzgoff's lot was meant to do, because at that point, and with no prior warning, the bridge doors blew inwards.

* * *

There had been no order in the headlong charge through *Sunstompa*. Myrin had led the attack insofar as everyone there deferred to him, but he had not insisted on a place at the front. Speed was of the essence – the fastest got into combat first, and the rest would catch up when they could. The same held true when they reached the bridge, and although Myrin fully intended to end Uzgul's life himself, he did not manage to be the first, or the second, or even the tenth through the doors.

It turned out that his crew were not going to be taking the glory. Several aeldari bodies were already lying at the feet of Uzgul da Magnificent by the time Myrin laid eyes on it, and the ork was breaking another corsair's neck with its bare hands. It was enormous – perhaps half again as tall as an aeldari if it rose from its brutish stoop, with fists nearly the size of Myrin's torso – and clad in a riot of colours and fabrics that made even its followers look drab. Precious gems glittered in its nose and ears, and entire panels of its clothes were covered in the teeth the creatures used as currency, but the most sickening and enraging form of self-decoration were the multiple spirit stones dangling from its neck as crude pendants, worn as rings on its massive fingers, and even – Myrin choked back his rage – used as cufflinks on its coat. It looked up as Myrin bellowed its primitive name, and he saw the spark of recognition in its bestial features. It knew who he was.

Myrin's sorrow at the lost lives was eclipsed by twin flares of rage and fierce excitement at the thought of finally slaying this beast that had polluted the galaxy for so long. He cut down three onrushing orks without thought, easily evading their clumsy swings and letting his void sabre taste their flesh, before snapping a shot off with his fusion pistol at their chieftain.

Uzgul, however, did not move like his underlings. The huge ork was shockingly fast, and had already dodged aside from where the blast was aimed. Myrin thought Uzgul was simply running, but then the ork snatched down an enormous two-handed axe from the top of what Myrin realised was a throne, and lunged into the attack.

'Bladesworn, to me!' Myrin shouted, rolling aside from a swing that sounded like the air was being torn in two by the axe blade. Issarel was there immediately, thrusting with a power sword, but the energised blade was turned aside by hidden armour within Uzgul's coat, and the Bladesworn had to leap backwards to avoid Uzgul's counterstrike. The ork was ferociously fast, Myrin realised, and fully capable of killing him with a single blow. He grinned savagely at the challenge, and launched a lightning-quick series of cuts with his void sabre that Uzgul mainly caught on the haft of its axe, then whirled at the last moment to lose a few threads of a golden epaulette to the tip of Myrin's blade. Xela, who had darted in behind Uzgul with her knives, flipped athletically out of reach again and left the freebooter kaptin to bury its axe in the floor panels with a frustrated roar.

Gazruk heard Uzgul's roar of rage, and looked up from clubbing another skrawnie in the head to see the head skrawnie and two of its nobz – one with a plethora of knives and a weird shell-like thing on its back, the other clutching a pair of swords like skreamers had – attacking the kaptin from all sides. It was tempting to leave them to it, as memories rose up of thinly veiled threats and Uzgul kicking his machine, but Gazruk wasn't the sort of coward who let others settle his scores for him.

'No ya don't,' he muttered, and hurled one of his inventions.

The lifta-cube landed at the shellback's feet, and activated a targeted field that thrust the skrawnie upwards and held it pinned against the ceiling while it thrashed its arms in surprise and impotent rage. Gazruk chuckled, then had to duck as another one of the other gits tried to decapitate him. He activated his wrist-burna this time, and the skrawnie came to a staggering halt with its torso half-severed and the stink of burning flesh filling the air. The zoggin' thing was slower after that, and barely even moved before Gazruk staved in its skull.

He looked up to check on the shellback, just in time to see it disappear.

'Wot da zog…?' Gazruk muttered, the fight around him forgotten for a second. The skrawnie hadn't gone through the ceiling, or anything like that. It was simply *gone*. It was like it had tellyported, but Gazruk didn't think the skrawnies knew how to tellyport…

It reappeared next to his lifta-cube, stepping out of nothing as swiftly, smoothly, and disconcertingly as it had disappeared into it. Gazruk caught a momentary flash of sharp teeth as it smiled, then it kicked the gadget across the floor towards him, and suddenly *he* was being crushed against the ceiling.

'Dat does it!' Gazruk raged, grabbing for his control belt. Did this zoggin' skrawnie really think he'd create a device he couldn't turn off? However, his fingers brushed against something else instead.

The kill switch for Da Machine.

Incorporating it hadn't even been an intentional thing, not really. Gazruk had this, well, call it a *need*, to not necessarily make things blow up, but definitely to make sure that they *could* blow up. He just thought better if he was building stuff around a bomb, for some reason. There was an awful lot of power flowing through Da Machine, and while using it to find skrawnies had definitely been an entirely valid use for it, it had felt like such a waste for it not to also have the potential to go bang. It hadn't taken much by the way of rewiring and, to be honest, Gazruk felt like the result was a far truer reflection of what he'd intended in the first place. Besides, it also meant that he had a handy distraction if Uzgul turned on him, plus it would ensure that if the kaptin tried to off him and get some other mek to operate it in Gazruk's place, he'd never be finding another skrawnie with it again.

Finding skrawnies wasn't the problem now, though – the gits were already here, and causing all manner of havoc. And possibly Gazruk should have thought about it a little longer, or a little harder, but he'd just been made to look a fool by a skrawnie, and he wasn't having that.

He pressed the button.

The decking panels of the bridge blasted upwards without warning in multiple places as tongues of flame erupted from beneath them. Combatants who weren't sent flying or imme-diately incinerated were knocked sprawling, then clawed for handholds as the floor partially collapsed into the raging inferno that now filled the chamber below. Still, on the upside – quite literally – Gazruk himself was currently pinned to the ceiling, and so was well away from the initial effects, other than a shard of decking metal nearly giving him a new eyebrow. His hand found the lifta-cube's controls on the second try, just before it slid through a rent in the floor, and he dropped down to what remained of the deck. It creaked alarmingly as he hit it, but just about held beneath his feet.

Say what you liked about unexpected detonations – and Gazruk's previous warbosses certainly had – but they could drastically change the course of a fight. The skrawnies, who had previously been doing what Gazruk would have grudgingly conceded was 'alright' against the bridge krew, were thrown totally off their stride. The Bukkaneers, on the other hand, accepted surprise explosions as something that just happened in fights – even fights that took place on spaceships – and carried on without missing a beat, resulting in a sudden and violent turnaround as various skrawnies fell with choppas buried in their necks or with gaping slugga wounds in their chests.

Even the skrawnie kaptin and his nobz were affected. The kaptin and the shellback stumbled, while the skreamer, whose swords had just taken off one corner of Uzgul's hat and the tip of his ear, and only missed removing half of his head along with it thanks to the kaptin's superb reflexes, suddenly lost its footing as the deck panel onto which it had staggered gave way…

It only took a moment.

Myrin had called for his Bladesworn to join him because he knew they would only have got involved anyway, and so it was best if he could plan for it. However, he was prepared to admit that Uzgul was a formidable adversary, and that possibly – just possibly – he might have been overwhelmed had he faced the massive ork by himself. Myrin had managed to land a shot with his fusion pistol, leaving a smoking wound in Uzgul's shoulder, but the freebooter kaptin was holding its own against the three of them despite the injury. Nonetheless, they were wearing it down, and getting closer to landing a truly telling blow, when half of the floor exploded.

Myrin ducked as a piece of panelling flew through where his head had been a moment before, and sufficient heat washed over him to scorch his finery, and even register through the void suit he wore beneath. He didn't waste time wondering what had happened. It could have been anything from a piece of orkish machinery suffering a critical overload, to a torpedo from one of his ships striking just below the bridge. The cause was unimportant compared to the effect, which was to knock him and his Bladesworn off balance while Uzgul, far heavier than any of them, kept its feet without trouble. The beast bellowed with rage, and swung for Issarel.

It was a brutal blow, but Issarel saw it coming. On steady footing, they would have been able to lean back without a problem, causing Uzgul to miss by a couple of crucial inches. However, when dealing in such fine margins, any mistake was disastrous. Issarel's right foot went through the floor, and what should have been a sure-footed evasion sent them lurching into the path of Uzgul's weapon instead.

There were no second chances against an ork of Uzgul's size. Myrin and his Bladesworn had wounded it, bloodied it, but those were little more than nicks which might slow it down over time. When Uzgul's weapon finally connected, it was instantly lethal. Time seemed to slow down for Myrin, sufficient for him to see the details in all their horror, but not enough to do anything about it. Issarel's armour and body parted before the axe head with an audible *crunch*, and they flew backwards to hit a bulkhead, then smeared down to the floor, still in one piece more by a technicality than anything else. A brave warrior, broken apart by a single misstep.

Myrin screamed without words, a feral yell of challenge and vengeance that tore out from between his teeth as he threw himself at Uzgul. The ork whirled back towards him, but only succeeded in presenting its massive chest as a target for Myrin's void sabre. The blade sheared through a decorative chain and the coat leather beneath it, then plunged on to pierce the brute's skin and thrust deep into its flesh. Myrin felt the edge grate along a rib bone, then the lack of resistance as the tip punctured a lung and slid in halfway to the hilt. Uzgul bellowed as pain overloaded its senses, finally giving Myrin a window for a clear shot. He brought his fusion pistol up to trigger it point-blank into the ork's face–

Even wounded, Uzgul's incapacitation lasted only for a moment. It slammed one arm down, knocking Myrin's fusion pistol from his grasp with a sickening snap and white-hot spear of breaking bone in his wrist, half-spinning him away with the force of it. Myrin's other hand was torn from his void sabre's grip, but fury had a hold of him sufficient to numb the pain. He rolled with the impact, came fully around, and leaped into the air to lash out with one boot in retaliation.

A kick to the chest – or even the face – of Uzgul would have been a pointless endeavour; the ork was simply too big and too strong to pay much attention to an unarmed blow from any aeldari. However, the toe of Myrin's boot was not aimed for a hard plane of muscle, or even a nerve ending or pressure point. Instead, it struck the protruding pommel of his void sabre, and slammed the blade into the ork's chest to the hilt. Uzgul gave a great, gasping cough, its bestial eyes widening in surprise and pain, and what might just have been fear. Myrin landed on his broken wrist and groaned, but grinned at the thought that he might have inflicted the beast's deathblow.

'You will die on my blade!' he shouted triumphantly, struggling to push himself up. Huge though the ork was, Myrin's void sabre was still anathematic to life, and the tendrils of its influence would soon start creeping through Uzgul's tissues.

Xela, it seemed, was not content to wait.

She launched herself at Uzgul from behind, and her knives hacked downwards into the ork's back like climbing irons dug into a rock face. Uzgul roared and spun, throwing Xela off, but her knives remained embedded. She landed and rolled, coming up to her feet not far from Myrin with two more blades drawn and a snarl on her face. She threw herself forward into a sprint directly towards the freebooter kaptin, leaping over a missing floor panel. Uzgul bellowed and brought its massive axe down, but Xela blinked out of the way and appeared behind it. Uzgul sensed her arrival somehow and swung again, still deadly fast despite its wounds, but Xela's blink pack carried her out of danger once more, back to her original position.

Uzgul was too slow to reposition itself, disorientated from thrashing back and forth in pursuit of this black-clad menace. Myrin, groping for his fusion pistol with his uninjured arm, saw Xela spin a knife through her fingers and bunch her legs beneath her, ready to spring and take Uzgul's back again, this time to drag the razor's edge of her blade across the ork's throat and spray its blood over its own throne.

The blast of electricity struck Xela in the back. She screamed, her muscles cramping as the discharge washed through her. Myrin's head snapped around to see another ork, this one festooned with gadgets and clutching a massive spanner, lowering a sparking device that looked like the unholy union of a gun and a high-voltage maintenance tool.

Uzgul needed only a second. It spun back, more ponderous now but still deadly, whipping its axe towards Xela. Myrin's second-in-command activated her blink pack to warp out of the way–

–and it sparked.

Confusion crossed Xela's face for a moment, which rapidly morphed into an expression Myrin had never seen on her features before.

Panic.

Darkness swirled up around Xela, darkness with the faintest afterimage suggestion of grasping, taloned hands. Her eyes met Myrin's for a moment, silently pleading for help that he could not give, and then she was gone, just as Uzgul's axe swept through the space where she had been.

But this time, she did not reappear.

'Xela!' Myrin screamed. He launched himself to his feet, fusion pistol forgotten, Uzgul forgotten, reaching for the empty space where the shade runner had been a mere moment before, as though he could plunge his hands into it and haul her back out. She couldn't be gone. Myrin had said farewell to fellow warriors and lovers both former and current over the years, and had felt like something was being pared off his soul each time, but nothing like this. It was impossible. In his very core, down beneath the swagger and bravado that had even him convinced most of the time, Myrin Stormdawn had assumed from the moment he first appointed Xela as his second that when the time came for him to die, she would be standing over him and sighing in disappointment. Not this, not just *disappearing*–

Uzgul's next blow took him in the chest. Not with the axe head – the massive ork had misjudged its swing slightly – but with the haft. Myrin's feet left the floor before he'd even registered the first impact. The second impact came a moment later, when he struck the arm of Uzgul's throne. There was a momentary blinding pain in his back, and a *crack* that seemed to echo through his skull, and then he was staring up at the ceiling, draped across the throne's seat. He tried to roll off it, to find his fusion pistol, to force his battered body to keep *fighting*.

His body did not respond. His arms flailed weakly, but nothing below his chest moved.

Panic reached for him with choking hands as he tried again. It wasn't just that he couldn't move; he couldn't *feel*. There was no sensation from anything below his breastbone…

Gazruk shook his head in quiet disbelief. A skrawnie kaptin and two of its nobz out for blood, and Uzgul da Magnificent had still managed to scrag 'em. Of course, Gazruk had played his own part in that, by zapping one of them with his volta-blasta so its tellyporting device overloaded, and knocking another one off balance when the floor exploded. Thinking of which…

'Da skrawnies blew up Da Machine, kaptin!' Gazruk said, eager to head the truth off before it could make matters even worse. He cast a quick eye around the bridge to see if any of the gits were still on their feet and looking to put any more holes in him, but the krew had – just about – come out on top. 'Reckon dey must've worked out how we tracked 'em down, an' wanted to make sure we couldn't do it again!'

'Is dat so?' Uzgul asked, fumbling at the hilt of the sword in his chest. He managed to get hold of the narrow, blood-slicked thing at the second attempt, pulled it out with a grunt of effort and disgust, and threw it to one side. He blinked a couple of times, and stared suspiciously after it. 'Dat felt weird.'

'Well, you got stabbed, kaptin,' Gazruk pointed out, prodding his own wound where a skrawnie had stuck a sword into him before he'd clubbed its skull into pieces with a large wrench. 'It don't usually feel great.'

'Nah, dis was different,' Uzgul insisted. 'Dat fing's dodgy.' He limped to the still-intact part of the bridge controls, avoiding the holes in the floor beneath which the flames were starting to die down, and picked up the shouta. 'Alright, ladz, dis is da kaptin. Dat's enough for one day. Take wot we got an' get back to da Dakkaplanet. Da skrawnies'll be froo dere ring before too long anyway, an' I've just killed da leader, so job's a good'un.' He dropped the handset, and rounded on what remained of the krew. 'Yoo lot! Get us movin'!'

'Yes, kaptin!' the krew barked as one – more or less – and ran to their stations. *Sunstompa* shuddered into motion again, shouldering aside the remnants of the skrawnie ship it had carved up, and heading for the system's interior. Gazruk, ever alert to the potential need to find a way off a ship, quickly scanned what readouts were still working.

'Huh,' he said in surprise. 'Da skrawnies ain't followin'.'

'Course dey ain't,' Uzgul said wearily. 'Dey know wot'd happen.'

Ya mean, dey'd kill wot's left of us? Gazruk's internal voice said as he took stock of the respective ship numbers. Still, he wasn't going to question what seemed to him to be a stroke of good fortune. Now all he had to do was hope that they'd scored enough skrawnie captives for Uzgul not to consider the entire thing a waste of time, and decide that it was Gazruk's fault…

'Well waddya know,' Uzgul grunted. 'Dat one's still alive.'

'Wot one?' Gazruk asked, whirling around in case the shellback had reappeared again. But no, it was the skrawnie kaptin, weakly clawing at its surroundings with its arms. Its legs, however, were very clearly not obeying its wishes any longer.

'Bad luck for yoo, my lad,' Uzgul said, drawing himself up with barely a wince and grinning at the skrawnie. 'Yoo ain't runnin' away now…'

TWENTY-EIGHT

+Taenar.+

This voice did not arrive at Taenar's ears by messenger wave. Taenar turned, startled, and found himself confronted by a ghostly form standing on his bridge. The rune-encrusted robes were familiar; the long-handled witchblade, smeared with blood, was less so.

'Farseer Caman,' Taenar said, inclining his head respectfully towards the psychic projection. Elthorn Caman had never appeared to him in this manner before – Taenar was usually summoned to see the farseer in person, if necessary – and despite the words that had saved *Dance of Dying Seasons* from destruction, Taenar could not help but wonder whether this was Caman delivering a sorrowful goodbye in person before calling for his death. For the farseer to have taken the field in Ilmaren's defence was a chilling illustration of how far the orkish assault must have penetrated into the craftworld before help arrived and distracted the attackers.

+You have completed your mission marvellously, Admiral Leotharan,+ Elthorn Caman said. +The orkish fleet is in disarray, thanks to the arrival of the Starsplinters.+

Taenar let out a deep breath, and felt tensions ease in his shoulders that he had not even been aware were there. He knew of his capabilities as a voidship captain and as a tactician, but he had never felt truly comfortable in the role he had been obliged to play as a covert agent. At first he had thought that it was simply because he had little experience at it, and he might give the game away and so fail in his task. After a while, he realised it was because he did not enjoy deceiving others – especially not those like Myrin Stormdawn, who seemed to approach the galaxy with such genuine verve, living their lives as fully and completely as they could, and daring events to stop them.

'Thank you, farseer,' Taenar said, deciding not to voice those thoughts. He could feel Ra'thar Kyldran's eyes on him, and could not help but wonder what the warlock's report of his conduct would be. Many things could be excused as necessary for the deception to work, but Taenar knew well enough that not every-thing he had done was because it was strictly *necessary*.

+Now it is time for you to return home,+ Caman said, and another wave of relief washed over Taenar. He had been prepared to give his life in defence of his craftworld – he still was – but he had been unable to rid himself of the creeping fear that he would, somehow, end up banished in reality rather than as a cover. Taenar's mission had come from Elthorn Caman, and although the implication was that it was approved by the Seer Council at large, Taenar had never spoken to any of the other farseers about it. What if Caman had died? What if they had been cast out? It was not impossible – even the legendary farseer Eldrad Ulthran had been banished from the craftworld of Ulthwé for finally and dramatically overstepping his authority in the pursuit of what he thought was right. If a similar situation were to have unfolded on Ilmaren, who was to say that the truth of Taenar's mission would be known, or indeed acknowledged? He was not naive enough to think that even the wisest and fairest of aeldari had not, at times, ignored certain truths that were inconvenient to them.

'Thank you, farseer,' he said again with genuine gratitude. Tendrils of regret still lingered within at the notion of giving up the freedom of the corsair life, and he would have been lying to himself if he did not acknowledge that it called to him. However, Taenar had lived all his life by the Paths of Asuryan apart from the last few months, and he still trusted in their wisdom.

Besides, so long as he never lost himself to the extent that he got locked into an individual Path, the Path of the Outcast – which in truth was no Path at all – would still be open to him, should he ever wish to take it. But if he abandoned his home in favour of the uncertain and fickle ways of the corsairs, who was to say that he would have the strength of self to hold himself together? There was perhaps scope for a little more flexibility in word and deed than the Paths allowed without falling into complete degeneracy, but Taenar was wise enough to know that the exact boundary might be beyond his ken.

+It is time to bring this to an end,+ Caman said, and Taenar nodded firmly.

'Of course.' He let part of himself bleed into the ship's circuits again, examining the conflict's disposition. He had to admit that the Badskab Bukkaneers had given a good account of themselves, and wrecked aeldari vessels leapt out at him like a drukhari knife in the dark. The orks were being torn apart now, though, their commanders unable to properly adapt to the change from attacking a large, slow-moving target to being taken in the flanks by a far more manoeuvrable force. 'There appear to be two main knots of resistance left. If we concentrate our fire on–'

+We will withdraw.+

Taenar took a moment to register what Caman had said, then hastily recalibrated his plans accordingly. 'The craftworld's defences would be an asset, but perhaps not best-suited to a fast-moving conflict, especially if the enemy breaks and flees. We can–'

+You misunderstand me, admiral. *We* will withdraw. Order your ships to disengage. We will be into the webway while the orks are still occupied with the Starsplinters.+

Taenar exchanged a glance with Faerys Asuthien, but judging by the shock on her face it seemed that he had not been mistaken in what he'd heard. 'Farseer Caman. You are suggesting that we should leave the Starsplinters to their fate?'

+I am suggesting nothing, admiral. This is an order. And the corsairs are as free to retreat to the webway as we are.+

'Farseer,' Faerys said, struggling to keep her voice steady. 'The corsairs are fighting with the admiral's ships as a part of their formation. If he pulls those ships out without warning then the results could be catastrophic! The orks are still dangerous, and they will not hesitate to capitalise on any weakness…'

Taenar did a lightning-fast estimate of what the impact would be if all Ilmaren ships broke away from the combat, and winced. 'The captain is correct. The Starsplinters could yet be overrun. Such a loss of life–'

+Not Ilmaren life, admiral, and therefore not our concern. This craftworld has suffered enough.+

The bridge doors hissed open, admitting Cithriel Shelwe-nin, covered in blood – orkish blood, from the stink of it.

'Admiral,' Shelwe-nin began. 'The boarders have been–' She broke off when she saw Elthorn Caman's projection, and came to a halt. 'Farseer.'

+Exarch,+ Caman greeted her in turn. +I am giving the admiral his orders to withdraw.+ They returned their attention to Taenar. +Do not let all this work go to waste for the sake of ties forged under a cloak of lies.+

Taenar ignored the small stab of guilt that sentence elicited. It was easy enough, given that the sensation was overtaken by a surge of irritation. 'What work? The matter of a few months?

Myrin's vendetta against the Bukkaneers led him here, nothing else!'

Ra'thar Kyldran smirked. 'You see? I told you he suspected nothing.'

Taenar whipped around to stare at the warlock. 'What did you say?'

+Taenar,+ Elthorn Caman said gently. +The Starsplinters would still be engaged in meaningless skirmishes with these creatures had the orks not hounded Starsplinter ships and attacked the Well of the Long Death, and jolted Myrin Stormdawn out of his self-serving hedonism and into self-serving vengeance instead. But of course, he needed to survive that battle.+

Taenar's eyes widened as the implications landed. 'But… *you* gave the orks the location of the Well? You arranged for them to get through the fissures?'

+Orks are simple beings,+ Caman said. +They take unexpected occurrences as a sign from their barbaric gods, without pausing to consider other explanations. Implanting knowledge into their brains was one of the most unpleasant things I have had to do, but the beasts were none the wiser as to the source of their sudden inspiration.+

Taenar gaped at them. 'Do you have any idea how many aeldari died during that battle?'

+The lives of renegades are of little concern to me compared to the lives of the craftworld I am sworn to protect, many of which would have been lost had Uzgul not been stopped here and now.+ Caman sighed, and suddenly even their psychic projection looked old. +This was not a short-term solution to an immediate problem, Taenar. Ilmaren could have taken a different route and avoided these orks today. Had we done so – had Uzgul's rise been allowed to continue without this battle taking place – then destiny places it as a far more terrible foe in the future, and one from which there would be little escape for us. We had to play the role of bait, here and now.+ They snorted. +Stormdawn rejected us because he thought we were not proactive. He merely did not understand the timescale over which such matters play out. There are fewer and fewer opportunities for bloodless victories in this galaxy. A small sacrifice today prevents a catastrophe tomorrow.+

'Then Uzgul is dead?' Taenar asked, searching his readouts for evidence of *Sunstompa*. He found it swiftly enough, since the idiosyncrasies in design of ork vessels made it easy to pinpoint individual ships. It was not destroyed – it was surrounded by wreckage, but aeldari wreckage. Taenar frowned, a sick feeling rising in his stomach as he tried to identify the lost vessel.

+Its fate is sealed,+ Caman said. +I can sense this much. It has taken a wound which it may disregard for the moment, but which will leach its strength. It will not be long before another ork overthrows it, at which point the risk to our people is greatly lessened.+

'That is *Light of Heaven*,' Taenar said, horrified. He turned back to Caman. 'Did Myrin board *Sunstompa*? Did he deal that wound? Was that why he, specifically, needed to be here?'

+The specifics are of no consequence,+ Elthorn Caman said. +Destiny has been guided into a new path.+ They tilted their head as though listening. +I understand that the orks are withdrawing. Excellent. Ilmaren will shortly be safely within the webway once more. I order you once again, admiral – withdraw your ships, and let the corsairs finish this battle alone, if that is their wish.+

The farseer was not wrong, Taenar realised. *Sunstompa* was veering away, its engines burning furiously, and the rest of the ork fleet were starting to disengage along with it. Clumsily and haphazardly, certainly, but disengaging nonetheless.

'We could crush them now,' he said, still staring at the readout that showed the freebooters' flagship. 'If all of our ships joined with the Starsplinters–'

+They will not,+ Caman interrupted. +Admiral, will you give your order?+

'No,' Taenar said immediately. The words shocked him, but he felt no desire to withdraw them. Caman's ghostly features turned to Faerys.

+Captain Asuthien. I hereby remove the admiral from command. You are to broadcast to all ships, and–+

Faerys drew herself up.

'The admiral speaks for me, farseer.'

Taenar stared at her in amazement. Faerys Asuthien was a loyal servant to Ilmaren, just as he had been. He had not expected this.

'I have flown with these aeldari and fought by their side,' Faerys continued firmly, staring Caman down with creditable determination. 'They are wild and they are reckless, but they are not evil. And they deserve better than to be treated as our unknowing tools, abandoned to die while Ilmaren flees.'

Caman sighed. +Very well. Warlock Kyldran?+

Taenar looked at Ra'thar, but there was no doubt there, no hesitation. Taenar considered appealing to him for a moment, but disregarded the notion almost instantly. Ra'thar was a son of Ilmaren to the bone. He had barely tolerated the corsairs amongst whom he had been forced to spend time, let alone developed any sort of bond. So far as the warlock was concerned, the Starsplinters – and Myrin Stormdawn in particular – had served their purpose, and therefore they were no longer of any interest. There was no use calling on him.

'Exarch Shelwe-nin,' Taenar said instead. 'Are you content with the number of orks slain today?'

'Not at all,' Cithriel Shelwe-nin said, her voice instantly hot and thick. Exarchs lived only for combat, and while they could mostly restrain those desires, they could never eliminate them.

'The ork warlord is allegedly wounded, but still alive,' Taenar said. His pulse was pounding, and he could not make himself look away from Elthorn Caman's face, but nor could he prevent himself from speaking. 'What say you that we pursue that ship and finish the job?'

'To fight and slay such a beast would be a great honour,' Cithriel replied, stepping forward eagerly. 'I am with you, admiral.'

'I cannot allow this,' Ra'thar Kyldran said angrily. He too took a step towards Taenar, one hand reaching out for his shoulder. 'You must–'

Taenar had served as an Aspect Warrior of the Striking Scorpions, and his reflexes were still faster than most, but Cithriel Shelwe-nin moved with a speed that even his eyes could not follow. Her claw – de-energised, but still strong enough to crack bones should she wish it – gripped Ra'thar's outstretched wrist, while the teeth of her chainsword were resting against the flesh of his throat with her finger poised to activated the whirling blades.

'Peace, warlock,' Cithriel hissed. 'I have been promised blood. You wore an aspect once, so you should know better than to think that I would accept the insult to my god were I to now be denied it.'

+Taenar,+ Caman said sharply. +There is no need for this!+

'I'm afraid there is, farseer,' Taenar said with a sorrow that hollowed him out. He dared not stop in case the full enormity of what he was doing reared up and struck him. All he knew was if he let himself be talked out of this, of what he knew to be *right*, then his life thereafter would be empty of anything except regrets. One of the galaxy's lesser species might be able to forget such a mistake, to move on and bury it under new experiences or novel narcotics, but Taenar knew better. 'I stand upon a turning point for my soul, and I must take the path that calls to me.'

+That will be the Path of the Outcast,+ Caman said, their voice heavy with warning. +This time it will be no act, no deception.+

'I am not certain that it ever was,' Taenar said with sudden realisation. He looked at Ra'thar Kyldran – the warlock's expression was furious, but he made no move. Ra'thar knew better than to test an exarch when one already had her blade to his throat, psychic abilities or no. 'Regardless, I cannot stand by and let good aeldari souls be extinguished. I cannot accede to this hierarchy of worth, where our lives are valued as greater than theirs simply by dint of our place of origin, or their choice of where to live those lives!'

+You will simply cause other lives to be lost instead,+ Caman said as Taenar fed power to the aether drives once more, and *Dance of Dying Seasons* began to break formation with the rest of the Ilmaren fleet.

'You appear to have found a way to live with your choices,' Taenar said stubbornly. 'I must do the same.'

+I am guided by foresight.+

'As am I,' Taenar replied. 'I can foresee what will happen to me if I do not do this, and to frame it in a way you can understand, farseer, I am prioritising my life.' *Dance of Dying Seasons'* sensors flashed him an alert, and he grimaced. 'Tell the rest of the fleet to hold their fire, or you will lose a ship and all the lives aboard it to no purpose at all!'

+Release Ra'thar,+ Caman said. +Do not drag him into this with you.+

Taenar did not look around. 'Farseer, if you will order the fleet not to fire on us or the Starsplinters, and you instruct Ra'thar not to interfere with this ship, then he can take a shuttle and return to Ilmaren immediately. Otherwise, we must keep him with us.'

+Very well,+ Caman agreed, although Taenar could hear disdainful anger bubbling under their clipped tones. +Ra'thar, leave them to their fate, whatever that may prove to be.+

'As you wish, farseer,' Ra'thar Kyldran replied. He eyed Cithriel. 'Exarch, would you mind? I will not stand between you and your desired bloodshed.'

Cithriel smiled a predator's smile, but she released the warlock and lowered her chainblade. Ra'thar hesitated for a moment as though he wished to address Taenar, but he must have reconsidered, for he stormed off the bridge instead with his robes swirling around him. Caman shook their head, and then their image disappeared as well, leaving Taenar unchallenged on his bridge.

Time to make the most of it.

'Fellow captains!' Taenar declared, broadcasting to every ship within range. He had no authority but empty bluster, and he knew exactly how fractured the corsairs could be, but he had to try. 'The orks are routed! We can finish them, and free the captives they hold, but we must harry them now before they can regroup!'

He received answering shouts from Starsplinter barons and baronesses – they were already locked in the fight, and could conceive of no other course of action save pressing home their advantage and confirming kills. However, Taenar knew they would not be enough on their own.

'Ships of my fleet!' he continued, trying to find a way to get his message across without laying bare the deception that had lain at the heart of their mission to begin with. 'Ilmaren commands us to stay. We will be welcomed back, but the price is to abandon our new allies to their fate – to run and hide again, as we have done so many times before, and turn our faces away from the suffering of our kin. That price is too steep for me. I will not blame you if you choose to pay it in order to see your home again, but I pray that you will not.'

'Don't stop there, admiral,' Faerys suggested, starting to bring *Dance of Dying Seasons* around. 'We're going to need all the help we can get.'

'Ships of Ilmaren!' Taenar declared as Faerys fed power to the aetheric engines. 'We came here to free aeldari captives held by the orks. Those captives now include your friends and family, taken as slaves from Ilmaren itself. The craftworld will abandon them and call them acceptable losses for its overall survival, but I cannot accept that! The Starsplinters can put aside factional differences for the good of all. I say it is time to do the same!'

He cut the transmission, and turned to Faerys. 'Now get us out of here, before Caman decides to shoot us down for insurrection after all.'

'Aye, sir!' Faerys answered, and *Dance of Dying Seasons* lurched forwards. One or two of the Ilmaren ships began to shift as well, before their progress was rapidly arrested. Taenar could not be sure what had happened there. Had some captains made to follow him, but then been ordered back by Elthorn Caman? Had he sparked a struggle between captains and their officers, as loyalty to the species warred with obedience to the craftworld?

'Taenar.'

Taenar stiffened. That was Arissys Caellanar's voice.

'These are the vessels on which I believe the majority of our captives were placed.'

'You no longer consider me a traitor?' Taenar asked as his ship's sensors picked out the fleeing ork craft highlighted by Caellanar's transmission.

'I do not know. But I know that I have been ordered to remain with the craftworld, and so these souls will be lost if you cannot aid them.'

Taenar sighed in relief. 'Thank you. Guard Ilmaren well. A piece of my heart goes with it, but my ship and my spirit cannot.'

'*Farewell, Leotharan,*' Caellanar said, her voice stern with warning. '*Should we cross paths again, I suspect that no one will order me to hold my fire.*'

Taenar pushed her words from his mind. He could mourn the loss of his home later. 'Prioritise boarding these vessels,' he broadcast to anyone listening to him, highlighting the same vessels Caellanar had identified. 'They are likely to contain aeldari captives taken from the craftworld.'

'*Ilmaren and its ships are abandoning us!*' came a reply from Arrerith Elwin. '*Why should we aid them?*'

'We do not need them to win this battle,' Taenar said tightly, willing himself to sound convinced on both a personal and a tactical level. He cast a glance at Faerys, who returned a look which eloquently but silently communicated that she felt it was too close to call. 'Besides,' he added, 'the craftworld has abandoned these captives as well. If Ilmaren has no need for warriors, bonesingers, warlocks, and healers, perhaps the Starsplinters do?'

The new shape of the combat was becoming apparent. A solid group of ork ships, with *Sunstompa* at their core, were burning hard for the system's interior. The Starsplinters, having focused on destroying those enemies who had remained to fight, were now starting to peel off in pursuit of the remnants of the Bukkaneer fleet. Ork vessels moved fast, despite their ungainly appearance, since the creatures prioritised powerful engines and speed – even if not manoeuvrability – nearly as much as they did destructive weaponry. However, Taenar knew that they could be overhauled. He began to plot out the chase, predicting which ships would strike where, observing cruisers that had lined up for kill shots on the fleeing orks now altering their headings with the intention of landing boarding craft on the ships he had highlighted. He was glad to see that most of his original fleet had joined the pursuit, with only a few drifting hesitantly back towards Ilmaren as it made for the webway gate. More surprisingly, he noted that a few vessels from Ilmaren's defensive fleet had thrown all powers to their drives and were surging in pursuit of the orks as well. Perhaps loyalty to species over craftworld was possible even without fighting alongside the corsairs first.

'The boarders will likely lose as many lives as they rescue, if not more,' Cithriel said from beside him. 'Entering an ork ship is like stepping into hell.'

'I can quite believe it,' Taenar agreed. 'However, those will be corsairs eager to face that challenge, rather than craftworlders abducted against their will.'

Cithriel nodded hungrily. 'And I would join them.' She hesitated for a moment, then pointed. 'Admiral. You have marked the ork flagship for boarding rather than destruction, but Admiral Caellanar did not indicate that she thought any number of captives were on it.'

'Myrin boarded it,' Taenar said, his throat tight. 'I am sure of it. He boarded it and dealt the ork chieftain the wound of which Farseer Caman spoke, but the ship still flees.'

'So the prince is most likely dead,' Cithriel said flatly.

'Most likely,' Taenar acknowledged. 'But perhaps not, and I will not abandon him until I know for sure.' He had always admired Stormdawn, even when they had both served in the Ilmaren fleet, albeit in a relatively abstract and distanced way – the account he had given of feeling betrayed by Myrin's desertion was a truthful one. But now... Myrin Stormdawn was far from perfect, Taenar could admit that, but he was gloriously, vigorously *imperfect*. There was far more to the aeldari spirit than that which existed within the boundaries of a craftworld, Taenar had realised, and he intended to explore it to find out all the ways in which he could be imperfect too. However, first he had to find out how imperfectly Myrin had attempted to slay Uzgul the Magnificent.

'You intend to board that vessel?' Cithriel asked.

'I do,' Taenar confirmed. 'But I am not Myrin Stormdawn, and I do not seek to match myself against the ork commander, especially not injured as I am.' He looked at her. 'Luckily, I have one of the greatest warriors I have ever met aboard my ship. I trust that I can count upon you to lead the assault.'

'Admiral, I would consider it the gravest of insults if you did not,' Cithriel replied, her voice hoarse as the battle lust began to wash over her. Taenar had felt echoes of that when he had followed the Path of the Warrior, and he knew how compelling the song of Kaela Mensha Khaine was even to someone like him. For an exarch, lost on the Path, it was a siren song that would not be denied.

'I will do my utmost to get us there as soon as possible,' he promised. Truthfully, he wanted no other vessel's crew to board *Sunstompa* first. If Myrin was injured or taken captive then he would be an easy target for any baron or baroness looking to advance themselves within the Starsplinters' ranks through his death, and Taenar could not countenance that. Not simply for his own heart's wellbeing, either. Myrin had accepted him and his ships, but other would-be rulers might have their own ideas.

There was no reason for the other Starsplinter commanders to follow Taenar's lead, let alone his orders, but it seemed that force of personality and determination to see the orks destroyed was sufficient, at least for now. Taenar had no true foresight with which to weigh his words, merely a warrior's instincts, an admiral's tactical nous, and a damaged warship under his command. It would have to do.

'Forwards!' he shouted. 'To victory!'

TWENTY-NINE

Farseer Elthorn Caman finished wiping the blood from their witch-blade, sheathed it, and automatically reached into their pouch of runes. It was a dangerous habit, but the call of destiny was hard to ignore. There was always the balance to be struck between assessment and action, of course. Always the risk of moving too soon and too hastily, leading to disaster, weighed against getting lost in the never-ending skeins of possibilities and awaiting the perfect moment at which to tip the scales in your favour, and so failing to achieve anything at all. Still, in the aftermath of such a conflict, it seemed only wise to assess matters again…

'Caman!'

The voice was that of Taevela Dumeril, a fellow farseer, approaching at the head of what remained of her Guardian squad. They were a mere handful of ragged warriors, none uninjured despite the presence and protection of such a powerful psychic. Such had been the viciousness and violence of the arakhia's assault. However, with them was another figure, neither farseer nor Guardian.

'Farseer Dumeril,' Elthorn Caman said, inclining their head in brief acknowledgement of their peer. Then they turned their attention to the newcomer. 'Warlock Kyldran. I am glad to see that you made it back unscathed.'

'One of the few who has returned at all,' Dumeril said bitterly. 'I did not come here as an escort to your agent, Caman. I need answers. Why has Admiral Leotharan abandoned us in favour of the corsairs? And why have the majority of his ships gone with him?'

'If the Seer Council requires an update on the operation–' Caman began, eyeing the Guardians, but Dumeril cut them off.

'Damn the Seer Council! And damn you, Elthorn!' she added venomously, stepping closer. 'You are not the only one who can divine potential futures, yet you act recklessly as though you alone hold the keys to our salvation! You sent Leotharan away without consulting the council, and now he, all those ships, and their captains may be lost to us for good!'

Caman noticed Ra'thar Kyldran stiffen slightly at the revelation that they had not waited for the Seer Council's approval before acting. They sighed. This entire conversation was regrettable, and was exactly why the disagreements of farseers should be kept away from the eyes and ears of the rest of the craftworld. It was important that those guided had complete trust in those doing the guiding, otherwise how could anything be achieved?

'It was a matter of extreme urgency. I ascertained the actions that needed to be taken, and I could not wait for the council's motions or approval,' Caman said firmly. 'Besides, you will note that Ilmaren is saved. The ork fleet is routed and in retreat. We did at least agree that the ork known as Uzgul posed a great threat in the future, and that it needed eliminating. This has been achieved.'

'At what cost?' Dumeril demanded, throwing her arm out to gesture broadly towards the direction in which the orkish fleet was retreating. 'Yes, Uzgul posed a threat, but that threat only came about because *we* influenced its rise, in order to blunt the threat of the Cult of the Seven Moons! Now we have not only lost an admiral and his ships, but also strengthened a corsair warband with no reason to love us!'

'Especially since Leotharan will undoubtedly inform Stormdawn of our manipulation of both him and the orks to bring them both to this point,' Ra'thar Kyldran put in.

'How were the orks manipulated?' Dumeril asked, casting a sharp glance at Kyldran. 'To bring them here?'

Caman raised a hand to wave questions and concerns away. 'The Cult of the Seven Moons were the primary threat at that point. Leaving them unchecked could have spelled disaster for us.' They fingered the runes in their pouch, aching to cast them and see what new shape the future had flowed into now it had passed this chokepoint. 'We eliminated an enemy that sought to destroy us and all those like us, in favour of a future threat more akin to a force of nature – severe, violent, but less imminent, and less targeted. Now that threat in turn has been removed.'

'And so Myrin Stormdawn, a gifted commander who knows our capabilities and had previously merely abandoned us, will now be actively after our blood,' Dumeril said, her voice dripping with contempt. 'You have set us to merely lurch from one potential catastrophe to the next.'

'I have averted *actual* catastrophes!' Caman snapped. 'What would you have me do? When one branching fate leads us to an imperfect result, I should simply step away and let events take their course, even if such inaction ruins us completely? I am no coward, to wash my hands of events when they do not unfold exactly as I would like!' They hissed in frustration. 'Myrin Stormdawn is still aeldari. Unlike the followers of Chaos, or the orks, it may at least still be possible to reason with him, perhaps even buy him off, with some confidence that he would honour such a bargain.'

'I would have preferred to face him with Admiral Leotharan

and his ships on our side,' Dumeril said pointedly, but Caman snorted.

'Leotharan's heart was already wandering. I could sense it, even if he could not. That was why I selected him.' They had not counted on quite so many of Taenar's captains being of a similar mindset, but such were the uncertainties of foretelling. They gestured to Ra'thar Kyldran. 'Warlock, how swiftly would you say that Taenar Leotharan adopted the corsair lifestyle?'

'He appeared quite at home, farseer,' Kyldran replied with regret. 'I voiced my concerns to him, but he was adamant that he was merely playing a role, even when the truth seemed obvious to me. Stormdawn got his claws into the admiral early, and hard.'

'A managed loss of what may well have been inevitable,' Caman concluded, turning their attention back to Dumeril. Actually scrying into the future's possibilities was only part of a farseer's role. An important secondary one was convincing others – including other farseers – that the path you had chosen was the correct one, and that everything had indeed proceeded as you intended. Otherwise, your people might be denied your influence when they needed it the most. 'Countless aeldari have followed the yearnings in their hearts, and sampled outcast life for a while. Many return to their homes in time. To seek to tie them to us against their will would merely make the break, when it came, all the more bitter.' They sighed. 'Such as it was with Myrin Stormdawn. He may be lost to us for good, although I hold out hope that this is not the case. Taenar Leotharan, though… Let him and his captains taste the heady fruits of this supposed freedom, and when his maturity matches his undoubted military skill, he will likely lead them back as a fuller and more rounded individual, ready to take a prominent role in our craftworld's future.'

'A future that you will not be shaping,' Taevela Dumeril said, her voice barbed. 'I will be speaking to the rest of the Seer Council.'

'Do so,' Caman retorted. 'You may find that those who appreciate results outnumber your puritan idealists!' They stared Dumeril down until she turned away in disgust, followed by her squad, one or two of whom cast looks back at Caman as their group moved away.

'Do not speak of our role in directing the orks to the Well of the Long Death,' Caman said to Kyldran, once the others were out of earshot. 'I need the Seer Council to be concentrating on actions and results, not get mired in the sort of ethical conundrums that Dumeril likes to throw up. She would push back against any course of action that does not meet her standards, and celebrate herself for her compassion while our enemies burn Ilmaren around her.'

'Of course, farseer,' Ra'thar Kyldran said, but Caman could sense doubt behind the warlock's eyes that had not been there before. Kyldran was a blunt tool, better suited to destruction than divination, but he had been loyal so far. Distrust would dent his usefulness. Thankfully, he was not the only tool with which Caman had to work.

They pulled out a handful of runes, and cast them. Such a thing should properly be done in a divination trance in a farseer's own quarters, free from disturbance and distraction. That was how most did it, which was precisely why Caman chose not to. What others viewed as distraction, Caman viewed as essential context. It was far too easy to get lost in lofty contemplation, and forget the reality of a situation. Here, in a dome damaged by the orkish attack, in which the acrid smell of smoke drifted on the artificial breeze and mixed with the sharp scent of aeldari blood, was where the future of Ilmaren could best be ascertained.

Elthorn Caman took a deep breath, steadied their spirit, and plunged into the skeins of fate to determine how the nature of the galaxy had changed.

THIRTY

They'd nearly made it back to the Dakkaplanet, but they were being hunted. It was not a sensation with which Gazruk was familiar, and he did not like it one bit.

Gazruk had always considered himself to be an ork able to interpret data. He could examine trends and work out the root cause; he could consider facts to not only draw well-reasoned conclusions, but also formulate sensible and practical plans to enact moving forwards. He knew how to spot anomalies and adapt accordingly. Meks who couldn't do that had a tendency to be blown up by their own malfunctioning equipment, and that was not a fate to which Gazruk would fall. The fact that other orks got blown up by malfunctioning equipment on which Gazruk might possibly have worked at some point was neither here nor there. Or, well, it *was* here *and* there, and a few other places besides, but that was nothing to do with him.

Anyway, the point was that Gazruk Hackspanna might be aboard a kill krooozer that got boarded by skrawnies whose ship had been destroyed, and who then made it as far as the bridge and stuck a sword into Uzgul da Magnificent, and he'd accept that as an anomaly. This obviously wasn't a common occurrence, historically, or the kaptin probably wouldn't still be alive. However, you had to be open to the possibility of the situation changing.

If, for example, *Sunstompa* got overhauled by skrawnies in the aftermath of that same battle – if, in fact, the Badskab Bukkaneers had decided that the battle was over, but the skrawnies had other ideas and had chased them down to demonstrate that difference of opinion – and it got boarded *again*… Well, in that case, Gazruk would have to consider his options. Orks shouldn't get boarded by skrawnies, that was fairly obvious. Gazruk had taken part in his share of boarding actions, and they were hot, noisy, brutal, and extremely fun, which was exactly the sort of thing that seemed completely at odds with how most skrawnies acted. Being on a kill kroozer that had been boarded by skrawnies twice was a concern, because it implied that they might stick a sword into Uzgul again, and would probably quite happily shank any other orks they found nearby. Gazruk didn't much fancy having all his limbs chopped off by skrawnie blades or those zippy pointy discs their guns fired. It would make it very hard to do his work.

All in all, when the port guns got blown up sufficient that a skrawnie kroozer was able to make it alongside without taking damage, and then word came over the shoutas that some very angry skrawnies had come aboard and set about killing as many orks as they could find on a direct route to the bridge, it seemed to Gazruk that being elsewhere was probably good not only for his general chances of continuing to have his head attached, but also for the future of orkdom in general. A freebooter kaptin could easily be replaced – even one as charismatic and commanding as Uzgul – but there was only one Gazruk Hackspanna in the galaxy, and Gazruk liked things that were one-of-a-kind, particularly when they were him.

'Get yerselves togevva!' Uzgul was bellowing at what remained of his bridge krew. The kaptin had recovered some of his swagger, and was brandishing his massive choppa as though it weighed nothing while his boyz ran to and fro, grabbing weapons and spare ammo off the dead in preparation for the incoming assault, but Gazruk could see beneath the surface. Uzgul was still favouring the wound he'd taken, which seemed to be bothering him far more than Gazruk's similar injury, almost as though the skrawnie leader's sword had some sort of poison on it. Gazruk wouldn't put it past them, the crafty little gits. He half-wanted to grab the thing and take a look at it, but it was stashed behind the throne not far from where the skrawnie leader itself had been hastily impaled to the wall via a spike through its hands, and something told him that Uzgul wouldn't appreciate Gazruk poking around his newly acquired trophies.

All in all, there was only one thing for it.

'Be right back, kaptin!' Gazruk said cheerfully as Uzgul bellowed instructions at the orks who'd been in charge of steering until fighting off intruders had become the priority. 'I got just da fing for dis!'

He took a step to the side and dropped through a hole in the deck to what remained of the chamber below, where Da Machine had been. There was nothing here that would help, of course, but that wasn't the point. The point was to get just a few seconds before Uzgul got suspicious – enough of a head start that the kaptin would quickly decide that the incoming skrawnies were a higher priority than one absent badmek. Gazruk landed on the uneven, heat-warped decking and made for the hole where the chamber's door had been blasted outwards by the explosion, deliberately not looking at the wreckage of Da Machine on the way…

'Boss?' Bashgut said in surprise, popping up from behind some wrecked panelling. Gazruk nearly took his spanner's head off with a swing from his wrench before he realised who it was, then just stared at Bashgut in surprise for a moment.

'Wot... didn't you get blowed up?'

'Nah, I'd just gone out to empty da snotlings out of da fans,' Bashgut said. 'Dunno how dey got back in dere, I swear I cleaned da damned fings out–'

'So wot're you doin' back?' Gazruk demanded, weighing up potential courses of action.

'Well, I fort I might be able to fix it...'

Gazruk looked around. Da Machine was in ruins. It was barely recognisable as having ever had any sort of form and function beyond that of a scrapheap of blasted parts. '*Yoo* woz gonna fix *dis*?'

'Well, ya don't know unless ya try, right?' Bashgut said hopefully.

'No, I guess *yoo* don't,' Gazruk muttered, searching for inspiration. He found it in a large chunk of metal that had once been part of the inkremental defuser. It was about the right length, width, and shape to possibly be a gun of the more experimental sort, with appropriate protrusions that looked a bit like a handle. He plucked it off the floor and threw it to Bashgut, who caught it.

'Wot's dis?'

'Kustom mega-blasta,' Gazruk said instantly. He pointed at the somewhat bent ladder that still led up to the bridge. 'Now get up dere an' tell da kaptin dat I'll be back up wiv some more dakka in a few seconds.'

'Don't look like no kustom mega-blasta I've ever seen,' Bashgut said dubiously.

'Dat's cos it's *kustom*,' Gazruk said with exasperation. 'We don't call 'em *standard* mega-blastas, do we? Now get up dat ladder!'

'Yes, boss!' Bashgut yelped, and obeyed with alacrity. Gazruk waited until the spanner's boots had disappeared out of sight, then instantly turned and made for the door.

'Boss?'

'For Mork's sake, wot?' Gazruk snarled, rounding on his new interrupter, which proved to be Snip the grot. It was somewhat singed, but was peering out from behind a vent covering where it had apparently been hiding. 'I swear to da gods, if yoo don't get outta my way–'

'Shuttle, boss?' Snip said hopefully, its outsized ears quivering.

Gazruk's eyes narrowed, and he grabbed the squawking grot out of its hiding place by the neck. 'Wot're yoo talkin' about, ya little git?'

'Nice handy shuttle?' Snip said, somehow managing to sound ingratiating while also asphyxiating. 'Dat sounds like da sort of fing a sensible mek like yerself would be after right now, no disrespect intended!'

Gazruk glanced upwards without thinking, but there was no sign that Uzgul's ears had picked up any sign of betrayal. 'An' wot? I can find a shuttle wivout ya.'

'Need someone to go first round corners?' Snip rasped, starting to turn purple. 'Extra pair of eyes to look out for sneaky skrawnies? Somefing to throw at 'em if dey turn up, wot can also sort wires an' such for ya if da shuttle ain't quite up to scratch when ya get dere?'

Gazruk scowled at it, but loosened his grip slightly. 'Wot's yer game, runt?'

'No games, boss,' Snip managed, wheezing. 'Just don't fancy gettin' shanked by a skrawnie, an' also wanna keep workin' for da best mek in da galaxy!'

That was blatant flattery, but Gazruk realised that he didn't really care. Snip had proved itself to be fairly useful, as grots went – certainly better at wiring than Bashgut – and yes, another pair of eyes *might* be useful.

Guttural roars echoed from above, accompanied by the heavy thunder of the few shootas that there were still living hands to wield, immediately answered by chilling war cries. The skrawnies had arrived.

'Alright, grot,' Gazruk said, hurling it towards the door. 'Time to make yerself useful! Dis ain't gonna be da end for Gazruk Hackspanna...'

THIRTY-ONE

Taenar had never been part of a boarding action before, and he wasn't sure if it was symbolic or foolish that his first time was not at the behest of a farseer or a superior officer, but on his own initiative and for his own purposes. Nor was this the desperate cut-and-thrust of the brawl in the Starsplinters' base, where there were no clear sides and confusion had been as prominent an emotion as anything else, or the tightly controlled pressure of a void war, where a captain took decisions and reacted to threats in a manner that seemed almost insulated from the very real events that were happening, until the moment at which the ship was blasted open to hard vacuum. This was close combat against orks, some of the most dangerous enemies in a galaxy full of danger, and every moment might be a sudden and painful last.

He had no time to adapt, though. It was kill or be killed, and the orks were making it abundantly clear which option they preferred.

Taenar just managed to sidestep a downward blow from a crude bladed weapon with a head nearly the size of his upper body, and slashed his power sword across the ork's chest in return. The energy-wreathed blade sliced straight through the ork's vest and bit deep into first skin and then muscle, showering

Taenar in the brute's thick blood. The ork howled, and tried to club Taenar with the barrel of the huge pistol in its other hand while it brought the cleaver back for a second blow. Taenar managed to wrench his blade around and hack through the creature's wrist before the ork could strike him, sending its gun hand skittering across the uneven flooring in another spray of blood, then slashed at its thigh. The ork's leg gave out beneath it, and it toppled forwards and sideways with a startled roar that was abruptly truncated when Taenar's desperate upswing met its descending neck with enough combined force to decapitate the beast.

The other orks were already dead, and Cithriel Shelwe-nin and her Striking Scorpions were advancing again, trusting to martial skill and the protection of their warsuits over the usual methodology of their aspect. They were normally ambush predators who would strike from the shadows at unwary foes, but the close quarters of the ork ship and the fact that the aeldari were the ones pressing on made that all but impossible. Taenar followed, the shrine's clicking battle cant already returning to him.

They were not alone, of course, since a single below-strength squad of Striking Scorpions would have been overwhelmed within minutes, no matter their skill. *Dance of Dying Seasons'* combat teams formed the force's bulk, cutting the orks down from whatever distance they could manage with concentrated fire from shuriken catapults and scatter laser platforms. Assault squads, similarly equipped to the Striking Scorpions with blades and shuriken pistols, would charge forward to meet whatever orks made it past the withering hail of razor-sharp projectiles and laser bolts. Many were former Aspect Warriors, like Taenar, while others were perhaps considering following that Path in the future. Neither their skills, weapons, nor armour were the equal of the Striking Scorpions', but time and time again they threw back the orks' ragged resistance, and so the boarding party continued to force its way deeper into *Sunstompa*'s guts, trusting to speed to keep them from being pinned in place and overwhelmed.

'Are we nearly there?' Cithriel sent to Taenar. The exarch was prowling ahead restlessly, but was restraining herself enough to not become separated from the rest of them.

'There is nothing approaching a standardised design when it comes to orkish vessels, but we must be close,' Taenar replied. It was infuriatingly true. All aeldari captains knew it was very difficult to target specific locations such as field generators, bridges, or sometimes even engines on ork ships.

'And if the beast we seek is not present?' Cithriel demanded. The exarch's voice had taken on a thick, grating quality, testament to how tightly Kaela Mensha Khaine had hold of her soul.

'It will be, or it will already be dead, or it will come to meet us first,' Taenar said confidently. It took a lot to make orks run, since they did not seem overly concerned by death, but sometimes their spirits broke, and sometimes their commander was capable of grasping the notion of a strategic withdrawal. This option seemed to Taenar to be by far the most likely explanation for the Bukkaneers' flight in the aftermath of *Light of Heaven*'s destruction, but he had no doubt that Uzgul would stand and fight when it learned that there were intruders aboard its ship. To do otherwise would surely be seen as cowardice by its underlings.

'More prey,' Cithriel said suddenly, and the exarch's form blurred into action once more. She leaped up and vaulted off the side of the corridor, so she was already flipping over the heads of the half a dozen orks before they even charged around the corner. The beasts slowed for a moment and looked upwards in bewilderment, only for Cithriel to land amongst them, her mandiblasters spitting death. Two orks staggered backwards, clutching at their eyes, while the exarch dealt with their companions. Her scorpion claw flashed out twice, plunging deep into chests and emerging dripping with gore, and her chainblade removed two more heads in a single balletic sweep, far more graceful than anything Taenar could have ever managed. The other Scorpions took the two blinded orks down with a hail of short-ranged shuriken fire before they had any chance to recover, and Cithriel advanced to the next junction.

'There is a large door that way, surrounded by orkish glyphs,' she reported, the tassels of her helm swaying as she glanced around the corner to the right. She immediately slipped back into cover, then chanced a slightly longer look, but no hail of fire or roars of rage greeted her. 'They look like the ones for command, firepower, speed, and so on, as well as many others. From this angle, I cannot see what is beyond.'

'Almost certainly the bridge,' Taenar concluded. 'Bring up the starcannon.'

They had one of the powerful weapons with them on a support platform, for just such a purpose. It had a far slower rate of fire than the scatter lasers, but the ravening energy of its plasma bolts could make short work of even the thickest doors. However, Cithriel waved it back. 'No need. The door has already been destroyed. Probably the work of Stormdawn and his team.'

Taenar took a deep breath. 'Very well then. On my mark, swift and silent as we can, for as long as we can. There is no reason to alert them to our presence before we have to.'

He looked around. The helms of his boarding team gave him no insight into their expressions, but he could read their body language as though they were lines of script laid out in front of him. Each one of them was tense, but steadfast. There was no weakness or fear here, simply determination to achieve the goal that had brought them here, edged with the thirst for battle that all aeldari felt when the Bloody-Handed God raised his head.

Taenar pointed his blade, and they charged. However, Uzgul da Magnificent was not so easily taken unawares, and he chose not to wait.

The aeldari were halfway to the door when the orks swarmed out. Tiny red eyes above massive, foam-flecked tusks, large-calibre weapons spitting out streams of shells, and garish clothing adorned with the orkish skull-and-bones motif that was the hallmark of these pirates, the Badskab Bukkaneers came to welcome death, either for themselves or their enemies. There was no time for thought, and there was no time for fear. Taenar simply hurled himself at the beasts, trusting that the orks' huge frames would at least help shield him from the bullets of their own kind, even as they tried to cut him down. He stitched a line of shuriken across the face of the first ork, blinding it and punching into its brain. It fell like a marionette with the strings cut, and then he was over its body and into the next. The half-healed wounds on his torso screamed at him, but they were merely ghostly possibilities of the agonies to come should he be too slow, and so he kept moving, kept swaying, kept ducking and dodging, kept finding the gaps in his enemies' defences, and angling his blade to sever limbs and open arteries.

Nonetheless, Taenar would have been dead without the Striking Scorpions, and especially without Cithriel Shelwe-nin. The Aspect Warriors and their exarch were the pinnacle of grace and lethality, and the ork charge blunted itself on them, green meeting green and erupting into red. Taenar and the other warriors moved behind them, trying to keep pace as best they could, plugging gaps and fighting off those who sought to flank Shelwe-nin and her fighters. The orks fought as viciously as ever, but there seemed almost a hint of desperation in their actions. They were used to being the predators, the ones who cornered their victims, gunned them down, looted the corpses and enslaved the survivors. They had little experience at being brought to bay in this manner, and their wild swings and furious howls spoke of their disbelief at this turn of events.

Point-blank shuriken fire from over Taenar's shoulder shredded another ork before it even got to him. The one behind it pointed what looked like a bit of junk at him, and appeared to be scrabbling around in an attempt to find a non-existent firing mechanism. Taenar hacked it down before it realised its mistake, and nearly severed its head from its shoulders, constantly doing the desperate mid-fight arithmetic of how long to take to ensure one foe was fully incapacitated without leaving himself open to the next. He nearly misjudged it, and only the sturdy shoulder plate of his armour saved him from losing an arm to a shot from the huge hand cannon wielded by the next foe. The impact still numbed his nerves, and his shuriken pistol fell from his hand, but he managed to sidestep the ork's downward swing so the blade of its weapon crashed into the deck beneath. Taenar leaped upwards, vaulting off the beast's thick arm and landing behind it, then lashing out backwards to drive his blade into its back. He twisted his weapon, slicing through protective bone and severing its spinal cord.

And then, as fast as it had begun, the combat ended. Taenar looked around with weapons raised and breath coming fast, waiting for the next howling monstrosity trying to murder him, but none appeared. The last of them were being cut down by his companions, or slinking away nursing the stumps of limbs, harried by blasts from the surviving scatter lasers.

'Did we get Uzgul?' he asked, looking around. However, despite the prevalence of garishly attired orks – and far too many of his own boarding party's bodies, mingled in amongst the dead – he couldn't see any corpse that looked impressive enough for him to be sure that it was their quarry.

The floor tilted beneath their feet, and the distant thrumming of the engines, transmitted through the ship's superstructure, took on a different note.

Taenar ran for the bridge without thinking, but he was not the first, nor the fastest. The remaining Striking Scorpions were ahead of him, and they were first through the ragged gap where the doors had previously been blown inwards. Taenar followed on their heels, but he was no match for their speed.

That was why he lived.

A firestorm engulfed the Aspect Warriors in an indiscriminate hail of explosive projectiles that achieved with volume what it lacked in accuracy. Taenar ducked sideways instinctively, taking cover behind the remnants of one door and wincing as the metal against which he was leaning shuddered and vibrated under the impacts, waiting for his moment. As soon as the barrage stopped, and was replaced by the rapid, hollow clicking of a primitive firearm repeatedly trying to empty a chamber that remained stubbornly unfilled, he moved.

The Striking Scorpions had run into the teeth of the fusillade, the expert ambush predators themselves ambushed by their quarry's cunning, and their broken bodies were strewn across the floor, along with many orks and some aeldari Taenar recognised from Myrin's crew. Even Cithriel had been hit, and although it seemed the exarch's armour had not been breached as such, the sheer force of impact had apparently blown out her left knee. She staggered sideways, raising her claw to pepper her adversary with shuriken, only for the ancient weapon to be smashed into uselessness by the blade of a massive, two-handed axe wielded by the largest ork Taenar had ever seen.

There was no doubt that this was Uzgul the Magnificent. Had it not been a monster responsible for the death and suffering of countless aeldari then Taenar might have marvelled at its size and swiftness, but there was no time for study, not even to get a better read on his foe before he struck.

Taenar attacked with a scream, swiping at the beast's ribs with his powerblade before Uzgul could take Cithriel's head from her shoulders. His sword cut through the fabric of Uzgul's coat with ease, but encountered hidden armour within. Taenar tried to slide the weapon around this obstacle and into the ork's flesh, but he had lost his element of surprise – Uzgul's hand flashed out and grabbed Taenar by the neck, hoisting him off the deck. The multiple barrels of the massive weapon attached to Uzgul's forearm were glowing so hot that Taenar's helm flashed an alert at him, but he was more concerned with the huge axe in the ork's other hand. Uzgul's mouth and eyes were open in rage, purplish tongue shaping a bellow of hatred as the kaptin of the Badskab Bukkaneers swept its weapon forward to cleave Taenar in half.

Cithriel Shelwe-nin lunged upwards, and her screaming chain-sword took Uzgul's axe hand off at the wrist, mid-swing.

Blood sprayed out from the ork's abruptly truncated arm, and the axe clattered to the deck. Uzgul roared in pain and rage, and the bridge spun around Taenar as he was hurled away, colliding with Cithriel. He grabbed desperately at the deck to slow himself as they slid across it in a tangle of limbs, managing to get purchase just before he pitched clean through a massive rent torn in the metal through which the room below could be seen.

'Bring it down!' Cithriel shouted. The remainder of *Dance of Dying Seasons'* boarding team were pouring into the room, weapons raised, and the exarch was not so proud as to demand the right to kill the ork chieftain when she could barely walk.

Uzgul looked up and saw the weapons being brought to bear

on it. It snarled with a glint of gold-plated tusks, then brought its remaining fist down on a massive red button on a control panel.

Alarms immediately began wailing, a sound that grabbed the hindbrain in fingers of ice, because what could be so terrifying, so dangerous, that *orks* needed an alarm for it? The boarding team froze for a moment, trying to assess what new threat was about to assault them. Taenar, struggling back to his feet, saw Uzgul's face twist into a brutish, amused leer.

'Boss!' Snip squeaked. 'Somefing's happening on da planet!'

Gazruk was busy trying to steer the tiny shuttle – little more than a maintenance pod that meks like him used to perform repairs and improvements on the outside of *Sunstompa* – but he spared a glance out of a viewport to see what Snip was on about. That was the Dakkaplanet, after all, and Uzgul had been so very obviously wrong about how it might work that maybe he'd been wrong about *that* too and had actually unknowingly been right…

Far below, there was a tiny puff of smoke. It was undoubtedly very large if you were down there and standing next to the mountain it was coming out of, but up here it was the sort of inconsequential detail you wouldn't even notice unless you were a grot with its face pressed up against a viewport, going *ooh* and *aah* at all the bright explosions.

'Zoggin' idiot,' Gazruk said with all the confidence of a mek who'd been proven correct after all and had never actually doubted his assessment of the situation, thank you *very* much. He returned his attention to getting away unnoticed – not that hard, given that the skrawnies were concentrating on the Bukkaneer ships that were actually large enough to hurt them. 'Gun-cano? I knew dat wouldn't work…'

* * *

For a moment, both aeldari and ork stood frozen on the bridge in taut, expectant silence. Then, as nothing more actually happened – no new wave of warriors emerged to attack, and the walls didn't start sliding inwards in some ingenious trap to crush the invaders – the leer started to slip off Uzgul's face.

Someone fired a shuriken catapult. Several of the projectiles ricocheted off the Bukkaneer's armour, but others sunk into its flesh with new sprays of blood. Uzgul roared feral defiance, the brutal and triumphant warrior transforming into a mere beast at bay, and whatever spell had been cast by the alarm broke. The boarding party opened fire as one.

No ork could survive that, no matter how imposing. Uzgul managed to throw a lever and send sparks flying by plunging its fist into the control panel in a desperate dying spasm, but the hail of shuriken and energy bolts tore it apart at an exponential rate. A mere second or so later, its lifeless body collapsed to the deck in various seared chunks.

'Myrin!' Taenar shouted, scrambling back to his feet and looking desperately around. 'Myrin!'

'Here.'

The voice was weak, breathy, and hoarse, but it was real. Taenar whirled until his eyes finally lighted on a pitiful figure: Myrin Stormdawn's broken form, hanging limply against the wall from hands impaled on a single metal spike. Myrin raised his head with obvious effort and blinked at him, trying to focus through an eye nearly swollen shut. One side of his face was distended, marred with the beginnings of purplish bruises where a massive fist had struck him.

'Taenar? Is that you?' he asked. Then his eyebrows lowered distrustfully, so far as they could with his injuries. 'Is this a rescue attempt, or are you here to drag me back to Ilmaren?'

'You're alive!' Taenar exclaimed with desperate gratitude. He pulled his helm loose and rushed to the Starsplinter prince. 'Someone help me! And no, Ilmaren has fled,' he added to Myrin, not bothering to keep the bitterness from his voice. 'It seems that Elthorn Caman was manipulating us both for their own ends in ways I could never have predicted.' That much, at least, was the honest truth.

'I saw you,' Myrin managed, his eyes blazing. 'I saw your ship fleeing for the craftworld.'

'Because Saraan Skyhand left us to be killed by orks!' Taenar snapped, which was also true. 'But we can discuss this later. We need to get you down from there.'

'I cannot feel my legs,' Myrin said with feigned nonchalance that was belied by his gritted teeth. 'I think my back may be broken. I can, unfortunately in this context, feel my hands...'

'Hold him!' Taenar ordered the warrior who came up beside him. He reached up and wrenched out the spike that had been pinning Myrin's hands to the wall, and Stormdawn slumped forwards and down with an agonised gasp. 'I see Issarel,' Taenar continued, looking around grimly at the fallen bodies. 'Where are Xela and Jhanandra?'

'Jhanandra went down with the ship. Xela is lost to the warp,' Myrin said through rasping breaths. 'However, we have a more pressing problem. You should not have come for me.'

'Well, we do now need to get off this ship again,' Taenar admitted.

'And quickly,' Myrin said. He lifted one punctured, bleeding hand, and gestured clumsily towards the bridge's viewport. 'Very quickly.'

Taenar gasped. His attention had been first on Uzgul, then on Myrin, but now he saw that the planet towards which the orkish fleet had fled was rising towards them fast.

'Uzgul set the ship on a collision course moments before

you reached the bridge,' Myrin said. 'Now it has destroyed the controls, so we cannot correct it.'

He threw an arm clumsily around Taenar's shoulders. 'You may have killed Uzgul the Magnificent, but the beast will yet be the death of us all.'

THIRTY-TWO

'Back to the shuttles!' Taenar ordered, replacing his helm with the hand he wasn't using to help support Myrin. The neck joint hissed briefly as its airtight seal engaged once more.

'There are more orks coming!' one of the rearguard shouted from where they'd taken up position by the door. Sure enough, Taenar could hear the thunder of boots and guttural, howling war cries. It was no surprise – his boarding party was vastly outnumbered by the crew of this vessel, not least because they'd had to leave a fair portion of their strength behind to hold the landing bay where their Vampire Raiders had set down. They had relied on speed, while the majority of the ork crew lumbered after them around the ship like a body's defences chasing a fast-moving infection, but now there was nowhere left to run.

Except… Taenar cast a glance behind him, at the ruined floor. If they could drop down through there to the level below, could they maybe outflank their pursuit.

'It would take too long,' Cithriel said. The limping exarch had seen Taenar's look, and had correctly interpreted it. 'We could retrace our steps to the landing bay on this level, but I do not trust that we could manage the same feat through this accursed labyrinth from a different starting point. Certainly not in time,' she added with a meaningful nod towards the growing planet.

'Here they come!' a rearguard shouted, and the spitting fire of shuriken catapults began, echoed by roars of pain and anger. A scatter laser opened up as well, but Taenar knew better than to think they could hold out indefinitely. Aeldari weapons were far more efficient with their ammunition than those of most other races, but he was grimly aware that they would undoubtedly run out of shuriken and laser charges before the orks ran out of eager bodies. Besides which, both sides were going to run out of time well before then, as the ship broke up during a catastrophic atmospheric entry.

'When your ships appeared to save me that first time, I was ready to sing my death hymn,' Myrin murmured from beside him. 'You bought me some more life, and for that, at least, I thank you.'

'I saved you then on Elthorn Caman's orders,' Taenar said, the words coming out more harshly than he had intended. 'You deserve to know. They foresaw your role in saving Ilmaren, so long as you stayed alive, and so I was ordered to ensure that came to pass.'

Myrin stiffened. He tried to release his hold on Taenar's shoulders, and Taenar had to support him with both arms to prevent Myrin from falling backwards to the deck. Myrin pawed clumsily at Taenar's grasp, trying to prise himself free with hands that lacked any strength or dexterity.

'Xela tried to tell me,' Myrin spat, his face twisted into an expression of hatred and betrayal that plunged into Taenar's heart like a dagger. He steeled himself, wishing that Myrin could see the anguish on his face, yet guiltily grateful for the blank mask of the void suit helm to hide behind.

'I refused to believe her,' Myrin continued. 'I could not bring myself to fully–'

'Worse, Ilmaren enabled that ork attack on the Well of the Long Death,' Taenar interrupted him. 'Their purpose was to ensure that you would seek out the Bukkaneers' destruction. That part, I beg you to believe, I had no knowledge of.'

'Why tell me this?' Myrin whispered, his eyes dead and empty. 'Why ensure that I spend my last moments choking on bitter ashes?'

'To ensure that you have spite and fire enough to *live*!' Taenar snapped. 'Ilmaren was willing to abandon you now you have served their purpose, but I have abandoned them, in truth this time, to save you. Hate me if you must, but do not slip away!'

'Live for what?' Myrin demanded with a hollow laugh. 'To be butchered by orks, or crushed by this wretched vessel crashing into a planet?'

'Neither,' Taenar said with as much confidence as he could muster. He raised his voice. 'Everyone void-seal your armour! Patch holes, take spares from the dead. Whatever it takes!'

'What is your plan?' Cithriel asked, inspecting the leg of her armour. Her warsuit appeared to be intact, despite her injury, and she grunted in satisfaction.

'It is death to stay aboard, so we leave in the only manner we can,' Taenar said, hoping that if he spoke with enough conviction then it would minimise any flaws in his plan. He pointed at the main viewport. 'Collect all the grenades we have. With those and the starcannon, we might have a chance of breaching our way out of here.'

'Into the void?' Cithriel said dubiously. 'I am a warrior. I would rather die fighting.'

'You need not die today,' Taenar said. 'If you remain aboard then your armour will be lost to this planet, and no other warrior will ever find it to take up arms against the aeldari's enemies. Grenades!' he shouted, pointing at the viewport.

'Ready the starcannon! And salvage as many spirit stones from the dead as you can!'

'I fear my armour is in poor repair,' Myrin said acidly. Taenar ran his hands swiftly over the corsair's body, trying not to wince at the lack of life in Stormdawn's legs and lower body.

'The main suit is not broken,' he said. 'But you will need new gloves, and a new helm.' He laid Myrin down as gently as he could and wrenched gloves loose from one of Myrin's own Starsplinters, who lay dead mere yards away. The blow that had broken the luckless aeldari's neck had also shattered their helm's faceplate, however, but Taenar's eyes lighted on another corpse, that of Issarel. The duellist's twin swords had spilled from nerveless hands, and their body had nearly been bisected, but their helm was intact. Taenar scrambled to them and twisted it loose, haste warring with the necessity not to damage the seal, then gingerly prised the Bladesworn's spirit stone loose from the front of their armour. He made his way back to Myrin, noticing with unease as he did so that he was starting to feel the tug of the planet's gravity.

'Hold out your hands,' he instructed Myrin. Stormdawn looked at him with hollow disdain, but finally did as he was instructed. Myrin winced in pain as Taenar tugged the gloves on over his abused flesh, but there was no time to waste – the team at the chokepoint that was the bridge's entrance were holding the orks at bay, but Taenar could tell from the clipped exchanges over messenger waves that they were close to being overrun.

He opened a channel to the landing bay. 'This is Admiral Leotharan to Vampire crews, Admiral Leotharan to Vampire crews, come in.'

There was no reply.

'And so we die here after all?' Myrin said bleakly.

Taenar hissed in frustration, and forced Issarel's helm over

Stormdawn's outraged expression, perhaps slightly more force-fully than was necessary.

'I did not place all our lives at risk to rescue you, simply to give up now!' he snapped. Myrin's helm seal clicked, and Taenar turned around. 'Breach it!'

The vessel was starting to shake as they hit the very upper levels of the planet's atmosphere. It would not be long before the entire ship was glowing red-hot. They had to get out now, while they still had any hope.

The collected grenades, secured to a single point at the edge of the viewport, detonated as one with a thunderous boom. The starcannon fired immediately: one shot, a second shot, a third–

A section of the viewport exploded inwards, showering the aeldari with chunks of transparent material. Taenar gestured wildly towards it.

'Out! Get clear of the ship! Scatter lasers to full-auto! And someone help me with the prince!'

One of his warriors raced to him, and between them they dragged Myrin's protesting form to the viewport while the rest of the boarding party clambered out through the hole, levering themselves clear over the viewport's edge. The abandoned sup-port weapons at the door continued blazing. It pained Taenar to have to adopt the orks' stratagems of volume of fire over accu-racy against them, but all the scatter lasers had to do was keep the orks at bay for long enough.

'Go!' Taenar shouted to the other warrior. They were the last few remaining.

'I am not eager to take my chances with being hurled into the void!' Myrin protested.

'It's that, the orks, or the planet!' Taenar snapped. He hoisted Myrin up through the gap, then turned to face the bridge door just as the first orks came through, smashing the scatter lasers aside. A shot crashed into the viewport beside him. He waited just long enough to see their expressions as they realised the fate that their kaptin had sealed for them, then threw the last grenade he had kept back for just this purpose.

He was through the gap before the explosion came, tucking his legs up and away from the edges of the blast. Myrin was grimly hanging on, the thin atmosphere buffeting him thanks to the speed at which they were travelling. Others of Taenar's boarding party had already launched themselves off from the ship, though that was not a risk-free action without any means of directing themselves and with the ship accelerating towards them. Taenar saw a luckless individual collide with a metallic strut and pinwheel away, probably unconscious and possibly dead.

'Leotharan to *Dance of Dying Seasons*!' he broadcast. 'We require retrieval from the ork ship entering the planet's atmosphere! We are in free fall! I repeat, we are in free fall!'

He waited no longer. He grabbed Myrin's arms.

'I need you to trust me.'

'I have no option,' Myrin replied. Taenar sighed.

'That will have to do.'

He leaped away from the ork ship as hard and as fast as he could, dragging Myrin with him.

'Admiral!'

'Faerys!' Taenar exclaimed in relief as the ork cruiser burned past him. 'Hurry! We are–'

'We can't do it, admiral.'

Taenar's heart froze. 'What?'

'With the damage we've taken, we can't make it to you. We would break up in the atmosphere. I'm sorry.'

Taenar swallowed through a thick throat. Myrin was laughing, wild and harsh, but Taenar refused to give up hope. 'Are there no Vampire craft that can reach us?'

'*Not if the ones that took you there are lost, we–*'
'*I have them.*'

That was a new voice, cutting in on the messenger feed. Taenar looked up – and there was definitely an 'up', now, as the planet continued to swell beneath them – and saw the familiar shape of an aeldari cruiser descending recklessly fast towards them, silhouetted against the light of the system's star.

'*Anyone who can hear me, activate a beacon,*' the new captain declared. '*We will reach all of you that we can find.*'

Taenar activated his armour's locator with a thought, then winced in anticipation as the rear end of the ork ship approached. 'Brace yourself,' he said, tightening his grip on Myrin's forearms.

The stern of the cruiser flashed past them, and the furious fire of the drives caught Taenar and his warriors in a blast of superheat. Taenar screamed as his armour's sensors flashed to red – it felt like the void suit was melting into his skin, and the sheer power threw him upwards as fast as it drove *Sunstompa* downwards. He and Myrin pinwheeled through the sky, the darkness of space above them and the glare of the sun whipping around to be replaced by the planet below and the fire of the cruiser's thrusters, over and over again, nearly dislodging Taenar's grip as they were buffeted about. His eyes were stinging from the sweat suddenly pouring down his brow, but he closed them tight, gritted his teeth and held grimly on.

Arms seized him from behind, across his chest. Taenar looked around wildly, wondering if another of his crew had been thrown into them, but he was being *held*, his and Myrin's momentum slowing into something far steadier.

'Stop squirming,' a voice scolded in his ear. 'Aemesa! Get the other one, I haven't got enough power for three!'

Another shape descended out of the sun. For a moment, Taenar thought it had six limbs, but then the upper pair were revealed to be the grav-vanes of a jet pack. Such a device would not have the same power or range as the wings of a Swooping Hawk, but it would suffice for null-gravity manoeuvres, or dropping into combat from a transport craft, or, in this case, for the operator to latch their arms around a fellow aeldari who was in free fall, and haul them laboriously upwards again.

'You can let go of him,' another voice said, presumably Aemesa. 'I have him.'

'No,' Taenar said. He honestly wasn't sure how easily he could make his fingers unclench, in any case. 'Not until he is safe.'

'Then don't thrash around,' said the corsair who had hold of Taenar. 'This should be over soon.'

Taenar looked upwards. The Starsplinter cruiser – a pirate vessel, not one of the ones he still thought of as 'his' – was holding position above them, while jet pack-wearing corsairs flew like insects boiling out of a hive to snatch their fellows from the air. As he rose towards the ship, and more details became clear out of its silhouette, Taenar could make out its individual markings. He frowned in recognition, and the tide of relief that had washed over him rapidly withdrew, to be replaced by a clinging dread.

'What captain do you serve?' he asked, bile rising in his throat.

'*You'll meet them in a moment,*' Aemesa replied, matter-of-factly. Taenar clenched his jaw, but save for releasing his hold on Myrin and somehow wriggling out of his rescuer's grip to fall to the planet far below, there was nothing for him to do but be carried meekly to his fate.

The cruiser's bay from which the jet pack-equipped corsairs were launching and returning was apparently open to the air, but atmospherically shielded. Despite the damage it had taken, Taenar's armour registered the change in pressure as they crossed into the craftworld-standard atmosphere within. He and Myrin were dropped unceremoniously almost as soon as there was deck beneath them, and Myrin cried out in alarm as his unresponsive legs buckled beneath him.

'He's injured!' Taenar yelled at the corsairs, trying to take Myrin's weight so he did not collapse completely, but they had already turned and dived out of the bay again. Taenar cursed virulently and let Myrin down as gently as he could, then prised loose his helm. 'Prince Myrin needs a healer!'

'And he will get one, craftworlder,' said a voice. Taenar whirled around, his fears confirmed.

'Skyhand,' he said heavily. The captain of *The Yearning Stars* stood a few paces away from him, one hand on the hilt of their blade. 'Why did you save me?'

'Well, you apparently wouldn't let go of *him*,' Saraan Skyhand said, gesturing to Myrin. They snorted. 'But it was my mistake. I left orks to do an aeldari's job, and you survived.' They studied him for a moment, weighing him with their eyes. 'Besides, you were not fired upon by Ilmaren. It looked as though they would have welcomed you back. Instead, you defied them to come and kill slavers, and took some of their ships away with you in the process. That I can respect.'

Taenar inclined his head cautiously. 'I doubt I will get the same indulgence from them again, but I would not change my decision. No aeldari deserves to live in chains, no matter their origin, or the nature of their captor.'

Skyhand nodded in agreement. 'And I am no seer, but I know better than to push the threads of fate too far. Live, then, at least until you cross me again.' They turned away, apparently unconcerned by any vengeance Taenar might see fit to wreak – although he had neither the energy nor the spite for it – and raised their voice. 'Healer! We need a healer here!'

Taenar turned away from them and kneeled down next to

Myrin, then popped Myrin's helm loose and drew it gently off to reveal the wild-eyed, pain-wracked face beneath.

'I should be angry that one of my captains tried to get another killed,' Myrin said, his voice low and fierce despite the sweat beading his forehead. He turned his gaze on Taenar, eyes smouldering. 'But I find my anger is reserved for betrayal of a different kind.'

'Every word I said that mattered was true, to the best of my knowledge,' Taenar insisted, fighting down the nagging sensation that he was lying, and that he knew it. 'My ships and I came to help you and do your bidding. I had no knowledge of Ilmaren's intentions other than you be kept alive, and that at least did not seem at odds with your own ambitions.'

'And now you claim to have abandoned Ilmaren for real?' Myrin asked sourly.

Taenar sighed. 'I already had. I just had not realised it.'

Myrin closed his eyes, but said nothing. Taenar heard footsteps, and looked around to see two aeldari approaching – one with the distinctive pallor of Commorragh – with Saraan Skyhand behind them. 'Who are they?' he demanded.

'Healers, craftworlder,' Skyhand replied. 'Ours do not wear robes like yours, to denote their Path.'

'Because some of us did not learn our craft on a Path of any sort,' the former drukhari said with a grin that exposed sharpened teeth into which had been set tiny red gems. Narrow, multi-jointed metal arms unfolded from his back, tipped with various medical devices. 'Do not concern yourself, captain. The prince is in good hands.'

'Baron,' Myrin said, opening his eyes. 'You are speaking to Baron Leotharan of the Starsplinters. And Baronex Skyhand,' he added, looking past the healers towards the captain of *The Yearning Stars*. 'It is the least I can do for their roles in saving my life.'

Taenar breathed out.

'We will speak again when I am healed, baron,' Myrin said, his eyes returning to Taenar's face and not leaving it as the healers lifted him in an anti-grav field. 'We will speak about a great many things.'

Taenar watched the Prince of the Starsplinters as he was borne away to whatever passed for a healing chamber aboard a corsair ship. No, he corrected himself, aboard *this* corsair ship. His ships were corsair ships now in truth. He had abandoned Ilmaren, and knowing to what lengths they were prepared to go in order to secure their own survival, he had no idea whether he even wanted to return. For the first time in decades, he was rudderless.

But he was also now a corsair baron. And if there was one thing that he had learned in his time with the Starsplinters so far, it was that those who stood still risked losing any ability to chart their own course at all.

Limping footsteps drew his attention to the approach of Cithriel Shelwe-nin. The exarch had removed her helm as well and her face was drawn with pain, yet Taenar had rarely seen it more alive.

'I have never departed an enemy vessel like that before,' Cithriel said, her eyes alight. 'You have a talent for the dramatic, admiral.'

'It's baron, now,' Taenar corrected her. 'And while I'm glad it worked, I hope to never have to do it again.' He walked cautiously to the edge of the landing bay, and looked down at the planet below. A series of distant explosions marked *Sunstompa* disintegrating and breaking up as it hit the top of the planet's troposphere.

'Baronex Skyhand,' he said, pointing downwards at large scars in the landscape. 'The orks were fleeing for this planet. I believe I can see evidence of their handiwork on it, which suggests to me that this is where they would be putting their slaves to work. I think it is time to do what the prince led us here to do in the first place.'

Saraan Skyhand came up alongside him. Taenar tensed, ready for them to attempt to shove him over the edge and let him fall to his death, but the other corsair simply nodded.

'I agree.' Their face took on an eager, hungry expression. 'I believe the rest of the freebooter fleet is either destroyed or in the final stages of being scattered. I will give orders to commence scanning the surface, and look for our enemies' vulnerabilities.'

'Good,' Taenar said. He tried to push his regret and anger about Ilmaren to the back of his mind, along with the jumble of confused feelings about Myrin Stormdawn and the Starsplinters in general, but they refused to sit neatly. He wanted to destroy something.

Luckily, an obvious target was at hand.

'Let them look to the skies,' Baron Taenar Leotharan said. 'It will show them no mercy.'

THIRTY-THREE

When the heavens lit up over the slave camps and the work stations, the orks and grots charged with fulfilling Uzgul da Magnificent's vision for the Dakkaplanet cheered. They didn't know what the explosions were, but they cheered on the basis that it was probably the boss doing some krumpin' somewhere up there in space, and also that explosions were generally good for a laugh anyway. Those who saw the fireball that streaked down from the sky cheered as well, even if they coughed a bit later when a mighty gust of wind carried a storm of dust and dirt that lodged in the throat and fouled up engine intakes. Then they went back to lashing the skrawnie slaves to digging, because no one wanted Uzgul to come back and get angry that things hadn't been done.

On that front, at least, they did not have to worry, since Uzgul da Magnificent never did come back. Others came instead – tall, slim shapes that dropped from the dust-obscured sky, or emerged from the shadows, or jumped out of skimmers moving faster than the eye could easily follow. They appeared everywhere an ork held a whip or a grot wielded a skrawnie-prodder.

And murder came with them.

EPILOGUE

On the lower slopes of the highest mountain of what had once been known as the Dakkaplanet, until the orks had been exterminated from it, lay wreckage.

Much of *Sunstompa* had broken away during its descent, and much of that had burned up and been vaporised. It was a mighty ship, however, and a great deal of it still hammered into the ground, blasting huge impact craters and throwing up great clouds of pulverised rock. Nothing on board survived – not even orks, the galaxy's great survivors, were that resilient. What was left when the dust settled was barely recognisable as a ship, but here and there were a few pieces that, through accidents of structural integrity and air resistance, had remained slightly more intact.

In the crumpled remains of the bridge, which had come to rest roughly one-third of the way up the mountain, the air shimmered. It whirled and vibrated, as though afflicted by a sickness, then spat out a black-clad figure.

Xela Flickerstep screamed, lashing out with corroded blades at empty air, until she stumbled into a wall. She stopped, eyes wild and wide, then cut at herself in a frenzy until she had sheared away the sparking blink pack attached to her back. It fell to what remained of the deck, and she kicked it away with a shrieked Commorraghan curse.

She looked around. All trace of the ice-cold warrior was gone, replaced by a feral animal. Her void suit was cut to rags, and the pale flesh beneath was covered with unnatural claw marks. Xela whirled from stance to stance, knives poised, until finally she seemed to accept that nothing was about to attack her.

She relaxed, ever so slightly at first. Then, like a dam that first cracked and finally burst under pressure, she collapsed bonelessly to the deck and managed to unclench her fingers enough to release the hilts of her blades. She screamed again, not a battle cry this time, but the animal sobbing of a being that has passed through horror and out the other side, and no longer has any idea what to do now the horror has ended.

Finally, the sobs subsided. Xela Flickerstep slowly unfolded upwards again, still panting, and looked about her with eyes that were now more capable of interpreting what they saw. She took in the twisted ceiling above her and the mangled deck, and the bodies of orks and aeldari mashed together by the force of the impact, now crawling with insects.

She craned her neck and peered out of the crumpled slit of the viewport, glimpsing a mountainside blasted bare by the impact and a faint sliver of star-studded sky.

'Hello?' Xela Flickerstep called, but no one answered. Her fingers moved reflexively, but there was nothing in them, so she squatted down and picked up her knives, then paused and looked at them. They were pitted, scored, and worn down, more vaguely sharp stubs of metal than elegant implements of the hekatarii arts, but they were all she had. She sheathed one in the myriad of empty scabbards on her belt and left the other to twirl absent-mindedly through her fingers.

She glanced at her blink pack, then shuddered.

It took abused muscles and wounded flesh longer than it should have to prise her way out, and the air was repeatedly split by curses rarely heard outside the darkest corners of Commorragh. Finally, after hauling herself away from the wreckage – every drukhari instinctively knew to avoid sites that would attract scavengers of any sort, unless they were to be the ones doing the scavenging – Xela found a rock to set her back against, and sat upon the ground.

Far above, the stars stared down at her. Uncaring, but not hostile. Remote. Utterly irrelevant to her presence on this planet.

Xela tilted her head back until it rested on the rock against which she was sitting, and stared back.

ABOUT THE AUTHOR

Mike Brooks is a science fiction and fantasy author who lives in Nottingham. His recent work for Black Library includes the Warhammer 40,000 novels *Voidscarred, Lelith Hesperax: Queen of Knives, Da Big Dakka* and *The Lion: Son of the Forest*. He has also written *Brutal Kunnin, Harrowmaster, Huron Blackheart: Master of the Maelstrom, Warboss, Da Gobbo's Revenge* and the Horus Heresy Primarchs novel *Alpharius: Head of the Hydra* as well as many others. When not writing, he plays guitar and sings in a punk band, and DJs wherever anyone will tolerate him.